THE DISORDER *of* LONGING

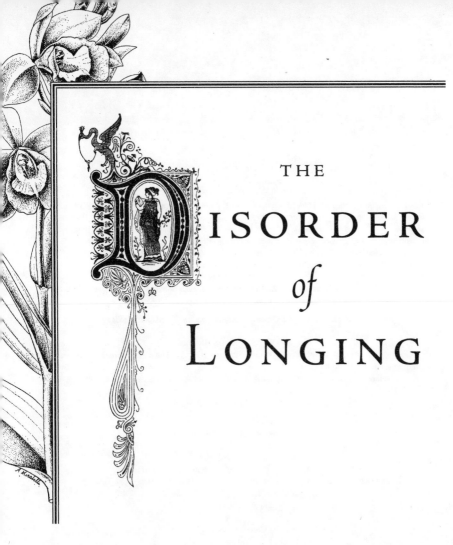

THE DISORDER *of* LONGING

Natasha Bauman

G. P. PUTNAM'S SONS   NEW YORK

PUTNAM

G. P. PUTNAM'S SONS
Publishers Since 1838
Published by the Penguin Group
Penguin Group (USA) Inc., 375 Hudson Street, New York, New York 10014, USA • Penguin Group (Canada), 90 Eglinton Avenue East, Suite 700, Toronto, Ontario M4P 2Y3, Canada (a division of Pearson Canada Inc.) • Penguin Books Ltd, 80 Strand, London WC2R 0RL, England • Penguin Ireland, 25 St Stephen's Green, Dublin 2, Ireland (a division of Penguin Books Ltd) • Penguin Group (Australia), 250 Camberwell Road, Camberwell, Victoria 3124, Australia (a division of Pearson Australia Group Pty Ltd) • Penguin Books India Pvt Ltd, 11 Community Centre, Panchsheel Park, New Delhi–110 017, India • Penguin Group (NZ), 67 Apollo Drive, Rosedale, North Shore 0632, New Zealand (a division of Pearson New Zealand Ltd) • Penguin Books (South Africa) (Pty) Ltd, 24 Sturdee Avenue, Rosebank, Johannesburg 2196, South Africa

Penguin Books Ltd, Registered Offices: 80 Strand, London WC2R 0RL, England

Library of Congress Cataloging-in-Publication Data

Bauman, Natasha.
The disorder of longing : a novel / Natasha Bauman.
p. cm.
ISBN-13: 978-0-399-15495-9
1. Boston (Mass.)—History—19th century—Fiction. 2. Brazil—Fiction.
3. Self-realization—Fiction. 4. Sex—Religious aspects—Tantrism—Fiction. I. Title.
PS3602.A96274D47 2008 2008006586
813'.6—dc22

Printed in the United States of America
1 3 5 7 9 10 8 6 4 2

Book design by Nicole LaRoche

Illustrations from F. C. Hoehne's Flora Brasilica

For my mother, Doreen Bauman

And in memory of my father, James Bauman,

and my aunt, Lorrie Tussman

Part One

A hysterical woman is a pitiful and unfortunate object . . . capricious in character, whimsical in conduct, excitable, impatient, obstinate, and frivolous—a regular Gordian knot for friends and physicians to unravel. She possesses a most variable and imaginative disposition, which, in spite of all that can be done, keeps her in a continued whirl of excitement from morning until night.

—Dr. Charles P. Uhle,
Godey's Lady's Book, 1870

A.J. Silveira. del.

The State of the Atmosphere

It was officially spring, yet the sun had been stingy, staying hidden away for weeks. On this morning, though, a sudden change in the weather woke Ada Pryce from a sound sleep. She rose from her bed and leaned out the window, allowing the sun to tickle her face and neck. Her room felt dank and close in contrast to the outdoors. The urgent need to be outside in the thick of this ripping day overtook her, so she pulled a cornflower blue wool walking suit from her armoire and dressed hurriedly, taking little care as she pinned her thick copper hair under a feathered hat.

It was the sun's fault, she told herself, the sun was the reason she was about to commit an unforgivable offense.

Mercifully, none of the house staff saw her as she made her way quietly down the front stairs, through the long hallway, across the octagonal foyer, and out the door. The three-story stone house cast a long shadow, preventing the sun from touching her. Her skirts snapped against her boots as she walked over the brick sidewalk along Marlborough, then stepped onto the cobblestone street, where at last she felt the full warmth of the morning sun. Once she stood in its glow, she found it impossible to turn back to the house. She crossed the street quickly, almost leaping over the horse droppings that had not yet been picked up by the men hired to keep her street clean, and headed toward Commonwealth Avenue. On reaching the Avenue Mall, she turned left toward the Public Gardens. It was a Thursday morning, and the streets of Boston were busy with carriages, horses, vendors, and men hurrying on foot to their workplaces. Ada was energized by the activity, so that her feet moved in a merry tempo, her heels clicking against the bricks in a tapping rhythm that pleased her. At the entrance to the Gardens, she felt the tension in her shoulders dissipate. She stifled the urge to laugh out loud. She had made her escape.

Governesses were already out with their tiny charges; they gathered forces with other governesses, their hordes of children forming large circles of ecstatic play around the pond, while the women watched and gossiped. A few younger men walked quickly through the park, headed somewhere, while older men strolled with one another, meeting to discuss their past accomplishments, no doubt. Then there were other men, of all ages, who seemed to be in the park because they had no purpose, nothing more important to do with their day. In spite of the perfect weather, many of these people looked forlorn.

Ada sat on an empty bench. At first she held her back straight, but soon her spine settled against the bench, relaxing into the support it offered her. The purposeless and shabby few who walked past were the ones who drew her eye. As she watched them, she tried to imagine what their lives might be. Were they alone in the world, living in a small room, at times going hungry? Had some horrible tragedy brought them so low, were they drug fiends or had they committed some other awful offense?

Suddenly, a blister of activity erupted behind her. Turning her body to face the back of the bench, she saw a group of cyclists coming along the dirt path. As they pulled closer, their bloomers and knickerbockers came into focus. It was a band of women, laughing excitedly as they gained speed on the downside of a slight hill, their tires crunching across the dirt. The governesses pulled the children in close, moving them away from the possible threat the wild riders posed. The governesses' bonneted heads tilted as they whispered behind the fingers of their gloved hands, surely appalled by these probable suffragists. What other sort of woman would get dressed up in such unfeminine vestment and dare to part her legs in order to straddle the seat of a bicycle?

Ada jumped up from her bench and moved toward the path. The women slowed down, yelping and laughing in delight, eventually coming to a stop not far from Ada. She walked toward them, drawn by the frenzy of joy that hovered about them, and by the wonderful contraptions they rode. She felt her nerve ends opening, blossoming with the thrill of this event. It must be a cycling school. She had heard this was a new rage among the more daring women. They were in love with the freedom offered them when they cycled. Ada wanted to be near them, to ask them what it felt like to ride a bicycle.

She drew closer to the women, stepping into their open circle. "Good morning," she said, and was surprised to hear her voice tremble as she spoke. The women smiled at her, bidding her good morning in return. But before Ada could ask them how they came to ride these bikes here, what class they belonged to, how she might join, out of the corner of her eye she saw a woman running along the edge of the pond, her arms raised in a wild salute, tracing a flurry of motion against the backdrop of the still water. Her simple striped dress and white bonnet clearly announced her status as a member of the serving class. As she ran and waved, it became apparent that she was headed straight for Ada, that it was Ada's attention she wanted.

The young woman came up closer, and Ada saw then that it was her own lady's maid, Katie. "Mrs. Pryce. Oh, thank the good Lord."

She pulled Ada away from the cyclists, and they collapsed on the bench together. Katie was out of breath, her blond curls springing out from under her white cap, her smooth young face shiny with sweat. Her voice rose and fell with the melody of Irish as she spoke. "Edith saw you cross the street as she was coming back from the market, and ever since we have been running about ever so madly trying to find you."

Ada reached out to pat her maid's hand, and in that moment, the riders got back onto their bikes and rode away, one after another, the gravel flying out from their balloon tires as they sailed away, waving to Ada as they went. It seemed possible to Ada that they were headed directly for the surface of the sun with all the freedom their wheels gave them. She turned reluctantly away from the cyclists as their figures receded. "I'm fine, Katie," she said. "What on earth is all the fuss about?"

"Well, ma'am." She stared at Ada, as if the answer were obvious and needn't be said aloud. But Ada tilted her head, waiting for Katie to continue. "You left the house all on your own, without a word to a soul. Edith told me and Mary, and then of course Ettie heard, and she insisted I was to find you straightaway. So I ran in the direction Edith said you were gone. I was behind you on the Mall, but I lost you when you came into the Gardens."

"But why couldn't you have let me be?"

All the kinetic energy that had been driving Katie suddenly seemed to drain from her. "Let you be?" She didn't seem to know what else to say.

"Sometimes I just want to go for a walk, all on my own," Ada said.

"Oh, dear me," Katie said.

As they walked back to the house together, Ada took Katie's arm, pulling her back. "I don't care if they're worried. I am going to enjoy the clear skies while I'm out here with no other purpose but to enjoy them. Walk slowly with me, please?"

Katie stopped, and the two women faced each other where they stood at the edge of the park. "You know I will come walking with you anytime you please, Ada." Ada encouraged this familiarity between herself and her maid, though it caused some discomfort for Katie. But now Katie said her mistress's first name with assuredness, as if she were speaking to her child.

It made Ada smile. "Of course you will, Katie. And thank you. But sometimes I just get the urge to walk down the Mall by myself. It's very different, you know, the feeling one gets when one walks entirely alone." Ada knew Katie walked by herself frequently, and that she probably rather wouldn't. But Katie didn't know what it was like never to be allowed to be on one's own simply because of one's station and sex. It was, in Ada's opinion, simply ridiculous.

When they turned the corner onto Marlborough, and the Ruskin Gothic house in which she lived came into view, Ada's breathing became more constricted. The sun shone now on the cream-colored Nova Scotia sandstone facade. She could feel the heat emanating from the stone as they climbed the steps, but it didn't warm her. The instant they were inside the foyer, the entire house staff appeared there, save George. The short and wispy young Edith, the more substantial but equally young Mary, and the older, sterner Ettie all fluttered about them, asking Ada over and over if everything was all right, if there was anything they could do for her. Ada smiled and thanked them, but shooed them away. She took herself up the front stairs and to her bedroom on the second floor. The clock on her dresser read five minutes after ten. The most exciting event of her day had lasted less than fifty-five minutes.

DINNER THAT EVENING, taken alone at the long ebony dining table, her back to the matching carved ebony-encased fireplace, made Ada wish she were supping with the bicycle club members. In front of her, on the other side of the expansive room, was an alcove inlaid with stained glass. Whenever Edward, her husband of four years, was at home, Ettie lit a lamp on the other side of the alcove, and bands of colored light danced across the dining room. But Edward had taken to dining at the Club recently, and when he was out, the lamp did not burn. Dining away from home had become such a habit with him that he occasionally failed to inform Ada whether he would dine at home or not. She expected to be alone.

Katie appeared at the table to pick up Ada's last dishes. "Thank you so much, Katie," Ada said. "Please tell Ettie it was delicious."

"Of course. She'll be pleased to know you liked it." Ada never failed to compliment Ettie, even though she knew the cook was only happy when Edward ate her food. It was a wasted meal if the man of the house wasn't there to judge and offer approval.

"Katie, tell me something," Ada said.

Katie stood next to the table, gripping the dirty dishes. "Certainly."

"Does George know about my escape this morning?"

Katie blinked twice before she answered. "I am afraid Ettie told him, ma'am."

"I see. Thank you, then. I'll be in my office if Edward returns in the next hour."

BY THE TIME Edward came home, the mild weather had taken a drastic turn, unnerving Ada. The sun had removed itself again, and a storm brewed. A spring electrical storm was nothing extraordinary. The sudden graying of the skies over Boston, the whinnying of horses and barking of dogs, the pressing down of the atmosphere, all were occurrences common enough to cause nothing more than simple, instinctive responses. But Ada imagined the turn in the weather to be a punishment for her morning perambulations. The electrical charges seemed to course up through the soles of her feet, spread throughout her body's tributaries, then emerge out the top of her skull like the clean upthrust of a knife. She left her office and went downstairs, hoping the activity would soothe her. Just as she stepped into the front hallway, holding on to her head in an effort to keep it of a piece, Edward appeared in the foyer.

He shook off his wet umbrella and peeled himself out of his raincoat with the help of his man, George, who had reached him before Ada was able to move an inch. George always moved more quickly than any middle-aged and overweight man should, Ada thought. It wasn't until Edward stepped into the hallway and walked toward her where she stood now in front of the parlor door that she noticed he was carrying something. He held a wooden box in front of him, out of the top of which poked spots of color. The spots bounced with Edward's stride. His footsteps echoed across the parquet floor, then silenced when he stepped onto the Chinese wool runner. Ada waited, motionless. Her brain was unable to put the bits of color into a recognizable form until Edward reached her and extended the box. He leaned toward her over his load, a grin spreading out across his face.

The box contained half a dozen orchids, none the same. One had delicate petals of yellow with orange spots, another large pink petals, one was purple, one red, one brown with white, and another vivid orange with burgundy streaks. The petals and sepals were all of different shapes, and in assorted arrangements. The leaves varied from pale to deep green, from long and pointed to round and rubbery. What they all had in common was simply this: not one of them was lovely. Each one of them was rangy, spindly, lacking in the pleasing qualities that constitute true beauty. Their necks were long and skinny, their florescences somehow too hard. If Edward had brought these home for her, she wouldn't want to disappoint him by not seeming overjoyed at the gift. Ada turned her gaze up from the flowers and looked at her husband's face, steeling herself for her performance.

There was something of the sublime in the look he wore as he continued to gaze on the orchids. He seemed so happy to have brought these plants home. She knew then that the flowers were not for her. They were Edward's own conquest. Ada was relieved that the orchids had caused a distraction, and that they had nothing to do with her. Everyone gathered around as Edward showed his flowers to them all.

"I must congratulate you, sir," George said to Edward. "You have, I trust, managed to find the best, as you always do."

Edward laughed and clapped his man on the back. "You know me well, don't you?" George reached out his arms, and Edward gave the box over to his man's keeping. George certainly wouldn't bother Edward with the story of Ada's solitary walk just now. But it would be only a temporary reprieve. Ada knew that, as soon as the time was right, he would relay the story to his master. And surely Edward would demand to know why his pampered wife had had reason to walk by herself to the Public Gardens, putting herself at risk without anyone along to protect her or go for help should something horrid happen. For now, though, he was happy with his orchids, and there was no mention of Ada's earlier misbehavior.

"I need to take care of these beauties," Edward told her. "Excuse me."

Ada went to the kitchen to check on final preparations for the next day's meals, but before she was able to speak with Ettie, a commotion echoed from the foyer. Back in the hallway, she saw Franz Locke, a partner from Edward's firm, and three strange men. For an instant, they all stood in front of the open front door as lightning flashed across the sky behind them, turning them briefly to silhouettes. Then the door was closed, and the men became flesh again. Franz, to Ada, was just another one of the men from Edward's law firm and club, one of the many men who had so much to say to her husband, and yet so little to say to her. But the three strangers were like no one she had ever seen before. Their clothing was coarse and seemed sun worn, as if they did some sort of physical labor in the clothes they wore. Their hair was not cut finely, nor were their faces clean shaven.

These men's voices triggered a thrill of familiarity in her, warming her spine and drawing her toward them. They filled the wide hallway with a largeness and energy that so delighted her, it took her a moment to register that one of the men was white, another was an African, and the third a dark-skinned man whose race was indecipherable to Ada.

Finally, Edward noticed her standing there and stopped to introduce her to the men. William Parrish was the African, Walter Kebble the white man, and from his name, she imagined that Jao da Cunha, the third man, no doubt was Brazilian. They smiled at her, tipping their rumpled hats, all of them greeting her at once, their voices bouncing off the wood paneling. "I'm so pleased to meet you," she said to them, addressing them as formally as she would any of her society acquaintances. She reached out her hand and, one by one, they shook it. Her crisp crinoline skirts and the rigid bodice of her waistcoat, with its turnover collar, all seemed overdone next to the relaxed attire of these comfortable men. Her fingers tugged at her collar as she tried to think of something to say that would draw them into conversation.

"You have a lovely home," Walter said. "We promise we'll do our best not to spoil it with our coarseness." His face seemed serious, but there was a twinkle in his eye.

Ada smiled at him and the others. "Please, make yourselves at home."

Before anyone was tempted to take the conversation further, Edward piloted the men toward his office. As they passed by her, they ruffled the air, stirring up a scent redolent of the jungle, of the open air in the dead of night, of unnamed places and unidentified species, of undiscovered natural wonders.

"Good night, then, my dear," Edward said. As he lingered in front of the open pocket doors, she could see the box of orchids behind him on the cabochon-cut malachite inlaid oak table. It would have been natural for her to be worried about the table with the ragged box placed there, but Ada wanted to ask him something about the plants. Edward saw her trying to formulate a question, and smiled at her, believing he knew what she was about to ask. "Don't worry. I'll move them. The table will be fine." He reached out and patted her hand. Though he exerted no undue pressure, the gesture suggested that he was pushing her away. "Sleep well." As he pulled the pocket door out of its space in the wall, the orchid hunters bade her good night.

"Good night," she called back to them. Did her voice sound too emotional, did it hint at her sense of abandonment? Just before the door touched the wall, Ada saw Edward watching her. His brow was furrowed, his mouth turned down at the corners. The scent of the men lingered there; Ada breathed it in in an effort to fill up on it. She stood outside the office, listening to their rich voices and their quick laughter, not realizing or caring then that this was the first time non-whites had ever crossed the threshold of her front door and entered a room not reserved for the use of servants. She would have been happy to stay there all evening, but fear of being discovered spying on them finally sent her away.

UPSTAIRS IN HER ROOM, Ada dressed herself in her peach silk nightdress and settled into the thickness of her bed linens with *Pride and Prejudice.* But she found herself turning the pages of the book without remembering anything she had read. The multiple ribbons of her gown scratched at her neck, distracting her from the words on the page. Occasionally, the men's voices, or their sudden laughter, drifted up from the floor below. The rain tapping on the window, together with the distant sound of the men's voices, made her feel a loneliness that reminded her of all the hours of her childhood she had spent alone in her nursery while her parents entertained guests downstairs. She untied the ribbons and opened the high neck of her nightdress. Now that she was no longer a child, why couldn't she walk on her own in the park, and why shouldn't she be down there, in Edward's office, sharing in the exotic discussion the men were no doubt immersed in at this moment? She hadn't chosen to grow into a woman; why should she be punished for it?

She couldn't read, but neither could she sleep. Instead, she paced her room in her bare feet, feeling the difference between the silk carpet and the peg and groove wood on the soles of her feet, occupying herself with this trivial sensuality to keep from screaming out loud. Later, when his guests had gone, and Ada heard Edward on the landing near her door, she stopped where she stood, bracing herself, gripping the carpet with her toes as she waited for him to come in and reprimand her. Certainly George had told him the story of her escape by now. She tied the ribbons of her gown quickly, pulling them tightly across her neck lest Edward should see them undone and reprimand her for that, too. Sweat gathered on her upper lip as she waited for her door to creak open.

After a moment, Ada heard her husband open and then close his own bedroom door. When he stopped moving about his room, and the whole house became silent, she blew out her lamp and slipped down under her counterpane, certain she would sleep finally. Instead, she tossed across the length and width of her mattress, flipping from front to back, side to side. She thought of the cyclists in the park, in their bloomers. And she thought of the rough men there, in her own home. What did they talk about in that room, without her? Why were men always so secretive about the things they discussed in the rooms they occupied away from women?

Finally, the rain ceased. She slipped from her bed and walked to her window.

Throwing back the maroon brocade curtains, she leaned her head against the glass. It chilled her skin, causing bumps to rise up along her head and down her neck. Her window looked onto the small garden and out to the carriage house. In the darkness, the garden's color was erased, it was nothing but shades of gray and black. But suddenly, a thin wedge of light brought smudges of color to the wet yard. Ada's eyes followed the light to its source. The carriage house. What was the stable man doing in there so late?

Whatever might be amiss in the carriage house was no business of hers.

It must have been the lingering restiveness that caused her to walk downstairs and out the back door without thinking about why she did it. Dressed only in her slippers and nightdress, she trod across the rain-slicked garden path. A breeze lifted off the river, chilling her. She stopped and looked up. Ada listened to the stars; they were so bright she almost believed she could hear them crackling as they glittered above her.

A surprising, submerged moan cut across the landscape of twinkling sound, like the hum of a Gregorian chant. As she moved closer, she recognized the cause of the uneven groan. Ada cocked her head, listening for a repetition. It came again, this time even more guttural. She followed the voice; it led her to the carriage house and the bit of light that shimmered across the garden.

As she closed in on the building, the moan was joined by a deeper, clearly masculine-sounding grunt. Without taking another step, she knew that this must be Katie and Liam, the stable man. Liam was young, Irish like Katie, with a firm body and strong hands that were so different from Edward's, or any of the men Ada had known. Ada was seized by the longing to watch them in the act. Though she understood this desire was irregular, and the awareness caused her a certain anxiety, she made no effort to censor herself.

She followed the thin beam of light to the closest window, but it was too high for her to see through. She found a metal basin nearby and carried it over to the window. Quietly stepping up onto the upended basin, she peeked into the corner of the window, and was surprised by the clear view she now had. Katie and Liam were in a stack of hay behind the carriage, completely naked, their clothes underneath them, protecting them from the sharp ends of the hay. The horses gave them no notice; apparently they were accustomed to the disturbance. The lovers lay facing each other, on their sides, Katie's leg thrown up over Liam's hip. Ada dropped her head quickly below the window frame, embarrassed, even out here, alone in the dark. But the continuing sighs held her there, incapable of leaving. When she regained her nerve and peeked in again, Katie was in the final surge of her crisis, her head thrown back, her mouth slack, her eyes wild. The light from the lantern flickered over her as her moans became rapid and high-pitched.

Liam climaxed with her. Both of their faces, in the uneven light, seemed to jump back and forth between expressions of bliss and a sort of pure rage, as if the crisis induced something akin to agony.

Their breathing soon evened; as they began to quiet, Ada felt a growing panic at the thought of being discovered. She replaced the basin and hurried away from the stable, to the safety of the back porch. As she entered the quiet of her house, her own quick and uneven breathing echoed through the back hallway, sounding as loud as if she had been breathing into a megaphone. Back in her bed, under the watchful eyes of the carved cupids on her headboard, she fought for the comfort of sleep, but instead was plagued by visions of Katie and Liam.

WHEN KATIE CAME into her room carrying a basin of warm water the next morning, Ada felt herself flush. She had to turn her face away, look out the window, to avoid eye contact.

"Thank you, Katie," she said.

"Of course. How are you this lovely day?"

Ada imagined it must seem lovely to Katie, after the evening she had spent with Liam. Ada would feel ready to slay dragons this morning if she had spent a similar evening with Edward. An image of Katie's face, thrown back in the moment of crisis, superimposed itself over Katie's smile.

"I'm fine," she told Katie. "But I am concerned about the progress we're making on the new linen closets. Could you see to that, and let me know what might be causing the delays? It is becoming an irritation to me now." She knew her behavior toward Katie was uncalled for. She even recognized that she was jealous of her maid's satisfied lust. But somehow she was unable to stop herself.

Ada didn't look to see Katie's face. "Of course, Mrs. Pryce. Right away," Katie said, exiting the room quickly. Her absence did not serve to relieve Ada of the specific memories that insinuated themselves into her consciousness now. Witnessing the act of sexual congress between her maid and her husband's groomsman inspired in Ada memories of her college years, and things best left unremembered.

She stirred herself, and rose to dress. The water Katie had brought was still slightly warm. Without allowing herself to engage in the sensuality of the procedure, she wiped down her breasts and underarms and crotch with the mildly scented water. She dried herself with a soft Turkish towel, wriggled her way into her corset and corset cover, drawers, petticoats, and stockings, then slid her arms into the muttonchop sleeves of her heavy pink silk housedress. After her beige kid boots were laced, she sat at her dressing table to check herself in the looking glass. The face that looked back at her rested on a long, elegant neck, above a body that was just lush enough to cause men's thoughts to shift briefly to unseemly territory when they first laid eyes on her, and even after. But Ada didn't see that in the image reflected back at her. She simply looked for the imperfections in her dress and hair, then moved to correct them.

Downstairs, Ada walked into the front parlor first. The strange orchids, preening themselves on the table behind the gold sofa, caused her to forget why she had come into the room. She moved closer to the plants, drawn by the ugliest of the group. Its petals and sepals were a bright purple, and at the center of the florescence was an obscene-looking protuberance of crimson. Its pot, and those of the other plants, rested on a clay trough, which in turn was on a strip of felt, the whole thing designed to minimize damage to her table. She wasn't concerned about the inlaid cherry table. Her home was filled with fine furniture, but she wasn't possessive of it. It struck her as odd, though, that Edward had gone to so much trouble to set up these strange flowers, giving them pride of place in the most important room in the house. Certainly they did not belong here of all places.

Ada turned away from the plants and tried for a moment to remember her mission here, but failing, left the room, putting thoughts of orchids out of her mind.

The sunroom was Ada's favorite room in the house. She often read there, under the glass windows that stretched across the whole of the south wall and then curved up, forming a portion of the ceiling. The brightness of the place buoyed her spirits. Nothing was more relaxing than reading a book on the sofa and looking up at the ceiling occasionally to find a cloud drifting above her. She went in now, eager to spend time alone there, but was surprised to find Edward inside, eating his breakfast. Ettie hovered over him, her plump face glowing with the thrill of serving her master. A shaft of orange sun cut across the heavy mahogany table, encircled the silver serving tray, and refracted back across Ettie's face as she arranged the food.

"Ada, darling," Edward said. "I'm glad to see you. Sit with me. I have news."

Ettie left, and soon thereafter Edith appeared with coffee and warm scones for Ada. Edward waited to speak until Edith had gone, as if what he was about to say was too precious, or perhaps too subversive, for the ears of his servants. "I do so hope you appreciate the orchids I brought home."

"Of course, Edward. I was just looking at them. They're stunning." The sun warmed her cold hands. She wanted to take off her boots and put her feet into the circle of sun, to warm her chilly toes.

"They are the finest in Boston," Edward was saying. "I'll be the envy of my club when the others see what I am up to."

"What you're up to, darling?" She took a bite of well-buttered scone, savoring the sensation of the butter melting on her tongue.

"I'm building a collection. Those six plants are only the beginning of a grand experiment."

"Why, this is all so sudden, Edward, darling."

Edward leaned across the table and tapped Ada's hand absently as he spoke. "Not really. I have been discussing it with Franz for weeks. He started his collection earlier than I have done. I shall have to assert myself to catch up to him. Within the next few weeks I will increase the number of plants I have tenfold, and I'll build a greenhouse for them. And then we shall have a dinner."

"A dinner?" Outside, the clouds suddenly parted and the whole room seemed to expand with the infusion of light. Ada lifted her face and closed her eyes for a moment.

"Yes. And your mother will come."

Her eyes opened wide. "My mother?" Before she had even finished speaking, Ada understood why her mother would attend. Beatrice Caswell was a member in good standing of the uppermost tier of Boston Brahmans.

People paid attention when she walked into a room. They held their breath when she opened her mouth to speak. And when she spoke directly to any one of them, it was an occasion fit to recount in the family records, to keep for posterity. Edward meant to impress his mother-in-law with his as yet incomplete orchid collection.

"Of course your mother, my dear. Absolutely your mother. And the orchid hunters will come as well."

"The orchid hunters?"

"Yes, yes. The men who came with Franz last night."

It all made sense to Ada now. Their clothes, their ruggedness, even their scent. Those men slept out under the stars, in search of rare orchids for rich men. It was thrilling and strange to her at once. The thought of having William, Jao, and Walter to dinner, of having the opportunity to sit at table with them, was more exciting even than her walk in the park and the pack of cyclists who had crossed her path.

"I shall be happy to entertain them, Edward. And my mother."

"It will be a grand evening." He leaned forward and kissed her cheek, then settled back into his seat, throwing his arm across the back of the chair. He looked so comfortable that way, as if he hadn't a worry in his world.

"These orchid men, Edward. Will they hunt orchids for you?" She purposely didn't say their names. She didn't want Edward to know that she remembered them.

Edward's eyes seemed to focus more acutely. "I don't know that it will be them, but yes, I will hire men to go to the tropics for me. I intend to become a serious collector of orchids, so of course I must have hunters go out for me, the sooner the better." He stood then, taking hold of her hand. "Come see them with me."

They went to the front parlor together. Edward picked up an orchid whose petals and sepals were pink, with the center protrusion rimmed in deep red. "This is the Ruby-lipped *Cattleya labiata*," he said. "Isn't she wondrous?"

Wondrous, yes, Ada thought, wondrously absurd.

"You wouldn't want to hunt them yourself?" she asked him.

His face fell all at once, then lifted itself up again, his cheeks rising, his eyebrows shooting up above his glasses. "Why, Ada. I have responsibilities. To you and to the firm. I can't go traipsing around the world. I am a gentleman, after all." He turned back to admire his *Cattleya*.

"Of course. Of course you are, dear. I just thought the adventure might be a temptation to you."

"I choose to maintain mastery over my baser desires. Please don't bother yourself with the details of how the orchids come to be here. Just appreciate them for the beauty they bring to our household." He set the *Cattleya* back in its place. "Unfortunately, this flower is not the *Cattleya labiata vera*," he said. "The true *labiata* flower was first brought to Europe in 1818. William Swainson discovered it in Brazil, in the Organ Mountains. He sent specimens to England, along with other tropical plants."

Edward and Ada returned to the sunroom, where he told the rest of the story of the *Cattleya labiata vera*. Swainson's *Cattleyas* were not in bloom when he brought them home, and perhaps he didn't know they would transform themselves into beautiful flowers. But a William Cattley cultivated them, and in November of 1818, one bloomed. The plant became popular when other plants bloomed in other collections, including that of the Glasgow Botanic Garden.

"But Swainson," Edward said, "seems to have disappeared, without bothering to tell anyone exactly where he found the plants."

In 1836, another orchid hunter, a Dr. Gardner, claimed to have found the orchids on top of Gavea Mountain, about fifteen miles from Rio de Janeiro. But the orchids were growing on the face of the mountain, impossible to get at. As Gardner himself said, they were far from the reach of the greedy collector. But he found others, across from the Gavea, on the mountain called Pedra Bonita. "On the edge of a precipice on the eastern side," he wrote, "we found, covered with its large rose-colored flowers, the splendid *Cattleya labiata*. It was with much difficulty and no little danger that I could obtain about a dozen specimens."

But in the end, it turned out that Gardner had never really found the *Cattleya labiata vera* after all. Someone took the trouble to check out the dried specimens at Kew Gardens. R. A. Rolfe, the editor of the *Orchid*

Review, concluded that Gardner's specimens were *Laelia lobata*, not the prized *Cattleya labiata* at all. No one was able to find the flower again, and its slippery existence became like an icon of the Gothic sensibilities of the time, shrouded in mystery, alone on a misty mountain.

"The question everyone asks now is 'How did Swainson manage to find the flowers, and why did he disappear without explaining it to anyone?' " Edward told Ada. He was silent for a moment, pondering his own questions.

"Some members of my Orchid Society plan to send hunters out just to search for the missing plants," he told her. Ada thought this a lavish and careless gesture. It was an act that suggested that its patron was willing to go the distance, that his obsession with orchids was complete, that he would do anything in his futile attempt to satiate this strange desire, including risk other men's lives. "I want to be the one to find that plant." His lips remained nearly immobile as he spoke the words.

Edith came in, quickly setting out fresh coffee and more scones and biscuits. Ada felt as though her insides were swimming in the black liquid, but not knowing what else to do with herself, she took another cup of the stuff and settled into her chair. Edward walked about the sunny space, examining it as if noticing it for the first time. She watched him silently; the occasional cloud cast shadows across him as he paced in and out of the light. "I should think this is a better place for the orchids. I will have George move them here today," he said.

Ada looked out the window to the garden, but the usual calming sensation didn't overcome her. Her sunroom would now be overtaken by the plants that had so recently bewitched her husband. Edward sat again in his chair, and she poured more coffee for him, willing her hands to remain steady.

"Ada, darling." His voice was rich with what sounded to her like kindness. "I hear you went on a foray yesterday morning." So all the talk of orchids had simply been preamble to this, the real purpose of their meeting.

She stood reflexively, grabbing her cup and saucer, stepping out from her chair, ready to carry the dishes to Ettie. Edith or Mary would be by to gather them; there was no reason for Ada to do so herself. She sat down again, still holding her filigreed cream china cup and plate. Edward watched her without speaking. She felt cornered. Finally, she had to speak to fill the silence. "I simply went for a walk because the weather was so lovely." At first she had wanted to tell him about the cyclists, to suggest to him that she might take lessons, but now she realized mention of the event would be a serious blunder.

He stroked his chin and leaned toward her. "You should always take someone with you. You and Katie get along so well. Take her. We will have no more of you wandering off by yourself." He pressed his hands into his knees, rose, kissed her cheek, and was gone.

Ethics of Marriage

That evening, immediately upon his return from the Club, Edward had come to Ada's bedroom, and now they lingered together, face-to-face, on Ada's thick mattress, as if their two bodies had become one. They were so still, it seemed as if they were sleeping sitting up, entwined. Her legs were wrapped around Edward's waist; he sat with his legs forward underneath her, in a V. He held her torso against his own. They were not sweating, nor were they breathing hard. The room was cool and silent.

But then, like a butterfly gently disturbing the glassy stillness of a pond, Edward slowly lifted his hips, and his pelvis rose up against Ada's. Her body quivered in response, but piece by piece, the subtle movement rising from her thighs and continuing up through her pubis, her torso, disturbing her breasts slightly, finally relaxing into her neck. The ripple completed itself when Ada released a small whimper and tilted her head back. Wanting to please her husband, she fought the desire to push to orgasm, willed her muscles to stop contracting, her hips to remain in position.

"I'm sorry," she said. "I'm sorry." She tried to control the release of her breath so it wouldn't be audible to her husband. The effort made her dizzy. Her head felt like an impossible weight on her thin neck as she pulled it forward, straightening herself. She returned her cheek to its place against her husband's neck. Her thick auburn hair settled onto his shoulder and chest.

Edward stroked her hair and tried to quiet her with pure sound. "Shh, shh." He said it over and over until their joined bodies returned to stasis and Ada's breathing became invisible again. The clock on the dresser was loud, animated, in contrast to the bodies on the bed. Its ticking eased Ada's active mind, moving her away from thoughts of sexual arousal, allowing her to sink into a sort of trance as she sat motionless in her husband's wiry arms. A last bit of the setting sun flashed through a slit in the brocade curtains and cut across her hair, lighting it as if it had been set afire. Edward and Ada remained there, tangled together yet immobile, until the sun moved past her, settling its light onto an empty space on the mattress. Finally, when Edward felt satiated, they separated from each other and tidied up, replacing their nightclothes and smoothing the sheets, then climbing back into the carved walnut bed, their heads resting side by side beneath the pair of wooden cupids. There was no need to wash up.

EDWARD STAYED WITH ADA till morning instead of returning to his own room afterward. During the past three years, Ada had spent many nights alone in her bed longing for the warmth of her husband next to her. But now that he was there, on this night, she wished to be alone, to stretch herself out across the bed, dangling her arm over one side, her foot over the other. Edward slept flat on his back, his eyes closed, his face emitting a sort of ecstatic contentment. She moved herself away from the crevasse created by her husband's weight on the mattress and banished herself to a narrow strip along the side of the bed. In no time at all, Edward was snoring softly.

Ada closed her eyes, hoping for a spiritual bliss to overtake her, followed by sleep. Instead, a vivid scenario played out in her mind a hundred different ways, keeping her awake most of the night. In every variant of the scene she imagined, the end result was orgasm. But this was achieved only in her imagination, and her body could not rest for wanting it in reality.

Just before Edward left her room the next morning, he leaned over to touch her cheek. He held his hand there as he looked into her eyes. He was close enough for her to catch his scent, but when she breathed in deeply, the absence of odor surprised her. When he removed his hand from her face, he let out a contented sigh.

He drummed his fingers across a book that sat on the bedside table. "Don't forget to review it."

She watched his tall, sinewy form as he crossed her threshold, then disappeared beyond her door. He was a handsome man, but he seemed to want to contain and control his very attractiveness. Ada wanted to run her fingers across it, caress it with her tongue, she wanted to watch the sweat bead up and drip down the slopes and valleys of it. But Edward would have none of that.

Ada lifted herself from the dry, neat bed. The wooden floor was cool beneath her bare feet as she moved slowly to her window. She pushed back the curtains in one angry thrust. But what she had hoped for wasn't there; the sun was hidden behind dark clouds and the shadows of clouds. Her shoulders slumped as she turned back to her bed.

In an effort to ward off a bout of ennui, she picked up the book Edward wanted her to read. She fingered the gold lettering on the blue leather cover. *Karezza: Ethics of Marriage*, by Alice Bunker Stockham. Stockham was a medical doctor who believed that if a man and woman engaged in intercourse without orgasm, they would come to a deeper understanding of each other, their marriage, and spiritual life. She had come to her philosophy through an examination of Tantric yoga. Edward believed this connection to Eastern spiritualism made the book and the philosophy both exotic and sacred.

Knowing she could not sit and read the book from front to back, having already tried and failed on several occasions, Ada opened it instead to a random spot and began reading from the middle of the page.

> During a lengthy period of perfect control, the whole being of each is merged into the other, and an exquisite exaltation experienced. This may be accompanied by a quiet motion, entirely under subordination of the will, so that the thrill of passion for either may not go beyond a pleasurable exchange. Unless procreation is desired, let the final propagative orgasm be entirely avoided. With abundant time and mutual reciprocity the interchange becomes satisfactory and complete without emission or crisis. In the course of an hour the physical tension subsides, the spiritual exaltation increases, and not uncommonly visions of a transcendent life are seen and consciousness of new powers experienced.

She tried to remember when she had last experienced crisis. There was snow outside the window when he appeared in her bedroom that morning more than a year ago, holding the book out to her. If she had known that day was looming, she would have made an effort to remember the last time. But because she had had no warning, their old lives as young husband and wife had seemed destined to last and even expand, so each individual experience folded itself into the next, becoming a blur of successive moments absent of articulation.

Ada imagined tearing the pages out of *Karezza: Ethics of Marriage*, one by one, and dropping them into her fireplace. The paper was of good quality, and creamy white. It would probably burn bright blue. Edward might come in to find her on her knees, in front of the fireplace, her face lit by the book's glow. At first he would be struck by her bright profile. But then he would see that she was burning his beloved book. She didn't try to imagine what he would do when the truth became apparent to him.

Suddenly, as she leaned over the pages of the book, staring at them without trying to read the words written there, Ada had a vision of her old friend Alice Blackwell. What would Alice think of this book? she wondered. Would she deride Ada for reading it, or would she see a certain value in it?

As a girl, Ada had attended the Chauncy Hall School in Boston, a private school that prepared girls for Boston University. There she met Alice Blackwell, an outspoken suffragette and editor of *Woman's Journal*, and her aunts, the Blackwell sisters, both physicians, when they came to speak to the girls at the school. Ada was taken with Alice and the sisters, who saw in her a good pupil. She was soon regularly invited, along with some of the other students, to tea at their sister-in-law, Lucy Stone Blackwell's, and to hear Alice speak on the Woman Question. Ada became involved with the politics of women in Boston to the extent that, by the time she was eighteen, she had marginalized herself from the pool of available men. What man of her class was interested in a woman who wanted to be his equal? She didn't really notice the absence of men in her life until she went to university.

After she had finished school, Ada enrolled at Boston University, even though her mother thought it a waste of time. There, she was one of only a small number of women, and she was, of course, surrounded by men. She continued to see the Blackwells, and Lucy's daughter Alice, during college. But as she pursued her studies, she also came to recognize her desire to be desired by a man. Boston University had given her this as well as an education. Her sexual awakening made the work of the Blackwells and their like seem less urgent to her; she couldn't put the energy into the fight the way these women did. She wanted to laugh, and be around men who were disturbed by the sound of her laughter, to watch their faces when she threw her head back, and her breasts lifted themselves in response, her whole body shot through with the thrill of the laugh. It was at university that she learned to fulfill that desire, rather than the impossible desire for equal rights.

When she was twenty-two, finished with college and already declared a hopeless spinster by her mother, Ada met Edward at a Blackwell salon. As usual, there were mostly women there, and the men who did attend were all men whom she had always known, it seemed. They were strident and serious, and none of them was interesting to her. But then, in walked Edward, in the company of a couple who came frequently to the salons.

Edward was tall and lean; he entered the room with an air of authority. Whether he was in his element or not, Ada was sure he always worked to give the impression that he was at ease and in command. He was still far across the room from her, but as he was introduced, she could hear the boom of his voice. It seemed to drop onto the floor in front of him and roll through the floorboards and under her feet, vibrating up through her spine. As she watched him move, she felt as if the lower half of her torso had separated itself from the usual workings of her mind and taken on, against her will, a purely sensuous aspect.

When he finally made it across the room to her, and looked at her with eyes that were the gray of shale, she hooked her arm through his elbow and didn't let him leave her side until much later in the evening, when she was tired and ready to go. They talked about their families and their educations. Edward spoke of his aspirations in business and the law. They never did discuss the Woman Question or politics of any kind. Ada wasn't thinking about those things when she stood with him that afternoon. As she watched him speak, she imagined running her fingers through his fine brown hair, she imagined the feel of his body against hers, and these thoughts did not make her ashamed.

Alice approached them where they sat together in the back parlor late in the afternoon.

"Why, Ada, I thought you had left without saying goodbye." Alice tilted her finely chiseled face toward Ada, waiting for her to defend her disappearance.

"Where have you been hiding Edward, Alice? Why have I never met him until today?"

Alice looked at Edward as if seeing him for the first time.

"Ah, don't blame Alice, my dear Ada," Edward said. "She only just met me last week."

"Well, my dear sister, you should bring more like him into your world," Ada said.

Edward left soon afterward, and Ada sat with Alice for a bit. "Alice," she said to her old friend. "If Edward should call to ask for my address, please do give it to him."

"Of course. Perhaps you will ask him to come to a meeting with us."

Ada nodded her assent, but she never did ask Edward to do any such thing. That wasn't what she wanted from him. He sent his card around to her the next day, and she responded to it with considered haste.

Later, when they began to spend time together, her physical desires spread out before her like a map of her self. When they walked alongside each other, he placed his hand at the small of her back and left it there. She could feel it pulse with the desire to explore other reaches of her body. She shifted her back underneath his hand, letting him know that she enjoyed his touch. Whenever they went to the opera or theater together, whenever they attended a dinner party, she hoped for the opportunity to be alone with him at the end of the evening. But they were both members of a society that expected them to refrain from physical intimacy until they joined each other in their marriage bed, and Edward was nothing if not proper. Ada wasn't thinking about marriage, though. She chose Edward because his tall body and strong hands made her breath come quicker, because his brown hair felt like silk, because when his eyes rested on her breasts she felt a familiar ache. None of these things were reason to marry a man.

It finally happened one evening after they saw Fanny Davenport in *Cleopatra* at the Tremont Street Theatre. Something about Fanny's bare neck, holding the asp to it in her grand suicidal gesture, excited both Ada and Edward. They were alone together in the box, and Edward allowed his hand to touch Ada's own bare neck. The sensation distracted her; the electrical charge that ran from her neck to her groin made it impossible to listen to Fanny, or think of anything other than Edward's fingers.

After the final curtain, they climbed into the hansom cab in silence. As the horse clopped along Tremont, headed for Beatrice's house off Louisburg Square, Edward touched her neck again.

"Don't take me home," she said suddenly.

"Where shall I take you?"

"Take me to a hotel."

She saw his face change, switching between desire and fear. "Ada. I simply cannot."

But she insisted, and she won. The driver turned the cab, and the horses headed south.

Ada didn't ask Edward how he knew of a hotel where they would not be questioned in regard to their marital status or their lack of luggage. She didn't care whether or not he had taken another woman there. She didn't mind at all that their room was simple, or the neighborhood a working-class one. She only cared that he took her into the bed there, and they at last revealed their bodies to each other, and at last, she tasted his skin, and felt the touch of his tongue on her own skin. Her monthly began toward dawn, but she wasn't ashamed of the trace of blood she left behind on the linens in that strange room.

On the way home, in the cab, Edward took her hand in his. "I am so sorry. I hope you don't think my intentions were not honorable. Please forgive me."

"Don't be silly," she said. "I wanted to do that as much as you did. We're both free adults, Edward. Aren't we?"

"Well, of course. But it is a bit irregular."

"Certainly you have noticed by now that I'm drawn to the irregular."

Even after he dropped her at her mother's house and she tiptoed into her room, where she relived in her imagination the experience of the night before, Ada never once thought that she and Edward would now have to be married. She hoped only to have more hotel room adventures, and to continue everything else as it was. She never thought about what Edward's passions might be outside his desire for her. Did he believe in the things she prized? If someone had told her at the time that no, Edward really wasn't concerned about votes for women or the Negro question, and that yes, he was content with the status quo, would that have changed things? Would her life have taken a different turn?

It was her mother who pushed her to marry Edward.

Shortly after the night of *Cleopatra*, on one of the rare evenings when she and her mother were home alone, Beatrice arranged that they eat dinner together. Usually, their house was full of callers, or Beatrice went out, leaving Ada to her own devices. But tonight, there they were, just the two of them. As she entered the vast dining room where her mother sat alone at the end of a Brazilian cherry table big enough to seat eighteen, Ada had the suspicion that the dinner was not just a family event, but rather, that it had an agenda. She felt her skin crawl under her heavy silks as she sat down at the corner of the table, to her mother's left. She wanted to stick her fingers inside her dress and scratch at herself, but she knew if she did, her mother would slap at her hands until she stopped.

The scraping of silver against china echoed along the length of the table. The precise moment after the last food had been dished up, and the last servant vacated the room, Beatrice, dressed to go out after dinner in deep blue satin, a long string of pearls dangling from her neck and down below the edge of the table, leaned her narrow chest forward and addressed her daughter. "I approve of Edward, you know."

"What?" Ada's breath became shallow, and she felt sweat beading on her forehead.

"I never saw myself as one of those mothers who might encourage her daughter to stay with her, to care for her in her old age and never marry herself."

Suddenly, Ada's skin stopped itching, but her hands grew clammy. She had to wipe them on her napkin. "What are you saying, Mother?"

"You should marry Edward."

Ada's voice was thin. "What you mean is that you don't want me to continue to live with you."

"I don't mind having you here. You're delightful, and this house is big enough for ten of you." Beatrice leaned back in her chair, taking up the end of the long rope of pearls and resting it neatly in her lap. "What I object to is the *idea* of you being here. You are too old and too intelligent to continue living in a house that isn't yours to run as you see fit."

"I don't believe I've known him long enough to even think of marriage," Ada said. Every word she uttered made her feel short of breath, as if she had just run from her room upstairs to join her mother at table. She pushed each sound out, then struggled to breathe before voicing the next.

Her mother shook her head at Ada. "You are nearly past marrying age, Ada, my dear. And you are a headstrong girl. If you don't marry Edward,

I'm afraid that you will never find a man of his caliber who will consider you for his wife."

Ada had always thought she was destined for a life more interesting than that of a wife and mother. But, of course, any such interesting life would have to be funded by her mother. This realization was sudden, and alarming. Her mother was not about to pay for her to live a modern life, one which Beatrice herself had not been free to enjoy until she became a widow. But she argued anyway, believing for another moment that she could shape her own future if she tried hard enough.

"Mother, I am not certain Edward and I should marry. I'm not certain I should marry anyone."

"I knew college would fill your head with nonsense. What a mistake it was to allow you to go. But your father always wanted you to attend, since you were our only child. So, of course, I honored his wishes after he died." Beatrice leaned forward in her chair and looked even more directly into Ada's eyes. "But that's behind you now. Let me put it to you simply. I will not have my only child, my daughter, live life as a spinster. I simply will not have it. If you have someone else in mind who is ready to marry you, please, tell him to come forward and present himself to me."

The words were right there, just inside her lips and ready to come bursting out. Mother, I will not marry him, or anyone. She meant to say them, but somehow she didn't. And the moment when she might have found it in her to stand up to her mother passed with the changing of the light in the room.

Beatrice had particular ideas about the way a household worked, and the place that household and its members held in the larger social structure. A single young woman did not constitute a household, though a single widow did. Her ideas were fixed, crystallized with all the points polished to perfection. Her mother was telling her that she was to marry Edward, and remove herself from her childhood home. Ada understood what this meant. She had seen it before. There were distant cousins, a stray aunt here and there, who had defied their parents' wishes, and had been cut out of the will. Their fates were far from pleasant. Ada knew she wasn't equipped to live a life of struggle and financial hardship. She had had no training in the arts of genteel poverty. As the light thinned, and the colors in the dining room grayed, Ada decided that her life would be easier than all those others, whether she grew to regret this decision or not.

Edward asked Ada to marry him the very next time Ada saw him. Certainly he had been speaking with Beatrice. Ada wondered if Beatrice somehow knew about the night in the hotel room, after *Cleopatra*. Perhaps her mother had extracted a confession from Edward, or maybe he had felt compelled to admit to his sin, to offer the story to Beatrice as penance. In any case, sure that she had no other choice, Ada said yes to Edward and even grew to believe she was overjoyed at her good fortune. Her days of adventuring were over; her four years at college had come upon her and then washed away faster than the turning of a single tide. It was time to be a wife.

AFTER ADA AND EDWARD were married, she didn't sever her ties with the Blackwells, but she did eventually stop going to the lectures regularly. Her contact with them was gradually, almost without notice, limited to quick lunchtime visits when the sisters were in town, and while her husband was at the office, doing the important work of their marriage—the work that made their lives possible. She came to understand that the lectures, the talking, were women's games, just as Edward would later insist. The work of those who could afford to invest their time in such pursuits.

So, Ada's unusual ideas about single womanhood were subdued, submerged, and supplanted, first by simple physical desire, then by her mother's will. When the brief period of desire she had shared with Edward early in their marriage ended, and Karezza had taken its place, Ada developed an agreement with herself, with the routine of her days. She would place her passions within the confines of small, inconsequential but solid acts and concerns. The household, the staff, ordered and restrained intimacy with her husband. It was necessary to learn to be happy with these things.

ADA TURNED HER ATTENTION back to *Karezza*. Edward would ask her about it later, so she should read enough to keep up her end of a conversation. At least Karezza was a reliable form of pregnancy prevention. For this, Ada was grateful. The book fell open, and she read what she found there.

> The institution of marriage becomes ideal when the desire and pleasure of the wife calls forth the desire and pleasure of the husband—when a single code of ethics governs their relation. When offspring is desired, then surely it is for woman to command and man to obey.

That was enough. Unable to read another word, Ada threw the book down on the table. Edward would do most of the talking, anyway. She would simply nod and agree, making herself seem the agreeable, childless wife Stockham would approve of. Was that all it would take—the birth of a child—for her to find herself in charge of her life once again? The idea seemed absurd to Ada.

She dressed herself in a taffeta bodice and India twill skirt and went to the stairs. Her right hand brushed lightly along the ornately carved mahogany rail as she descended the front stairs. The wood was silky to the touch; its sensuality caused her to lift her hand away and walk the rest of the way down holding only her own skirts.

She filled her day with the house linen project, and devoted a brief interlude to preliminary preparations for the dinner party. Her own dinner that evening was again a solitary affair. She would have asked Katie to sit and eat with her, but she knew George would report such behavior to Edward, and at the very least, there would be no hope of ever sharing a meal with Katie again.

After dinner, as Ada sat in the chair under her bedroom window and read the stories of Edgar Allan Poe rather than the wisdom of Alice Stockham, she heard a commotion downstairs. She went down to find Edward in the sunroom, bearing another box of orchids, and accompanied by Franz and Walter, the white orchid hunter. Walter was setting up some large metal contraption.

Ada, delighted to find Walter in her house again, walked brazenly into the room, holding out her hand. "Hello, Franz, how are you?" He kissed her hand, and then she turned and held it out to Walter to kiss. "It's lovely to see you again, Walter." Franz and Edward interrupted their labors and watched her as if she were a naughty child who needed attention, as if they were waiting to make sure she didn't go too far.

"It's nice to see you again, Mrs. Pryce," Walter said. Then he kissed her hand.

"Please, call me Ada." Ada sensed that Edward and Franz had stopped breathing. "What is that monstrous thing that's filling my sunroom?" she asked Walter, smiling as she spoke.

"It's a heater, for the orchids, Ada," Walter said, smiling back at her.

Edward was so eager to discuss his orchids, he seemed to excuse his wife's forward behavior with Walter. "They need to be kept warm, and they can't tolerate direct sunlight," he told her. "So we're going to install the heater, and drape the glass with a tarpaulin." He pointed to the roll of burlap on the floor. "Franz and Walter have helped me to expand my collection. I need a proper place for them." That was when she allowed herself to look at the box on the table under the window. A new collection of orchids rested there, preening, it seemed to her, gloating over their usurpation of her sunroom.

Ada felt a rage gurgle up in her stomach. What right did Edward and his horrid plants have to take away this room, to eliminate the thing about it that so pleased her? Now where would she go when she needed to feel the warmth of the sun? She wanted to stomp out, to make a fuss that he would never forget. But she also wanted to stay as long as he would allow her. She wanted to hear what Walter might have to say for himself, she wanted to linger in this now-male space for a moment longer.

"We're about to make a mess in here, my dear," Edward said. "You might not enjoy it."

Franz laughed and stroked the curls at the end of his mustache. "I know if this were Emmy's room, she would be in tears at this moment. You're a brave girl to be in here at all, Ada."

Ada recognized Edward's directive. She bade the men good night, smiling as she did so, and left.

She returned to her chair and to Poe. Even after she had changed into her nightdress and climbed into her bed with the book, the banging continued. As the night deepened, the sounds that echoed through the house as the men tore apart her sunroom became a suiting backdrop to the tone of Poe's odd stories. When she put the book away, the clatter kept her from sleeping, but she remained in her bed, never considering asking Edward to stop work for the night. Ada remembered Stockham's claim that a woman who was a mother could command a man to do her will. Did that explain Franz's comment about his wife, Emmy? He wouldn't consider transforming *her* sunroom, Ada knew that. But was it because Emmy was a mother? It was possible Edward would only begin to treat her like an adult when she became a mother.

The work in the sunroom continued past midnight. When it finally stopped, and Ada heard the guests leave and Edward retire to his room, she went to her window. It was hard to tell how long she had been looking at the stars when a weak light appeared in the carriage house window. She was tempted to sneak outside, but Edward still moved about in his room, so she got back into her bed, pulled up her gown, and ground her pelvis into the mattress. In the end, she slept very little, and was exhausted when she woke the next morning.

TERRESTRIALS *and* EPIPHYTALS

They stood together, Ada and Edward, in the sunroom, gazing on the orchids. There were more than two dozen orchids now, all set out along a large table that had been placed under the windows. The burlap compressed the light, making the room hazy, the sound muffled. "What is it about them that so fascinates you?" Ada asked.

Edward hardly hesitated. It was as if he anticipated the question, and had planned his response. "Someone who hasn't experienced this sort of passion may find it difficult to understand what it means to be the best at something. It's a crucial challenge."

Ada didn't try to disabuse him of his belief that she had no such experience. She didn't even let her husband's comment settle into her consciousness. "So you want to be the best."

"I would like to be known as the man with the rarest orchid collection in Boston."

"I think, if I were a man, I would want to be known as the one who helped women to get the vote and Africans to become equal citizens." She averted her gaze as she waited for his response.

Edward leaned forward to take his wife's hands in his own, and she looked at him again. "The difference between your passion, if you will, and mine is that mine is practical. I actually have rare orchids under my roof at this very moment, and the prospect of obtaining more is one hundred percent realizable."

She tugged at her hands, freeing them from Edward's grasp, and dropped them to her sides, resisting a sudden urge to strangle the Ruby-lipped *Cattleya.* Edward's voice cut into her fantasy.

"Do you remember what that one is called?"

She turned to her husband. *"Cattleya,"* she said, holding her hands behind her back now.

"Excellent. *Cattleya labiata* to be precise." He crossed the room, heading for her.

"But not *vera*," Ada said.

"Bravo!" Edward grinned at his wife. "I married the smartest girl in Boston." He came up next to her and encircled her small corseted waist with his long hands. "The slipper orchids," he said, indicating the purple-cupped orchid, "are terrestrials. Because they grow in the earth."

"Don't all orchids grow in the earth?" The lower petal of the purple flower was shaped like a hip bath, or a china cup, even. A faerie might have sipped wine from it. At its center was a slight protrusion, a simple swelling that seemed to usher from the internal workings of the flower. This would be the sex of the plant, Ada thought. The bit of flower that was fundamental to procreation. It was crisscrossed with blue veins. She reached out to touch it; its flesh was surprisingly thick and spongy. Ada's fingers recoiled from the sensation as though she had touched some humanoid piece of flesh.

But at the same time that the plants repelled her, she imagined what it must be like for Walter, or William, or Jao, when they first happened upon one of the creatures in the jungle. Were they warmed by a sense of jubilation? Did they feel pride? Did they feel as if they had conquered nature after a manner?

"No," Edward was saying to her. "That's the miracle of orchids. Some of them attach themselves to trees, or to rocks, and their roots thrive on air.

Take this one, for example." He picked up an orange flower with strangely curling petals that resembled vines. "This grows in rocks. See how I have placed its roots on chips of wood? There is no soil in this pot. These are epiphytals." He handed it to Ada and leaned in toward her as she examined its roots. She felt his breath on her neck, and suddenly an image of Katie and Liam in the stable crossed her consciousness. She felt the atoms in her groin shift.

"I want to make my collection the best for my son."

The vision of Katie and Liam dissolved, and Ada felt the hairs on her neck rise. He was thinking of children, yet he never discussed them with her. He had never uttered the words "my son" in front of her; he knew full well her reticence regarding motherhood. Besides, it wasn't possible for her to get pregnant as long as they practiced Karezza.

"Do you want children soon, my dear?" she asked.

He didn't look at her when he answered. "Not until I'm sure you're ready."

Without another word to her, he left for his club. Though it was still early, Ada was suddenly exhausted to her very marrow. She went up to bed. Just after she blew out her lantern, she felt a strong urge to cry. Instead, she went to her window, threw it open, and leaned out of it to look up at the stars. She imagined that she might somehow travel across the Milky Way. When she slept, she dreamed of spinning planets and crackling stars. When she awoke, she wondered if dreaming of stars brought her closer to Stockham's ideal of spiritual awareness.

Early the next afternoon Ada walked down the hall, past the sunroom. She had had no intention of entering it now that it was no longer hers, but she stopped, then turned back, putting her kid leather boot on the threshold of the room, and stayed there, hovering, contemplating whether or not she should enter. Finally, she stepped in, softly, trying to prevent her shoes from making a sound as she walked across the rosewood parquetry. The room that had once lifted her spirits was draped in drab cloth and smelled of bark and loam and the dankness of ill-lit places. The plants seemed to taunt her. What did they want from her? Suddenly, Ada imagined that, to Edward, these plants served as some sort of replacement for the children that they did not have.

She noticed a watering can under the orchids' table. The plants did look thirsty, perhaps she should water them. Putting thoughts of children out of her mind, Ada hummed to herself as she tipped the heavy can over each of the orchids, one by one, careful not to overdo it. They weren't so terrible, she thought. Just odd, harmless flowers.

But when she lifted the can to water the purple slipper orchid, it looked different. The protrusions that before had signaled its sex to her now were like pustules, ulcerations. Following an urge to wipe the thing clean, to obliterate its abnormal sexuality, she let the water gush until the offending flower rested in puddles of water, its pot soaked through.

The watering relieved the flowers of their droopiness, except for the purple slipper. The excess of water exacerbated that plant's condition. The slipper looked as if it were attempting to lie down in its bed, to retire from the responsibility of always standing at attention. But its protuberances were more pronounced now, as if they were mocking Ada. Disturbed by this, she set the watering can down on a shelf at the other end of the room and turned her back on the plants.

She went to the kitchen, meaning to check with Ettie about the pantry. Instead, she found the kitchen empty except for Liam and Katie, who stood together near the back door, his hand touching the curly hairs that fell free of her chignon. He dropped his hand and went back outside the instant he saw Ada. For a moment, she wished she had entered the kitchen more stealthily, so that she might have watched them in the daylight.

"Oh, Ada. Good day," Katie said as she turned away from the door. She didn't let on that she was surprised or embarrassed. "Would you be needing anything?"

"Thanks. No. I was just looking for Ettie."

"She's gone to the market. She wouldn't stand for me going. She was all in a twist about the meat. Said it wasn't good enough for the likes of Mr. Pryce."

"Oh, never mind about her," Ada said. "She enjoys being angry." Suddenly, Ada saw an opportunity in Ettie's absence. "When did she leave?"

"Not fifteen minutes ago."

"Where's George?" Ada asked.

"Oh, gone as well, tending to some important business for the Mister. You know."

"So neither one of them will be back for a while. Come sit with me in the dining room, and we'll have lunch together."

"Oh, Ada, are you sure? I've so much to do. Edith and Mary will be in a snit if they see the likes of me dining with you."

"Then let's ask them to join us."

THE FOUR WOMEN dined on lamb stew, fruit, cheese, and mincemeat pie. They drank from the Pryce wine cellar. At first the three maids were quiet and respectful, saying "Yes, ma'am" and "Thank you ever so much, ma'am" every time they took a spoonful of food from a platter or filled their water glasses. They sat with their backs straight in their chairs, fearful of appearing too comfortable in front of their employer. But Ada insisted on refilling their wineglasses, again and again, and soon all of them were draped across their chairs, or leaning on the table, telling one another stories.

"Oh, yes," Edith was saying. Her cap was next to her on an empty chair now, her sandy hair loose around her shoulders. "That Tommy over at the Coffins', he is the handsomest boy. But they say he's a faithless one. I don't care. I enjoy it whenever I have the chance to watch him wiggle his arse across the yard." Edith leaped up from the table and sashayed down the length of it, shaking her bum as she went. "And I'd enjoy seeing him in the raw, I would," she said as she returned to her seat.

All the women roared. Ada was forced to take in great gulps of air before she could speak, she had laughed so hard. "I want to see this Tommy. I must see him. And his arse."

"Oh, we'll show him to you, Ada. He comes by here every so often," Katie said.

"Do you have a sweetheart, Mary?" Ada asked.

Mary turned a shade of red that nearly matched the wine she held to her mouth. Ada reached over and patted the girl's hand. Edith said something under her breath, but Ada didn't catch it. Mary set her glass down. "I fancy the boy who works in the public stables," she whispered. "Patrick."

"Why, Mary. You never did tell me," Katie said.

"I knew," said Edith. Mary shot Edith a look that shut her up.

"Lovely Irish boy, he is," Katie said. "Does he fancy you?"

"I don't know. I'm too shy around him." Mary waved her napkin in front of her face, trying to stir up a wind and cool her cheeks.

"Well, we can take care of that," Edith said. "Let's go there." She tugged at Mary's hand, trying to get her to stand, but Mary pulled back, remaining in her seat.

"Oh, yes," Ada said. "Let's go talk to the lad. We'll tell him to get his arse over here." She rose as if to go right then, but her body wavered, and she dropped back down into her chair. Her actions caused a new round of raucous laughter. Ada laughed along with them. "Well, I'm afraid I've had a bit too much wine."

"Thank the sweet Lord we can't manage a stroll over there," Mary said. "It would have been the death of me, for certain." She grabbed her glass and took a great gulp of wine.

"But let me give you some advice," Ada said to her. Everyone stopped talking and listened silently as their mistress spoke. Mary gripped her glass and stared solemnly at her employer. "Next time you have reason to pass by the stables, when you see him, you swish your skirts so that he catches a glimpse of your leg. That will bring him running to you." She pulled up her own skirts, sticking her legs out away from the table so the girls could see, and pumped them as though she were riding a bicycle.

They all laughed hard at that—even Mary—so the house echoed with the unfamiliar sound of spirited mirth. Ada was certain she hadn't laughed this hard since college. She almost didn't hear it when the pocket door slid open and George stuck his head in, just in time to catch Ada with her legs up in the air in front of her where she sat, her skirts above her knees.

"Oh, excuse me, madame," he said, making no effort to conceal the displeasure that registered on his face. "I didn't realize." He was gone without another word, but the laughter stopped abruptly, and within an instant, the girls were clearing the table, and then moving to the kitchen to wash up. Ada followed after them, carrying a stack of plates. All of them had sobered up with George's arrival, it seemed.

Edith heard Ada walking behind her, and turned back. "Please, don't do that, madame," she said quietly, reaching out her hand to take the plates. Ada acquiesced and handed them to her, then stood and watched as the girls disappeared into the kitchen. She was left on her own in the now quiet house.

It didn't surprise Ada when Edward knocked on her bedroom door that night. She had been expecting him. He settled himself into her overstuffed chair. He looked uncomfortable in it, still dressed in the smoking suit he had worn to the Club. He gazed at her without speaking for some moments. She waited.

Finally, he leaned forward. "What were you thinking, Ada, allowing the household staff to drink wine with you in the middle of the day?"

"They are good girls, Edward. It can't hurt to let them enjoy themselves occasionally."

"Of course not. But that isn't what I am referring to. It is not your station to entertain them. Let them entertain themselves with their own kind, Ada. These people talk. Soon enough, all the maids in Boston will know what you did, and so will their mistresses. What will they think? What will their husbands think of my wife?" He stopped talking and looked into her empty fireplace.

"I'm sorry, Edward. I meant you no harm. But I simply don't understand why you care what other people might say about our little party. I don't care."

"Oh, my dear girl. That sense of independence is an admirable quality in you. But it is one you must use with discrimination. Sometimes you simply must care what other people say. This incident is hardly worthy of you. Quite frankly, I'm worried about you. First the walk in the park, now this." He stood up and went to her bedside. "Is something wrong?"

His concern pinched his forehead. He looked in agony, so that Ada felt remorse for her recent missteps. She put her hand on his and stroked it. "I am so sorry to have worried you, Edward." She kissed the back of his hand. "Please forgive me." She tugged gently on his hand until he sat down on the bed next to her.

He touched the top of her hair. The gesture had a quality of gentleness that calmed Ada, that made her want to pull him closer. She took his face in her hands and kissed him, and he reached around to unbutton her housedress. Karezza seemed different in this moment. She felt now as if she were performing a service that was crucial to her husband's survival. She held him in her arms as though he were a vulnerable child, and she felt the satisfaction of a sacred duty fulfilled when she managed an hour of sexual intercourse without orgasm.

ADA SLEPT ALONE that night, and her dream landscape was lush as a hothouse. She could have slept till late in the morning, but early, not long after sunrise, a strangled sort of bellow interrupted her imaginings. Ada shot up in her bed. It was Edward, yelling something incomprehensible. She threw her thick linen robe over her silk gown and rushed out of her room and down the stairs. She found him in the sunroom, George hovering at his side like a shorter, rounder shadow of his employer. The bellow had reduced itself to a pained whimper that sounded like that of a lost dog.

Edward was holding the purple slipper, the orchid she had overwatered, in his hands. It looked now as if it had passed through the desert and was dying of thirst. "This was a very valuable flower. How could this have happened? Who has been in here?" he demanded of George.

Ada felt as if all the blood in her body had pooled in her feet, making them weigh one hundred pounds in themselves. She could not move. George turned his puffy cheeks to Ada, glancing at her over his half-glasses briefly as she stood frozen in the doorway. But he didn't answer Edward;

he simply shook his head. It was only when Edward spoke again that Ada realized she had been holding her breath.

"All right. All right. Go about your business, then. I'll try to figure out if I have done something wrong."

"Yes, of course, sir," George said. He bowed slightly to Edward before he turned and walked toward the door. He didn't look at Ada as she stepped into the room to allow him to pass; she imagined his snub to be quite purposeful.

Ada went to her husband and encircled him in her arms. "Oh, my dear, I am so sorry."

"Oh, well, I shall just have to get busy on that greenhouse so that this does not happen again." He turned to his wife and kissed her forehead. "I must go to work. Please, if you would, keep an eye on the creatures for me, would you? Don't let anyone else in here. I'll clean the place myself."

"Of course, Edward."

Edward left Ada to go back to her routine. But whenever she encountered George that day, and even the next, she sensed a rigidness in him that went beyond his usual formality. Was he still angry about her lunch with the girls, or had he seen her enter the sunroom the night before? She would never know, but she feigned innocence, and never faltered in her performance. There was no guilt attached to this performance, for the simple fact was that George had somehow become her tormentor, the one who was always there, ready to report back to her husband whenever Ada refused to behave according to a formula she didn't really understand. How could anyone tolerate such an offense? She felt perfectly justified in her betrayal of George, even as she understood that Edward probably knew all along that his own wife was the one to blame for the violence against his beloved orchid.

THE GIRLS MOPED around for days after their notorious lunch together. "Ettie gave us a good talking-to for our inappropriate behavior," Katie told Ada. "She's taken away our free Sunday."

Ada tried to talk to Ettie, to get her to relax the rules a bit. "It wasn't their fault," she insisted. "I led them into it."

"Nevertheless, they know better." Ettie ceased rolling out her pie dough and turned to Ada. "They should have stopped you doing what you did. It is right that they should suffer for their indiscretions." She gripped the rolling pin as she glared at her mistress, daring her, Ada supposed, to disagree. But Ada knew not to pursue it with Ettie. If she did, Ettie would be certain to complain to George, who would report back to Edward.

"Of course, you're right, Ettie. I stand corrected."

Feeling stifled in all other pursuits, Ada concentrated her efforts on preparing for Edward's party. His orchid collection had grown to almost five dozen flowers, the greenhouse was close to completion, and he was nearly ready to display his collection to the world. She needed to keep her own planning abreast of his progress.

Since the purpose of the dinner was really to show off to Beatrice, the plans could not go ahead until Ada had secured her mother's commitment and they had agreed upon a date. But this wasn't an easy thing to do. Ada exchanged a number of phone calls with Elizabeth, her mother's lady's maid. She penciled dates into her calendar and erased them a total of six times. Edward checked on her progress regularly. "Has Beatrice committed yet?" he asked her, always trying to sound nonchalant, never quite succeeding. At last, Ada felt compelled to pay a personal visit to her mother, just so that she might report her success to Edward.

Ada sent a messenger to Beatrice's house, warning her mother of her impending arrival, and one hour later, Liam drove her to her childhood home off Louisburg Square. Desirous of her mother's approval, or at least of avoiding her mother's disapproval, she had dressed herself carefully in a finely embroidered shantung shirtwaist and a walking skirt the color of the sea. As Beatrice's parlor maid—yet another new one, Ada thought her name was Sarah—ushered her into the foyer, Ada straightened her shirtwaist, smoothing it so that her mother would notice the tiny embroidered rosebuds rather than the wrinkles.

Sarah—yes, she was sure it was Sarah—took her into the parlor. Ada had been waiting for what seemed a very long time when the maid came back.

"Mrs. Pryce? Mrs. Caswell has asked you to come to her room. I'll see you up."

Ada walked past her old room without turning her head to take a peek. Sarah left her at the doorway to her mother's room. Ada found Beatrice sitting in front of her dressing table, dousing her face with powder from a silver box. Ada's mother was a tall woman who had not gained the weight that attached itself to most women of her age. She remained as thin as she had been all of Ada's life, and her hair was still dark. Her thinness, Ada thought, made her more forbidding than she would have been had she grown softer. Beatrice motioned with her free hand for Ada to sit down in the chair in front of the table.

She adjusted her mirror so she could see her daughter's reflection as she drew lines around her eyes with kohl. "What is the emergency that brings you running here on such short notice, my dear child? As you can see, I am getting ready for an engagement."

"Of course, Mother. I won't keep you long. I just wanted to ask you, face-to-face, to honor Edward and me with your presence at the unveiling of his Orchid House. It will be a lovely evening."

"Why do you need me there?"

"This is very important to Edward, Mother. He is proud of his collection. And you are our closest family member. Edward's family won't travel from Philadelphia, of course. Perhaps next year they'll come. But we wouldn't think of unveiling the orchids now without your presence."

Beatrice studied her thinning skin, lifting it with her fingers and sighing when she released it and it dropped down again.

"I will have to have Elizabeth consult my books."

"I've already spoken with her, Mother. She says you're free on the thirteenth."

"All right, then. I promise I will be there on the thirteenth."

"You won't change your plans if something more interesting comes along?"

Ada watched Beatrice's eyes narrow in the mirror. "I can't imagine why I would do such a thing."

"Of course you wouldn't. I'm sorry. I'm all nerves over this dinner."

Beatrice leaned back on her bench and rounded her eyes, watching her own gaze in the glass. "You must give more dinners, my child. You have too little practice at this sort of thing."

"Perhaps I should," Ada said. She stood then and leaned over to kiss her mother's forehead. Beatrice reached back and patted her daughter's hand, her eyes still on her own reflection. Throughout the visit, her mother did not once turn away from the mirror. Ada said goodbye to Beatrice's image in the glass and went home to give Edward the news.

Once Beatrice had agreed to a date, Edward participated in preparations for the dinner by fussing over his orchids and the greenhouse construction whenever he was at home. If Ada needed to consult him about the guest list for the event, or about some household problem that related to the dinner, she knew to find him in the sunroom. Little more than a week before the party, she still couldn't decide between turnips and parsnips or turnips and potatoes to serve with the roasted ducks and scalloped oysters. Edward had always been sensitive to Beatrice's likes and dislikes, so she felt it appropriate to seek his advice.

He stood in a deep shadow thrown across the room by the burlap that covered most of the expanse of glass. As she walked toward him, she had an odd vision of the orchids as extensions of Edward's own fingers. He stretched his hand toward her, and from across the room, the winding tendrils of an orchid's roots seemed to touch her arm.

When she asked him the question, it was impossible to tell whether or not he was looking at her. "What should I serve, Edward? I simply can't decide between turnips and parsnips, or turnips and potatoes."

"All three, I'd say," Edward told her without hesitation. "That way everyone will be happy." He knew without her saying it that she was concerned only with pleasing her mother.

"Why, of course. You're absolutely right. Turnips, parsnips, *and* potatoes," she said.

"Don't let your own mother frighten you, my dear. She's only human, after all."

Ada's eyes widened as her vision blurred for an instant. "What?"

But Edward had already turned his attention back to his plants. "Do you know Darwin's work on orchids?" he asked her as he examined the flowers before him.

"No. I only know him from *On the Origin of Species*," she said.

"Of course. Of course. But after that, he wrote *On the Various Contrivances by Which British and Foreign Orchids Are Fertilised by Insects, and On the Good Effects of Intercrossing*. Published in 1862." Ada wasn't surprised that her husband could so easily recite this cumbersome title. He was, after all, a lawyer. This sort of information was to him as Shakespeare had once been to her, she imagined. "I've been studying it," he went on. "He made remarkable discoveries about the ways in which orchids adapted themselves. Beatrice will be interested in this, no doubt." He took the book from the end table and leafed through it. "Take a look at this," he said, his exhilaration reflected in his rising voice, yet subtly muffled by the burlap.

Edward pointed to Darwin's sketch, Figure One. Ada gazed on it as Edward carried on. "He removed the sepals and petals in order to study the labellum, which, of course, is the landing platform for the pollinator." Ada imagined it as a sort of molestation of the flower, a tearing away of the layers that were meant to protect the flower's secret places from invaders such as Darwin's probing fingers. "The slightest touch caused the membrane to rupture transversely in a sinuous line," Edward was saying. And again, Ada could think of nothing but a man's clumsy touch, causing irreparable damage, yet pleasing the man. Pleasing him, of all things.

Suddenly, Ada noticed the hammering and banging coming from the garden, where workmen were busily trying to finish Edward's greenhouse on schedule. Edward seemed to notice it at the same time.

"I must go check on their progress," he said.

He hadn't allowed her to enter the greenhouse since construction had begun. "I want you to be as surprised as everyone else," he said. It seemed to Ada to represent another way for Edward to keep her separate from this secret world of orchids that had become so important to him so suddenly. And now that the orchids would be moving outside to this new habitat,

Edward would become yet more distant from her, and her world inside this house.

After he had gone from the sunroom, Ada went back to the kitchen to consult with Ettie regarding plans for the dinner. She felt a certain fear at being the final arbiter of its organization. It was to be, after all, a small dinner, only ten of them altogether. But what if she were to fail Edward in this small but important endeavor? Would her husband ever forgive her if the dinner was not an unqualified success?

FINALLY, several days before the party, the plants were removed from the sunroom. At the thought of regaining her beloved room, Ada felt a slight tingle in her spine, like dozens of delicate fingers drumming the length of her back. Edward had hired special workers to move the plants into their new home. He hovered, and scolded, as they carefully transported each plant. Ada hovered alongside him, and watched silently as the disposition of the sunroom gradually declined from that of a sultry and overdressed entertainer to that of a down-at-heel dowager. The life in the room was all drained out. Her sunroom wasn't, now, the place she had dreamed so long of reclaiming from the orchids.

She stood there after Edward had followed the plants outside, staring at the disheveled room, wondering what she should do. She wanted to follow Edward out to the Orchid House, but he wouldn't allow it. "I want to watch your face the first time you see them all properly arranged," was his reason for banishing her. She looked out the window just as Edward opened the greenhouse door, then quickly closed it behind him. Burlap covered the greenhouse glass, and she hadn't had even a glimpse of the interior.

Unable to move from the spot where she stood, she called out Katie's name. Katie ran into the room, a look of dread on her face. "Ma'am, is everything all right?"

"I'm sorry. I didn't mean to frighten you. Everything is fine, I just need this mess taken care of, please." Katie left to fetch Edith and Mary. Ada stood, considering the space, the trails of loam and small bits of browned leaves, the wilted and dropped flowers. A withered florescence the color of dried blood peeked from under the sideboard. She picked it up and put it to her nose, sucking in the fading fragrance. Without knowing why, she put the flower into her pocket, then hurried out of the room, her boot heels snapping crisply against the wooden floor.

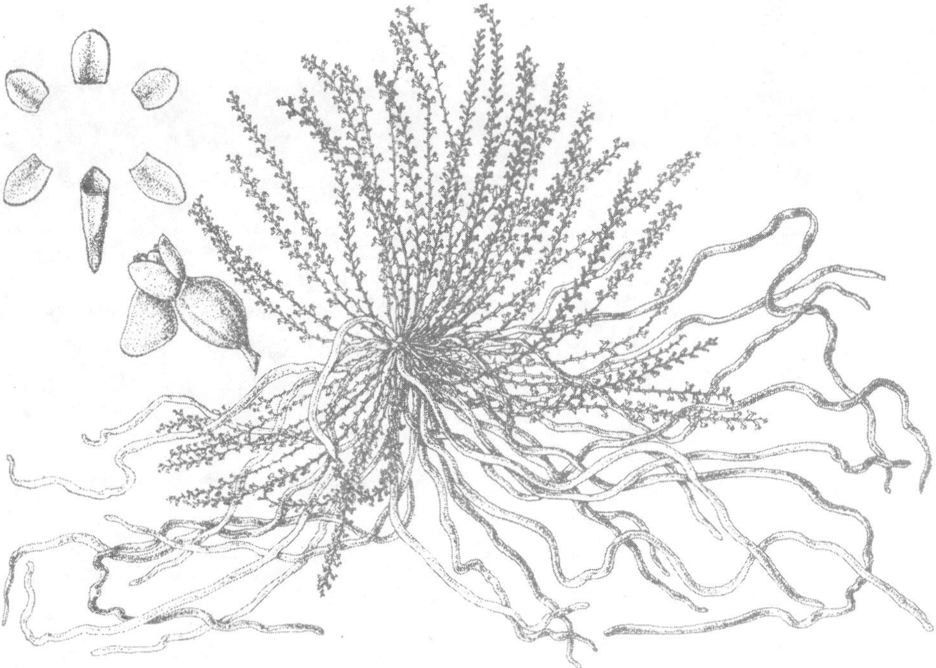

The Thousand Eyes

The afternoon of the big event found Ada in the kitchen, checking up on Ettie and the girls, making sure nothing had gone wrong with any element of the dinner. George and Katie were busy setting up the dining room. "Everything will be lovely," Ettie insisted as she and Mary and Edith rushed about. Ada knew she was making them nervous, breathing down their necks as they worked, trying to help them but making matters worse. She couldn't stop herself, though. Finally, just to keep her hands busy, she went to the sideboard and polished the already-polished silver.

She sensed a shift in the air when her mother arrived. It wasn't possible that she heard her mother's entrance from all the way back in the kitchen, but still she knew the instant her mother was there.

Ada stepped into the foyer just as Beatrice breezed into the house, precisely on time, the rustle of her skirts telegraphing the flurry of activity that always surrounded her, the importance she attached to the whirl of her busy life. As she walked her mother down the hallway and into the front parlor, her stomach suddenly developed the collywobbles.

The rest of them came in bunches. Emmy and Franz Locke arrived within seconds of Minnie Lovell and her husband, Anderson Lovell, partner in Edward and Franz's law firm—at least in name—but most important, president of the Orchid Society. Minutes later, Walter Kebble, William Parrish, and Jao da Cunha arrived. Ada's heart quickened as Katie brought the three men down the hallway toward her. Their presence made all the effort worth it.

After the guests had had some time to unwind in the parlor, Edward led them into the dining room. Ada took a sharp breath in as she walked into the room. Seeing it in its final presentation shocked her. She had changed her mind several times about which china, silver, and glassware to use, and what centerpiece would most impress her mother. The glassware caused her the most trouble. Her mother had given her a complete set of Thousand Eye wine and water glasses as a wedding gift. Ada knew she should use it to please her mother, but she had always hated the stuff. Its very name suggested to her that her mother had sent a spy into her house in the form of the glassware, that those thousand eyes watched her every move, assessing for Beatrice whether or not Ada was performing to her expectations. She resisted placing it on her table until the very last minute, at which time she instructed Edith and Mary to set the things out. Ada didn't want to touch the bumpy surfaces of the milky blue glasses until it was absolutely necessary. But seeing them laid out around the table now, Ada was struck by their strange beauty.

At the center of the table, the girls placed a large crystal bowl. Ada had filled the bowl with water in which floated the tops of blood-colored Moutan peonies she had purchased herself that morning at Van Oot's nursery. The cuts in the bowl reflected the light from the candelabra on each side of it, creating a snowflake pattern that glittered inward onto the peonies and outward to the table and across the Thousand Eye glasses. A lamp burned on the other side of the stained glass alcove. The two light and glass patterns, on the table and from the wall behind it, conflated, giving the room the quality of some many-hued arcadia. As she gazed on the effect, Ada knew she had done it right.

Ada arranged her guests at the table amid compliments on her centerpiece. Edward beamed at her from across the room as she seated herself at the foot of the table. A wife sat on one side of her, so that Edward would not accuse her later of having ignored the wives, and an orchid hunter on the other. The wife she had chosen to sit next to was Minnie Lovell. Minnie was a woman slightly past forty. She had two children closing in on adulthood, she had a big house, many servants, a lot of money, and a husband who was rarely around. She was secure in herself, and seemed unafraid to do what she wanted and to say what she thought. In spite of her commanding presence, she was impressed by Ada's college degree. For all these reasons, Ada did not mind spending the evening seated next to her.

"The peonies are wonderful," Minnie said. "Just splendid, my dear."

On her other side, wonderfully, mercifully, sat Walter Kebble, the white orchid hunter. "They are, indeed," he said to her. "Impressive." Hearing such a compliment from an orchid hunter filled Ada with a sense of accomplishment. The peonies were her pièce de résistance, certainly.

Down the table to her right, on the other side of Walter, Beatrice sat between Emmy and Anderson. Ada had always thought Emmy to be a pale, insubstantial-looking woman, in spite of the great deal of attention she paid to her hair and dress and jewels. She was in her mid-twenties, the mother of a two-year-old, and devoted to her husband and to doing all that Franz Locke wanted and demanded from her. She talked about little else. Beatrice would be thoroughly bored by her. And Anderson was a man who needed to be carefully steered away from topics that concerned his many accomplishments. Ada told herself that seating her mother between these two was in no way malicious, but rather it was a compliment. Beatrice was the only person present with the talent to force them to seem more interesting than they really were.

To her left, on the other side of Minnie, Ada had seated Jao, Franz, then William, and finally, Edward was at the head of the table.

As soon as their glasses had all been filled with wine, Anderson felt inspired to make a toast to Edward. "A man who is about to impress Boston as a formidable orchid collector." It was a generous toast, given that he was Edward's most obvious competitor. The company raised their glasses, and all the many Thousand Eyes refracted across the table and back to Ada.

As the wine flowed, and Beatrice drank, she seemed not to notice the Thousand Eye glasses, or remember that they had been her purchase. Perhaps Elizabeth was the one who had acquired them for her, and Beatrice had never even seen them. Ada's mother ate her duck and turnips and potatoes, but she did so with restraint, had no seconds, and offered no compliments. Ada clutched her own wine goblet, allowing the bumps to make indentations on her palms, as she watched her mother's reluctant approach to her plate.

"This is simply delicious," Emmy cooed.

Beatrice's left eyebrow arched slightly, and she turned her attention to Anderson. "You must let me know next time you have an orchid show," she said to him. "I believe I missed your last one."

As the orchid hunters drank more wine, they seemed to grow more at ease with this group that was not of their class. Soon enough, Walter leaned forward across the table so that he could regale Minnie and Ada with stories of his adventuring. Though he was probably in his early thirties, Walter looked considerably older than the other two orchid men; his skin had the look of the hide of some cragged and weary animal. His hair was a dark blond, and it shot out in every direction from his skull. It was evident he had not paid a visit to a barber who knew his trade in quite some time. Perhaps it had been lopped off with a machete, or some other fierce instrument. Certainly not by a pair of well-sharpened shears. But Walter was tall, and it was apparent, even though he was covered up with an ill-fitting suit of brown wool, that the man was a mass of muscle. Ada thought of wild horses when she looked at him, and the thought made her feel as if a strange airy space had inserted itself into her midriff; the space discomfited her, needed to be filled quickly, with almost anything.

She took a handful of grapes from the fruit platter and placed them in her mouth one by one, chewing them slowly while she listened to Walter. "We had traveled for thirteen days through the jungle, with a native guide leading the way. I couldn't have told you to save my life how to get out of there. And when we finally arrive in a remote little village, exhausted and hungry, what do you think we find?" Ada held a grape in front of her mouth, suspended, until he answered his own question. Everyone at the table was listening to him now. "Another group of American orchid hunters, who had arrived there only hours before us." The whole company groaned, and Walter held his chest out a little, basking in the attention.

Minnie reached over and patted his hand. "I hope we aren't boring you too much in staid old Boston."

"Oh, no, ma'am. Not a bit. I need a touch of calm now and then. It reenergizes me. And I appreciate your hospitality." He nodded at Ada; she bowed her head to him.

"Ada is a charming hostess, isn't she?" Minnie said.

"Indeed she is, ma'am." Walter winked at Ada. Ada looked immediately to Edward, to see if he had been watching. But he was engrossed in conversation with Franz now. She smiled at Walter. "Would you like more duck, Walter?" He took a large slice from the proffered platter. Ada watched him as he took generous bites and chewed his food as though he truly reveled in it.

Beatrice's voice suddenly rose above the others at the table. "Tell me more about your orchids, you two," she said to Edward and Franz.

Edward and Franz were only too happy to oblige Beatrice. As they regaled her with their theories of successful orchid cultivation, inspired by Darwin, and bragged about their prize plants, Ada turned her attentions back to Minnie and Walter.

Occasionally, her eyes and ears drifted to the other side of the table, where Jao and William were entertaining Franz and Anderson. Jao's voice seemed to jump out at her. Its pulse soothed her, made her want to listen to him. She tried to train her ears to his voice as she kept her face turned toward Minnie and Walter. What was he saying?

"I can't wait to go back," she thought he said. She turned her head just long enough to catch a glimpse of him. The candlelight threw a line across his angled face, dividing it in two. The side closest to her shone like something polished. Ada imagined him under the moonlight. Here at this table he seemed all wrong. She turned away from him before he could catch her watching him, but she continued to notice the strains of his voice as it floated across the table.

Walter shared his stories throughout the meal. He told Ada and Minnie that when he was in the Amazon last, he had encountered some rough characters. "But these rough ones were not, as one might expect, the natives. They were other orchid hunters, sent out by rich Americans and English lords and European princes, to find the rarest orchids. These collectors do not appreciate competition. And their minions take this attitude to heart. There were some nasty barroom encounters. I came to fisticuffs on numerous occasions. I finally took to avoiding white men altogether, and swearing my native assistants to secrecy."

Minnie slapped her hand on the table. "Oh, but that is simply appalling. To think that you can't trust one another out there in the wilds."

"It doesn't surprise me a bit. You can't trust one another here in the city. It would only stand to reason that it would be worse out in the jungle," Ada said.

Walter smiled at her. "That is the simple truth of it, I'm afraid. Each one of them is out to be the first, the best, and the richest. Everyone else be hanged."

Ada looked around the table, checking again, as she should, to be sure everyone had what they needed, and everyone had someone to talk to. Even though she was a reluctant hostess, she knew how to size up the status of her table quickly and expertly. Laughter and excited conversation, the contented scraping of forks across plates, and sighs of fulfillment drifted across the table. There was only one detail that needed correcting. She motioned to George to bring more wine. The lilt of Jao's voice wafted over again, but she still couldn't tell what he was saying. When George began to refill glasses, she turned back to Walter, leaning in close to him and speaking quietly. "So you will be keeping your next expedition secret, I imagine?"

"I won't be giving away many details, no. I don't want anyone to know what I'm looking for, or even who has sent me."

"Why are you here, then? Hasn't the Orchid Society hired all of you to find the *labiata vera*?" Ada asked.

Walter smiled and swallowed his wine without speaking.

"Oh, but you can trust us, please do tell all," said Minnie. Ada would never have presumed to be so obvious, but she was glad Minnie had said the words. Maybe Walter would tell her something that would keep her awake nights imagining the excitement of the journey, and wishing she might go along. Or perhaps he would haunt her dreams.

"This is undoubtedly true, but I don't trust myself, so I keep my mouth shut." Walter lifted his glass in a pantomimed toast. Minnie and Ada raised their own glasses to him, and watched him silently as he emptied his glass of its wine all at once.

Feeling as though she might be giving Walter too much attention, Ada turned to Minnie. "Tell us about Averel. How is he doing at university?"

"Oh, he surprises me. He's suddenly discovered a love of Shakespeare," Minnie said. "I never would have imagined that about him. You would have to know my boy, Walter."

"Ah, Shakespeare," Jao said suddenly. "Anyone who reads Shakespeare is destined to be bewitched."

Walter laughed, and shouted out to the table, "Jao forever tells me these infernal stories. Romeo and Juliet. Hamlet. Why should I concern myself with Hamlet and his problems? He never has answered me that."

Everyone laughed in sympathy with Walter. Ada heard Jao's laugh hovering, low, beneath the others, underscoring the waves of sound.

Imagine. The man loved Shakespeare.

I'll Take You Home Again

Shakespeare reminded Ada of freedom. His plays had been so much a part of the best time of her life, a time when she did what she pleased with few restrictions, a time when she had believed everything was possible. William Shakespeare had been right there in the thick of it with her.

There were thirteen women in the Liberal Arts program at Boston University, all of them imbued with the sense that they were doing something beyond the pale. Something that was, really, simply shocking. They were giddy with the thrill of it. It was like the smell of the earth after the first spring rain, when the ground has finally softened and become willing to give up its redolence, to release itself from its frozen winter abstention. They could smell the fecundity of their own minds. Ada didn't understand the boys who stayed out late drinking and didn't find the time to do their reading. She would not squander the gift of education. How could she when others had fought so hard for her right to be here? The thirteen of them could not indulge themselves the way the young men did.

Ada loved her Shakespeare class beyond all other

classes. She was always eager to see Professor Arlington, to hear his voice. As he lectured, she listened without seeing or feeling. Though her face grew flushed in the closeness of the lecture hall, she could not have told anyone, had they asked, whether it was warm or chilly in the room. She didn't see the patterns the sun and its shadows made as they frolicked through the windows and across the floor and desks and blackboard. She didn't see the great globe at the front of the room. She didn't even hear the other pens scratching, the other papers shuffling, the occasional cough. She heard only the basso of that voice that had so much to say. So much that she wanted to know.

Professor Arlington was in his thirties. He had thick reddish hair, the curls of which refused to decide where they should fall, and so they bolted every which way about his head. He wore wire-rimmed glasses over his smallish gray eyes. His voice boomed across the room as he beseeched them to "touch me with noble anger, and let not women's weapons, waterdrops, stain my man's cheeks." She looked in her book quickly as he spoke, trying to find the passage so she could see it and hear it at once, doubling the words so that they echoed both on the page and in the ethers. At times he told them where to look first, and she could leisurely read with him as he admonished them to "release me from my bands with the help of your good hands. Gentle breath of yours my sails must fill, or else my project fails."

When they came together so effortlessly, the words both written and spoken, she felt the tug of a fine silver cord connecting her to the book, the voice, and the eternity over which those words would wander. She wondered sometimes if she loved college and the friends she had there simply because of Shakespeare. Was it that awakening in her the plays inspired that created the person who flowered in the company of her classmates?

Moira Sumner, who sat next to her in the Shakespeare course, became her closest friend. Moira was a tall blond woman who always seemed to be enveloped in a gust of her own wind. She moved with the air of a woman who would rather be out rowing or playing croquet than sitting in a classroom. That first year, the two women were seen together so frequently, their friends referred to them as Moida. They walked together in the Common after class, discussing *Hamlet* or *Richard III*; they went together to social events with other classmates, both men and women. Eventually no one would dream of inviting one without the other.

One weekend in late fall, Moira invited Ada and their large group of friends, along with Professor Arlington, to Redruth, her family's country home on Cape Cod. Ada took a train to the Cape on her own, and a cab picked her up at the station. Pressing her face into the small window of the cab, she watched the estuaries and ponds and bits of sea as they passed by. The odors of salt and fog crept in through the floorboards. The breeze chilled her even through the blanket she had wrapped around her legs, yet at the same time it made her feel alive, and glad that she was alone for this bit of time.

The trap delivered her to the rambling Queen Ann house that stood, solitary, in a landscape of dying grass against sea. Bayley and his crew rushed out to greet her before she had both feet on the ground. They came across the wide yard like waves of black and white, all pushing and shouting and bumping up against one another. Ada felt jolted by this contrast to her silent journey. Her head felt laden with the clamor. She turned away from them and pulled her bag from inside the trap, but Bayley reached to take the bag from her. His hand touched hers. His was still warm, and it seemed to thaw her own in the square inch of contact. He picked up her carpetbag and buckled under the weight. He exaggerated the effect then, allowing his body to sink down to the ground. "Help me!" he shouted at his mates, feigning distress. Ralph rushed to him and reached down to help him up, but instead he suddenly dropped down, sprawling on top of Bayley, as if, weighted down by Ada's bag, Bayley had become unmovable.

"What on earth have you brought? A dumbbell?" shouted Ralph.

"No. Of course not. Just my Shakespeare."

Bayley and his boys laughed at this, uproariously. "You are going to saddle your merrymaking with Shakespeare?" asked Bayley.

Moira and the women didn't laugh loudly at this joke. They giggled politely, but the boys were so beside themselves, none of them noticed the women's reticence. The boys clearly didn't understand that this opportunity to study at university was something to be squeezed tightly for every drop of juice it had to offer. These women believed that they were changing the world for other women, and even that they were special women, and the world would bend for them, yet still they lived with a sense of urgency because somewhere, hidden away from their conscious thought, was the sense that this could not go on forever.

"You won't have time to study Shakespeare here, Ada." Bayley stood up and reached to pick up the bag, lurching his body forward, exaggerating the weight of it, and stumbling into Ralph, who walked in front of him.

"Oh, my man, you are going to break my bones with that thing!" The laughter was punch-drunk now, and even the women guffawed. But still, as they looked at one another, eyes moist with the jollity of it all, there was a silent recognition. They were laughing at Ralph and Bayley because they were silly, carefree. But the girls would never have the luxury of knowing that the world was waiting for them to come and show it what they had learned at university. Ada could see it in the way they refused to move in closer to the tight inner circle of men; they remained out on the periphery, in their own wider and looser circle. Their learning would always be a sort of secret, guilty gift, if not an angry one, and for many of them, the books in their carpetbags would one day be relegated to a place of furtive pleasure.

Moira escorted Ada to her bedroom on the second floor. The rooms and hallways seemed to be connected haphazardly; the wooden floors rolled up and down, and the stairways listed to one side or the other. The house smelled of age commingled with the unceasing assault of saltwater-heavy breezes. Ada took a massive gulp of the air. It offered some sort of unidentifiable comfort. They walked past sections of the house that were themed, the mariners' rooms, the nature walk, the hallway of family portraits, the Oriental area. There were a dozen bedrooms in the old place, plenty of room for the crew that Moira invited. Ada's bedroom, with its hodgepodge of themes represented by artifacts from India, France, Turkey, Ireland, and the Eastern seaboard of the United States, looked out over the back garden, which still, though autumn was well advanced, had some late-blooming flowers lending color to the expanse of green. She sat in the window seat and looked out her open window to the sea in an effort to restore the energy that had been depleted on the train and hansom ride out.

Moira came in then, interrupting her reverie. "We should change for dinner," she said.

Ada was loath to rise from the window seat, but her ingrained sense of propriety forced her to her feet in the end. "What shall I wear?"

"Oh, something outré, I'd say. It is just us, Ada. No old folks to tell us how to behave. We get to be as we wish to be, who we really are."

After Moira was gone, Ada spread all the contents of her large carpetbag across her bed. Squinting her eyes and regarding the assorted garments with the distorted perspective a painter might use, she came up with an ensemble that would have made the men of Araby drool, that would have made Moll Flanders blush.

She unbuttoned the thirty-three tiny cloth-covered buttons that ran from her throat to her pubis, peeled the heavy dress from her body, and hurried herself out of her layers of undergarments. Finally, fully naked, she went to the washstand and wet a hand towel. She washed off her underarms and dripped water across her chest. Her nipples tightened and popped out, startled by the chill. She pulled her thinnest, softest corset from the tangle of items on her bed, an abbreviated corset of maroon silk that pulled together with only two buttons in the front. She covered the corset with a thin black silk blouse that was meant to be worn over another, sturdier sort of corset. But the maroon looked delectable peeking out from the sheerest of covering the blouse provided. A velvet skirt that Moira had given her completed the effect. It was imported from Eastern Europe, a thing covered with silk embroidery the colors of a darkened rainbow. The fabric of the skirt clung to her legs, for there was nothing on them to prevent its doing so. She threw a host of beaded and bangled and clanging bracelets onto her arms. Her hair, though, fell out of its eternally declining bun, so in the end she let it have its own way and went to face her boon companions with her hair trailing down her back.

They had thrown themselves across the comfortable, full furniture in the parlor. No one sat with back upright. Moira reclined on a sofa, her bare feet flung across Bayley's lap. Bayley held onto one of her ankles as he talked, expansively, with his other hand punctuating the air.

"Marx says," Bayley was opining as Ada walked in, "the working man—" He stopped when he saw her. Everyone turned to look at her. Professor Arlington, who was prone on the floor, supported by a raft of large, soft pillows, jumped to his feet. Once standing, he seemed surprised by his own sudden movement, and struggled to find a reason for it. Finally, he reached his hand out to her.

"You look lovely, Ada. May I offer you some of my cushions? It seems all the other seats have been claimed."

Ada accepted the offer and lowered herself to the floor. "Please, go on," she said to Bayley. "What were you saying about Marx?"

Moira gave Bayley's arm a quick flick with the back of her hand. He smiled at her apologetically and struggled to pick up his train of thought.

"Marx said . . . He said that labor is not a part of the worker's life. It is a sacrifice of his life."

Arlington nodded his head. "I have to say that Marx, though he was not a laborer himself, certainly knew what he was talking about."

Ada looked up from her reclining position on the cushions into the professor's face. It made her nervous that he was here with them. But everyone knew that about Professor Arlington. He was the sort who did things with his students—he made friends with them, they invited him into their homes. He saw her looking at him and smiled. She smiled back. "Professor Arlington," she began.

"Please. You make me feel far too old. Call me Frederick."

Ada felt then as if she and Frederick—yes, Frederick—were floating on their raft of pillows, and the raft was moving away from the society of their fellows. It was moving quickly, and soon Bayley and Moira and all the other people around them were far removed. Certainly no one there could hear them now, nor were any of them aware of anything that was happening on the little float of cushions.

"I imagine you're right," she said to him.

His eyes hadn't turned from hers. "I know I'm right. My father was one of those laborers. I watched him sacrifice his life every day."

"Oh, really? What did your father do?"

"He worked in the mines. In Nova Scotia."

Ada imagined a man, much like Frederick, only with a face streaked with the black of coal, and wearing rough workman's clothes, and she felt her face flush.

"He sacrificed comfort and health so that I might go to university and make a living lecturing rather than swinging a pickax."

Ada had never known a man who worked with his hands. The men in her life did things in offices, behind closed doors. They did things with banknotes and commercial properties and commodities of all sorts. They did things she did not understand, but she was certain they were the very things Marx wrote about, and protested against. She wondered, on occasion, if there were people suffering in some distant location because of the profits her father had been able to reap on some investment. She imagined entire families of six, eight, ten, working till their bones ached so that they could eat before going to bed. Perhaps their toil had made it possible for her mother to entertain one hundred people in her ballroom.

These were parties for which her mother drew up plans for placement of the food. She opened a large journal, laid it flat, and drew up a map of the tables, a diagram that spread across both sides of the book. She had models of the Arc de Triomphe constructed from aspic, one at each end of a table thirty feet long. This long table offered up tureens of rabbit soup, and giant platters covered with dozens of roasted pheasant with lemon glaze. Each of the tureens and the platters cost as much as many laborers earned in a year. More than one hundred candles and gas lamps caused a glittering of silver and a sparkling of crystal that tired the eyes of some of the older guests. Specially skilled people came to decorate the ballroom, with specially painted lengths of canvas that reflected her mother's chosen theme. Finally, her mother would hire an orchestra to play waltzes so the guests might sweep around the ballroom in their expensive formal attire, the ladies' exalted skirts hovering, and then rushing to catch up to the precious bodies that controlled them. And, invariably, late in the evening, the orchestra played a couple of songs that conjured up images of the working life. A life no one in the room, save the servants, could understand. But the music was lovely, and the lovely couples danced to it.

There was the song made to words from Mark Twain:

Conductor, when you receive a fare,
Punch in the presence of the passenjare!
A blue trip slip for an eight-cent fare,
A buff trip slip for a six-cent fare,
A pink trip slip for a three-cent fare,
Punch in the presence of the passenjare!
Punch, brothers! punch with care,
Punch in the presence of the passenjare.
Punch, brothers! punch with care!
Punch in the presence of the passenjare!

Certainly, none of the dancers in her mother's ballroom thought of the conductor as anything other than the reason for an uptempo song. But for some reason, it had always bedeviled Ada. When she met the Stones and the Blackwells, she believed she had come to understand why.

But now, here, sitting with Frederick Arlington, she was as close as she had ever been to the life of a real laborer and as far as she could imagine from her mother's ballroom. She ventured a question, unsure whether she was overstepping her bounds, but feeling compelled nonetheless. "Did you, before you went to university, work at some sort of physical labor?"

Arlington pulled his attention away from the other conversations going on around him. "Yes, I did. I helped my father in the mines on occasion, when the work was heavy and the family was short on funds. I know what it was like. But he—" He stopped speaking and looked down at his smooth hands for a moment before continuing. "He didn't like it when I went down with him. He asked me less frequently than he should have by all rights. I regret that I didn't help him more."

Ada's idea of who Arlington was forever altered in that moment. She settled in next to him, feeling somehow physically safe seated at his side.

One of the students went to the piano and began to play and sing. The raft Ada floated on suddenly pulled back into the room, and she noticed the people around her. The student, an Irish boy named Colin, one of the very few Irish Ada knew to attend college, sang with a sweet voice. Westendorf's "I'll Take You Home Again, Kathleen."

I'll take you home again, Kathleen,
Across the ocean wild and wide,
To where your heart has ever been,
Since first you were my bonnie bride.
The roses all have left your cheek,
I've watched them fade away and die;
Your voice is sad when e'er you speak,
And tears bedim your loving eyes.
Oh! I will take you back, Kathleen,
To where your heart will feel no pain,
And when the fields are fresh and green,
I'll take you to your home again.

Shadow Dancing

Edward stood in his place at the head of the table and tapped his Thousand Eye glass with his knife. "We have come to the moment that I, at least, have been waiting for." Everyone laughed politely at his self-effacing joke. "It's time for the official unveiling."

They all walked to the back of the house and down the stairs. Outside the night was black, but a light emanated through the greenhouse glass, sending a refracting corridor of light across the shadowy garden. Beatrice came abreast of her daughter in the darkness of the garden. "Is it as wonderful as he says?"

Ada was speechless. Her mother had caught her in a moment of weakness. But finally she held her head high and spoke with a steady voice. "I haven't seen it. Edward wanted me to be as surprised as everyone else."

Beatrice laughed, her voice tinkling in the night air. "Oh, well, then." And she moved away into the group, leaving her daughter alone.

Suddenly, on the path, in the midst of the flowers that were gray in the night, Edward took his wife's hand and twirled her under his arm, a bit of spontaneous dancing that was so unlike him. Then he pulled Ada up close to the greenhouse door and swung it open with a force that was almost too much for the heavy door to withstand. Small flames from gaslights pulsated along the four walls of the conservatory, casting cavorting shadows on the hundreds of orchids that swelled across the reaches of the cavernous room. Hundreds of shapes, colors, sizes, and scents crushed against the available space, and overflowed, to occlude each of Ada's senses.

The dinner guests moved into the room behind Ada. There was a momentary hush as they took in the rush of visceral stimuli. And then they all seemed to gasp in unison. Minnie was the first to utter intelligible words. "This is just too fantastic, Edward."

Anderson Lovell pumped Edward's hand. "Quite a show, old bloke," he said. "Quite a show, I must say."

But Ada didn't stop to listen to what they said. How could she have, when the sublime was there, offering itself to her? Every one of her guests, and her husband as well, seemed to fall out of focus, both visually and aurally. Only the orchids were articulated. She brushed her face against a chocolate brown flower whose petals were traversed by yellow veins. She saw then that Edward had labeled each plant. In purple calligraphy on pink card stock, he had written: *Vanda Cathcartii*, India, rare. She sniffed the flower and imagined that this was the smell of India in the apex of monsoon season, when all the senses were assaulted by the chaos of the ethers. She felt a shock travel down her spine, as though lightning bolts had stored their energy in the petals of this flower, and her touch ignited their force.

The orchids instilled in her a strange longing to be away. Just away. Somewhere other than this place where days were made from the ordering of the larder, and the directing of the small domestic staff, and the tending to Edward's needs and demands. The purchase of linens and new objets d'art, the arrangement of flowers and papers and place settings at the dinner table. The organization of menus and the handing out of calling cards, and the sitting through luncheons with women who did not read Shakespeare, and the endless nights alone in bed, with the occasional interruption caused by Edward's visitations. She would go where these flowers came from if she could create her own destiny. She would most certainly go away from all this. She would dive into a field of chocolate brown orchids, and she would eat them for sustenance, and breathe their scent; she would bathe in them, and before long she would speak their language.

"Ada?"

She turned slowly to find Edward staring at her. He must have said her name more than once. He wanted her to raise her glass in a toast. Katie had brought champagne into the greenhouse, and it was time for Ada to perform her role. She pulled her face away from the *Vanda* and smiled at the small crowd gathered around her and Edward. Then she went to stand with Edward and the three orchid hunters in front of a camera Edward had set up. The five of them stood perfectly still as George pushed the button on the box. When the pictures were developed, Ada thought there was something ghostly about the light that hovered around the orchid hunters.

After the last photograph was taken, and people had begun to mill, carefully, under Edward's watchful eye, about the Orchid House, Ada sensed the dangerous stirring of air that always accompanied her mother's approach. Beatrice had somehow ended up standing at the fringe of the group, separated from Edward by a number of guests. But all she needed to do was nod toward Edward and take half a step forward, and the Pryces' guests opened up a pathway in the greenhouse that allowed her immediate access to Edward. It all happened in one unified movement, as if they were an organic whole that had been genetically wired to behave this way. Beatrice nodded and smiled at her lessers as she swept forward.

"You've done a fantastic job, my son," she said to him. Her numerous strings of pearls and onyx and amethyst clanked against one another as she leaned forward to study the plants. "Without doubt, I will be bragging about you to my friends."

Edward's face broadened and spread into the most open smile Ada had ever seen on it. Now everyone in Boston would know that he had a collection that impressed even the jaded Beatrice. Beatrice's word was more valuable than money in the bank.

Ada's mother bent her head over the creatures, examining them with a finely developed critical eye. "They are quite fascinating," she pronounced. Beatrice reached out her hand, not bothering to ask permission, and caressed several of the orchids. As her fingertips fluttered across the petals, Ada imagined her mother suddenly snapping the heads off each orchid, one by one, as Edward stood by, helpless to stop her.

"You should be quite proud." She leaned in close to Edward. "Don't let Anderson know I said it, but I daresay you have the most exquisite orchids of any I've yet seen. You've managed to educate yourself on these matters very quickly, I see," Beatrice said. Ada watched as Edward's chest expanded in circumference. Her mother was no expert on orchids, but she knew enough about everything that was important to Boston Brahmans to be able to make pronouncements about many different things, and for her pronouncements to carry weight. Beatrice was always very careful with her compliments. She used superlatives rarely. The compliments she uttered now were something to be remembered for many years to come. Had Ada ever accomplished anything that moved her mother to use such terms with her?

BACK IN THE HOUSE, Beatrice walked to the parlor with Ada, Minnie, and Emmy. Ada watched her hover there, as if her mother's feet weren't quite touching the ground. Her mother assumed the position from which she could most easily escape the present company, and hurry on to join her more relevant companions in some late-night event. The moment Emmy started to talk about her daughter, Beatrice headed for the door. Ada's mother never pretended to enjoy children. Discussion of children always sent her running. Ada couldn't say whether she felt the same, whether a similar dread of children played a part in her decision not to have a child. "It's been lovely, my dear," Beatrice said to her daughter. "But you know how full my calendar is these days. I must be off." Her mother had fulfilled her end of the bargain, Ada knew, having stayed for the better part of the evening.

Ada rang for Katie, who came to help Ada escort Beatrice to her waiting carriage. Katie walked with her back straight, her head high. The image of Katie's head thrown back in the throes of crisis superimposed itself over the proper girl who appeared in the foyer. Ada felt a warm flush rise from her neck and into her face as her mother kissed her cheek.

"Why on earth are you blushing, my dear?" Beatrice patted her daughter's cheek, but didn't wait for a response. Katie took Beatrice to the carriage while Ada watched from the front steps. Her mother disappeared into her carriage, turning her attention away from her daughter and toward her next engagement.

Ada returned to Minnie and Emmy in the parlor, though she wanted to be in Edward's office with the men. Her father had let her puff on his pipe once when she was small. As she recalled, there was a certain comfort in the taste of the thing, even though it had made her cough. She might like to, just once more, light up a pipe and smoke as she listened to men's stories about the jungle, and about travel aboard ships, and about living in places that had no parlors or drawing rooms or chattering wives.

Katie, Mary, and Edith hurried in and out with teapots and desserts and returned to clean up after the women. Neither Emmy nor Minnie paid the servants any mind as they moved silently about them. "What was your favorite flower?" Minnie asked Ada. Ada looked up toward Minnie, but her eyes swept across Emmy's face first. Emmy seemed to wince at Minnie's question.

"Might we talk about something else?" Emmy asked. "I have had my fill of orchids."

Suddenly, as she looked at the young mother sitting across from her, holding her teacup and staring into it as if it held the secrets of the universe, Ada felt certain that Emmy blamed the flowers for everything that might be wrong in her marriage and her life.

"Perhaps Emmy's right," said Ada. "Let's talk about something else."

Minnie was energetic and intelligent. Her company made up for the dullness of Emmy's. But still, Ada regretted that she could not sit down with the men and talk to Jao about Shakespeare, or to any of the orchid hunters about what it was really like to travel so far and to live such raw lives in the service of a desire that was ultimately so very flimsy.

After Minnie and Anderson and Emmy and Franz had left, the orchid hunters lingered with Edward in his office. Ada stayed in the parlor, listening to the sounds of their voices as they drifted through the walls. She felt like a child drawn by the music of the Pied Piper. But she wanted to hear the words, not just the melody of their voices. There was no resisting; she followed the sound to the door of Edward's office and leaned close until her cheek was almost touching the wood. Still, she could only make out their laughter, and an occasional isolated word removed from all context. She reached her hand out and placed it on the door handle. It was as if her hand were acting of its own accord. She watched, waiting to see what it would do. It gripped the handle, then slid the door open. Smiling, she stepped into the room.

The men fell silent. They were gathered casually around the fireplace, Edward leaning against one end of the mantel, Jao against the other, both of their faces reflected in the angled gilt-framed mirror. William and Walter were each seated in armchairs in front of the fire. All of them held cigars, and the room was thick with the woody fragrance. Ada watched their frozen arrangement, pleased with the aesthetics of the composition, the determined masculinity and the sweet secrecy of it.

"Yes, Ada dear?" Edward said at last.

"I've come to wish you good night. And to tell you what a pleasure it was to have your company this evening," she said to the orchid hunters.

They all blustered about, until Walter took the lead. He ambled over to her and, for the second time, kissed her proffered hand. "It was an honor to be your guest," he said. The others quickly repeated the ritual. Edward watched, his mouth set in a grim line.

HE CAME TO HER room that night, even though her light was out. He lit her lamp, then sat in her chair, still dressed in his dinner clothes. "I am quite concerned about you, my dear." He rubbed his forehead as he spoke.

"Why? Because I came into your office to say good night to your orchid hunters?"

"That, as well as your solitary stroll in the park, your luncheon with the servants, and the other incident with Walter, in the sunroom. Ada, this is simply beneath you, all of this strange activity. Is there something that is making you unhappy?"

A soft chuckle escaped her chest. "Unhappy? It makes me happy to do those things."

"But Ada, it is so highly irregular. You know better. I must insist that you watch yourself in future. As your husband, I demand it."

He left then, but instead of dwelling on her husband's ultimatum, Ada went to sleep beneath the cupids floating above her head, and dreamed of the lovely orchid hunters.

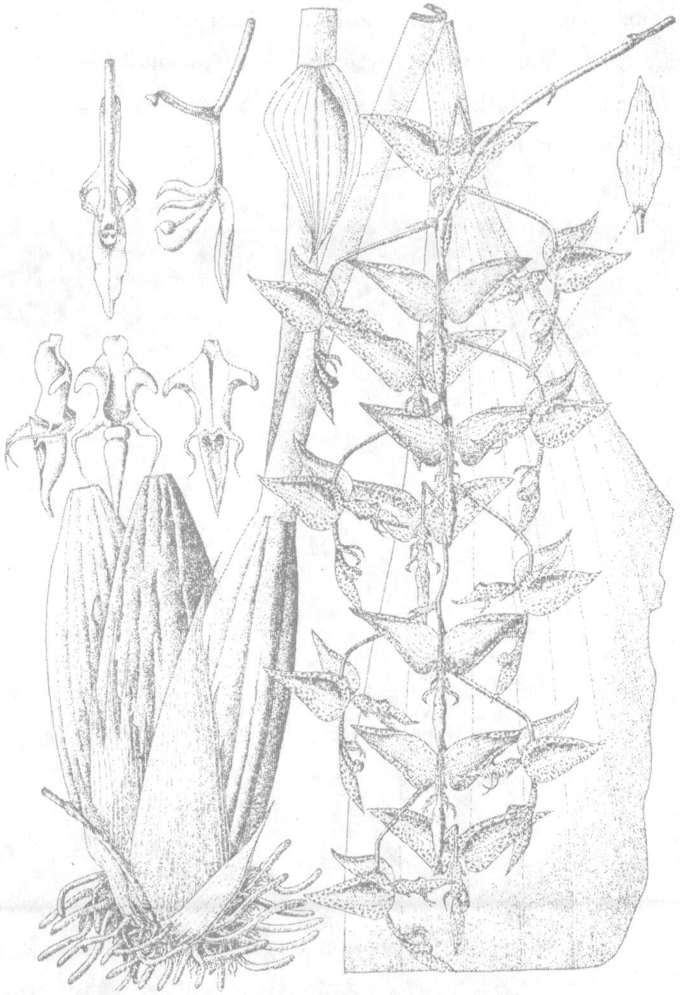

Use *and* Disuse *of* Parts

In the weeks immediately following the dinner party, life in the Pryce household returned to its usual rhythms. With the orchids gone from the sunroom, Ada saw them only when Edward invited her to join him in the Orchid House. Even though her attitude toward them had changed completely on the evening of the dinner party, when she stepped across the threshold of the greenhouse and into their moist habitat, their role in her life remained limited. She continued to read *Karezza*, for Edward's sake, and made inelegant attempts to embrace Stockham's philosophy. But Karezza and her household duties alone were not enough to hold her interest.

On a day when Edward was at work, and the monotony of her domestic duties put her nerves on edge more than usual, Ada took the greenhouse key from Edward's desk drawer and went out back. She had waited for George to leave on some errand, and for Ettie to be busy in the kitchen, before she went on this expedition. But now, as she unlocked the door and stepped into the glass-enclosed space, she felt eyes on her back, and her skin prickled. She didn't know whether or not Edward would mind her visit to the Orchid House, but lately, anything she did without his knowledge might be seen as suspect, as some covert activity bound to make her subject to recrimination.

Once she was alone inside, though, her fear of discovery vanished.

Edward's arrangement of the plants was brilliant. It would have been impossible for anyone with sight to walk into this place and not be moved by the spectacle. She had been in the greenhouse three or four times since the dinner party, and each time the collection had grown. Now, as she walked toward them, the orchids seemed to beckon and taunt her at once. When Edward first brought them home, they had represented to Ada a betrayal of some kind. Edward had excluded her from his passion for the flowers, and they had blossomed under his tender care, mocking her, it seemed, as they usurped her sunroom and flowered in its warmth. But now some part of them had come to suggest faraway places and the touch of the orchid hunter. These creatures had seen the jungles of India and Brazil and Africa. They had been tenderly collected and transported by men who were certainly as strangely wonderful as the men who had come into her home for dinner. Perhaps if she spent time with the plants, something of their adventures, some remnant of these ruddy places and the unsettling men who found them, would leach into Ada's own blood.

Some of the flowers emitted a sweet odor, but that was overwhelmed by the richness of bark and loam and running water, of flagstone, and the teak that lined the base of the house. The scents were emanations of a botanical drama that unfolded before her, but whose machinations were too minute, or too complicated, for her to comprehend. She longed to curl up in a ball right there and sleep so that dreams of wild places would overtake her.

The orchids displayed their beauty flagrantly; they craned their necks at her and seemed to welcome her as she walked the aisle. She could see now the intelligence of their structure, of their pattern and color. A plant with a long stem that rose up and then curved over in an arc, with small intricate orange-speckled flowers running the length of the stem, stopped her. What sort of brilliance went into the design of such a thing? She ceased breathing while she considered it.

. . .

Edward dined with her that evening. His face softened when she talked to him about his orchids. "They are stunning, Edward. I am so proud of you for having such a good eye."

"I am well on my way, am I not?" He folded his napkin and rested his hand on the perfect rectangle, then smiled across the table at his wife.

The room echoed with the sound of Ada's fork against her plate before she spoke again. "I think I might be interested in learning more about them. Would I be allowed to go to your Orchid Society?"

"Ada, darling, you know it's for men only."

The old sense of outrage that had once bubbled up in her gut when she attended meetings at the Blackwells' visited her now. What did her womanhood have to do with participating in the Orchid Society? What about a woman's presence should be threatening to these plant enthusiasts? Because she knew these archaic rules were not Edward's fault, she made an effort to hold her tongue, but it was unsuccessful. "Why on earth are women banned from your society? Why, Edward? It makes no sense to me."

"Of course, my love. They have no idea what they are missing in you. I believe you would be an intelligent, and a lovely, addition to the membership. But, alas, it can't be." Ada couldn't think of the right words to say before Edward spoke again. "There is a lecture series offered to women, though, my dear. You might learn a great deal from it, Ada. I'll find out about it for you at the Club."

"Are you going tonight?"

"Yes. Franz and I have some further arrangements to make regarding the collectors we sent to South America."

"Well, thank you for dining with me. And thank you for looking into the lectures." She waited for a moment before posing her next question, then tried to ask it with an air of nonchalance. "Did you hire the collectors who came to dinner?"

"Not all of them together. Just William. The others were hired before we could get to them."

Just William. Not Jao. Or Walter. That omission bothered her for some reason. "I'm sorry. Are you disappointed?"

"At first I was disturbed, but we found another man who is top-notch. They left three weeks ago." Three weeks they had been gone, and Edward had not uttered a word about it to Ada. "They should be there by now," he said happily, ignorant of the effect his secretiveness had on his wife. "They are probably even well into their hunt."

He pushed his chair back then, and Ada knew that her time with her husband was now at an end. But later that night, he knocked on her bedroom door. As he sat on the edge of her bed, he held out a pamphlet to her. Without knowing what the words on the paper said, Ada was instantly reminded of the many tracts she had seen when she still traveled in the Blackwell circles. But the content of those leaflets had always caused her such unease. What inhered in them was a reminder of her inferior status as a woman, of a fight that must be attended to, and of the energies she lacked for such a fight. As she touched Edward's proffered pamphlet, she thought now that the real reason she had resisted the fight was not because she lacked the energy or the belief, but rather that she was disappointed in the inability of mankind to see the absurdity, the simple unfairness of woman's position. At some point in her life, her disappointment had paralyzed her, and she had simply stepped back from the problem.

Ada unfolded the paper in her hand and read.

LADIES!

Learn about the Exotic Orchid, and be the envy of your Circle!

> Discover why such Fantastic sums of Money are being spent on these Rare Beauties, and what you must know if you are to truly understand the ways of these Mysterious Plants.

This leaflet possessed a quality of amity. Ada was determined to go to the lectures and learn everything there was to learn about orchids. The first one was in a month's time; she would find it hard to wait.

"This is just what I wanted, Edward. Thank you, darling."

He touched his hand to Ada's face. "I can't tell you how much it means to me that you have taken such an interest, Ada. I know you will be an apt pupil. I am eager to discuss orchid propagation with you."

He put his hand inside her gown then, and let his fingers flutter across her breast. She remembered something Stockham had written in her book: that the blending of a married couple in sexual consummation is fulfillment of natural law, much like the fructifying principle in plants. She lay back on the bed, and his fingers moved down, pushing her legs apart.

She was dry. Darwin had theorized about the use and disuse of parts, suggesting that those things that were unused weakened and disappeared altogether. Could her own sexual apparatus fall into disuse so permanently that it might wither away? Edward pushed his fingers into her and wiggled them, in a hurry, it seemed, for her to moisten. But there would be no crisis, so what did he rush toward? Was this the way he touched his orchids? One of his slipper orchids had a labellum that resembled nothing so much as a human tongue. The fleshy outthrust, designed to lure pollinating insects, had at first seemed lewd to Ada. But Edward had marveled over it as he showed it off to her. Was he reminded of her own labia when he looked at the tonguey petal? Suddenly, the idea made her feel as if her vagina were an orchid labellum. She curled her body around his, her arms and legs the sepals and petals, her torso a sturdy stem. Let him desire his flowers, then, she thought, as he enters me. And I, like a flower, will be inscrutable in my response to his stunted act of pollination.

WHEN SHE AWOKE the next morning, she was startled to sense Edward still there in the bed with her. She got up quietly and went about her toilette carefully so as not to wake him. But he roused as she was pinning her hair.

"You look lovely, my dear." He sat up to watch her. "I shall miss you."

"Miss me?"

Edward rubbed his hand across his face, then looked at her with sleepy eyes. "Didn't I tell you?"

"No. Tell me what?"

"I'm to go to New York for the office. I'll be gone for three weeks."

Ada set the silver-handled brush down on the dressing table and turned to Edward. "I see."

"Please forgive me. For some infernal reason, I thought I told you. What a lout I am."

"Don't be silly. When do you leave?"

"The Saturday after next." He got up from the bed and went to her, put his hand on her shoulder. "Will you be a dear and see that my orchids are well tended? Liam will water them, of course. But just check on them for me? I'll take you to the Orchid House and show you the ropes."

"Certainly, Edward. I'll be happy to. And while you're gone, I shall attend the lectures. When you return, perhaps I shall know nearly as much about orchids as you know now."

ADA FOUND HERSELF eager for the orchid lectures to begin and for Edward to be gone on his New York trip; the anticipation of both events made her excitable. It occurred to her that the wait might be made easier if she had her own orchid to cultivate. She had some extra money left from her clothing allowance, so Edward need not even know. She enlisted Liam to drive her to the nursery where she had bought the blood-colored Moutan peonies for the dinner party.

When she first walked into the large warehouse, the scents of floral perfumes and decaying minerals encircled her, and she felt the tension in her head subside instantly. Mr. Van Oot, a rotund middle-aged gentleman, looked up at her expectantly from the table near the entrance. She smiled at him, and spoke as if she knew exactly what she was talking about. "Mr. Van Oot. I am so glad to see you. I was wondering, might you have a wonderful *Odontoglossum* for me? I find myself suddenly wanting one desperately."

He smiled at her then, his lips curving upward so that they engaged his cheeks, and offered up dimples that deepened into trenches. "You are very lucky today, Mrs.— I am so sorry. I don't believe I learned your name last time you were here."

"Oh. Forgive me," Ada said. "I am Mrs. Webber." Ada was surprised by how easily the lie formed itself on her lips, and how smoothly she uttered it.

"Of course. Well, Mrs. Webber, I have two *Odontoglossum*, both very beautiful." His smile disappeared and his eyes narrowed. "They are quite expensive, I must warn you."

"The price is of little concern to me."

"This way." The entire northern side of the house was devoted to orchids in all their stages. Some were just green leaves waiting to sprout their stems and flowers, others were naked roots, and others still were flaunting their radical and conscious blossoms. The scent of them filled her nostrils with a sweetness that held heat within its aroma.

They strolled past dozens upon dozens of bedecked and baroque plants, each urging them to stop and consider such intricacy. Her skirts snapped like sails on a blustery day as they wrapped themselves around her legs. She rode the wind of her willpower down the entire length of the glass house until, in the far corner, before they made it to the *Odontoglossum*, she spotted a *Vanda* with lilac blossoms crosshatched with a velvety crimson. The blossoms, six of them, were small and dainty, forming a progression along the single stem that held them in such order.

"I like this one," she said. Her voice was crisp, and her gaze steady. Van Oot stopped and followed her, not bothering to remind her of his *Odontoglossum*.

"That one is one hundred and twenty-five dollars," he said, waiting calmly, no doubt to see if the price would send her away.

She didn't even draw in a breath. But still, he continued to talk, as if he was afraid to let the space of silence open up too wide. "I have had royalty in here inquiring about my *Vanda*. They would be fit to be tied if they knew I was selling this to you without giving them a chance at it first."

"Ah, well, there will be others for them to buy, won't there?"

His hand had been moving toward the flower, but it stopped for an instant, then dropped to his side. He turned to face her square on. "You must understand this orchid mania. They don't want others. They want the best. You're getting the best."

"Ah. If that's so, then I don't suppose I should mind parting with all this money." She opened her purse then, a sign that negotiations had ceased. When she took the money from her bag and counted it out to Van Oot, she felt a kind of power that was entirely unknown to her. She gave him two fifty-dollar bills, a twenty, and five one-dollar coins. As much as Katie earned in four months.

"Mrs. Webber, it has been a pleasure helping you to find a flower that will make you truly proud. Please do not hesitate to return whenever you fancy another of nature's most beautiful creatures. I am at your service. May I call someone to carry it to your carriage?"

"No. Thank you. I want to take it myself."

She shook the dealer's hand and walked out with her plant. Van Oot had wrapped the whole thing carefully in brown paper, covering the brilliant blossoms, hiding them from public view.

Outside, Liam still sat in the driver's seat, facing away from her. The early summer sun shone across the cobblestones, whose smooth surfaces sent rays to bounce obliquely into Ada's eyes. She shielded them, and stood still, holding her *Vanda* out in front of her, waiting for her eyes to adjust to the brightness so she could pick her carriage out of the crowd of carriages waiting in the streets. A man lurched onto her path. He seemed to have come out of nowhere. She couldn't make out his features, but as he thrust himself in front of her, she could see he was a Negro, and that his clothes were worn, and his skin seemed to have been too long out of doors. She stepped quickly to the side to avoid him, but he dodged in the same direction, and they almost collided. She held out her orchid to protect it. "I'm so sorry," she said.

"Ma'am. Please, you've got to help." The sun washed across him, and Ada shielded her eyes.

Suddenly, Liam materialized before her. "Now see here," he said. "Leave the lady alone." Liam pushed at the black man and put his hand out for Ada to take. She couldn't think what else to do, so she held her orchid firmly in front of her and took Liam's hand.

At home, when she climbed out of the carriage, she was still gripping the orchid. She walked away from Liam and went into the foyer alone, setting the plant down on the window seat in order to divest herself of her coat and hat. She unwound the scarf that held her hat around her neck, and removed the pins that kept it attached to her hair, eager to finish with herself so she could unwrap her plant. She peeled the paper back and regarded the purple-spotted thing. It seemed to turn its many-headed neck to her, beseeching. Suddenly, she realized there was no safe place for her to keep it. Certainly Edward would be furious if he knew she had taken it upon herself to invest in this novelty. And if George discovered it, he would be sure to tell Edward all about it. She wrapped up the plant again.

Of course she couldn't keep it in the Orchid House. Nor could she put it anywhere in the house. Even her own bedroom wasn't safe. She stood there in the foyer, alone, holding the tender package, her mind emptied. She couldn't think clearly enough to make a decision about where to step, or in what direction to walk if she did move forward. All the possibilities roiled about her, while she remained inert in the center of the fugue. She forgot she was standing in her own house and was aware only of the weight and sense of the veiled flower in her hands. Time seemed to expand out from her and then snap back in, contracted into a bubble-like minuteness. Her place in the sequence of events seemed meaningless, or nonexistent. And the orchid, what was it for? She held it and looked at it, but it seemed to be something she couldn't place, its purpose eluding her.

Finally, Katie appeared. "Miss? Ada? Are you all right?"

Ada let loose a single laugh that served as the clearing away of a blocked force field. The strength of it shook her loose from her timeless or time-bound breach. "Oh, Katie, I am so happy to see you." Here she stepped out of the small space that had contained her indecision.

She held the plant in front of her, motioning for Katie to follow her up the back stairs. All the way up to the third floor and along the length of the hallway there, Katie walked alongside her mistress without ever acknowledging the package. When they reached Katie's room, Ada stopped and stood respectfully outside it, unwilling to go in without Katie's permission. She felt Katie come up next to her and stand quietly, hesitantly.

Ada turned to her. "Katie, I would like to ask you to help me with something."

"Certainly, Ada."

"May we go into your room?'

Katie nodded, and waited for Ada to go in ahead of her. The back of Ada's neck grow hot. Once safely inside, the door closed, she nodded down at the brown package. "It's an orchid. A very special one. I want to try to raise it on my own. But Edward simply must not know." Ada felt nervous as she continued. A touch of regret, perhaps, for this pointless covert act? "I know it seems odd, but I love this plant. And Edward simply wouldn't understand. I would have to answer no end of questions about why I took it upon myself to invest in such a rare creature. I simply don't want to have to explain myself. And I want to see if I can do it."

"Well, of course. I'll do whatsoever you ask of me."

Ada continued to explain herself as if she hadn't heard Katie. "Edward never comes into this room, and so the plant will be only mine if I keep it here. I just feel the need—it's strange, I know—but I need to have something of mine that has nothing to do with him. I don't want him to tell me how to care for it. I don't want his disapproval if I ruin it. I need to know if I can do it myself. I simply must. I will care for it, of course. You need do nothing. Please. You understand, don't you?"

"Indeed. It's all quite fine, miss."

Ada motioned to the nightstand next to Katie's bed. Katie nodded her head, and Ada placed the flower on top of the nightstand. "Ah. It's beautiful, isn't it?"

Katie nodded. "Yes. Why, yes it is." She turned to go then, as if she sensed Ada's desire to be alone. "If you'll excuse me? I should get back downstairs."

"Please. Don't let me keep you." Katie had gone by the time Ada turned her face back to her flower. She leaned into the *Vanda* and imagined that its blossoms were small faces. It was then she remembered the Negro man in front of Van Oot's. A vision of the man jumped out at her, obscuring her view of the orchid. His face had come into clear focus for an instant as she was leaving, hadn't it? Now the memory of that instant triggered another memory. She knew this man. He was William, the orchid hunter. What had he been saying to her? That he needed her help? Had he perhaps followed her there? No, that was silly. He was an orchid hunter. He had business with Van Oot, certainly. Running into her there was clearly a coincidence. But still, why did he ask for her help? Why had he seemed so desperate?

She felt as though she were being pressed by a weight that made it difficult to move or even to breathe properly. She looked at the plant and felt it was simply out of her league; she didn't know what she was doing with it or why she wanted it.

As she crossed the threshold that led out of Katie's room, she felt the weight settle in her stomach. She went down to the kitchen and fixed herself a bicarbonate of soda, but it didn't relieve the discomfort. She tried eating a piece of toast, but it had no effect either. The disturbance in her stomach occupied her for some time, distracting her from thoughts of her new *Vanda* and the image of William's stricken face.

The Secret World of Men

The light from the near-full moon slipped through the sides of Ada's bedroom curtains, and she failed in her attempts to rearrange them in any way that obliterated it completely. The sounds from outside and inside the house were relentless. A creaking of the wood frame of the house, sudden bursts of wind disturbing the trees, a dog's lonely howl, erratic clopping of horses' hooves along the cobblestones, small objects tossed about gardens and streets, battering against fences and walls. The carriage house remained dark, leaving Ada with nothing to divert her attentions from the cacophony. This night was bound to be another battle for the comfort of sleep.

The next morning, after having slept what seemed like mere moments, Ada was wakened early by a sharp slant of sun jutting in through the slit in the curtains and cutting clean across her face. The day was calm, the blustering wind had soothed itself. She pulled herself from her bed and dressed in a plain mustard yellow poplin dress in preparation for mundane domestic matters. Edward had already gone to his office when she set to work.

As Ada tried to help Katie clean out the larder, the sound of horses and a carriage interrupted their quiet conversation. She peered through the back door window to see a delivery wagon with a large wooden box atop its flatbed. The box had to contain orchids—what else would it be? She had the delivery men carry it out to the Orchid House. After they had gone, she sat in the moist, glassed-in space, looking at the box, delivered directly from Brazil. How perfectly far away that country was from Boston and the order of things here. She leaned her face against the wood and tried to separate the smell of the wood from the smell of the plants inside. Would Edward be terribly angry with her were she to pry the lid off the box and remove the orchids? She wanted nothing more than to peek inside.

Finally, she climbed up to her room and dressed herself for town. Not wanting to take Liam away from the tasks Edward had set for him, she ordered a hansom cab to be sent round, and directed the driver to take her to Edward's offices. When she stepped into the paneled and carpeted reception area, Henry, the secretary, hurried over to her.

"Mrs. Pryce. What a pleasure. Mr. Pryce is in a meeting. May I get you some tea?" He was tall and thin as a rope, and his nervousness made him seem too young to be in his position.

"Oh, of course, Henry." It would probably make him unhappy if she didn't allow him to perform this ritual for her, so she agreed to the tea, and forced herself to hold her tongue until it had been served. At last, her hat and gloves removed, a biscuit in one hand, a fine china cup in the other, she spoke.

"Would you take a message in to Mr. Pryce for me? It's not urgent, but he may wish to hear my news right away, nonetheless." Henry brought her writing paper and pen. She wrote the words down—*The orchids are here*—folded the note twice, and handed it to Henry.

Edward stood in front of her in less than five minutes, Franz at his elbow. They were both carrying their hats and gloves and their walking sticks, ready to go out.

"Ada," Edward said as he hurried to his wife, his face glowing. "Franz is coming with us," he said. "Thank you for bringing the news."

"Oh, yes. It's terribly exciting. I can't wait to see," said Franz. The men each took one of her arms and they walked together, the three of them, out to the street, to the waiting hansom cab.

Ada began to feel as if she were being carried along within a bubble of prescience. Edward had not said anything to her about this shipment of orchids. She had no reason to believe he looked forward to it more than he had to any of his others. But it was as if her appearance at his office was not only appreciated but expected, as if she were in on the grand experiment that was surely being conducted by these orchid-possessed men. Perhaps her coming here had gained her some secret access to the world of men.

Edward allowed her to accompany him and Franz out to the Orchid House. The men took a crowbar to the box and pried the lid off. Ada hovered over a far end of the box. When the lid had been lifted and thrown aside, onto the floor, Edward allowed himself a display of enthusiasm.

"Well, I'll say, old boy, we've done it this time, haven't we?"

Franz laughed, a thin, excited laugh that seemed to come from high up in his chest. "We never would have found the *Cattleya* if old Walter hadn't met his end, I daresay." He seemed to have forgotten that Ada was in the room. Edward touched Franz's elbow. Franz turned to Ada, who was staring at Edward. "His time was up, I'm afraid. Nothing anyone could have done about it. It was unfortunate for him. But in the end, quite a good thing for us," said Franz.

Walter, the man whom she had sat next to at the dinner party? He met his end? Suddenly, the sense of him came to her, robust with living. He had reminded her of wild horses, hadn't he? But here was Franz, talking about Walter's death as if it was just another minor topic for discussion. Ada managed to find her voice. "But why was it good for you for him to die?"

"Oh, he was hunting for Lovell. He never would have let us in on his discoveries. But when he died, our man was able to move in for us." Edward put his hand out to hold Ada's arm. "I'm sorry. I didn't mention it to you because I knew it would upset you that someone actually lost his life on an orchid hunt."

"Ah, but he was a fool. He put himself in harm's way," said Franz.

"But how? How did he die?"

"Fell off a bloody mountaintop, the idiot."

"Now, Franz," Edward said.

Ada wondered whether her husband was objecting to the language rather than Franz's criticism of Walter. Why were they both so nonchalant about this man's death? "It's all right, Edward. It's not as though I have never heard the word *bloody* in my lifetime. I can bear it."

Edward turned from her and addressed Franz. "Well, then. Shall we examine the flower?"

Ada took a step toward her husband. Words of protest, even grief, were there, just inside her lips and ready to dance out. But Edward looked at her and spoke quickly, before the words had freed themselves from her mouth. "It's all well enough, Ada. Walter had no family. Lovell saw to that before he hired him." Ada bit her lip and turned her head back to the shipping box.

Edward reached into the box and began to extricate the plants from their packaging, which was a tangle of roots and leaves from other, valueless, plants. None of them was in flower; they all looked rather miserable. He pulled out one parched and scraggly plant and held it up to Franz. He seemed to have forgotten Ada was there. "I think this is it." Before Franz could examine the thing, Edward carried it over to his worktable and laid it out tenderly. He removed a huge leather-bound volume from the shelf above and opened it. Ada could see it was full of hand-drawn illustrations of orchids. Edward leafed through the book until he found the *Cattleya labiata vera.* He examined the picture, then the plant on the table, and then repeated the exercise again and again. Finally, he stepped back. "What do you think, Franz?"

Franz's hands were shaking as he moved to take Edward's place. Finally, he made his pronouncement. "We shall have to cultivate it to be certain, I'm afraid."

So this would be the thing that would consume Edward now. The cultivation of a single plant that had just survived thousands of miles inside a wooden box, which was again inside the dank hold of a worn-out cargo ship. Had a man really died for this?

That night, Ada had a dream. She was in a ballroom as big as Boston Common. It was impossible to see from one end to the other. It seemed as though there were several balls being conducted at once. One orchestra played for the Brahmans, who swept across the room in their best evening dress. Another, stranger orchestra, with instruments that seemed mismatched—a harpsichord and an African drum, a Spanish guitar and an oboe—played for a group of women who shouted something at the dancers. The yelling women wore bloomers, their distorted faces signaled anger. In yet another part of the great room, people touched and kissed and slid up against one another. Ada seemed to be in this part of the ballroom, or to want to be there when she found herself at the other end. Was she involved in the touching, or was she just watching? She couldn't tell. But she sensed that there were orchids in the room, perhaps behind her. The awareness of the orchids distracted her from everything else; she felt the desire to locate them. And then she saw Walter, dancing with a woman whose dress looked like the petals of the *Cattleya*.

When she woke, Ada remembered that, after the dinner party, she had thought Walter might haunt her dreams. Now here he was, bullying his way into her nighttime. She woke from the dream feeling tired, as if it had made her work too hard in her sleep.

When she finally heard the house stirring, George and Ettie and Katie at their labors, she lifted herself from the wearying bed and put a heavy silk robe over her thin silk nightgown.

She walked along the long narrow hall to the north side of the house, up the back stairs, and into Katie's room. Her *Vanda* seemed to bend toward her slightly as she moved across the room. It turned again, reaching ever for her, as she lifted herself up onto Katie's high bed. Ada perched herself on the very edge of the bed, then leaned her face into the orchid. As she came closer to the petals and sepals and labellum, they moved out of focus, their outlines dimmed and the many colors fused. She felt suspended in a solution of color, and she longed for it to grow to a size that could envelop her entire body. She wanted to run the velvety textures across the length and breadth of her skin's surface. Her face burst into warmth, radiant with some perverse longing.

"Beg pardon."

Ada jerked her head to the door, where Katie was standing stock-still, her hands stiff at her sides. Her eyes were wide and her mouth slightly open.

Ada wasn't sure what she had been doing at the moment she was interrupted by Katie's voice. She hoped she was simply sniffing her plant. But Katie looked so unnerved. Perhaps she had done something unseemly. But what?

"Yes, Katie?" She straightened herself and leaned away from the flower.

Katie was holding the silver tray. She walked toward Ada and held the tray toward her. Ada slowly picked up the calling card sitting in the center of the gleaming surface. Emmy Locke.

"Emmy Locke? Whatever is she doing here? I don't want to see Emmy Locke!" Ada stood and walked past Katie.

As she turned into the hallway, Katie hurried after her. "Shall I tell her you are indisposed, then?"

"No. No. I imagine I must see her. But I should change first. Let her wait wherever she is most comfortable, and I'll be down." Her robe sliced the air like the quick cut of a knife through melon as she turned and walked away from Katie.

Ada was angry as she dressed. What business did Emmy have here? They were not real friends. Their only connection was their husbands' love of orchids. She threw open the door of her armoire. One dress stood out for her. It was new, ordered from Paris. A red silk shantung with sleeves that revealed the shape of her shoulders and arms, a drastic departure from the muttonchop sleeves that had been popular for too long. Ada knew if she wore this dress out, people would whisper about her as she walked by. They would be so appalled, their whispers would be pointedly loud, so that she could hear their disapproval and, the hope was, be moved to cease her unruly behavior. She didn't stop to wonder why she wanted to wear this dress to meet Emmy, but simply stepping into it made her feel better.

She found Katie in the kitchen. "Now, where's Mrs. Locke?"

"She's in the front parlor. She asked to be there. Shall I bring tea? Ettie has already made up a tray."

"Please, do. Thank you."

• • •

ADA FOUND EMMY sitting straight-backed, staring at the fireplace. It struck her that she herself could never wait for people without something to read. Ada always asked to wait in the library so that she wouldn't be stuck like this, staring into space for thirty minutes while some rude woman or another primped and bothered herself. Emmy turned her head at the sound of Ada's skirts in the room, and then rose to greet her.

"Emmy. How delightful to see you!"

"Ada, I am so sorry to surprise you this way, but I simply must speak to you."

"Of course. Sit down. Tea is coming. Then we'll talk." Their skirts touched as they stood near each other, Ada's lively red diminishing the warmth of Emmy's yellow skirts. Emmy didn't seem to notice Ada's dress.

After Katie had served them and left without speaking, Emmy dispensed with the small talk.

"I had a very strange visitor yesterday, Ada. Do you remember the Negro man who was at your Orchid House party?" Ada nodded, and felt the room grow suddenly hot. "He showed up at my back door yesterday afternoon."

"What? Whatever for?"

"He said he needed to speak with me. But I, well, he frightened me. He looked desperate. I sent him away. But now I am not sure I should have done so."

"Why do you say that?" Ada pulled at the neckline of her dress, in an effort to let air enter wherever it could.

"I have a bad feeling. I can't say what it is." She picked up the pink teacup from the silver tray and took a sip. The china clinked against the tray as she set the cup back down. "I came here because I thought, since he had been here before, maybe he came by your house first. I thought perhaps you knew something I didn't know." She stopped speaking and looked at Ada.

"No, he didn't come by here." Ada couldn't say why, but she didn't mention her encounter with William in front of Van Oot's.

Emmy fidgeted in her chair. Her dress rustled against the heavy satin upholstery. "I can't get the man out of my mind now. And I'm simply afraid this orchid thing has gone too far, Ada. Franz has changed. I don't like it one bit. Surely you have noticed that Edward has changed as well?"

"I don't know, Emmy," she said. "I'm certain I don't know quite what you mean."

The two women grew silent. Ada looked down at the red shantung of her dress and ran her fingers across the embossing. "What did you want to do? I mean, why did you come to me?"

"I want to find this man and speak to him. I thought you might know how to reach him. He was on your guest list."

"Yes. Yes, he was. Of course." Her fingers were moving rapidly across the silk now. "But, Emmy, think this through. What is it you want to say to this man?"

"I simply want to know why he came to my house looking so desperate."

"But, Emmy," Ada said, "we have no idea what this is about. Suppose he's a dangerous man?"

"Do you think that, Ada?"

"No. No, I don't. But we have to be careful nonetheless. We can't just go running off to some horrid part of the city asking questions about nothing, and not knowing why, can we?"

"Just tell me where I can find him, and I will go on my own."

Ada's hands caressed the fabric of her dress. "I ordered this dress from Paris. It only just arrived last week. Isn't it gorgeous?"

Emmy looked at Ada's bare shoulders, her eyebrows raised slightly. "Yes, of course it is, Ada. It looks lovely on you."

Ada smoothed the fabric with the palms of both hands, then looked at Emmy. "I can't imagine what any of this is about, or why you are so fretful about it all. But I will find out where to reach him, and I'll send him a message. I'll let you know when he answers."

"Oh, Ada, thank you. This is a relief." Emmy took a biscuit from the tray, then leaned over to touch Ada's dress. "This is simply exquisite. Who was your dressmaker? You must share with me."

• • •

EVERY NERVE END in her body seemed to be unraveling. The instant Emmy was gone, images of William outside Van Oot's greenhouse visited Ada. He had looked like a man who sought consolation but had failed miserably. But how could she help him? Why had she promised to do this thing for Emmy?

Upstairs in her office, she rummaged in her desk until she found the book containing the guest list for the dinner party. William Parrish's invitation had been sent round to an address in a part of Boston that Ada had never had reason to see. She called the messenger service, then sat down to compose a note. It said, simply,

Dear Mr. Parrish,

I would like to speak with you if I might. Please reply to this message if you can meet me Monday. I will arrange a time and location if I hear from you.

A. P.

She put her note in an envelope and sealed it with her green wax. Then she waited thirty minutes for the messenger to take it. Unable to read, she alternately paced and picked at the embroidery on her dress for the entire half hour.

After the messenger had gone off with her note, there was to be nothing for her but more waiting. Ada tried to calculate the hours and minutes it should take to hear a response. She imagined she should allow two hours at minimum. But if he wasn't at the address she had for him, it could take considerably longer for the messenger to track William down. It was possible she wouldn't get a response today at all. The tick of the Ansonia Utopia crystal clock in her office seemed synchronous with her steps as she walked from there and across the hall to the library. The library clock's mechanism advanced in a counterpoint to the clock in her office. The two together danced against the clicking and the lifting of her heels. The twin tickings seemed in conspiracy to drive Ada mad with waiting.

She didn't want George to intercept William's message when it came. His loyalty was to Edward, and he would report back to her husband. What on earth would Edward say to all this? Surely he would see it as some sort of affront against good manners, or worse. She went looking for Katie. Her gait was hurried, in spite of the heaviness of the dress and her underskirts as they wrapped around her hot legs. As she rushed down the front stairs, for the first time in her life she imagined how freeing it would be to take to the stairs wearing a pair of bloomers rather than these heavy skirts.

She found Katie outside, at the side of the house, pulling in the laundry from the line. Ada simply asked Katie to stay inside and answer the service door for the rest of the afternoon, without explaining why. She didn't explain because, convinced that the entire business was moving beyond the pale somehow, she was at a loss how to put it to Katie. What could she possibly say about the planned meeting with William? She didn't know what it was about herself.

STILL WAITING FOR a response to her note, Ada took tea alone in her office. The cakes Ettie had spread across the china plate weren't appealing to her, but she ate them from nervousness. As she chewed rapidly on a triangle of biscuit, there was a sudden commotion coming from downstairs, at the front entrance. George's loud voice hitched itself onto the wind that came in from out of doors and drifted all the way up to her office. "Sir," he was saying. "How good to see you at this hour." There was a shuffling about as George no doubt relieved Edward of his coat and other excess paraphernalia.

Ada felt the biscuit suddenly go dry in her throat and stick itself there. It was necessary for her to succumb to a coughing fit in order to dislodge it. Certainly everyone in the house could hear her loud hacking. But no one came to her rescue, or to scold her for her rudeness. The sounds down in the foyer seemed to have receded to the back of the house. Perhaps Edward was taking George out to the Orchid House. She grabbed her cup and took a gulp of Earl Grey. The cooled tea finally pushed the knot of biscuit down and into her stomach. But her heart did not stop its dissonant pumping. Why was her husband's arrival in his own home causing her such anxiety? Should she go out to the Orchid House to welcome him? Why had he not asked after her?

She stood in the center of her office, her chilly teacup in her hands. Cold droplets of sweat traversed the ethers, it seemed, materializing on her upper lip and under her arms. At last, she managed to find the will to move herself toward the study doorway and down the stairs. She heard the back door slam shut, so she turned in that direction, knowing that Edward would be walking toward his orchids. Just as her hand reached out to open the back door that led to the garden, the kitchen door chimes rang. The impulse to fear was instinctive.

She listened for the sound of voices coming from the side of the house. It was Katie answering the chimes, bless her, and a man at the door. There was no way of telling what they said, she was too far away. But the man's voice was deep, and it reverberated across the kitchen and along the hallways of the large house, clanging against the walls and filling up each room as it came across open doors. Surely the voice was big enough and of sufficient gravity to reach all the way out to the Orchid House. And if Edward should look out into the yard, he would be able to make out William, standing there at the side of the house.

By the time Katie came down the hallway with the silver tray, Ada had clenched and unclenched her teeth enough to make her ears hurt. She took Katie's elbow and led her back toward the kitchen and away from the back door.

"Ma'am, there is a Mr. William." Katie walked and held out the tray as she talked. She sounded winded as she spoke. "He wanted to wait for your reply."

Ada reached out and took the folded paper from the tray. It was her own original note, with a reply written in a shaky hand beneath.

Where and when? was all it said.

Ada dipped the gold-ink pen and scribbled again at the bottom of the page:

African Meeting House. Monday morning. Ten o'clock.

"Take this to him, and ask him to tell you yes or no. That's all I need to know from him. Just yes or no. And then send him away as quickly as possible." She handed the note back to Katie. Today was Friday. This Saturday and Sunday would be Edward's last week's end at home before his trip to New York, so Ada had been forced to choose Monday for the meeting. But now she would have to wait three interminable days to find out what William wanted of her.

She spent those days on the linen project she had created for herself, styled after the sorts of things she had seen her mother do throughout her childhood. Katie took Ada to the washroom at the back of the house. They walked side by side down the long back hallway, their booted heels clicking against the wide floor planks, soft, well-tended kid next to rough, worn black leather. The washroom was big, open, with floor-to-ceiling windows along the north wall. Even though the day was gray, this room was bright. In the flood of light, Ada felt as if she were washing away, melting into its pool and diluting into nothingness.

The center of the room held a wooden worktable fifteen feet long. It was piled with baskets and folded clothing, sorted by color. Edith and Mary stood at the table, folding and organizing. The maids of all work curtsied to Ada as she entered. They seemed like apparitions, hoverers in the whiteness all around them. It took a moment for Ada to bring them into her focus.

"Hello, Edith, hello, Mary." She blinked at them as she spoke.

The two maids had avoided any sort of familiarity since George had caught them dining with Ada. If anything, they were more reticent with her now than they had been before the luncheon. "Hello, ma'am," they said to her, in unison. Ada didn't try to dissuade them from their formality. It would only bring trouble for all of them.

Metal racks with bars for hanging clothing ran the length of the east wall. Katie and Ada walked along them together, and stopped in front of the electric washing machine. It consisted of a base with elaborate piping and chrome dials, to which was attached a large metal drum. The motor caused the drum to rock back and forth. Once the wash was complete, the clothes had to be removed and put through a wringer by hand.

"I've removed the linens from all the armoires and closets. I have the sheets, towels, tablecloths, napkins, washrags, table runners, quilts, everything, as you can see. It's all right here. Except what you're using now, of course. These here"—Katie indicated stacks of linens folded and piled on the table—"have all been washed and sorted first by purpose and then by color. These"—and she pointed to the baskets—"have yet to be washed and sorted. But you could begin going through them if you'd like, even before we're finished. To see what you want to keep and what you would like replaced?"

The linens gave the big room a whiteness that called to mind heaven as described by some romantic writers. Certainly heaven would be decorated with the flutterings of the finest lawn and ecru linens, embroidered with cherubs and edged in filet lace. She nodded at Katie. A task. One she had little interest in, but which would give her purpose, make her feel productive, at least until Monday, when she was due to meet William, or the following Saturday, when Edward would leave for New York. "Yes. I will do that," she said.

That night, Edward didn't come home for dinner. Ada went to bed alone. After she had changed into her nightdress, she looked out her window, hoping to see a light in the carriage house. It was early, and she knew they wouldn't dare be in there already, but still she checked. Disappointed, she went to the small bookshelf she kept in her room, but found nothing she wanted to read at the moment. Finally, she pulled out her Shakespeare and carried it to her bed. None of the plays drew her in. Instead, she flipped through the pages, examining the casts of characters. When she came to *The Winter's Tale*, she ran her fingers along the characters' names—Hermione, Leontes. . . . It wasn't possible for her to see those names and not remember her time at Redruth. She held the Shakespeare up against her breasts, curling herself around it, and allowed herself the luxury of this forbidden remembrance.

A Frozen Queen

After breakfast the second day at Redruth, they went about the serious work of organizing a *tableaux vivant*. Moira divided the lot of them into three groups, each to do one of the Bard's plays. She had cast the parts. "That way, there will be no one to blame but your hostess," she told them all as she assigned the roles. "And Professor Arlington will be the judge, of course."

Moira's group got *A Midsummer Night's Dream*, with Moira as Titania, Queen of the Fairies. Bayley was to be Hamlet, in his last deadly scene. Ada and her group would portray *The Winter's Tale*. Moira had cast Ada as the sculpture of Hermione, the queen whose grief over her husband's false accusations had frozen her into a statue. The three groups separated, unwilling to allow any of the members of the other groups to see what they had come up with for their scene. Ada took charge of her group. She led them down the hallways, away from the fireplaces in the parlor and dining room, and into the unheated reaches of the old house. At last she found what she was looking for. Upstairs, at the end of the servants' wing, was a room filled with worktables and dressmakers' forms.

Someone in this family's employ was obviously a seamstress. Ada and Mimi, a tall thin girl who was to play Hermione's daughter, went through the cupboards and sideboards until they found fabric and glitter and satin cord and all manner of things to create the illusion of Hermione as a statue.

"We'll take these to my room," Ada said.

"Oh, yes, let's do," said Henry. The sandy-haired boy with wide-set brown eyes had been cast by Moira to play Hermione's husband, the king Leontes.

Mimi poked Henry in the side. "You will come with us to Ada's room in your dreams, Henry. Meanwhile, go work on your costume with Polixenes."

"You can't be serious," Henry said. "Do you really expect Arthur and me to make our costumes?"

Ada clutched Henry's arm as she spoke to him. "Do you really expect Mimi and me to make our own costumes and yours as well?" She pinched his arm for effect.

"Ouch! Now, why would you go and do that?"

"Off with you two, now," said Mimi. The two women hurried out of the room and down the hallway, leaving the men to find their own way through the maze.

The fire in Ada's room roared, its flames sending heat to every corner. The two young women worked together to make both costumes, but Ada's demanded the most attention. Hermione, a woman turned to statue and back to woman, would have to stun the audience. Mimi arranged Ada in a sheath of white they had made from a fabric that gripped her body. Ada had sprinkled the gown with silver glitter to give an impression of silver-flecked marble, or ice, to suggest the otherworldly. Mimi made sure that the dress would stay in place, and not fall from Ada's body as she held her pose. "You are simply divine in this, Ada."

AFTER DINNER, the men moved some of the furniture to create a staging area in the huge drawing room, leaving the rest in place for the audience members. The room was so large, their voices bounced off the opposite walls and echoed back to them faintly when their talk and laughter grew loud. Heat from the fireplaces at each end of the room couldn't spread far enough to meet in the middle. But the excitement of the entertainment warmed the players.

They all came to the parlor draped in robes and blankets so that their costuming would not be revealed until they took the stage. Once they had all assembled in the great room, Arlington stood in front of them, the only one still dressed in his street clothes. He seemed suddenly less assured than he did when he faced them in a classroom or lecture hall. He fidgeted with his lapels and cleared his throat before he spoke.

"I have decided," Arlington began. The voice didn't boom as it did at university. It hovered in front of him, struggling to extend itself out farther. His students leaned forward as he spoke, eager to catch every word. "That *The Winter's Tale* shall go first." He stroked his chin as the players rose from their sofas and chairs and disappeared behind the velvet curtains.

Ada corraled her group in whispers. Someone had erected a curtain of cut silk velvet to separate the stage from the rest of the room. The group settled into the positions that best pleased her before they called for the curtain to be pulled back. She felt hot, sure that she was about to begin perspiring, but at the moment when she saw just a strip of the audience between the opening in the velvet, she suddenly felt cool and solid. When they were at last revealed, she stood, at the focal point of the scene, surrounded by students playing her daughter, her husband, her friend. Ada felt as though she really were somehow representing Hermione here tonight. Hermione's husband's cruelty caused her to cease to grow, or act, even to breathe, and yet she did not cease to exist. What did that say, then, about women and their obeisance toward men? Was Hermione's forgiveness of Leontes a weakness, a stupidity? Or was it something to be celebrated, her desire to be loyal and to unite her family? Ada couldn't say. But the idea of Hermione, as she comes to life and speaks to her husband, always made Ada feel unmoored. Now, pretending to be Hermione, she wanted to turn to the student playing Leontes and give him a piece of her mind for having treated her so unkindly.

As she was having these unjust thoughts about her ersatz husband, she sensed Arlington was suffering the sight of her in her cool white. The fabric of her gown was heavy, but it was, at the same time, sheer, and it seemed, she knew, merely a shadow to her body. The musculature of her thighs and the tension in her buttocks were evident in bas-relief through the shimmer of the dress. The outline of Ada's form was so well revealed, the dress gave the impression that it was transparent, though in truth it was not. At some point, after she had been standing still long enough for her muscles to grow weary, after she had begun to hope that this particular entertainment would be finished shortly, Ada allowed her eyes to dart about the room, and she caught Arlington in the act of gawking at her body. When he saw her gaze turn to him, he looked away from her quickly. He pulled a handkerchief from his breast pocket and wiped his brow. Ada, on the other hand, did not feel flustered. She felt an odd sense of power over her professor. There was an element of the euphoric in that, an unfamiliar element, which Ada felt instantly comfortable with. She could be happy feeling this way forever.

"All right. Thank you, *Winter's Tale*. *Hamlet* is the next group, please." As the others burst into wild applause, Ada walked out of the scene and moved toward Arlington, cutting close to him so that he could not avoid looking at her. He looked, he did, but he looked away quickly again. Ada passed him. She felt sure, now that her back was to him, that he was looking at her again. She threw her shoulders back so that her breasts were high, and allowed her backside the freedom to sashay with the movement of her legs as she walked. She draped herself across the sofa, stretching her legs and her bare feet out in front of her without consideration for what harm she might be doing the furniture, or the young men surrounding her. She did it simply so that if Arlington were to look at her now, he would be devastated by the line of her thighs beneath the fine fabric.

The curtains opened again, and Ada watched Arlington force his attention onto the *Hamlet* tableau. Bayley as Hamlet, and his school fellows, playing Laertes and Claudius and Gertrude, were strewn across the floor, swords and poison goblets pitched at their sides. Arlington lingered over them for so long, Elizabeth, who was playing Gertrude, began to giggle. She was lying on her stomach, her arms akimbo over her head. Her back rose and fell quickly as she struggled to keep from laughing. "Enough of that, now," Arlington scolded. "You are dead, remember?" Elizabeth giggled frequently in class. Ada thought this made her silly, and imagined that Arlington disapproved of it as much as she.

Moira's group went finally. Bayley came over and sat next to Ada, crossing the boundaries of the private tableau she had created on the sofa. She had to pull her arms and legs in to make room for Bayley, who sat closer to her than was really necessary. Moira had gone all out for the *Midsummer Night's Dream* scene. A burlap bag was strung up above their heads, and Mimi (too gracious of her, really, Ada thought) shook the rope, causing glitter to rain over their heads. Moira was all got up, from head to toe, in colorful, diaphanous fabrics that revealed nothing of her figure, with a set of gauzy wings attached to her back. She was accompanied by her king, done up in rough burlap and leaves and twigs, and Colin, the Irish singer, as Bottom as an ass, complete with butcher paper ears. Arlington spent a long time scrutinizing their pastiche.

The room grew silent. Ada looked at the other players who sat around her, watching the final competitors. She saw anxiety in their faces, in the tension of their muscles as they held their positions, as if they were not breathing. She wanted to laugh out loud suddenly. All of these young people desperately needed to be Arlington's favorite, to be his darling. Here, in this graceful, expansive home, as they garnished their bodies with what they imagined to be the garb of their literary characters, they hoped to be actually seen. Seen to have the ability not only to speak and write their brilliance, but to give it form. Making it visual would make it simple. This one is the genius, see? See it clearly. They all wanted that just as much as she did, Ada was sure.

Finally, finally, Arlington turned away from the *Midsummer*'s cast. "Thank you all. You were marvelous, every one of you. I must say, you have outdone all the other classes who have come before you. Applaud yourselves."

The applause was reticent. They all wanted to know who would get the honors. How silly, Ada thought. This is supposed to be an entertainment.

"I have chosen, with great difficulty, I assure you." Arlington paused here. "I have chosen *Hamlet*."

Ada forgot, instantly, that she had judged this whole affair to be silly. She was suddenly angry. She had been sure Arlington would choose her group. Hers was by far the best. And the way he had been staring at her. Perhaps he was simply trying to cover up the desire he felt for her. She joined the press of students who were putting on their best faces and congratulating the winners. She wondered if Arlington had, possibly, chosen *Hamlet* not because he was distancing himself from Ada, but simply because the *Hamlet* tableau was headed up by, and starred, a man. Arlington was, like all other men, used to a world that was by, about, and for men only. Throughout the rest of the evening, she felt an undercurrent of anger regarding Arlington's choice of winner.

It was late when she finally went to her room, after the singing and the drinking had slowed down and then trailed off to a finish, and people began to wander up to their rooms. But when she got into her nightgown and crawled into her bed, she was wide awake. Unable to sleep, debating with herself whether or not she should turn on the electric light and read, she noticed a light coming from out in the garden beneath her window.

The light did an unsteady dance through her window and along her walls and high ceiling. The bouncing glow filled her with an odd sense of joy, which drew her to leave her bed and walk across the cold wood floor to her window. Her white silk gown charged with electricity as she walked, and clung neatly to her body. She leaned her face against the rippled glass. A man walked toward the edge of the lawn, carrying a lantern. He stopped at the low wall and looked out toward the ocean. A shimmer of light cut across his face. The rest of him was hard to see, but that bit of face was bright, and it obviously belonged to Arlington. Her breath fogged a patch of the glass.

What possessed her? She had been so angry with him after the *tableaux*, but now all she thought of was how it felt to rest with him in the bank of cushions. She took her heavy blue chenille robe from the armoire and threw it over her gown. Without debating with herself, she picked up her own lantern, lit it, and went out the door.

He watched her as she walked across the great expanse of lawn. He puffed on a pipe, but otherwise he didn't move. Did he know who he was looking at? she wondered. He smiled at her when she came close. She smiled back, the most radiant smile in her repertoire, she knew. "I couldn't sleep," she said.

"Nor could I. It's a lovely night. We may as well enjoy it."

They stood together and faced the ocean, as if that was the reason they both had come to this particular spot. Ada took in a deep breath. "Don't you love the smell of the sea?" she asked him. She wished she might have said it more poetically, so that she might show off her facility with words just for him. But they were failing her at this moment.

"Everything about it," he said, "the smell, the sound, the color, conspires in a reckless siren call, I think. We want to become part of it, but if we do, we are finished."

"Exactly so. That is it exactly."

"Shall we walk down?" he asked. He tapped the tobacco out of his pipe and put it into his breast pocket.

"Oh, yes. That would be grand."

They walked together in silence. When they reached the edge of the water, he took her arm and steered her to the south. A foghorn keened. The water lapped across the pebbles, and their feet crunched over them.

"Have you found yourself a man to marry yet?"

The question seemed so odd, set against this ocean and this wakeful night. She hadn't been thinking about anything of the kind. She laughed at him and stopped walking. "Certainly not. I have my studies to think about."

"But you must mean to find yourself a husband."

"I am not concerned with finding a husband. My mother would be horrified, but it's true."

"Well, you are one in a million, Ada Caswell. You are indeed."

"I want to be like a man," she said, without knowing that was what she would be saying until it was out, released from her tongue and set free on the breeze.

"Oh, well, that will never do. You are much too beautiful to be a man."

She felt a ripple of anger, but again spoke before judging what her words should be. "I don't mean that at all. I mean I want the freedom you have. To marry or not marry, to travel on my own, to study and work. I want all that."

"Why would you, though? It's a difficult life for many of us."

"It's difficult to be locked away in a house with no one to talk to, too," she countered.

"Perhaps it's boring. But certainly it is comforting to know someone else will see to the damnable details of life."

Ada held her tongue then. No good could come from responding to him now, when she felt so disjointed by his talk. She began to walk again, and he stepped in alongside her.

"Tell me what it is you want from your life, then, Ada. If not a husband, what?"

"Just to do what I like. I don't want to run a household for some man. I want to study the law and use my brain. I want to write books about history. I want to explore the Antarctic."

He looked at her without speaking. It seemed to her that he was imagining, perhaps for the first time, what it would take for a woman to have such a life. He laughed then, a laugh that came from far inside his belly. "You will probably get everything you want. I wouldn't be a bit surprised."

She laughed with him. "Do you think it's possible?"

"There is always the rare one who breaks all the rules. Why shouldn't it be you?"

Suddenly, in response to those words, an image popped up in her mind: Ada in a wedding dress, Frederick the groom at her side. She laughed explosively in an effort to shake the image loose. But when Frederick laughed along with her, it seemed only to make the vision grow more vivid.

ADA TOOK THE heavy book off her breast and set it aside. Her curtains were still open. The night was dark, and she could see even from her bed that there was a light coming from the carriage house now. She crossed to her window and leaned out. They were there. Agitated, she hurried to her armoire and took out her robe, but just as she slipped it on, Edward appeared on her threshold.

"Edward. Darling. How nice to see you." Her face felt heated; she wiped her forehead as she spoke.

"Six days until I leave," he said.

Her thoughts were still outside, with Katie and Liam, when she took him by the hand, then led him to her bed. "I shall miss you."

He climbed into the covers with her and pulled at her clothes. His fingers seemed hurried, impatient. His urgency excited her.

He followed her with the pliability of an adolescent who is unfamiliar with the rituals of sex. She turned the gaslight down so that they could still see each other, but the light was appeasing. The bed spread out before them like an empty canvas, and Ada set to work creating a tableau there. She stretched herself diagonally across the green velvet spread, letting her hair fan out all around her, lifted her arms up over her head, and opened her legs so that her gown rose up to her hips, leaving her ungarmented vagina just inches from exposure. Edward leaned in close and lifted her nightgown up over her hips and then her head. He rolled over and across her body then, hoisting himself up onto his hands, and looked down at her for a moment. She spread her legs, exposing her own sepals. She could be anything an orchid could be to him. He put his hand between his legs and guided his penis toward its goal—her labellum, her landing platform.

But Ada wasn't ready; she put her hand down and pulled his hand from his penis, up to her breasts. "Edward, oh, Edward," she whispered. He did her bidding, fondling her breasts, his hands smooth and his touch quick. Tangled up in thoughts of Frederick and Katie and Liam, she forgot herself and took his head in her hands, forcing it down so that he would kiss her nipples. She led his tongue to her neck and her belly. At first he was hesitant, but she was persistent, and in the end, he did things to her he hadn't done since their first year. He kissed her lower back, ran his fingers along her rump, stroked her breasts with his hard penis. He got himself caught up in her long copper hair, and as she watched him through its veil, she thought she saw Frederick's face.

She let him enter her, but she struggled against the very idea of Karezza. She pushed up with her left hip, again and again, until she had forced their two bodies to rest on their sides. Then she swung her leg up over his hip, pinning him under it. His eyes sprung open, and he moved his lips to speak, but she put her hand over his mouth, then put her fingers inside it. "Suck my fingers," she said. As he followed her order, she turned him onto his back and slid herself on top of him, all the while keeping her fingers inside his mouth in order to feel the frantic groping of his tongue. She pushed herself up so that she had total control over the motion of her hips. Her hips rocked up and down slowly, so slowly that he grabbed her buttocks and pushed hard, trying to force her to move faster. She acquiesced, and moved rapidly then, keeping her eyes open and watching his face as he climaxed, her breasts dragging across his chest, sweat dropping from her face onto his. She burst into laughter as his face contorted and purpled, the full laughter of someone released from tension and allowed to run free.

When they were finished, Edward lay next to her for only a few moments. Ada smiled at him, but he was still and his face gave no indication that he was pleased. When he rose from her bed, he dressed in silence. He leaned over her and kissed her on the cheek with lips that felt hard and lacking heat. She looked into his eyes, encouraging him to look back at her, but he averted his gaze and walked out of her room without saying a word.

Ada looked away from the door through which her husband had just walked. The residue of sweat from their lovemaking turned icy. It commingled with the thick semen that leaked onto her thighs, but none of it was warm anymore. It seemed incongruous there on her body, chilly and tight. She went to the washbasin and dipped a towel into the cold water, then rubbed her breasts and her stomach and her crotch over and over, until the skin was raw and the smells no longer assaulted her senses.

THE NEXT DAY, Ada didn't see Edward until he returned from work. The moment he came home, he called her into his office. When she walked through his door, he remained seated behind his flamed mahogany twin pedestal desk. In all the times she had seen him sitting there, he had never looked small to her, but now the massive desk seemed to diminish him. He motioned to her to come sit; she crossed the room, conscious of her stride, then took the chair in front of his desk. He reached out and handed her a piece of paper without speaking.

He had written it all out for her, in the form of a list, as if she needed to be reminded of her affronts. As she read his list, he drummed his fingers on the embossed leather blotter and rocked in his sprung chair.

You walked alone in the Gardens.
Held out your hand to be kissed by Walter.
Had luncheon with the servant girls.
Entered my office unannounced while I entertained men. Again, held out hand to be kissed by questionable men.
Displayed blatant disregard for the teachings of Alice Stockham and the pursuit of perfection in the marriage bed.

"I'm worried," he was saying. "I must say I am terribly worried. So many offenses against good taste, Ada, in such a short time. What is happening to you?"

The paper felt moist in her hands. Her husband had given her a list that detailed her errors, her sins against the order of things. She gripped it as she spoke. "Why, Edward, do you really think something is happening to me?"

"Yes. And I've a mind to put off my trip to New York."

"You simply must not do that. Nothing will happen while you're gone. You have my word."

"Well, of course I haven't canceled the trip, it's not possible. But I have asked Ettie and George both to watch over you."

He was treating her like a child. She was tempted to have a tantrum, to fling herself across the desk and demand that she be treated as an adult. Instead, she held the list out. "Please don't worry. I've been chastened. I will think of you before I do anything at all, Edward. I promise you."

Edward tapped Ada's hand quickly, then pulled his hand away from hers, placing it carefully in front of him on the desk. "Keep the list. Put it next to your bed so that you will remember, every night before you go to bed, and every morning when you wake, what is expected of you."

Crossing Boundaries

When Ada had responded to William's message, she knew that she could not meet him anywhere where some member of any of Edward's societies or clubs or work might see her. Even if they didn't know William, the very idea that she would have some business with a Negro man would set tongues wagging all over Boston, and Edward would know all about it before she made it home, no doubt. So she had scribbled the name of the only public place she knew of in the West End: the African Meeting House on Joy Street. She had heard of it during her time in the Blackwell circles. Some of them were old enough to remember attending Abolition meetings there. The place had once been sacred to many of them.

William's answer had been yes. That yes had carried her through the three days she had to wait for this meeting. It was with her, a comforting sound, yes, the throaty *y* and the hissing *s.* She heard the single, drawn-out syllable repeat itself to her as she ate her breakfast in the kitchen while Ettie worked noisily about her; it gave her the courage to follow through with this meeting in spite of Edward's increasing concerns about her.

She left the house with Katie so that she wouldn't be reported missing. They told Ettie they were off on a shopping errand together, but they parted company at the Public Gardens, and there, Ada boarded a streetcar, alone, for perhaps the first time since she had finished college. By the time she got off the car, on the downward slope of Beacon Hill, the faces on the streets of Boston had changed from white to black.

She peeked her head inside the front door of the simple brick building that was the African Meeting House before stepping across the threshold, hesitant. A young African man sat behind a desk in the entryway, writing in a ledger. He lifted his head when he heard her footsteps.

He smiled. "Yes, ma'am? May I help you?" His tone was not deferential but rather forthright and comfortable. He didn't act as if he had been caught in the act of being human and suddenly needed to put on the show of subservience. His very attitude comforted Ada, making her feel less apologetic about showing up in this place.

"I'm here to see William Parrish. I believe he is expecting me."

The young man got up from his chair. "Would you follow me?"

She walked behind him into the large meeting room whose two-story-high windows washed the place in light, past a long, curving stairway of highly polished wood, then behind it, to a doorway. He tapped lightly on the door. Ada expected it to creak, but was surprised by the silence as it opened.

William stood before them. "Mrs. Pryce," he said. "Thank you for coming." He nodded at her escort. "Thank you, Esau." Esau left them then. William motioned for her to enter. It was a small space, with a table and four chairs, a writing desk with books spread all over its surface, leaded windows that ran from floor to ceiling on the west wall. William closed the door, held out a chair for Ada. She sat down without thinking that she was alone in the room with a black man, and should therefore be concerned. But she did think that because she was alone in the room with a black man, many people she knew would be concerned.

"Mr. Parrish, I'm not sure why I'm here. So, please, do tell me what is wrong. What is it you want to tell me?"

Just then there was a knock at the door. Esau brought in a teapot and a plate of biscuits, then swiftly left again.

"This is lovely, thank you," Ada said.

William poured the tea, passing Ada the biscuits before he spoke.

"It's about Walter Kebble, Mrs. Pryce. It's important that people know he was willfully murdered. He can't speak for himself now. So I must."

Ada would remember the words, all of them, their precise order, and the tilt of William's head, the outline of his form against the window, the sound of the birds outside, for the rest of her life. This moment she existed in the space between her life before and her life after. This was the information she needed to inspire her to climb out of the space, onto solid ground. But she would not realize it in this moment; that would come to her later.

"Murdered? I thought he fell off a mountaintop."

"Fell? No, he was pushed. I'm telling you this because I was there. I know."

"Did you see? Who pushed him?"

"I saw. All of us saw." William's face was grim, his eyes aimed directly into hers.

"But who did such a thing?"

He leaned toward her before he spoke. She pushed herself as far back into her chair as she could, feeling an only vaguely recognized desire to maintain control over the space between them. "You see, I'm one of those who go down to the tropics. I sleep out under the stars," he said. "I get bitten by spiders, I trip over snakes, I climb the mountains, I go hungry. I do all of these things because I like to live in the wilderness, and I like to be paid for doing what I enjoy. But I'm able to do it only because there are many powerful men who are wild about orchids."

A bird sang a long refrain just outside the tall window. Ada fought the urge to go open the window so she could find the bird, and tell William what sort it was that sang to them now. She resisted the desire to turn away from his words, his news, his worried face. Instead, she kept her gaze steady, locked in his own while the bird carried on singing. "So who murdered poor Walter?"

"I don't want to lose my job. But I do want to be able to sleep at night. This is my dilemma. I have not slept properly since that day. I see him falling, turning over and over in the air before he finally hits the ground. He falls for a long time, and he looks at me as he falls, asking me why I didn't do anything to help him. I'm very tired."

Ada sat still, determined not to make any noise that would distract him. His voice was soothing to her; it was like some forgotten melody whose notes she might remember if he went on long enough. She wanted him to continue, but was afraid he would stop if he heard the slightest sound. When he spoke again, finally, she breathed lightly, letting the air escape through her mouth in a thin, silent slip.

"Walter was my friend. We traveled the world together."

"How can I help you, William?" She did want to help him if she could.

"It was John Jefferson who pushed Walter off the mountain."

"Who is John Jefferson?" Ada had never heard the name, she was quite certain of this.

"One of the men who worked for your husband."

Ada felt as if her vocal cords had suddenly gone pliant. She had to fight to get them to make a shape around her words. "But why?" She held the edge of the table with both hands, as though it might keep her from falling onto the floor.

"Your husband and Franz Locke gave him the order. Walter and Jao found a valuable orchid. They were working for another man. Their employer would have claimed discovery, but John Jefferson and I followed them. We camped out near them, without their knowing it. We got up before dawn to go after the orchids. You must understand, we do this sort of thing all the time. It is to be expected. We were gone before they even arrived at the site. But they tracked us, and found us after two days. Walter came at us ahead of Jao and the others he was with. He confronted us, insisting that the orchids were theirs. I held back, I am ashamed to say. Before I knew what was happening, John had pushed Walter over the cliff, and said that any of the rest of us who objected would end up at the bottom of the mountain with Walter."

"But are you certain Mr. Pryce and Mr. Locke approved?"

He nodded. His eyes closed, as if he were too weary to keep them open.

"Can you prove it?"

He opened his eyes in order to train them on her. "No. But you can. That's why I sought you out."

"But what makes you think I would help you to implicate my husband?"

William leaned back in his chair, looking up to the ceiling for a moment before his gaze came back to Ada.

"I watched you at the dinner party at your home. I watched you and Mrs. Locke. I could see very clearly that neither of you is the sort of woman who would protect a murderer. And Walter liked you. He told me so, just before we left. He thought you to be a good woman. Not like most. Am I wrong?"

Ada stood. The chair, as it scraped across the wooden floor, drowned out the rush of her thoughts. She went to the window and pressed her face against it, searching for the bird. But the song had ceased and the bird, flown.

"What can I possibly do to prove my husband, as you say, is party to a murder?"

"You live in his home. You are surrounded by his papers and his acquaintances and fellow orchidists."

"But I'm only his wife. We are not business partners. There's very little that he tells me about his life outside our home."

"You know the orchids. I saw you in the Orchid House."

"Yes. But they aren't mine. And my access to them is controlled, just as my access to everything that is his is controlled." It was difficult for her to look square into his eyes, so her eyes darted between William and the window as she spoke to him.

"That makes things difficult, yes." William sighed and wiped his hand across his face. "Mrs. Pryce, I know I have little power as a black man speaking out against a rich white man. In fact, I would probably never take a public stance against your husband. But I believe that he had my good friend murdered, and I want him to know that I know. It's a matter of honor, I believe."

She looked into his tired eyes then; he looked back at her with a gaze that frightened her in some unnameable way. She nodded her head so slightly that, if she chose, she could later deny that she had actually done so at all.

William saw her to the front door. Just before she began to step away from him, she stopped to ask, "Do you have a telephone?"

"There is a telephone in the Meeting House. If you call here, someone can always reach me." He wrote the number on a pad he pulled from his coat pocket. "You were wise to choose this as our meeting place. I knew when I saw it written on your note that I had not been wrong about you." He held out the paper to her.

She took the phone number and put it inside her brocade handbag.

"May I escort you to your streetcar?" he asked her.

"I'm fine." She held her hand out to him. They shook, and then Ada walked by herself down Joy Street to the streetcar. People who passed her were not surprised by her presence there; her fine clothes and white skin didn't cause concern. Occasionally, passersby smiled and nodded, a couple of people even said hello to her. No one seemed disturbed by the fact that she was out alone. By the time she stepped onto the streetcar, she felt as if she was leaving a place that had welcomed her, unconditionally, even though the people here knew nothing about her history, her family, her failures.

She didn't want to go home to her house or her husband. She could imagine finding a small room to let on Joy Street and staying here, surrounded by her own orchids, for the rest of her days. But instead, she took the streetcar to Emmy Locke's house. When she knocked on the double doors, she was surprised to see Emmy appear in the entryway, behind her maid, her daughter Isabel hanging on to her skirts. The child's face was red and puffy from crying; Emmy looked distraught.

"Oh, Ada. You've come." She smiled, an effort, certainly, to appear as if Ada hadn't imposed upon her in the least. Ada felt the thrill that had buoyed her deflating, flattening out beneath her, as she stood smiling back at Emmy's forced smile.

"I am so sorry. I have caught you at an inconvenient time. I can come back another day."

"Nonsense. Sally, if you'll take Mrs. Pryce into the front parlor, I'll take Isabel back up to Anne."

"Nooo!" Isabel began to kick and scream, tearing at her mother's dress. Her shrill voice echoed across the wide space, bouncing from one highly polished, inlaid cherry wall to another, over and over. Ada fought the desire to put her hands over her ears, or even to scream back at the child. Instead, she smiled and followed Sally, while Emmy struggled to take the little girl upstairs.

Even when Ada was safely ensconced in the parlor, with the door closed, Isabel's protests were clearly audible. The muscles around her head began to contract. By the time the crying stopped, and Emmy appeared in the parlor, she had a full-blown headache.

"I am so sorry, Ada. We are having a difficult day."

"Please, Emmy. Don't apologize. I shouldn't have come without contacting you first."

"I'm glad you came. But I am sorry for the scene. Now you have seen us as we really are. Both the good and the bad of motherhood." She laughed. Ada's head tightened even more, seeming to restrict the flow of blood entirely.

"It's about William," Ada said.

Emmy's alabaster skin went, impossibly, even paler. "Oh. I see." Ada thought Emmy must be expecting some horrible news. It was almost as if she knew exactly what Ada would tell her.

"I am only here to tell you what William said to me. I do not, of course, know what is true and what isn't."

Ada told the story, leaving nothing out. Perhaps she intended to frighten Emmy. Or perhaps she meant to make her feel solidarity with Ada. It wasn't really clear to Ada herself what she wanted from Emmy. But finally, when she got to the part she was so eager to tell, the words came slowly; she had to force each one out. "William says that Edward and Franz ordered John Jefferson to kill Walter." It surprised her to find that, when she said the words, there was no sense of relief. In fact, she felt more agitated than she had at any time since she listened to William's story.

Emmy's face crumpled up, her eyes disappearing into her furrowed skin. "This is just dreadful, Ada. It can't be true, can it? What does he want us to do? Certainly we can't accuse our own husbands of, of . . ." She sat there, silent, unable to say the word she groped for.

Suddenly, Isabel's high, tinkling laughter floated down from the nursery window and into the parlor. The joyousness of it as it drifted lightly into the room caused both women to turn toward the window. Ada imagined Emmy longed to be in that nursery, where only the present moment held any weight, and there were no issues more pressing than what game to play next, how to relieve the pain of a stubbed toe or an incoming tooth, or when to head to the kitchen for a treat.

Certain that Emmy was about to invite her up to the nursery, Ada rose from her chair. "I really must get home. I'll send you a note if I learn anything you should know. Perhaps you could come visit me soon?"

"Yes. Yes, of course." Emmy straightened her skirts as she stood to accompany Ada to the door. "It was so nice of you to come by." She was suddenly behaving, Ada thought, as if this were a typical, routine visit. As if nothing Ada told her had ever been said. As if the world were still the way it had seemed not so long ago.

Ada ran from the streetcar to her house, hurrying now to get there before Edward came home. It wasn't until she stepped into the foyer and saw George in the hallway that Ada realized she had returned without Katie, and without so much as a package to explain her absence.

"Good afternoon, madame," George said to her, bowing slightly.

"Hello, George." He stepped forward to help her with her wrap. Had he been waiting there to catch her out? She made up the story on the spot. "I have been out looking for new furniture for the sunroom. It seems so drab now that the orchids are gone. I believe it needs redecorating."

"Well, that sounds like a worthy project." He took her jacket from her and moved to put it in the closet.

"Yes. It just came to me today. I can't wait to discuss it with Edward." Ada nodded her thanks to him, then left him there, careful as she walked away to maintain an air of indifference.

That evening before dinner, eager to tell Edward about her new project before George had a chance to tell him about it, Ada went to his office. "I've decided the sunroom needs to be redecorated. With the orchids gone, it seems drab. What do you think, dear?" She sat in front of his desk. He sat across from her, leaning back in his chair, his arms clasped together over his head.

"That's a splendid project for you. And then soon the orchid lectures will begin. You should be busy and happy while I'm gone. I approve." He leaned forward and opened his desk drawer. "How much money do you think you'll need?" He took out his checkbook. "I'll draw a draft for you."

Ada hadn't come to him looking for money. But suddenly the idea of it seemed right. Shouldn't she have her own money, to do with as she wished? Shouldn't she be able to purchase whatever wonderful thing she might find for the sunroom without having to wait for Edward's return? "Well, I will probably buy new sofas, chairs, a table, a rug, and a chaise. Perhaps a painting. I am thinking a jungle motif might be nice."

"Of course. As long as it's a tasteful jungle. Nothing too shocking. And we must have the best. I will give you seven hundred dollars. Will that do?" Ada hesitated only briefly. "Perhaps not," he said. "I'll make it eight hundred, then." Eight hundred dollars was a sum sufficient to furnish the room with some of the finest pieces available.

"That is more than generous, my dear."

"I look forward to finding a newly revived sunroom when I return from New York," he said. She watched him as he wrote the draft and wondered what it must be like to have that sort of power over money. Edward had also, no doubt, made out a bank draft to John Jefferson for his work collecting orchids. Had he given extra money to the man for killing Walter? He smiled at Ada as he handed her the check. In that smile was the answer to her question. This man who had shared her life for four years now could not have done something so base. She walked around to his side of the grand desk and leaned down to kiss him. He put his hand on her cheek. The touch of his hand on that sensitive skin was as light as the wafting of fine silk in a gentle breeze. Not the touch of a man who approved of murder for vanity's sake.

As Ada left him to his work, holding her check in her hand, the idea of having all that money at her disposal made her feel like telling someone. Some woman friend. But who? Once, Moira was the one she would have told. Now there was no one.

She took the draft up to her room and placed it on her bedside table, next to the list of her crimes. She would cash it the very next day, and keep the money in her trunk until she needed it. The trunk was hidden behind a tapestry in the corner of her room. It had belonged to Ada's own grandmother. Beatrice had been about to throw it out, but Ada rescued it and kept it hidden in her room until she married. Edward had hated the trunk the moment he laid eyes on it. Ada was only allowed to keep it on condition that it remain out of his sight. It was a smelly, crumbling trunk of camel-colored leather, stained in many places. Bulging, bloated stains of brown, and small, contained pimples of orange, dashes of gray, all spread out across the surface and the interior of the thing. She knew, without doubt, that Edward would never dream of opening the lid of this particular trunk, and once she had cashed the check and hidden the money inside it, this knowledge somehow made her feel secure.

WHEN EDWARD FINALLY LEFT for New York, it was as though the hemispheres of Ada's brain were divided into two camps, one side regretting his departure, the other rejoicing in it. She wanted him to stay so she could prove to him she was a good wife and that her transgressions were lapses that she would correct with great flair. But then again, she wanted him to go so she might spend a little time being herself rather than Edward's inadequate wife, so that she might allow herself to be just the person she meant to prove she was not.

That side of her brain that wanted to be Ada Caswell again won the very first day after Edward's departure. On a whim, she rang up Alice Stone Blackwell, who invited her to an afternoon in celebration of the Blackwell sisters' return to Boston.

The gathering fell on a thick summer day when the clouds were charcoal gray and pressing down hard so they touched the tips of the oak trees. The minute George left on some outside errands, Ada took a trolley to the Blackwells'. Because she felt as if she were somehow betraying her husband's trust, she didn't ask Liam to take her in the carriage. The anonymity of a trolley felt more in keeping with the nature of her escape.

The Blackwell house was full of women. At first, it didn't even occur to Ada that there was not a man to be had in the entire place. It only came to her slowly, as she moved about the parlor, greeting old friends, being introduced to new ones. Emily and Elizabeth Blackwell, the physicians, were in town from New York, staying with their niece Alice Stone Blackwell. They had suddenly grown old and frail, she thought. They certainly would not live to see women get the vote. The two women had gone to medical school, and had practiced medicine, and yet they could not be trusted to vote for their local or national representatives. And the hansom driver who had gone to school for fewer than five years, the man who spent his life cutting meat, the male servants in houses like this one and Ada's own? Every one of them could vote, if they cared to.

Ada watched the people gather around the sisters, moving toward and away from them at intervals, as though their movements had been choreographed. Emily was standing alone suddenly, for just a space like a breath in between words. Ada went over to her and put her arm around the woman whose stature was condensed by age, and whose skin had gone reed-like, rippling with the slightest movement. Before Ada could say anything, before the tears had a chance to move from thought to action, a young woman of perhaps twenty approached. She walked as if there were springs on her feet, and her feet were easily visible beneath the hemline of the trousers she wore. Her dark hair fell out in bunches from the sloppy chignon she seemed to have slapped onto her head.

"Emily!" the young woman called out, and stretched her arms in front of her to give the old woman a hug. Ada smiled at the intruder, but released her own grip on Emily and then moved away.

She went to sit with Alice, certain she would feel comforted being in the presence of her old friend. There was no small talk between them.

"We are making progress in our struggle, Ada. Don't you want to join us again?" Alice's urgent tone grated on Ada.

She didn't want to give Alice reason to believe she might recommit to the cause. Edward was the perfect excuse. "I don't know how Edward would feel about it."

Alice's face fell. "Oh, Ada. You of all people. I never thought I would hear you speak this way."

"Never mind, Alice. I'm just so happy to be here with you now. Let's just enjoy one another's company while we are in it."

Alice's mouth pinched itself in before she spoke. The words eked themselves out between her closed teeth. "I'll try, Ada. But I can't forget. I simply cannot ever forget that you have changed so much."

"I haven't really changed. I've just grown older." Ada felt cornered by her old friend. Her eyes scraped the room, looking for something to settle on, something that would pull her up from the sinking feeling that was encroaching on her.

"But you don't have children," Alice said, pulling Ada back to her. "You don't have those responsibilities, like other married women your age. There is nothing really stopping you. You just have to tell Edward that you are going to work for suffrage, and that's the end of it. What will he do, divorce you?"

"It's not that simple, Alice. It just isn't that simple," Ada said.

As they sat together in the Blackwells' plain but spacious parlor, Alice continued to prod, but her voice was nothing but an irritant, and Ada felt that other half of her brain taking over, the half that hadn't wanted her to come here. She nodded and whispered commiseration when Alice spoke in detail of the next action that would be taken at the state level, but she was thinking about her home and Edward's strange and wonderful orchids, Liam and Katie in the barn, about her restricted sex life with her husband, even dinner menus. If she kept her mind trained on these simple and necessary things, she wouldn't be seduced by the lost past that dogged her here in this company.

Later, she found herself sitting next to the young dark-haired woman in bloomers. After Alice had given up on her, the girl plopped herself into the empty space next to Ada. The pillows seemed to welcome the young body; they puffed themselves up and then settled themselves protectively about her. Ada pulled herself up, steeled herself, as if she needed to protect herself from the ease that seemed to encircle the creature in the pillows next to her. She wondered suddenly what Edward would say about a woman dressed in men's clothes. But immediately she realized there was nothing to wonder about. She knew. Exactly.

It was in that moment of realization that she reached out her hand. "Hello. I'm Ada Pryce."

The girl took Ada's hand in between both her own and squeezed it warmly. "I'm Margery Jordan. I'm very honored to make your acquaintance."

Ada couldn't stop the laugh from bubbling out into the ethers, and thus becoming audible. "Honored? To meet me? But why?"

"Well. I'm at Boston University. I hear stories about you. You, and the others who were there with you. It hasn't been all that long since you left."

Ada felt an involuntary sucking in of air, air that swooped down into her belly and lay there heavily, making it impossible for her to speak. While speechless, she had the realization that Margery Jordan was the name of a character in a Shakespeare play. She could hear Frederick pronounce the name in his basso, the syllables filling the classroom as he spoke. She couldn't remember in what context Frederick had said the name, or even what play the character was from. But the mere memory of the sound of it carried with it a physical pain that ran from the back of her neck down her spine and into her tailbone. She didn't have the mettle to ask Margery if she was taking Shakespeare with Frederick.

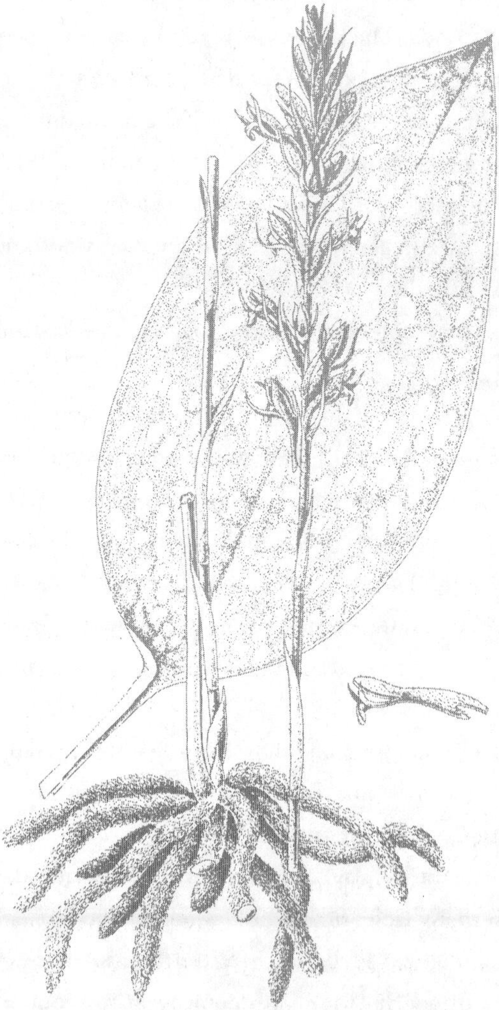

After *the* Play

The second night after the *tableaux vivant* at Moira's summer house, Ada found herself out on the patio with Frederick again. She had been unable to sleep, but this time it was the memory of her stroll with Frederick that kept her awake. So she repeated the previous evening's movements, while Frederick apparently did the same. She bumped into him as she rounded the corner of the house. The separate orbs of light from their lanterns met before they did, becoming a single halo around them both. Their shadows cut clean lines across the walkway, but Ada and Frederick didn't notice them. They were looking into each other's smiling faces.

"Have you come out to contemplate plans for your voyage to the Antarctic?" Frederick asked her.

"Wouldn't it be lovely if that were the case."

They walked together toward the water's edge as if they had planned to go there and had no need for further discussion of their plans now.

"Do you know how to swim?" he asked.

"No. I never have gone swimming. Do you?"

"Yes. I wouldn't mind going for a dip right now."

"I'll watch if you'd like to go in," she said.

"No. Not without your company."

"Oh. Well, perhaps one day I shall learn how." They gazed out at the sea, watching the moon as it rose up over the water, its white light bending across the waves. "Just think," she said, "the Antarctic is a world away, but the ocean here in front of us reaches all the way down there. We could board a ship and sail across this very sea to reach it. Perhaps the water in front of us now was lapping up against the shores of the Antarctic at this time last year." He looked at her without speaking. "What I am trying to say is, it makes the world seem so small." She didn't know how to say it to him, or even to herself, but what she meant was that it was all so vast, and yet even the smallest bits of matter, even invisible atoms, could cover the vastness, could claim both here and the place that was a world away. "It makes me feel small and yet eternal at the same time."

"That's because you are. You are both those things, my dear Ada."

"Perhaps we should swim together to the bottom of the world."

He leaned in toward her, placing his hand on her face. The light from the lamps flickered below, while the moonlight washed down over the crown of his head. The waves plashed across the sand. His mouth moved closer to hers, so that she could no longer make out his features. She smelled the cherry tobacco from his pipe, and then she tasted it as his mouth touched hers. There was nothing then but the taste of him and the scent of him.

She lifted her arms to wrap them around his neck. His face moved away from hers, and he settled his hands under her robe. She reached out to touch his cheek.

"Oh, Ada. What have I done?"

"What do you mean, what have you done?"

"I shouldn't be out here with you, kissing you."

"How can you say that? I want you to do it again." She knew he had a wife somewhere, a woman none of them had ever seen, but she refused to bring her between them. She pulled his face down, pushing her lips into his. The kiss this time was more pressing. She sucked at him as if she were competing with some unseen entity that would steal away anything she missed. She marked him with her tongue, laying claim. She felt the flow of her power over him. It moved out from her and encircled him, then pulled him closer. He didn't resist.

They went on like that, until at last Frederick roused himself.

"We should sleep, Ada. Let me walk you back to your room."

She didn't argue.

Their lamps bumped up against each other as they walked. She moved slowly, wanting the sensation of him next to her to last forever. But he stood outside her door, then walked away from her once she stepped across her threshold.

The third night Ada and Frederick walked together outside Moira's country house was different from the earlier occasions. They both appeared outside at the same time. It was evident to both of them that they had come in search of each other. So they dispensed, immediately, with pretext and subterfuge.

"I'm so glad you came," Frederick said to her.

"How could I have stayed away?"

Wordlessly, he took her elbow and steered her away from the house, and the scattered lights that still shone from a few of the windows. Neither one of them had brought a lantern; they let the moon guide them in their stroll. It wasn't until they had been walking together for some time that Ada noticed Frederick was carrying a blanket. She hurried her pace then, pulling Frederick along, eager to get to the beach so she could feel his body against hers as they lounged on Frederick's blanket.

They took off their shoes to walk to the water's edge. Ada sensed the blanket, spread out on the sand behind them; she longed to return to it. Instead, she hiked her skirts and they walked in the water together. It was cold, she was young. She didn't try to censor herself when the shock of the water hit her. She cried out, then laughed. The combination of cold and laughter made her lose her balance. Frederick caught her in his arms, pulling her toward him. They stood in the water, kissing, not caring that their clothes were getting wet.

Finally, Ada pulled away from him. "It's cold," she said.

"I'll warm you."

"Yes, do." Taking his hand, she led him away from the water. They settled onto the blanket. Ada shivered, leaning into Frederick's arms for warmth. He put his hands inside her coat. Without stopping long enough to feel clumsy, or to doubt herself, she began to unbutton her gown. She had put on a simple housedress with few buttons. Now, her shoulders were bare under her coat. He put his hands onto her shoulders, then stroked downward, forcing her dress to her waist. His head moved into the warm space inside her coat, and he found her nipples with his lips.

So this was what everyone was so afraid of, Ada thought. The thing her mother had warned her against, the thing no proper young woman would discuss. This is so delightful, it runs the risk of distracting the whole world from the work that keeps it running, so it must be hidden away to keep people productive, she decided. Ada made a pact with herself in that moment. She would pretend to the outside world that sex was unknown to her, and that she believed it should remain so until her wedding night. She would share her desire for this act, for this feeling, only with Frederick. And she would share it with him as often as possible.

SHE STILL STOOD in Alice Blackwell's drawing room, and Margery, who hadn't seemed to notice the fugue-like flight Ada's memory had taken her on, was still talking to her. Had she been talking for seconds, minutes? Ada couldn't tell. This loss of time and awareness made her feel vulnerable, as if she were on the edge of some great separation that would leave her alone in the world. "You must come by sometime," Margery was saying. "I would love to hear stories about what it was like. And maybe you would like to come to some of our suffragist meetings."

Ada nodded her head and smiled at the young woman. "I'm off to my cycling lesson now," Margery said. Ada caught her breath for an instant. Had Margery been one of the young women in the Public Gardens that day she had escaped to the park by herself? The idea that it might be so made her feel a vicarious pleasure, but at the same time she wanted to cut the young woman, to tell her that cycling was crass, too beyond the pale. She heard the words in her head as if Edward were whispering them to her: such unsuitable behavior for a woman.

"But, please," Margery was saying as she fished in a pocket of her trousers, like a man would, and pulled out a card. "Here's my calling card." She handed it to Ada and then waited. Ada was supposed to offer Margery her own calling card. She dipped her hand into her bag before she remembered that she hadn't brought the cards with her. Believing that coming to the Blackwells' somehow freed her of the usual social niceties that she viewed as strictures, she had left them at home.

"I'm sorry, I seem to have forgotten my cards."

"Oh, no matter. Please, though, you have my address, do me the honor of calling on me, would you?"

"Of course. I would love to talk with you about university." But in truth, she was terrified of dredging up memories of her time at Boston University. She had to stuff them away in a safe place even now, as she stood talking with Margery, in order to avoid the feeling of becoming momentarily disembodied, of being detached from the lineaments of time.

Out on the street, out of reach of the general guilt that seemed to shimmer around the Blackwell house, the breeze from the river cooled her, lifted her spirits. But the thought of going home distressed her. There was some other form of guilt palpitating within the walls of her home. Instead of returning directly there, Ada took a trolley to Williams & Sons Furniture to look for pieces for the sunroom. Edward had given her all that money, after all. She needed to do something with it. Perhaps a search for pieces for the room would calm her, thus easing her transition back into her domestic realm.

Inside the store, Ada looked over the huge inventory of furniture. It was all too heavy, ornate, far too lumbering for her sunroom. What she envisioned for that space was not here. But as she was about to turn and go, a rocker from Liberty & Co., of London, caught her eye. The chair was from the Aesthetic Movement, with clean lines that called to mind Japanese furniture. It was constructed of cherry, with inlaid brass and mother-of-pearl on the back panels, cut into lean floral designs. Raw silk upholstery in shades of purple and deep red lent comfort to the sleek construction. Its purchase made her feel flush with a sense of accomplishment.

When the chair was delivered the very next morning, Ada had the men put it in the sunroom, but when she sat in it there, it felt somehow wrong. It was too vibrant for this barren space. That afternoon, she had Liam carry it up to her bedroom. As she walked ahead of him to the staircase, she saw George watching them from down the hallway. Certainly there was nothing wrong with what she was doing, no reason for George to be disapproving of her. He smiled at her the instant their eyes met, then moved quickly away.

The rocker took pride of place in front of her bedroom window. Ada sat in it, alone in her room. The design was so flawless, the wood sculpted so finely, the chair made barely a whisper as it rolled back and forth across the peg and groove floor. What a perfect chair for reading. She went to her small bookshelf and examined her books. There was nothing there that suited her mood. She wondered how it was that, with all the books in her house, there was nothing she cared to read. Was she losing her interest in literature? Suddenly, she thought of Minnie Lovell and her love of books. She would visit her the next day and ask her for something wonderful to read. Certainly Minnie would inspire her. She gave a message to Liam to take round to the Lovells', warning her friend of her intended visit.

MINNIE OPENED THE DOOR herself when Ada showed up at her door at eleven the next morning. She pulled Ada into the parlor, and within minutes was plying her with tea and biscuits. Ada didn't even have to turn the subject to books. As they sipped their tea amid the splendor of Anderson's trips around the world, his African masks and New Guinean headdresses, his English compasses and Icelandic scrimshaw, Minnie brought it up herself.

"I went to the bookstore yesterday. I bought a whole bag of new books. If I keep reading so much, I'm bound to be more educated than my husband before I die."

Ada leaned forward and touched Minnie's soft hand. "I wouldn't be surprised if you have long since surpassed him, and all our husbands." The two women laughed together, but the laugh was biting, comprised of both irony and regret.

"I'm looking for something at the moment," Ada said. "I don't seem to want to read any of my own books. Do you have a suggestion?"

"I've just read *The Woman in White*. Wilkie Collins. It's a sensation novel, you know, from the sixties. It's not Shakespeare, but I found it to be a thrilling read. Let me give you my copy." Minnie went to the library herself rather than calling a servant, and came back with the book. "I can't wait to have someone intelligent to discuss it with."

Ada held the red leather volume in her hands, then lifted it close to her face so that she could smell its gilt-edged pages.

THAT NIGHT IN her room, she took the book to her new rocker and opened it. She forgot completely that it was a sensation novel, at least until Walter Hartright happened upon the Woman in White walking alone on the heath. When he sees her there, in the dark of night, he is aghast that a woman should be out alone at such an hour. His incredulity reminded Ada of the reaction she got when she walked alone in the Public Gardens. But Ada's story was a simple one; she wanted nothing more than to take a walk in the sunshine. The Woman in White, whom Hartright helps to find a carriage, is desperate; she may have escaped from an asylum. And she will, of course, draw Hartright into intrigues involving mayhem and murder.

Suddenly, Ada felt as if she could not read the book. She had no stomach for it under the circumstances. Minnie would have to wait until she read some other book before they had their intelligent conversation.

What if she, like this fictional woman, was also involved with a murderer? Shouldn't she be desperate, too?

William, and those words he spoke to her at the African Meeting House, came back to her. "It's about Walter Kebble, Mrs. Pryce," he had said. "It's important that people know he was willfully murdered. He can't speak for himself now. So I must." She had refused to consider the accusation ever since Edward gave her the banknote for the furniture, but now the memory of William's voice, the sadness in his eyes, tugged at her, just as the Woman in White's desperate eyes must have tugged at Hartright. Instead of inspiring her to read, Ada's visit to Minnie had inspired her to continue doubting her husband, to continue searching for a sign.

She rang the bell for Katie, who appeared within moments.

"Yes, ma'am?" she said as she pushed the door open.

"Katie, I need to go into the Orchid House. Will you tell me when George is gone? I don't want him to know."

Katie didn't answer right away. Instead, she twisted the front of her dress in between her hands. Ada got up from her rocker and went to her maid, taking her by the hand. "Katie, are you worried that this will get you into some sort of trouble?"

"Oh, Ada. I didn't want to say anything to you, but now I see I must. I overheard George speaking with Ettie this morning. He took her into his office, but I heard them when I walked by. He told her to keep an eye on you. He was suspicious about where you've been getting yourself off to since Mr. Pryce has been away."

"But he knows I went furniture shopping." She touched the back of her rocker, sliding her fingertips along the velvety surfaces of the wood.

"I don't believe he thinks that's the half of it," Katie said. "I'm sorry to be the one to tell you, but I do think he believes you go about too much on your own."

"Oh, dear Lord. All I want to do is go into the Orchid House, Katie. I'm not planning on leaving the house again today. I just don't want to go in while he is here. He watches everything I do." She shouldn't have been surprised. Edward had told her he had asked George and Ettie to watch her.

"I'm so sorry." Katie spoke as Ada paced. "I thought I should tell you. I never did mean to upset you."

"No. I'm glad you told me. You did the right thing." She patted Katie's arm. "Thank you."

"I'll be happy to come let you know if ever he goes out. And I'll try to learn where he's taking himself as well."

Within the hour, Katie was back in her room. "He's gone to speak to the haberdashers about some order or other of the Mister's."

"Good. I'll go out to the greenhouse, then." She looked at herself in the mirror and patted her hair. "I only want to have a moment to refresh myself in the company of the flowers. It's nothing suspicious, nothing improper. If Ettie knows, it's fine. I just don't want George watching everything I do. I simply cannot tolerate it."

"I understand, miss. I do."

"Will you tell me if he comes back?"

"Indeed."

As Ada walked down the back stairs and out into the yard, she thought how nice it would be to talk to Katie about William's suspicions, and to enlist her maid in her search for the truth. But it was impossible. She couldn't tell Katie anything about it. Not ever.

Her fear that George would return and catch her out hurried her walk across the yard. But when she stepped into the greenhouse, and the odor of bark and soil and moisture filled her nostrils, she forgot to worry. She walked up and down the lengths of the tables, stroking the petals, touching the loam, sniffing at the fragrant and odorless flowers alike. There were so many and their variety so overwhelming, she felt dizzy with sensory input.

The plants were like a mystical balm, soothing her the instant she walked through the door; she had to force herself to stay focused on her mission. Pulling herself away from the orchids, she went to the safe that Edward kept under the worktable in the far corner of the house. She had seen him open it on several occasions. She took the dial in her right hand, then closed her eyes. Emptying her mind of distraction, she conjured a picture of the lock in Edward's hand. It took less than a minute for her to remember the combination.

The safe creaked open. Ada instinctively glanced toward the greenhouse door. It was closed, the room still except for the gentle spray coming periodically from the automated irrigation system. Before she reached into the safe to pull out two leather-bound volumes, she studied their positioning so that she could return them to their precise locations.

She put the volumes on the table in front of her. One was a book Edward had allowed her to read; it contained his records of the plants' care and culture—their feeding schedules, their measurements, what sort of light they did well in, how much moisture they needed, how quickly they bloomed. The other she had never seen before. The leather was dusty blue, as if it had been well used. Was this something he usually kept at work? Why had she never seen it before?

Ada's hands shook slightly, just once, as she opened the cover and turned to the first page. In red-inked calligraphy, the letters tall and sinuous, were the words *Secrets of Orchid Culture—from the Studies of Several Orchid Enthusiasts.*

Her fingers touched the letters, following their curving lines; she hesitated to turn the page. The secrets might just be more measurements and dates and listings of genus and variety. But the secrets might be something more disturbing. Suddenly, she wasn't at all sure which sort of secret she was hoping to find. If she were to find some kind of proof of Edward's complicity in Walter's death, what would William really do with the evidence? But the instant the question arose, she pushed it aside, aware that William was impotent against her husband.

If she found something, it would simply serve to clarify her husband's true nature to her. And if she found nothing, she would stop doubting. Certainly the truth was all she was after.

Turning the frontispiece over hesitantly, she revealed the first page, which introduced the orchids themselves. Whoever had written it—was it Edward's handwriting? she couldn't be certain—wanted the reader to understand why orchids were so important. "They come to us from the mysterious region of the thirteenth parallel south latitude. It is a long and difficult journey from their hiding places to the hothouses of London and Boston. But they carry with them a mystique that makes the journey worth every step and every danger along the way."

A watercolor of a *Cattleya* with purple flowers interrupted the text. The page was dimpled from the paints. She touched the picture, her fingers rising and falling with the peaks and valleys of color. It was a lovely flower, one she didn't recognize. Was it from Franz's collection? Ada turned the page. The text picked up again. "Orchids are highly evolved, having graced the planet for millions of years. They hold their own against other jungle plants, animals of various sorts, extreme fluctuations in weather, drought and monsoon, disease and even absence of sunshine." She skimmed quickly then, moving through the pages in search of information that was more pertinent to her cause.

She slowed her pace again when she found the pages describing the sexual apparatus of the orchids. Had Edward been the author of these words? She imagined him, in a fever, writing to purge himself of his own base sexual desires.

"The orchid exists on a high spiritual plane, with the male and female parts of the flower being fused. The flower has solved the problem of the ages, having found a way to integrate these disparate energies, becoming one thing, both male and female, conjoined." This was what he wanted from Karezza, a perfect joining of male and female. If they were joined, he seemed to think, then the tug of desire would dissipate, the laws of attraction would become obsolete, and life would suddenly be pacific. But Ada knew none of this was possible. He hungered after something unattainable, insisting that she try to make his unreasonable quest a reality, in spite of the fact that she was powerless to do so.

Ada turned more pages, read more text, until the information flooded her brain and she felt a headache coming on. As she pressed her fingers against her temples, she was distracted by a movement from outside, disturbing her peripheral field of vision. She stood up and went closer to the window. It was Katie, running across the yard toward the Orchid

House. Ada closed the book gently, then quickly carried it to the safe, where she lined it up exactly as it had been when she first found it. She swung the door shut, spun the lock, and stood up before Katie opened the door.

"Oh, Ada." Katie was out of breath from running. "George is back."

"I was just about to come in. What perfect timing." She refused to allow Katie to see her anger, or her own fear of George. Before they stepped out the door together, Ada reached for Katie's arm. "Smile at me," she said. "And laugh. George should have no reason to be suspicious of us. I have every right to go into the Orchid House and enjoy the flowers."

The women were both smiling and laughing as they walked through the garden. Ada thought she saw George's shadow cross the small window next to the back door, but by the time they entered the hallway, there was no one to be seen.

Back in her room, in her rocker, she held *The Woman in White* but didn't read it. Instead, she thought of Edward and Walter and the mountaintop where Walter had known his last moment of life. She had found nothing in Edward's safe, and somehow that disappointed her. She wanted to do something for Walter. Not find her own husband guilty of his murder, of course. But she felt a need to find something that would resolve the issue, so that the dead man might rest in peace, so that she herself might cease wondering. She knew she would have to spend more time; she had only scratched the surface in this hunt for evidence. But evidence of what? Edward hadn't been with the men in the jungle. If someone had pushed Walter off the mountain, it wasn't Edward. Certainly it was possible that John Jefferson had simply assumed he had been ordered to do anything for the orchids, including commit murder. Edward couldn't be responsible for such an assumption.

She remembered the upcoming orchid lectures. Perhaps a firmer knowledge of orchid culture would help her find something to report back to William, would help her to understand where to look, and what to look for. She put her book away and picked up the pamphlet Edward had given her.

> Discover why such Fantastic sums of Money are being spent on these Rare Beauties, and what you must know if you are to truly understand the ways of these Mysterious Plants.

Money and mystery certainly did revolve around these plants, in degrees that were perhaps greater than she could handle.

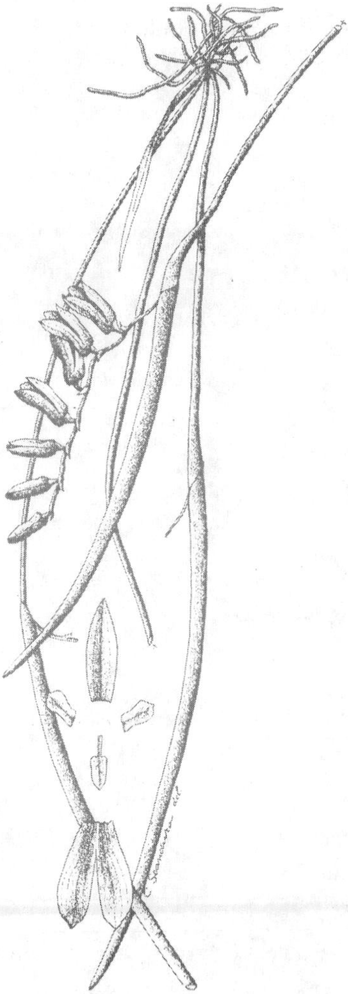

ORCHID CULTURE

The lecture was delivered by Everett Jones, a man in his thirties with long muttonchops that stood out a good three inches on each side of his face. He referred to himself as an active and enthusiastic member of the Orchid Society. He never mentioned what he did for a living. Perhaps, thought Ada, he is independently wealthy and this is all he really does. Mr. Jones was dressed carefully in clothes that seemed never to have carried a wrinkle or absorbed a drop of sweat. His hands were white and soft-looking. The walls behind his podium were covered with charts and illustrations. He pointed to them with a long wooden pointer as he spoke.

"There are two types of orchid," he said to the dozen or so members of the all-female audience, and went on to explain what Edward had already told her about terrestrials and epiphytals. As he spoke, Ada imagined the epiphytal orchids' survival, with their roots bared to the vagaries of the earth's rites and designs, as something noble. But she also believed it made them ardent. They were creatures that yearned after something. Yearning for something seemed such an accomplishment, even if it was simply the plain will to survive that was the impulse behind the desire. Still, it was desire.

Edward desired his orchids. Katie and Liam desired each other. She knew other men who desired success, others adventure. She knew women who simply desired approval from their mothers and husbands. And of course there were those who wanted the vote. But for Ada, what was it? Was it Edward, really? Surely she dove into this orchid culture in part because of her longing to be in his course, to have substance there. But what else was there for her to do, after all?

Once Everett Jones moved into new territory, Ada became engrossed in the content of the lectures and abandoned her own musings. "One must always plant an orchid in the same habitat from which it was removed. For example, if it was found on a branch, place it on a log." Here Jones distracted himself and went off on a wondrous ramble about orchid hunting. "It is far preferable to collect an orchid in the wild when it is in a dormant state. Their roots, as you already know, are either fibrous, tuberous, or fleshy. When they are in the state of excitement required for them to bloom, the roots become terribly fragile." He stopped then and looked out at the women. "I hope at least one among you is lucky enough to happen upon an orchid in the wild when it is in flower. But if you should ever do so, do not collect it. You must mark its place and return to it when it is once again dormant." Ada tried to imagine his smooth hands digging in the dirt but failed. Jones returned then to the business at hand: teaching women to cultivate orchids in greenhouses.

The other women wanted to chat, with one another and with Mr. Everett Jones, after the event. But Ada didn't want to dilute what she had learned by staying on to listen to the conversations of these women. She went to two more lectures while Edward was away in New York. After each one, she left as soon as she had greeted the women there briefly. She knew they talked about her once she had gone; she knew that some of the women knew Beatrice, and might even report back to her, somehow, that Ada had slighted them. But Beatrice's disapproval was something to which she had long since become accustomed. This would just be another item on the list of Ada's flaws her mother surely kept. She wondered then if Edward and

Beatrice ever compared notes on Ada's misdeeds. Perhaps Beatrice was the one who developed the idea for Edward to create a list of Ada's recent crimes.

ON THE AFTERNOON of Edward's return from New York, while Liam carried his bags to his room, Edward steered Ada toward the sunroom. He's eager to see what I've done to transform it, Ada thought. Her breath became rapid as they crossed the threshold of the room. She watched as his face fell and grew ashen. "I gave you money to redecorate," he said. "I looked forward to seeing what you had done with it when I returned. You've had an abundance of time, certainly, and no want of funds."

They stood together in the barren space, gazing into its fallow brightness. For an instant, Ada couldn't think what to say in her own defense. But finally, searching for truths about herself, she uttered one he might want to hear. "I was so engrossed in the lecture series, I forgot to involve myself in this room, my dear. In truth, I have spent time in the Orchid House, I've been so inspired." As she said the words, she knew they soothed him. Within half an hour, they were in her room practicing Karezza. Her nerves, on edge from his reproach, made it easy for her to participate in their sexual ritual without fear that she would slip toward crisis.

When they had finished, Edward sat up in her bed and gazed at her rocker, and she was obliged to tell him the story of how she came to purchase it. She defended her decision to buy the chair, but he seemed to appreciate its beauty and didn't reprimand her. "I can see why it caught your eye. You have a good one," he told her as he dressed to return to his room. "I look forward to seeing how you apply your talents to the sunroom." He kissed her forehead then and left her alone.

IN THE DAYS following Edward's return, Ada tried to focus on the sunroom, but doubts about his role in Walter's death cropped up incessantly, interfering with her thinking. William's face, and the words he said to her, would not leave her be. "I see him falling, turning over and over in the air before he finally hits the ground," William had told her. And when she was alone with her thoughts, Ada imagined she heard that very thud, the sickening compactness of an inert body making contact with the earth. This sound especially, coming at her quickly, in odd moments throughout the day, made her doubt her husband.

Finally, one afternoon when George had stepped out, she used the telephone on Edward's desk to call him at his office, with the flimsiest of pretexts. If he answered the phone, that meant he could not walk through the front door in less than forty minutes. It would buy her a small slice of time in which to continue her investigation. If she could prove Edward's innocence, she could still the sound that tormented her. It was a worthy pursuit, certainly.

"What do you think of an Oriental motif for the sunroom?" she asked him. "I think I've gone off the jungle idea."

"Certainly, my dear," Edward said without hesitation. Ada felt the cells of her body open up and relax when she heard the words. "As I said before, I believe in your talents and your taste. And I am very happy to see you're taking an increased interest in domestic matters."

The phone's earpiece felt heavy in her hand. She leaned in closer to the mouthpiece. "Edward, I am so lucky to have such an understanding husband."

She went to Edward's office door the instant she rang off, and turned the key on the inside, locking the door against George or even Katie, then checked the clock. She would give herself three quarters of an hour to search his papers.

As she reached under the desk to retrieve Edward's desk key from its hiding place along the drawer track, she was certain she could hear her own heartbeat. She opened the top desk drawer, pulling it out slowly, carefully. Before she did anything, she studied its contents.

The drawer contained wooden dividers on an angle that allowed Edward to file papers, while still being able to see a portion of the page. Each file had a paper label taped to it. The first one read: Household. Ada pulled all the papers out of it and placed them on the desk. She picked up the top sheet—a receipt from the butcher—examined it, then turned it facedown.

Next she found a receipt from Charlton's, for linens purchased by Katie. It listed them in a column on the left:

One dozen damask tablecloths
Four dozen damask napkins
Six pairs Holland sheets
Eight pairs servants' sheets

with prices on the right-hand side.

Next were five receipts from five different dressmakers. Apparently, Edward went through her personal receipts and grouped them together. Was he keeping track of how much money she put into her wardrobe? Her skin crept a bit with the realization that he observed her so closely, and that she had never known.

She looked at all the papers one by one, turning them facedown and placing them on the desk so that they would be in the exact order she found them in when she replaced them. Edward had filed receipts for food, dishes, cutlery, linens, cleaning supplies, objets d'art of lesser value, clothing for the household staff and Ada, candles and oil for the lamps, even boot-blacking. The receipts might tell the entire story of her domestic life. Ada examined the whole of the Household file without finding anything of interest. The next file, labeled Livery, was also devoid of anything that seemed to her to be suspicious. She looked at the clock on the mantelpiece; she was moving slower than she had counted on. Already half an hour had flown past.

She tried to move faster while still being regimented in her adherence to order. Edward was extremely well organized and neat; she could leave nothing out of place. But a sense of desperation made her want to just shuffle through the papers. Certainly, if she found whatever might prove something, one way or the other, about Walter's death, she would finally be able to relax. Maybe it wouldn't matter if Edward discovered her. Then she would be able to simply tell him the truth about what she was doing, and ask him straight out if he knew the details of Walter's death.

The third file was named Club. It included an accounting of membership dues, money spent on dinners and drinks there, and lists of special events. A few stray photographs were at the bottom of the file compartment. She pulled them out and studied them. Edward posed with other men from the Club. They sat together on sofas, or crowded around chairs, or were seated at tables. They held cigars, drinks, cards. Their suit coats were unbuttoned, or removed altogether, their faces open, their posture relaxed. Ada had never seen the inside of the rooms in the photographs. And she had never seen her own husband with the look that he wore in these photographs. It wasn't that he looked happier there, at his club. He looked to be some other person entirely. Why did he go to this dark and old-fashioned-looking place so often, and spend so much time with other men? And why could women never penetrate the veil that protected this world of men from their curiosity and desire?

It seemed logical to Ada that there could be only two reasons for keeping women at bay. Either the men were joy-filled when they were without women, or they were committing some sort of evil that they were ashamed to reveal to the women who would undoubtedly chastise them. She imagined Edward, in these very pictures, discussing the murder of Walter as he waited for the photographer to set up the shot. "So, are things in shape for the offing of that fellow in South America, old chap?" he might have been saying to Franz as they tugged on their cigars and loosened their shirts.

The photographs engrossed her, causing her to forget to look at the clock. It reached the hour, and the chime struck six times. Ada started. Carefully, she went about organizing the papers so that they were exactly as she had taken them from the drawer, but her hands shook as she did so. As she reorganized them, she heard, unmistakably, the sound of Edward's voice coming from the hallway. Her heart moved down to her feet, then up to her throat. She could hear his footsteps now. She threw the papers into the drawer, put the key under the desk, and ran to the door. She unlocked it and stepped out of the office just as Edward's head peered around the corner.

If he went to his desk, he would know immediately that someone had disturbed it. Ada's only hope was to keep him out of his office.

He was too far away for her to make out the expression on his face. His boot heels smacked against the wood, then silenced when he crossed the carpet runners. Ada walked toward him, and as they neared each other, she could see that he wore a worried scowl.

"Were you in my office?" He asked the question when he was still half a dozen paces away.

Ada worked to prevent her face from revealing the rapid succession of emotions she felt. Finally, she found a lie that seemed plausible. "I misplaced my copy of *Karezza*. I thought yours might be out in your office. I didn't find it, though." Had the response come quickly enough, or was it clear to Edward that she was lying? His response was slow in coming. Ada's hand went to her heart, reflexively, before she could stop herself.

"I believe I left it in my bedroom, so, no, you wouldn't find it in my office." His gaze on her face was hard, unyielding. His eyes were like small gray pebbles.

Ada exerted an effort to keep her voice even and light as she spoke. "When would you like dinner? Ettie and I came up with a lovely menu for this evening. She's cooking lamb in plum sauce."

"I'm going to eat at the Club tonight. I just came by to get one of the orchids. Have Katie get the book from my room."

"Oh, Edward, I would so like to have you stay in tonight." She wondered as soon as the words were out of her mouth why she had said them. Ada rarely complained about Edward's absences; she hoped he wouldn't notice how uncharacteristic her plea was.

"My darling Ada. I would be pleased to stay home with you but this is urgent. Remember the orchid that came from Brazil? We thought it was the *Cattleya labiata vera*. But we were wrong." He stroked her cheek briefly with his delicate fingers, then dropped his hand and moved past her. Ada watched him walk down the hallway. His walk was not quick. Was he thinking about something, or was he walking slowly because he was about to go into his office?

He slowed in front of the door and turned to go in. Ada took the five paces at a sprint, catching him by the hand before he had crossed the threshold. "Edward, do you have an hour before you go?" Her voice dropped to a whisper. "Might we go together to my room?"

"You seem all in a dither, Ada."

She carried on with her charade, eager now to convince him that she very much wanted him to stay with her, but her mind always half on the mess she had left in his office. "No, no. I'm not really. I just so want to spend some time with you." Unbounded passion never sat well with her husband, so Ada reeled herself in, cloaked herself in calm, and opened her arms to him. He fell into her embrace as if into a spell. But his submission was brief. His hand went out in front of him, palm toward her, as if to ward her off.

He freed himself from her. She stood alone, sensitive to the movement of the air around her. "I really must go," he said. He kissed her cheek and headed for the back hallway, apparently having forgotten his desire to enter his office. The pent-up breath escaped from her in such a rush, she hoped Edward hadn't heard it as he walked through the back door and out into the yard. After he had returned with his orchid, and then left the house, Ada waited ten minutes before she went into his office and cleared up the evidence of her desecrations.

In bed that night, Ada was alone, and wakeful yet again. She tossed herself across the mattress as she examined every possibility over and over—Edward might have told John Jefferson to kill anyone who got in his way, but then again it was not possible she was married to such a man, was it? Even though her marriage to Edward had been coerced, she had loved him well, she thought, but then issues with parenthood, strange sexual limitations, and even orchids had come between them. And he had changed, she believed. Now she had to wonder if he had killed a man over orchids. William's words, the timbre of his voice, sounded clearly in her head: "It's important that people know he was willfully murdered."

As she gazed at her ceiling, watching the patterns of light and dark that flicked across it, it seemed she was looking into the belly of loneliness itself, hovering just above her, waiting to devour her completely.

HOURS LATER, she was still awake, her eyes wide, staring at the random light patterns decorating her room, when her door creaked open. A lantern, thrust into the room, lit her startled face. She felt the light like a focused heat, burning her skin. The light came toward her, its bearer invisible behind the brightness.

"Ada?" The voice came thickly through the inky darkness. She imagined, for an instant, that Frederick Arlington stood on the other side of the glow, just as he had on those nights at Redruth. But of course it was Edward who set the lamp on the table and moved away from it, stepping into its orb, revealing himself, in his nightdress, to her. The image of Frederick melted away. Edward climbed slowly, almost stealthily, into her bed. He touched her lightly, fleetingly, on the thigh, as if he didn't want her to notice what he did to her, as if he was trying to get away with something, and in the surreptitious nature of his actions lay the thrill. The brief contact reverberated, creeping up her side, tracing a slick path of dread into her skin. Karezza was just a word, an Italian word meaning caress, but it echoed now as if a thousand mocking voices spoke it aloud. She wanted to be rid of it, the word, the book, the act itself. Even Edward's fingertips, as they skimmed across her body, seemed to be speaking the word again and again, whispering and shouting by turns. Karezza.

Some time into their static coitus, Ada began to feel as if she could not breathe. Her body was stiff, her feet numb, head heavy. His body against hers was an unbearable weight, the places where their skin touched burned. Again, she thought she heard the distant sound of a body making contact with the ground after falling some great distance. Was the man in her arms a murderer? Was it possible? Suddenly, she felt certain she would have fainted had she not leaned her head back to take in great, loud gulps of air. She pulled herself off of Edward, hanging her head over the side of the bed and breathing deeply, rhythmically.

"Dear God, Ada, what is it?" Edward's voice was strained, impatient.

"I don't know. I . . . I couldn't breathe. I'm sorry." Her breath escaped like the scraping of sandpaper against metal.

"Couldn't breathe? Why ever not?"

"I'm sorry, Edward. I don't know." The breaths became staccato, making Ada feel light-headed. The floor seemed to rise up toward the bed, close to her hanging head. She groaned.

"Ada, this simply must stop. You must try to control yourself."

She slid down onto the floor. "I can't," she whispered. "Can't breathe." She sucked in the air and it whistled as it struggled toward her lungs. Rising onto her knees, she crawled toward the window.

"Ada. Get up this instant."

Her fingers clawed the wood, trying to find purchase there so she could pull herself to the window. Edward's recriminations continued, but the words lost their meaning; she heard only a wave of sound as she struggled toward her goal. Finally, she made it to the wall, then pulled herself up to the windowsill. She thrust her head out and took gulps like those of a swimmer who has just surfaced from long minutes underwater. As she bit at the air, desperate to feel it fill her lungs, she felt Edward's hand on her shoulder. All in one smooth action, he spun her around to face him and slapped her across the face.

The quick snap of his hand against her cheek was painless at first. But it made time telescope in front of her. She saw Edward's hand fall to his side in a balletic motion, her view of it magnified, as if this whole event had been choreographed, as if both she and her husband knew their parts well, even understood them.

But then her face began to sting, and she cried out. Edward shook his hand and rubbed it across his chest.

"Tonight I learned that the orchid shipped to me from Brazil was not the rare plant I thought it to be. I came to you for solace. But what you greet me with is hysteria. Your behavior is disgraceful."

Though it might have felt good to do so, she didn't cry. Later, when Edward had gone from her room, she marveled at the fact that she had not dissolved into tears. She examined this small piece of herself and felt a swelling of pride. This was the memory she took to bed with her, allowing it to underlie her dreams, to soothe the sting of her injured cheek. The tears would signify nothing so much as her degradation, and so she had contained them.

THE MORNING FOLLOWING the incident in her bedroom, Ada went through the rituals of her day feeling as if a swarm of moths beat against her heart and her stomach. She found it difficult to concentrate. In an effort to soothe her nerves, she climbed the back stairs to visit her orchid. The door to Katie's room was slightly ajar, but not enough to reveal the flower to Ada. She pushed against the heavy wood until she could get a look at it.

It sat there, on the nightstand, calmly waiting for someone to appreciate its rarity. She took the three steps across the small room and bent her head down close to the orchid, allowing the petals to brush her cheek. Their cushiony flutter across her skin sent a spark through her spinal cord.

"What shall I call you?" she asked. She listened for a moment, patiently, then kissed the purple blossoms. As the pulpy flower touched her lips, it came to her. She would call her *Vanda* Ghost Flower. It suits her, Ada thought, because there is just a ghost of a whisper coming from someplace within her. A whisper of desire, desire to be somewhere else, with someone else, in some other life. The life that we were really meant to live before we made the mistakes, and put the desire behind us, relinquished it, in favor of the practicalities of life.

Her nerves weren't soothed by this brief, unsatisfactory visit, though. Without considering the consequences, Ada picked up the flower and carried it out of the room with her, hoping if she kept it close it might offer her more. The back stairs groaned under her feet, and she realized suddenly that what she was doing was mad. She reasoned then that she would keep the plant in her room for only an hour.

As she went to her bedside table to set the orchid down, she saw the list Edward had created, enumerating her delinquencies, lying on her bedside table. Ada hadn't left it there. George must have put it there while she was in Katie's room. She thought it a violation that he was free to enter her room at will. She set her Ghost Flower down and picked up the list, touching it gingerly. It had been amended to include her latest infraction.

You walked alone in the Gardens.
Held out your hand to be kissed by Walter.
Had luncheon with the servant girls.

Entered my office unannounced while I entertained men. Again, held out hand to be kissed by questionable men.

Displayed blatant disregard for the teachings of Alice Stockham and the pursuit of perfection in the marriage bed.

Collapsed into an unreasonable fit of hysteria during Karezza.

Ada didn't know what to do with this archive of her shortcomings. Did Edward want her to study it, to wear it close to her breast? She wanted to throw it into her fireplace, to prevent the possibility of its lengthening, but that would be an unforgivable act of sabotage, so she tucked it into the table drawer instead. Even though it was out of her sight, the fact of it stayed with her, gnawing at her nerves. She tried to distract herself with her orchid, but now she feared that George might discover her Ghost Flower and tell Edward about it. She hurried back to Katie's room and left the plant there as if it were a thing that might turn on her.

The World of Matter

She didn't see Edward at all that day; he left the house before she rose and came home after she had retired to her room. When she heard him in his room next door, she found herself holding her breath and tiptoeing about her own room. She picked up *Karezza* and read it absently, so that if he came into the room, he would have no cause to criticize her.

Stockham wrote that in the Karezza marriage,

> there is no bondage for either man or woman; it is a result of the recognition of the spiritual nature of man, and in this recognition he is enabled so to order his life that he is master of conditions. He causes the world of matter to serve him. He not only claims and appropriates the forces of nature, but in his new strength and power, in his knowledge of the all-potent spiritual forces, he breaks the bonds of supposed fleshly limitations. In the wisdom of spiritual knowledge, he acquires the conscious ability to divert his entire nature, his thoughts, his aspirations and desires into channels of effectiveness.

Ada could not see any way in which she might ever cause the world of matter to serve her. The very fact of her womanhood precluded any such power. The book would never save her; it couldn't even help her. Stockham herself had never been married. How could she understand what it was to bend one's will to one's husband? She put the book away; Edward never did come to her room.

HE LEFT EARLY again the next morning. Ada's anxiety increased. In an attempt at distraction, she dressed herself in her old yellow poplin and busied herself with the linens, moving them from the armoire outside the bathroom and into a large cupboard she had had built into the wall in the bathroom. She was down on her knees in front of the armoire, and she was beginning to sweat when Katie appeared in the hallway, holding out a small silver tray.

Ada looked up. The bottom of the tray was shiny, its glow refracting her own distorted face back to her. She scrambled to her feet and looked down at the tray. A cream-colored calling card lay, alone, on the burnished surface. She felt suddenly wobbly, and put her hand on the wall. Who would be calling on her today? Why now?

Still holding the wall, she picked up the card with her free hand and saw Margery Jordan's name there. In that instant she remembered that Margery Jordan was a witch in *The Second Part of Henry the Sixth*. The very idea that Margery was named after a witch put some sort of negative enchantment over Ada's associations with this young woman she hardly knew.

"Tell Miss Jordan I need to dress, will you, Katie? Send her to the library and give her some refreshment?"

Katie nodded and hurried downstairs.

Ada was angry when she went into her room to change. How dare this stranger burst in on her like this? She peeled off her light poplin and wedged herself into a corset and the most conservative dress she could find—a heavy, dark blue triple poplin walking dress and jacket. The dress swished about her legs and the parquet grumbled under her feet as she walked down the hallway toward the library.

As she opened the library doors, she saw the back of a woman in a conservative powder blue walking suit. Her arm was outreached, resting on a volume that was high above her head. Could this be the flamboyant Margery Jordan she had met at the Blackwells'? The woman turned suddenly and laughed. "Oh, dear, you caught me. I'm sorry, but I just couldn't resist. You have a wonderful library."

Ada breezed into the room. "Why, good afternoon, Margery. What a pleasant surprise." She put her hand out, but Margery turned and threw herself immediately into Ada's arms.

"It's so good of you to see me!" Ada felt herself melting into the woman's embrace. She might have rested there for a while, but Margery stood back then and looked around her. "You have a lovely home. You must be very happy here."

"Oh, why, thank you. Yes, Edward and I are quite contented."

Ada and Margery sat down together to the tea that Ettie had prepared and Katie delivered. The teapot and cups were a fine bone china purchased in England when Ada and Edward were on their European tour, shortly after their marriage. Ada looked across at Margery as she sipped her tea, and watched the painted floral pattern change angles as the cup tipped toward and away from her mouth. The low table separated them, a barrier that prevented their knees from touching.

"You must know, Ada," Margery was saying, "that I have heard about you from so many different quarters in my life, it has always seemed that I was destined to know you."

Ada raised her eyebrows and tilted her head at Margery, waiting for her to explain herself. "I mean, of course, I have known the Blackwells and Alice, and I have worked for suffrage with the same people you knew, and now I am at Boston University, reading English, just as you did."

"I am afraid I am not keeping myself abreast as I should. Is there any good news for women?"

"Well, we make headway little by little, as you must know. There is always something encouraging going on. But then, we have the conservative wing of the Association always holding us back. Now they are angry with Stanton because of *The Woman's Bible*."

"Elizabeth Cady Stanton?"

Margery nodded her head.

"What's *The Woman's Bible*?"

"She's working to interpret the Bible in a way that refuses to limit woman's role. She says the ways in which the Scripture are currently applied are perverted."

"The Association doesn't approve?" Ada asked.

"They are more than a little put out. I try to smooth it over with them. I told them I think it's wonderful. But they are trying to dissuade Stanton from disseminating it, before she has even finished it. They think it will harm the movement. We do have to come together, I believe, if we are going to be successful. She should publish whatever she sees fit, I say."

Katie came in then, quietly, to clear away the dishes. Margery looked at her and smiled. Ada looked at Katie, too, and saw her blush and take a step back. Ada had never entertained a single guest who had even so much as glanced at her domestic servants unless they had a complaint or a demand of some sort. Ada felt a warmth surge up into her belly. She smiled at Margery.

"Margery, this is Katie. She's from Ireland. Katie, this is Margery." It should have been Miss This and Miss That, but Ada had never been comfortable with those formalities, and she knew both Katie and Margery were not much for that sort of politesse either. So she dispensed with it without a second thought.

Margery reached her hand out to Katie. "How do you do?"

Katie wiped her hands quickly on her dress before extending her right hand to Margery. It took her a beat to respond to the question. "Oh, uh, ma'am, I am just fine, I daresay. And yourself?" She could hardly look at Margery as she spoke. Her eyes batted open and shut at a rapid pace, and she wiped her hands again when the handshake was finished. Then she curtsied.

"Oh, pshaw," said Margery. "You don't need to do that for the likes of me. I'm not royalty, after all." She laughed loudly, and Katie joined in once Ada laughed also.

The conversation ceased for a moment, and Katie loaded her tray. "I'll be back with fresh tea," she told them, and then hurried out.

"I'm afraid that was a first for Katie," Ada said. "My guests don't engage in conversation with her."

"I have never understood the idea behind pretending that servants don't exist," Margery said.

"I should correct myself and say it was almost a first. There was the afternoon I had lunch with her and the other girls. We drank wine together." Ada was surprised, even as she spoke, that she was sharing this story with Margery.

"Oh, that's lovely. Tell me what you talked about."

Ada told her everything, except that in the end George had caused them to terminate their luncheon, and that Edward had chastised her.

Ada must have made Margery feel comfortable with her, for at the end of her story, Margery burst out, suddenly and apropos of nothing, "Ada, tell me about your years at university. I hear about you from time to time, and I am just dying to hear it all straight from you."

"How do you hear about me? That's quite extraordinary."

"Well, I am taking a class from Professor Arlington. He says you were a firebrand."

Ada's hand flew reflexively to her throat. It seemed to her five minutes might have passed before she found the words to speak to Margery. "He says that, does he? I can't imagine why." She took her hand away from her throat and laughed. "He would be astounded if he saw me now. One might go so far as to call me simply dull." Ada gazed at Margery, whose skin suddenly seemed radiant to her. Imagine, she thought. At some time since Ada last saw Margery, the young woman had sat under Frederick's gaze; he had looked upon this same radiant skin. What did he think of Margery? she wondered.

"Oh, I will never believe that about you, Ada."

When Margery said these words, something adjusted itself in Ada's nervous system, a sudden fluttering of all the roadways in her body—her veins and arteries and even the sinews and skeletal structures. All these things that joined one part to another, or carried things from one region to another, seemed to be shifting direction. The movement threatened to choke off her airways. Was it fear, though, or was it excitement? She couldn't say, but it was, she was certain, all brought on by memories that this Margery Jordan character insisted upon stirring up. She had been, she knew, a firebrand in many ways. But what did it amount to, in the end?

Ada and her friends had tried to change it all, at least within the orbit of their own minute world. Women like Ada and Moira must have been a jolt to the machinations of proper Boston society. And perhaps the university was to blame for nurturing their uppity natures. But Ada had to put all of it aside when she finally earned her college degree and went out into the world. There was nothing for her to do with her knowledge and her energy. There was nothing for her to do but marry or grow old alone.

Moira had insisted they not marry. "If we marry, we'll become like them," she said to Ada. Ada knew quite well who "them" referred to. The women like her own mother, the Beatrices of Boston, whose social status and houses were more important to them than suffrage or education. Ada never knew Moira to fall for a man; throughout college she remained unattached.

They attended a suffrage lecture together one afternoon, before Ada met Edward at the Blackwells'. Afterward, they walked in the Gardens, just the two of them. "I shall never fall in love," she said to Ada. "Falling in love requires too much of women, and too little of men. I want to remain myself rather than become some man's wife. Our husbands wouldn't even allow us to walk alone in the Gardens together. Can you imagine?"

Ada had laughed at that. "I can't imagine marrying a man who wouldn't allow me to walk on my own wherever I pleased."

"I was nothing special, Margery. You must believe me," Ada said to her guest.

Here she was now, manager of her husband's house but with no pretensions to ownership, spending her days worrying about stocking the larder, making sure the house was cleaned by other people, the yard was tended by other people, that her husband had all the things he needed and wanted, and that everyone in her circle of friends and neighbors saw her as a fitting wife and upstanding citizen. She didn't need to worry herself with political issues or economic issues, because she could not vote and she did not work. Her brain cells had been allowed to go soft, and that softness manifested as a vague aching that went unremarked for the most part. But the day that Margery Jordan came to her door, the vague ache became that sudden shifting about of her body's conduits, and Ada was forced to take notice.

"Shall I give him your regards when I see him next?"

"What?" Ada said. She felt her breathing grow shallow. Was Margery referring to Frederick? Suddenly, it seemed imperative to Ada that Frederick know nothing about her. But, with Margery's presence in her life, Frederick was suddenly no longer just a memory. He still walked the streets of this very city, and breathed its air. She might run into him in the flesh at any moment. "Don't," she said, before Margery could respond to her query. "Don't tell him. I might like to surprise him with a visit. It would make me happy to see his face, after all these years. Your giving him my regards would spoil the surprise."

AT FIRST, upon their return from Redruth, when their affair was still brand-new, Ada and Frederick went to hotels whenever they could manage it. But their desire for each other increased, and their time together seemed always too brief and too infrequent. Eventually, Frederick rented a room in a discreet building not far from campus, and for the rest of the spring semester, they made fairly regular visits there. A few weeks before summer break, they went there together on a warm afternoon.

Ada was bursting with the wonder of it all—her first year in college, Shakespeare, her affair with Frederick. She wanted to dance down the street and declare the world perfect. Frederick made her feel as if she could be anything she wanted to be, as if she would never have to succumb to the dreary role of wife and mother. As they stood in the hallway of the apartment building and Frederick fiddled with the skeleton key, she bounced onto her toes and kissed him on the cheek.

"Ada, you must control yourself," he said after they were safe inside. "I can always say you are a student who is helping me with my research. But I don't know who would believe it if they saw you kissing me."

The scolding didn't discourage her. "I just feel so much joy, I can't stop myself sometimes." She threw herself onto the shabby settee, allowing her legs to rise up into the air, her dress to ride up her thighs. Laughter exploded from deep in her belly, and Frederick couldn't help laughing along with her. He sat next to her and pushed at her skirts, stroking her thighs above the line of her stockings.

"You are a beautiful woman," he said. "It hurts me sometimes to look at you. What can one man do with so much beauty?"

"Sink into it," she said. "Drown in it."

They rooted at each other then, removing clothing and dropping it onto the floor in scattered heaps. Their lovemaking was fast, propelled to breakneck speed by their limited time together. When it was finished, the sofa cushions had joined the stacks of clothing on the floor. Ada's hair was in knots, her hairpins everywhere she looked. She pushed her wet hair back from her forehead and threw her leg over Frederick's back.

Their ardor filled the room with a certain light, Ada thought. It had a blue tinge that she had never seen anywhere but in the rooms she shared with Frederick. This room delighted her; it made her feel as if she knew what it was like to live among the working classes. She imagined she could be happy living in just two or three rooms if she lived in them with Frederick. Why would she ever need anything more than her books and this man? "Let's keep this room forever," she said to him.

He removed her leg from his torso and pushed himself up off the sofa. As he bent over to retrieve his undergarments, Ada watched the muscles in his thighs and buttocks bunch up, then relax. The sweat glistened on his smooth skin. She wanted to bury her face in it. She gazed at him, silently, as he put on one garment after another, but she made no move to put on her own clothing. It felt too wonderful lying there naked, the sweat of his body still lingering on hers, the smell of semen ripe between her legs, the moistness of it all slicking her, making her tangy.

When he had pulled on his trousers and buttoned his shirt, he sat in the worn pink armchair, barefoot, and looked at her. "Ada, I am afraid this just cannot go on."

"What? This room? You want to meet somewhere more respectable?"

"Listen, my dear sweet Ada. You are almost finished with your year with me. You will be moving on. I think it's time we weaned ourselves from one another entirely. I am a married man, after all. This simply can't go on indefinitely."

"Frederick, what are you saying?"

"And I think it's best that we don't prolong this meeting. So I am going to leave, and that will be the end of our interlude. I must get back to my work; I've been neglecting it, devoting myself to you when I should be publishing my writings." He leaned over to put on his shoes without so much as a glance into her eyes.

Ada spoke to the top of his head. "I would never dream of keeping you from your work." She felt angry that he wasn't even looking at her. She wanted to grab a handful of his hair and pull his face toward hers.

"Ada, as I said before, you are a beautiful woman, devastatingly so." His voice was almost muffled by his bent posture. Ada strained to understand him. "But I must get back to the real world. As must you. You will be needing to find yourself a man who can marry you."

"I don't need to be married. I don't want a husband. I want you." She felt a pain at the back of her throat as she spoke.

"You are much too intelligent to believe that. You will find yourself a good man. And when you do, you will invite me and my wife to your wedding."

He rose to put on his jacket, still not looking at Ada. Ada cried then. It was the lack of eye contact that made her do it. She didn't want him to hear or see her cry, but she simply couldn't stop herself. When he had finally finished dressing himself, he went to her and wiped the tears from her cheeks. "You always knew it would come to this. Your intelligence, your sensibility, are what made this possible for us, for as long as it could last."

He kissed her forehead, then walked to the door. Ada watched his back as he turned the skeleton key that rested in the lock, then dropped his hand down to the doorknob and looked back at her. "Lock up when you leave, and slide the key under the door."

ADA STEERED THE CONVERSATION away from Frederick and back to issues of suffrage. Katie came in to clear away their dishes. Margery got up and began piling the dishes onto Katie's tray. "I'll do that, ma'am," Katie said.

"I'm sure you could use a little bit of extra help now and then, though." Margery kept right on helping Katie, and walked to the door with her.

"Oh, Ada is very kind. She never overworks any of us," Katie said. They walked out the library door together.

"I shall return," Margery sang out.

It was a full ten minutes before Margery came back. In that time, Ada did her best not to think about Frederick, or worry about what unkindness of fate brought this woman who knew him into her home, to remind her of him. Instead, she thought of reasons she could give for drawing her meeting with Margery to a close. In the end, though, there was no need. Margery left soon after she had finished her work in the kitchen.

TWO DAYS AFTER Margery Jordan's visit, as Ada sat in her rocker reading *Karezza*, Katie appeared in her room bearing a package wrapped in brown linen. "It came by messenger," she said as she handed the package to Ada.

Katie lingered while Ada removed the linen, and a card fell out.

To my new friend,

Here is an advance piece of The Woman's Bible *which Elizabeth gave to me herself. Very few people have seen it. I look forward to discussing it with you. Enjoy.*

Warmly,
Margery Jordan

"Goodness," Ada said to Katie. "She's sent me a bit of *The Woman's Bible*. What shall I do with it?" Ada ran her fingers across the book, but she did not turn the pages to look at the text inside.

"There's a woman's Bible? I've never heard of such a thing, to be sure."

"It's the Bible imagined from a woman's perspective," Ada said. "Written by a suffragist."

"Oh. Well, I never." Katie stared at the manuscript as she said the words. Ada pushed herself up from her rocker. Katie reached out to take the pages from Ada as she rose, holding them to her breast as she waited for Ada to gain her balance.

Ada let go of the book easily. It surprised her how happy she was to relinquish its care to Katie. "I don't have time to read it right now. Would you like to look at it?"

Katie's eyes grew as round as skipping stones and she clutched the book closer to her chest. "I . . . Oh, Ada. I couldn't."

"Don't be silly. Take it with you. Read it whenever you'd like." Ada felt as if the act of turning the manuscript over to her maid was a form of penance, and in return Edward might erase some of the entries from her list of infractions.

WHEN KATIE HAD GONE, dazed by the burden of the book she carried, Ada opened her table drawer and checked the list that she kept there, hoping perhaps to see that it had shortened as magically as it had lengthened. She pulled it out of the drawer carefully, holding it between her fingers gingerly as she read it. But it remained the same. Nothing had been spirited away from it.

She put it away again, but was left with a lingering sense that she must find a way to alter it, to cause Edward to replace the complaints he listed with commendations. Perhaps the sunroom might save her. If she could finally dedicate herself to the perfect completion of this task, it might cause her to correct the other things that had gone askew in her life.

She brought out a drawing pad, and on the same day she gave *The Woman's Bible* to Katie, she began to make small drawings of the sunroom, carefully decorating it with furnishings that existed only in her mind's eye. In each drawing, she included orchids, drawn from memory of the various species that populated Edward's greenhouse. If she were able to buy her own orchids to keep there, the room might come close to ideal beauty, and she might be truly happy.

She took to going out several afternoons a week to search for the things she had envisioned for the room, believing if she was dogged enough, eventually she would find the very pieces she had drawn. Soon after recommitting herself to the design scheme, Ada asked Edward to join her in her room one evening.

They had spoken only briefly since the day he had slapped her, and Ada felt nervous with him there now. She meant to share her drawings with him, to prove to him she was committed to her plans, to show him he might have a sort of faith in her, after all. But before she had a chance to mention her sketches, Edward rose from his chair and picked up Ada's copy of *Karezza* from her bedside table. He sat down again, and she watched his thin fingers poke in between the pages of the book. His hands were so clean and smooth they left her speechless, unable to say a word. Edward cleared his throat.

"I've been at my wits' end," he said, "trying to explain to myself why you have such difficulty with Karezza. But today, at the Club, I had an epiphany," he said. "I want to read something to you." He opened the book at the place where his index finger had been resting. " 'It is true that in Karezza,' " he read to her, " 'one experiences growth in the spiritual nature. This is attained through the habit of self-control and mastery, and through the desire of each for the best good of the other, and to the high aspirations accompanying the relation. Once having experience in Karezza, one will never return to the ordinary habits in which sensuality and selfishness so often predominate.' " He stopped reading to gaze at her, as if his eyes could imprint her mind with the meaning of the text. " 'All spiritual experience is growth in the knowledge of man's divinity, of his inseparable union with the omnipresent principle of life. He may come to a sudden awakening of his being which results in an instantaneous conversion.' " Suddenly, Edward's voice grew louder, adopting a sort of rhythmic cadence, like that of a preacher. " 'Or, it may slowly dawn upon his perception.' "

He let the book fall to his lap. "This is what I failed to see. The first time I read this book, I understood it, I was instantaneously converted, and I have never doubted. But now I see that, since you are a woman, it may take time for the absolute truth of Karezza to dawn on you. So, I want to take the time to teach you carefully, instead of assuming that you understand these principles immediately."

Ada shot up from her chair and moved toward Edward. She had been following a sudden impulse to slap him. If his chair had been one pace closer to hers, she would have done so. But she had that extra second to realize what she was doing, to recognize her own bad behavior, and to stop herself in time. Thankful for the breach, she walked past his chair to the fireplace, where she leaned against the marble mantelpiece. She rubbed her forehead with her hand, trying to calm her nerves.

"Ada, you must see that this is for the best. I am your husband, after all. I have the responsibility of seeing to it that you always seek to do what is right for you as a wife, and for us as husband and wife. You must find a way to forget your wayward notions regarding relations between husband and wife, and the blasted experience of the crisis. All that be hanged, until we're ready to have children."

Ada took her hand from her forehead. "Do you still want to have children, Edward?" She surprised herself with the question. She didn't know she had been thinking it.

"What sort of question is that? Of course I do. Isn't that why a man and woman get married?"

"Is it?"

She thought she saw his body stiffen, without its moving an inch. "Come now, Ada, you can't be serious."

"I am. Do men and women always get married expecting to become parents?"

He took the time to sigh before he spoke to her. "It's part of the natural order of things."

"I suppose it is."

"Do you still have doubts about being a mother? I thought that whole business was simply because our marriage was too new, because you weren't ready."

Ada didn't respond. She didn't believe she wanted children; she still, after four years of marriage, couldn't imagine herself a mother. What she wanted, she was sure, was sex the way it had been with Edward during the first year of their marriage, before things had become so different between them.

The Erratic Womb

Even though Beatrice had coerced Ada into marrying Edward, the first year of their marriage was passionate. Then, Ada had believed that she could spend the rest of her life lounging in bed with her handsome and well-to-do young husband. The happiness she felt when he moved his hands, his tongue, his body across her sensitive skin almost made her forget that she was a college graduate who had no prospects other than to become a wife. If she could keep him in bed, her legs wrapped around him into eternity, then she would accept the fact that society offered her no other options.

Edward seemed just as happy in that bed as she did. He had to leave it, of course, to do the work charged to him by his law firm, but he always came back to her as early as possible. She was happy to tend to the house while she waited for her rendezvous with her husband.

But then it happened. One morning, she lay in bed alone after Edward had left for the office. Suddenly, she felt sick. She ran to the chamber pot and retched into the thing. But it was a different sort of nausea than she had ever known. It felt as if her whole body was somehow weighted down by it. And her breasts were tender. It could only be that she was pregnant.

Her reaction was not what she had expected it to be. She was gripped by panic. Her heart began to race. When the nausea subsided, she found herself pacing her room, twisting her nightgown in her fingers, clenching her teeth.

Of course, he probably wanted to have children right away, and would be thrilled. Their parents would be thrilled. Everyone would approve. At the thought, she began to hyperventilate. She had to sit down and put her head between her knees to keep from fainting. As she sat there, leaning forward, the blood reentering her head, she entertained memories of her friends' and family's childbirth and childrearing experiences. An aunt had died in childbirth. Edward's mother had lost two of her children in her childbed. Ada's older cousin, Mildred, was saddled with five children. Ada never saw her looking anything but exhausted, and Mildred's once beautiful figure was only a memory. Ada's own mother had stopped at one child, and had told Ada throughout her childhood of the horrors of childbirth. This was as close as they ever got to discussing anything to do with sex and fertility.

Ada had never spoken to anyone other than Edward and Frederick about sex, and those conversations involved issues of pleasure rather than prevention of pregnancy. She had never spoken to anyone at all about methods for prevention of pregnancy. In fact, she hadn't thought that she would want to prevent a pregnancy. No one she knew had ever broached the idea in front of her. So her awakening was sudden, her reaction unqualified.

By late morning she had decided on a course of action. She washed and dressed herself. She found a rag in the hall linen closet and used it to wipe the vomit from the blue and white chamber pot. She wrapped the rag in newspaper and put it into a linen bag so she could throw it out away from the curious eyes of anyone residing in the Pryce household. Then she pulled the green silk cord that connected to Liam's bell out in the stable, and had him bring the carriage round to take her to her doctor's office. When

Liam was standing on the other side of the carriage, behind the horses, she deposited the package of vomit in the trash receptacle outside the doctor's building.

She had known Dr. Fentzling all her life, and she felt certain he would do whatever he could for her, so it was without fear that she told him she was pregnant, and she was not ready to be so. But she had forgotten that she was a married woman now. Suddenly, there was someone who had authority over her. "Have you discussed this with Edward?" Dr. Fentzling asked after he had examined her and determined she was, indeed, pregnant.

"Of course not. He would never let me go through with this."

"Ada." He pushed himself back in his chair and looked at her over the top of his glasses, his long white eyebrows knitting together as he gazed upon her. "I can't do this without Edward's approval."

She pleaded with him, but he could not be moved. He did, however, promise to say nothing to Edward regarding Ada's plight. "I'm not going to have the baby," she told him. "So it will not do to tell Edward anything about my visit here today." She knew the doctor would be quiet to save himself, but she couldn't resist the urge to threaten him, after his refusal of help in this crucial time.

By the time she got home she was in a panic. Whom could she turn to? Who would know what to do? She had no friends or family who would understand why she didn't want a baby. No one.

In the end, she told Katie.

"Oh, Mrs. Pryce." She grabbed Ada's hand and began to cry. "I'm so sorry you feel you can't keep it."

"Katie, don't cry. Please. It's just the way it is. Do you know someone reliable? A doctor, not a midwife. Someone with a good reputation? Surely you have heard of other maids whose mistresses have had the same problem."

"I have, indeed. I won't say who, I never would, but it is someone of your acquaintance. An upstanding lady by all accounts, who would go only to the best doctor. Just last year, she had this same problem. Her maid is a chatty one, and she gave me every detail. I've never told a soul, though.

I swear it." Ada knew Katie would never breathe a word of this to anyone. She was an unusual young woman; that was why Ada had hired her in the first place.

"We must hurry, though," Katie said. "This must be finished before ensoulment."

"Ensoulment? What's that?"

"Why, Mrs. Pryce, that's when the soul enters the unborn child's body. Up until then, it is not murder, or a sin, to . . . to . . ."

"Oh. Of course. Well, that shouldn't be a problem. I'll be finished here before there is a soul quickening my belly." She didn't know why she said the words, but as she uttered them, she surprised even herself. Why wasn't she thrilled to be with Edward's child? The fact that she was not thrilled disturbed her, yet it did not stop her from taking herself to the operating theater of a certain Dr. Massey within one week of her conversation with Katie.

The morning of the surgery, Ada saw Edward off to work, then she and Katie went together to the carriage Liam brought round for them.

Katie helped Ada walk across the icy pathway to the carriage. It was cold in the compartment. Ada and Katie huddled under the blankets. Katie patted her mistress reassuringly throughout the bumpy trip across Boston.

"Are you sure Liam won't suspect anything?"

"I told him it had to do with your monthlies not being right, and that you didn't want to bother Mr. Pryce with the womanly things. He believed me. Even if he were suspicious, though, he would never talk about you to anyone, I swear it."

Liam approached the building from the back, as directed by Katie. He remained with the carriage, while Katie and his employer went to the back entrance.

The waiting room was small, decorated like a domestic parlor. Ada and Katie sat together on a velvet sofa in front of the fireplace. When the nurse, Miss Higgins, a thin older woman dressed neatly in a simple white dress with a striped apron, came toward her, Ada's stomach churned. She stood up and walked arm in arm with the woman. The rustling of their dresses conjoined as they moved away from the familiar comfort of Katie. Ada turned to look at her lady's maid. The round face and curly sandy hair that forever refused to be constricted by a bun were reassuring to Ada. Katie smiled at her, her tentative grin framed by escaped curls, and Ada felt an overwhelming urge to beg Katie to come with her, but the morning sickness came on with a vengeance at that moment. Ada moaned and held her stomach. Miss Higgins rushed her into the theater and veered her toward a sink. Ada heaved into the copper basin while Miss Higgins stood patiently behind her.

"There, there, dear. This will all be over in an hour, and you will be feeling better by tomorrow." She wiped Ada's face for her, patted her hands. Ada wanted to collapse into the woman's arms, to be held there like a baby.

Dr. Massey was businesslike in his approach. He left the chatter to Miss Higgins. As she reclined on the operating table, her legs spread out in the stirrups, her lower half draped with a sheet, Ada tried to focus on Miss Higgins's voice and what she was saying. But she couldn't keep from examining the doctor's every move. First he gave her a shot of morphine to deaden the pain. When he picked up a large instrument that resembled a knife with a spoon at the end, she felt she would faint. Miss Higgins told her to relax, she told herself to relax. She was fine when the cold instrument invaded her pelvis, but at the first scraping of metal against tender tissue, she had to dig her nails into the table to keep from screaming.

"The morphine isn't working," she managed to say.

"I gave you the standard dosage," the doctor responded. "This will be over soon enough. Relax."

She waited in vain for the pain to subside. By the time the doctor had been gouging at her insides for some five minutes, Ada couldn't hope to control anything about herself. She moaned and she screamed and she cried, but the pain was so intense, she didn't even hear herself, and everything the doctor and Miss Higgins said or did disappeared into a bubble that existed outside her own circle of pain.

Katie and Miss Higgins hovered over her afterward as she lay on the bed. She was dizzy and her stomach felt as if someone had taken a cleaver to it. If she stood, surely every ounce of blood would drain out of her and onto the floor. After tying a thick rag between Ada's legs and up around her waist,

Miss Higgins brought her biscuits and tea. The doctor checked on her only once, then disappeared into the neighboring operating theater. Ada didn't want to think about whether or not he had another woman in there, about to undergo the same degradation just imposed on herself.

Finally, after what seemed like days and yet might have been only minutes, Katie helped Ada walk to the hallway and down the back stairs.

"What will Liam think if he sees me walking like I've been injured?" Ada asked.

"He will think you've had some mysterious woman's treatment, and he will be afraid to think beyond that."

Ada laughed, and regretted it; she grabbed her sides and quieted herself.

"We need to get you into bed," Katie said as she walked slowly and patiently alongside her struggling mistress. "We'll tell Mr. Pryce you've come down with the influenza."

Inside the carriage, Katie tucked Ada into the blankets. "Are you all right, Mrs. Pryce?"

Ada patted Katie's hands. "After today, it seems absurd that you should continue to call me Mrs. Pryce. I wish you would call me Ada. It would comfort me."

Katie sat up straight and looked at her mistress with widened eyes. "Oh. Well, surely, if you'd like, I'll oblige you, then. Just kick me, though, if I forget. 'Twon't be easy to remember, I daresay."

"Kick you I shall."

Once home, Ada went immediately to bed, trusting Katie to keep Edward and the other household help out of her room. The instant Katie left her alone, Ada was overtaken by tears. They stung her eyes, and when they went on and on without abatement, they began to weaken her. Though she still believed she had done what she must, an unexpected sense of profound sorrow suddenly overcame her. From that moment on, she was unable to pull herself out of her bed. She believed grief had laid her low. But by the third day after the abortion, she was feverish and her insides felt swollen. When she stood to pee in her chamber pot, the urine that filled it was tinged with red. The room spun around her and her body swayed precariously. She stumbled back to her bed and pitched herself into it.

Katie came in that third morning to check on her.

"How are you, Mrs. Pryce—Ada?" Ada tried to smile and say Fine, but she couldn't manage it. Katie went to her and put her hand on Ada's forehead. "Oh, my goodness, you're burning up, you are."

Katie straightened abruptly, paced two steps away from the bed, immediately turned and came back, and leaned over Ada again. "I need to bring you some herbs. You stay in bed. Don't you so much as move a muscle."

Katie brought her goldenseal tea. "The Indians use it for infection," she assured Ada. She washed her mistress's forehead and face with cool water, forced her to drink water. But within an hour, the entire bed was damp with Ada's sweat, and her head was hotter than it had been earlier. Ada was talking but making no sense. Katie called in a midwife, smuggling her into the room so that Ettie and George wouldn't see her and ask questions that Katie wouldn't know how to answer.

Afterward, Ada would vaguely remember the midwife standing in her doorway, but then nothing else. Seven days later, she woke to find Dr. Fentzling and Edward sitting in chairs pulled up next to her bed, looking tired and bedraggled. She moaned, and at that sound, both men jumped up from their chairs and leaned over her. Their faces were so close to her own, it seemed they might suffocate her. She wanted to push them away from her, but her arms weren't strong enough.

Dr. Fentzling felt her head. "The fever has broken," he said.

"Thank God. Oh, thank God," Edward said. He took both her hands and looked into his wife's eyes, while the doctor settled back into his chair, looking relieved and less tired all of a sudden.

"Ada. Oh, my darling Ada, you have come back to me." Edward seemed overwhelmed with emotion, even struggling to hold back tears. Ada felt as tired as she might if she were an old woman of ninety, and wanted to go back to sleep, without these men in her room. But within minutes, Katie came into the room, bringing Mary and Edith with her. They appeared, bearing sheets and warm water, as if they had received the news of Ada's recovery through the ethers. Ada turned her head toward the window and closed her eyes. But the three women roused her; together, they carried her to the easy chair in front of the fireplace. The men left while Mary and Edith changed the bed.

"I'll be back the minute you are finished here, sweet Ada," Edward said before he vanished.

"Would you like to wash?" Katie asked. "I'll help you walk to the basin."

Ada looked at Katie, but it was difficult to focus on her. The world of her bedroom, and the people in it, was blurry, indistinct. She closed her eyes again. "I think I'll wait. Just leave the water." If she did wash herself, she would do it without another soul in her room. "And, Katie, please tell Mr. Pryce to let me rest. I'll ring you when I am ready to see him."

When the bed was finally made and the women had gone from the room, Ada propped up her pillows and regarded her room. As she gazed about the large space, all the familiar objects it contained looked altered. Everything was now unfamiliar to her, as if it all suddenly signified something she couldn't understand. Their newly acquired strangeness seemed to suggest to Ada that she did not belong in this place, surrounded by these things. The mahogany washstand with its green marble top and china washbasin, the tall armoire shipped from London, the brocade curtains, and the cherry headboard with a pair of cupids carved across the top all seemed to have no meaning for her, to serve no purpose. Why were they so prized, why had she concerned herself with their acquisition? Ada wanted, suddenly, nothing more than to throw all the things out her window, to place her mattress on the floor and sleep with the stars miraculously showing themselves through the ceiling of her room. She did sleep then, and her dreams were of the ocean. She found herself in a room that floated on the sea, then submerged itself under the water. In this dream, Ada had no trouble breathing underwater.

LATER, Ada would learn, piece by piece, the story of her lost week. Katie, terrified when Ada lost consciousness, had told Edward that Ada was seriously ill. Edward called Dr. Fentzling, who told him that Ada had sought an abortion. Edward was furious with the doctor for not telling him immediately, but the anger was tempered by the doctor's success with Ada's infection. Neither Katie nor Liam ever revealed their part in the trip to see Dr. Massey, and later Ada told Edward that she had gone there alone, on the streetcar, and had hired a carriage to bring her home.

She had been in a delirium for one full week, and on several occasions, Edward came close to making burial plans for his wife. Beatrice had been at her bedside for some of that time, but had left, exhausted, before Ada revived. Ada had only one clear memory of her mother's visit. At some point, she opened her eyes. Beatrice reached out her hand to touch her daughter's cheek, and Ada's eyes rested for an instant on the bracelet on her mother's wrist. It was a bracelet made from the hair of Ada's dead father. Beatrice hadn't made it herself. She had had it made by one of the finest hair jewelry craftsmen in Boston. The intricate braidings were held together by a delicate etched gold clasp. Ada didn't remember seeing her mother's face, but a clear image of the gold clasp lingered.

Ada was just as happy that Beatrice had gone before she regained consciousness. Her mother's presence always distressed her. Edward, however, loving husband that he was, stayed home from work, at his wife's bedside, the entire week. He never reprimanded her for the abortion. Ada expected it, and waited for it, but it never came. Whatever the reason, Ada was grateful for his kindness, and she promised herself, in return, to recommit herself to her marriage. Edward's refusal to punish her for her actions caused her to see him differently. He was now something more than the man who gave her a home, who shared her bed. Edward had become a part of herself. A stronger, higher part, she thought.

The Perfectionists

Sometime after Ada regained her health, Edward came to her and sat beside her bed in the overstuffed chair. "I've been studying Male Continence," he told her. "There was a large group of people who advocated the practice, and who wrote about it extensively. It's a blessing sent to me, and a way to express the deep love I have for you, finally, without fear," he said. "You see," he said, "the husband does not allow himself to reach the propagation crisis, so in that way, the wife has no fear of impregnation."

Ada didn't have time to think clearly enough to prevent the laugh from escaping. It was a loud laugh that felt as if it came from deep within her belly.

"There is nothing funny about this, Ada. I will never forget that I almost lost you due to an unintended pregnancy."

Ada was caught off guard by his comment. Neither one of them ever spoke of the event. Unable to think of any appropriate response to his harsh reprimand, she changed the subject instead. "Who were these people who advocated Male Continence?" she asked him.

Edward didn't miss a beat. The subject of her abortion

seemed to be forgotten as quickly as it had arisen. "They called themselves the Perfectionists," he said. "Their beliefs were deeply held religious beliefs. They were biblical communists."

"Communists?" The word reminded her of college.

"Yes. They lived a communal lifestyle, and shared labor and profits."

"Well, I hope you don't plan to join them in their commune." She laughed again, but Edward didn't laugh with her.

"No. Of course not. Their society has disbanded, unfortunately. And I'm happy with my life here, with you. I just want to benefit from their discoveries in my own relations with my wife."

Edward didn't bring Ada things to read about the Perfectionists. He didn't spout their philosophies to her. He simply ceased to allow himself to climax, repeating over and over his claim that this simple act allowed him to enjoy his wife's physical attributes without fear or guilt. The boisterous sex life Ada had known with her husband became a memory, a blissful interstice in her life, one that would never be repeated. For the next two years, Edward refrained from having an orgasm, while Ada experienced this ecstatic crisis on her own, her husband watching, observing, waiting. The act became a performance for him, a scene in which his own role was obscure and difficult for Ada to truly enjoy. She wanted to hear him cry out, she wanted to feel the tensing and shudder of his body as he reached his own climax. She found herself trying to remember what it had been like. But the memory was difficult to grip, slippery as a wet floor under freshly powdered bare feet.

Now, as they sat together in her room, discussing the possibility of becoming parents after so long, she refused to oblige him by referring to the abortion, even obliquely. Best to stay on the topic of Karezza. "But why have we been practicing Karezza, if you want to have children? Why haven't we just had natural relations that lead to pregnancy?"

"I am waiting for the perfect time. I'm waiting until you and I are one hundred percent aligned in our spiritual and domestic goals. We still have time. You're still young."

Ada felt as if those goals lay at the far end of a labyrinth which she didn't have the wit to tackle. "But what if we never reach alignment?"

For an instant, he looked at a loss for words, as though he were momentarily stunned. But then he spoke with fervor. "We will. We simply have to work at it. We need to be as we were before, don't you think?" The question made him seem frightened, and Ada felt touched by his fear. "We need to get back to it, to the Karezza. I'm certain you will come to a full understanding, and you will embrace it as I have, my dear. Let's begin now, shall we?"

He got up and went to her, taking her by the hand. Ada smiled at him, and allowed herself to be led by her husband. Following him from the fireplace to the bed, holding his hand as they went, she was struck by his strong back, his height, and the force of his personality. As long as she was a good wife to him, certainly this man would always take care of her, never cast her aside. He went to great lengths to make their marriage something solid and of the spirit, she could see that now. She was lucky, really.

When they reached the bed, he finally smiled at her. His smile was tentative, as if he sought her approval. His vulnerability, the idea that he might need their marriage as much as she, was so surprising to her. Something fundamental shifted in Ada as he smiled at her; she realized that there were certain rules by which she must abide if she was ever to experience something like happiness.

From that day, she devoted herself to a deeper study of Karezza. The logic of the book sneaked up on Ada as she read further, until she came to believe that her sexual behavior was in essence base, and that her inability to find the ecstasy in the binding of souls rather than bodies was the only thing preventing her from finding happiness, or even simple satisfaction, in her marriage.

From then on, she performed her domestic duties cheerfully, always reminding herself that she was a blessed woman, that all her life needed was a deepening of her spiritual resolve. By the end of a week, or two perhaps, she had almost forgotten why she had committed so many transgressions, and her spiritual purpose seemed clarified, solidified. It was at the end of that period that she started to think about children.

It seemed clear to her, suddenly, that this was what she had been meant to work for all along: perfecting herself spiritually so that she might be worthy of motherhood. Would Karezza help her to be a good mother? And would Edward, grateful that she was a good mother to his children, finally give her some small bit of mastery over their marriage?

The contented smile and complacent attitude that Ada adopted then became a ritual during relations from that night. After a short time, Edward seemed to Ada to be, finally, contented with her and her performance as his wife. She began to enjoy their discussions of Karezza. He stayed home for dinner more frequently, and he even took her into his confidence regarding his orchids. Ada believed she had moved away from the naive belief that marriage was about passion; she had matured to become a woman who nurtured the spiritual side of her marriage, in preparation for another thirty or forty years of living with this man.

THE MISSION ADA had undertaken, on William's behalf, to implicate Edward in Walter's murder seemed now like some lunatic's fantasy. Not long after her marital epiphany, Ada received a message from William. It arrived in the early afternoon, while she was engrossed in her new duties as daytime keeper of the population in the Orchid House. When Katie, silver tray held aloft, pushed the greenhouse door open, Ada was humming to the flowers. She jumped the instant she caught the flash of silver in her peripheral vision. "Oh, Katie. You startled me."

"I'm sorry, ma'am. I have a message for you." Ada thanked her, then waited for her to leave before opening the rough card-stock paper. She knew right away it had to be from William. As she read the message inside, she could hear it spoken in William's own voice:

Anxiously awaiting word of your investigations. W.

Ada knew William was counting on her. But she had gone through all the pertinent files, hadn't she? There was nothing to be found. Her husband was being particularly kind to her. That, coupled with their newfound spiritual contentedness, made it impossible for Ada to contemplate her husband as murderer. But how could she tell William these things in a note?

She decided the honorable thing would be to pay him a visit at the meeting house and explain things to him in person, so that he might believe her. Perhaps Franz was the person they should be going after, in which case William should meet with Emmy instead of Ada.

Ada sealed her request for a meeting with green wax and placed it in Katie's hands inside of half an hour. She settled back into her household duties then, confident she had done the right thing.

Two days later, Ada again sat in the small office in the African Meeting House, in front of the same pile of books. William seemed agitated. He rubbed his hands together, then placed them in his lap, then wrung them together again.

"Have you learned anything that will help us?" he asked as soon as Ada had been served a cup of tea and they were left alone.

"William, that is why I wanted to come see you in person. I wanted to explain that I have gone through all of Edward's papers and I've found nothing that might connect him to Walter's death. I don't know what else I can do for you. I'm sorry."

"But perhaps the evidence isn't in his papers. Perhaps you need to get him to talk about things to you. Perhaps he will admit something, or give you information that might prove me to be wrong. If I am wrong, I want to know. Then I will go after John Jefferson, and I will hold him accountable, because I saw the man push Walter. I saw it with my very own eyes, Mrs. Pryce."

Ada straightened her back and leaned forward across the table. She felt her corset's whalebone cut into her ribs. "I don't believe Edward had anything to do with it."

"How can you be so certain?"

"I am his wife, after all. Who knows him better than I?"

William ran his hand across his face. When his hand fell away, his face looked tireder than it had just seconds before. "Sometimes those who are closest to us are the best at deceiving us."

Ada wondered if he might be referring to himself as well as to Edward.

Certainly William must feel great guilt over the death of his friend, after he himself had stolen his friend's orchids. "I think you might want to have Mrs. Locke examine her husband's papers. You might get somewhere with her," Ada said.

"That may be true, of course. But I'm not so sure I can convince her to do that. Would you be willing to speak to her about it?"

Ada saw Emmy then, in her mind's eye, with Isabel screaming and clinging to her skirts as she tried to go through Franz's papers. The thought seemed absurd. Ada had had a hard enough time without the distraction of a child. She shook her head at William slowly. "I don't know that I would have any influence on her. She has a child to worry about. I just don't think she wants to find her husband guilty of murder, really. What good would it do her?"

William looked out the window for a moment. The room became so quiet, the only sounds were from outside—the streetcars, the birds, even the slight rustle of the wind through the trees. He reached across the table and pulled an envelope out from a stack of papers. "I have a photograph here," he said. "May I show you?"

Ada's throat felt suddenly dry. She had to cough to ease the scratching sensation.

William held out a grainy black-and-white photo, mounted inside a thick cardboard frame. "That's Walter," he said. "Three days before he died. None of us imagined he was so near the end of his time."

Walter stood under a tree, surrounded by a group of Indians of all ages. He was taller than all of them, but he didn't seem to be taken with himself because of it, as many white men in a setting like this might have been. He seemed to want to be there with them. Everyone wore a serious face, but Ada sensed a bubbling up of laughter in all of them, a laughter that had to be contained for the half minute it took to snap the photograph. She imagined they all roared with laughter the instant the camera ignited its powder.

The tree in the background was broad, lush, its trunk as wide as a carriage. It had a solid, low branch running almost parallel to the ground. Ada imagined herself sitting on that branch, laughing along with the others after the photo had been taken. What must it have been like to spend so many months in the jungles with these people who were so different from her? she wondered. She might have slept in the tree. She might have come to know Walter and William better than she ever could here in Boston.

"Did he have plans for the future?" Ada asked.

"He was building a house in Brazil," William said. "He had a woman there." He handed her a dozen other pictures. Ada went through the photographs, carefully, studying each one for signs that might lead her to a point of certainty. "I worry that this business is becoming cutthroat, and that it will happen to someone else. Some of my other friends," he said. "I need to know exactly what led to Walter's murder. I can't rest until I know."

Though the pictures were in black and white, Ada thought she could see the colors of Brazil in them. She knew the reds there were redder than any red anywhere in Boston; she was certain the waters of the rivers and streams and ocean there were bluer than Wedgwood, bluer than her own eyes could ever hope to be.

She held on to the pictures as she spoke. "What will you do if you learn that Edward or Franz did tell Jefferson to push Walter? What can you do?"

"I am not naive enough to believe that I might succeed in having them imprisoned. But if I know the truth, I might let some other powerful orchid collectors, some of your husband's competitors, know what they are dealing with. Perhaps they can prevent this from happening in future expeditions, to other hunters. Justice has many guises, I think."

Finally, she set the pictures down. "All right, William. I'll speak to Emmy. I'll try to get her to understand about Walter. I will try. But I don't know that I will succeed."

"Trying is all I can ask of you," he said.

As she waited for the streetcar, Ada felt the same peacefulness in this neighborhood around Joy Street that she had felt last time. But now, at the same time, she felt the desire to get home to her husband and her house tugging at her. This was new. It was, she was certain, thanks to her recent realizations about Karezza. Edward had been so right; she had been wrong to doubt him. She felt comforted by her passionless desire, and resolved to express her gratitude by reading *Karezza* as soon as she got home.

At home, the comfort and solitude of her room beckoned Ada. She climbed into bed with the book, the only book that was important at the moment, and read.

> Intelligent married people, possessing lofty aims in life and desiring spiritual growth and development, have it in their power so to accord their marital relations as to give an untold impetus to all their faculties. This is given through the act of copulation when it is the outgrowth of the expressions of love, and is at the same time completely under the control of the will.

She could see so clearly now how this was true. She had taken control of her will, and her boredom had disappeared, while at the same time her interest in orchid culture had returned and her love of her husband reached a new peak. Alice Stockham was her personal savior.

For some reason, in spite of her sense of purpose and of peace, the memory of William's request nagged her in the coming days. Finally, she decided the only way to find total peace was to pay a visit to Emmy in order to pass the torch of the investigation to her.

When the maid opened the door of the Lockes' townhouse, all was quiet inside. Ada allowed Sally to escort her to the front parlor, where she waited for only a minute or two. Emmy was gracious about the impromptu visit. The two young wives discussed their homes, their husbands' orchids, recent parties they had attended. They ate biscuits and sandwiches, sipped tea. Ada asked after Isabel, whom Emmy reported on glowingly. Finally, after nearly an hour of this, Ada brought up the purpose of her visit.

She took a last small gulp of her tea, then set it down, leaning forward in her seat. Her skirts rustled, her petticoats rubbed against her calves. She felt her stockings droop. Emmy retracted back, pulling at the skirts of her pale blue housedress, straightening her spine. Ada suspected she knew what topic was next, and she didn't want to discuss it.

"I have been to see William again. I told him that I've been through Edward's papers and have found nothing to suggest there was a planned event involving Walter. He begged me to continue searching for evidence. I told him I had nowhere else to look."

Emmy looked away, then back into Ada's eyes. "You seem changed somehow, Ada."

Ada flushed. "I do?"

"Yes, indeed you do. You seem less nervous than usual."

"Oh, do you think of me as the nervous sort?"

"Well, yes. I'm sorry. I mean no disrespect to you, Ada."

Ada felt bothered. This was no compliment, really. But then, Emmy was just trying to distract her. "Nevertheless, I do have to ask you a favor. On William's behalf."

"Oh?" Emmy looked toward the window.

"He wants you to go through Franz's things. See what you might find. Give it the old college try, you know."

Emmy took a deep breath, then released it. With the release of air, she seemed to calm herself. Ada recognized it as the technique she and Edward employed in their Karezza practice. She felt suddenly certain that Emmy and Franz were also practitioners. "You're right, you know, Emmy."

"I'm right?"

"About my seeming less nervous. It's because Edward and I have been practicing a spiritual technique called Karezza."

Emmy's face relaxed, her eyes brightened. "Oh, Ada. Really? Franz and I practice Karezza as well."

Ada was overcome by an instantaneous image of Edward and Franz together, at the Club, discussing first their orchid obsession, then their experiences with Karezza. The image was not comforting.

Emmy interrupted her brooding. "Surely you can understand that with the deep bond between husband and wife that Karezza helps to develop, well . . . I mean, how could I betray Franz by spying on him? Or even suspecting him of such a thing?"

"I don't imagine you could. I'm so sorry, Emmy. Maybe William is just altogether wrong about this entire thing. Maybe Walter did simply fall."

"I think that may be the case, Ada." Emmy took a deep, calming breath and then spoke again. "Even if Edward or Franz, or even both of them, had something to do with this poor man's death, what could we do about it?"

Ada was surprised to hear Emmy equivocate even slightly from her resolve to hold Franz and Edward guiltless. But it didn't change her mind, or cause her to push Emmy to elaborate. If their husbands had not overtly sanctioned the murder, William would always believe their power and their money had nonetheless given Jefferson carte blanche to commit the act. And if they were guilty, it didn't matter. William, Emmy, and Ada would never be able to do anything to hold them accountable. No matter what the truth of that day on the mountain might be, no one would ever pay a price for Walter's death.

"When did you begin to practice Karezza?" Ada asked Emmy. In asking the question, she knew she had drawn her questing to a close. There would be no more of it.

"Only a few weeks ago. Ada, I can't tell you how it has improved my marriage. It is a miracle. Dr. Stockham is a genius, don't you agree?"

"A genius and a saint, I daresay."

THAT NIGHT, alone in her bed, sleep eluded Ada again. Did men fall asleep more quickly, she wondered, tired from their responsibilities and active lives? She threw back her curtains, allowing the nearly full moon to wash even the farthest corners of her room in light. The color in her room was erased; everything seemed black or white. When she saw the light in the carriage house, she turned away from her window, ashamed of the memory of her voyeurism. She paced the room, watching her shadow move across the walls and the mantelpiece. It grew larger, more grotesque, as she moved toward the far wall. If she had woken from a dream to see this shadow moving about her room, she would have been terrified.

Finally, hours later, she slept. In her dreams, she saw Walter everywhere, smiling the way he had at her dinner party. The white of his teeth was set off by the Brazilian sun. Red and purple orchids surrounded him, dancing in the tropical breezes. There was water nearby, she heard it lapping and gurgling. The sounds of children playing punctuated the scene. The tree from William's photograph of Walter figured in every bit of her dream; it managed to be everywhere at once. When she woke, she felt strangely reluctant to pull herself away from the lingering images.

Walter, his mouth open in a dazzling smile, seemed to walk with her throughout her day. Why had he suddenly come to bother her? Why did she feel guilty about his death? What had she to do with it, after all? Finally, in exasperation, she went to her office, where she wrote a note to William, telling him that she had tried with Emmy, but that nothing could come of it. She apologized for any false hope that she had given him, wished him well, then sealed the note with her green wax and sent it out into the streets with a boy she trusted.

She sought comfort in Karezza, and in Edward's presence when he came home. She was certain of her purpose in life now. That made everything easier for her. If she could know this kind of peace, then certainly she might handle the duties of motherhood with equanimity and grace. She would wait, though, to tell Edward until she was perfectly certain.

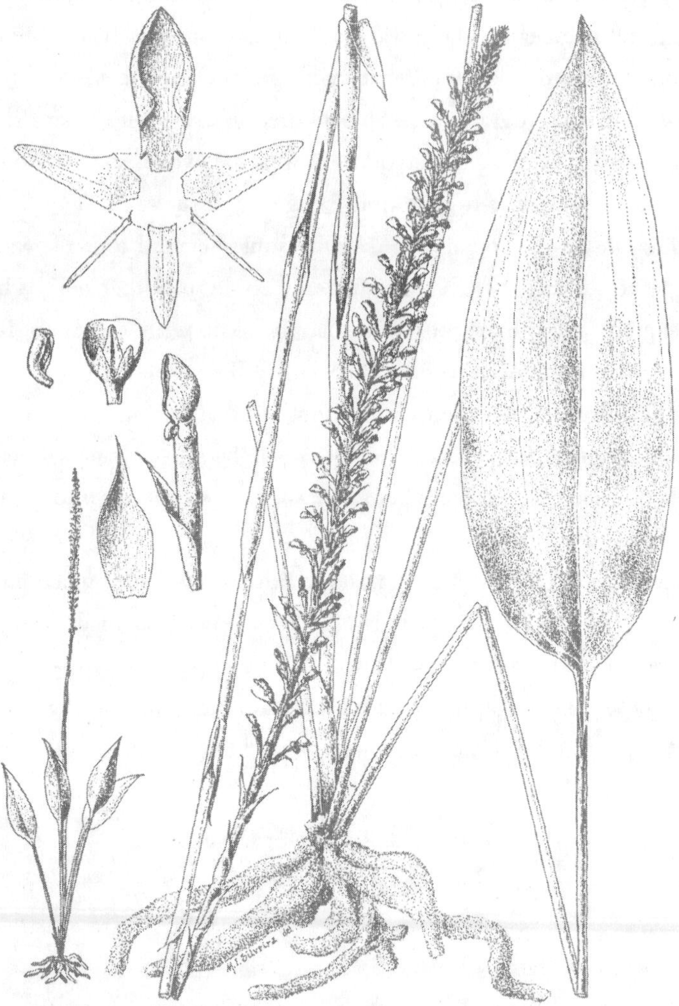

GENESIS

Katie walked around Ada's room, putting away her linens, straightening the detritus of Ada's studies, and talking excitedly about *The Woman's Bible*. "I never even thought about the passage in Genesis," she said. "It does say exactly what Stanton claims. God said, 'Let *us* make man in *our* image,' didn't he? Who did he mean by 'us'? I think he meant the father and the mother. Don't you think so?"

Katie gave off a heat in her excitement. Ada saw herself in her maid—a young woman full of the possibility inherent in suffrage, and everything it implied. But she was past all of that now. Still, perhaps this whole thing would serve someone like Katie better than it had served her. Perhaps Katie, free of the restrictions of the ruling class, would be better able to pursue her passions than Ada herself had ever been. "Yes. I think God did mean that. What god would give women the role that has been assigned us and be proud of his work?" Ada said. "It makes a great deal of sense to view the world the way Stanton sees it, I think."

"Why ever does it make people so angry, then? That

women want to be full citizens, I mean. I don't understand, not for the life of me."

"When we are able to answer that question, I imagine we will have the vote," Ada said.

The two women went downstairs to the kitchen together. Ada checked with Ettie to see what purchases she might need to approve, and she checked with Edith and Mary regarding their own chores. When all five women were in the kitchen, Katie continued to go on about *The Woman's Bible*.

"And when you think about it, you must agree that the Bible's teachings degrade women. You must read it when I'm finished. I swear, you can't help but be moved by it," she said to the others.

Edith shook her head. "I don't think it'll serve to make a difference in my life, whether I ever read that book or I don't. And what would my husband think?"

"We'll know that when you find one, won't we?" Mary said. "We don't read as well as you do, anyway," Mary told Katie. " 'Twould be nothing more than a chore for us. But I don't mind if you tell me about it."

Ettie went about her food preparations without speaking, shaking her head periodically to demonstrate her disapproval. When Ada left the kitchen to tend to correspondence in her office, the women were still carrying on about Stanton's Bible.

Ada was patient with Katie when she continued to talk about the book during the proceeding days; she enjoyed seeing her maid so passionate about the issue of a woman's place. She thought nothing of the minor disturbances Katie's zeal caused among the other women of the household staff—hadn't she and her friends at college argued for hours about issues such as this? Such discussion seemed to her to be a good thing. So it surprised her when Edward brought the subject up at dinner one evening. Edward sat at the head of the long ebony table, while Ada sat to his left, her back to the ebony fireplace.

"Ettie is complaining about friction among the girls on staff," he said. Then, without elaborating, he waited for Ada's response.

Ada had just pierced a morsel of goose with her rose-patterned silver fork. She set the fork down on her Pickard china plate. "I haven't heard of any friction."

"It seems that Katie is reading *The Woman's Bible*, of all things, and her incessant chatter about its principles is unsettling the others."

"Oh, goodness. That," Ada said. "She's simply excited because it's all so new to her. There's nothing harmful in it, my dear." She picked up her fork and ate the bit of goose. Ettie had cooked it perfectly; it felt like velvet on her tongue.

"I'm surprised that you would give Katie such a book, Ada. It can't serve any purpose to fill an Irish servant's mind with ideas about women as creators of the world."

"I don't know, Edward. What can it hurt?" She cut another bit off the goose on her plate, but before she put it into her mouth, she said, "Have you tasted the goose? Ettie has outdone herself."

"Please don't try to change the subject. Tell me, where did the book come from?"

Ada was about to tell him that it was just something she herself came across, but looking into his eyes, she sensed that he already knew where the book had come from, and he was somehow testing her.

"An acquaintance of mine, Margery Jordan, whom I met through the Blackwells, gave it to me. I didn't have much interest in it myself, so I loaned it to Katie."

"I hear about this friend of yours. Word is she is quite an untamed thing."

Ada felt something clamp down inside her brain when Edward said those words to her. She didn't answer him. "The real issue here is, you failed to see it when Katie caused disorder in the running of this household. That is your job, Ada. But Ettie found it necessary to come to me." He glared at her for a moment before dropping his gaze and stabbing at his own piece of goose.

"Oh. I see. Yes, of course, you're right, Edward, darling. I'll talk to Katie tomorrow."

They finished their meal without further conversation, other than to comment on the food, then excuse themselves, and wish each other good night. Ada was stunned by the coldness between them. She had made amends for her crimes, hadn't she? What was this nonsense about a book by a harmless suffragist?

MARGERY, the source of the new trouble, appeared at her door the very next afternoon. Ada found her in the library again, dressed in bloomers as she was the day Ada first met her. Margery excused herself for her casual dress. "I have a riding lesson this afternoon, and I won't have time to go home and change."

"May I have Katie bring you tea and biscuits? Fruit?" Ada asked her.

"Thank you, but no. I'm on my way to campus before my riding lesson. I wanted to ask you to come with me. I have a meeting scheduled with Professor Arlington."

Katie came in at that moment, before Ada had time to decline Margery's invitation. Margery went to Katie and threw her arms about the girl's shoulders. "How lovely to see you again, Katie."

"Oh, and it's a pleasure to see you as well, miss," Katie said.

"Please, call me Margery, for heaven's sake. How have you been since I saw you last?"

"Well, to tell you the truth, Margery, I have been reading *The Woman's Bible,* and I am both amazed and angry." Ada watched the two women, and heard their words, but her thoughts were on the awful possibility of seeing Frederick that very afternoon. How ever could she do such a thing?

"Why, how wonderful." Margery didn't ask Ada why she hadn't read the manuscript herself. "I have a brilliant idea. You come with us to university," she said to Katie. "Won't that be wonderful, Ada? Perhaps Katie might go there herself one day. We should show her around."

"Me? At university?" Katie looked at Ada with moist eyes.

"Of course, we shall show you around," Ada said to her maid. She wanted to strangle Margery for giving Katie such an idea. How would Katie qualify for university, even if she did have the funding to go? And worse, how dare Margery burst in on her and suggest that Ada might want to visit Frederick, of all people?

Margery went to Katie and helped her to peel her apron away from her simple peach poplin dress. "Let's find her a proper hat, shall we? She'll be lovely with the right hat and a shawl."

Ada wanted to stop the whole charade, tell them both that they were ridiculous, that no one was going to campus with Margery. But the whole event seemed to have wrested itself from her control, like a feral cat that would not be contained. In the end, she went with the other women and stepped into Margery's waiting carriage. There was nothing else she could have done.

Within fifteen minutes, they were parked outside Jacob Sleeper Hall. This was the building where she had had all her courses during her years at university. The building where she had first laid eyes on Frederick, where he held court with his students, and where she had seen him for the last time. After he had left her at the small apartment, Ada faced him in the lecture hall for three miserable weeks. For those three weeks, he treated her as he treated any other student, a turn of events so painful to her that she left class without speaking to him, even when Moira insisted upon staying to ask a question of their professor.

As they entered the hallways now, the three women together, their heels tapping out a ragged rhythm on the stone floors, Ada felt as if she had walked into this building to face Frederick's indifferent face and hard eyes just yesterday. They passed the lecture hall that was the scene of her education in both literature and the disorder of love, and continued toward Frederick's offices. When they reached his door, Margery burst through it without knocking.

Frederick was standing at one of the bookshelves that lined three walls of his office, pulling a volume down from a shelf just above his head. As he turned to see who was disturbing him, he kept his arm raised, the book suspended over his head precariously. He looked much the same as he had the last time Ada saw him, except that he seemed older. She hadn't imagined that the years would age him, somehow. He saw Margery first, and then only slowly turned to notice Ada. A minute change registered in his face, his eyes lifting slightly, his mouth puckering briefly at the corners as he realized who he was looking at. Then he moved to her, and reached out his hand to shake hers. Ada felt her breath stop completely when his fingertips first touched her own.

"Why, Ada Caswell. What a surprise to see you." His voice was maddeningly even.

Ada took his hand in hers, willing her own hand not to tremor. "I'm delighted to see you, Frederick."

Margery put her arm around Katie's shoulders. "And this is Katie Shaughnessy. Katie, this is Frederick Arlington, Shakespeare professor." Ada stepped back to allow Katie to come forward and shake his hand. As she moved away, it was as if she were riding a riptide that pulled her out, away from the safety of shore. She watched Frederick greet Katie. He swept his eyes across her body, sizing her up; his eyes seemed to grow sharper as he looked at her.

"Aren't I lucky that Margery has brought you along to grace my offices," he said to Ada's maid. He looked at all three of them then, but he took Katie by the arm and led her to his sofa as he spoke. "Please, sit down. I'll have my secretary bring coffee. What a wonderful surprise this is."

Margery's smile was as big as the room. "I have been dying to bring Ada here to see you, ever since the first minute I met her. I'm so happy to be here for your reunion."

Ada smiled at Margery, but she felt a tremor disturb the quality of the smile. Frederick reached out his hand to Margery, resting it on her shoulder. "It's quite lovely of you," he said, without so much as glancing at Ada. "It truly is." Margery beamed back at him, seemingly oblivious to the temperate nature of Frederick's welcome.

"I wanted to surprise you." She turned and looked at Ada then. "Ada wanted to surprise you. She gave me the idea. So I lied a little and asked for help with my paper." As Margery spoke, Ada contemplated how she might run from the room and never turn back.

The secretary brought coffee and biscuits then, and disappeared. Margery pulled Ada onto the sofa next to Katie. Frederick sat in the stuffed leather chair facing the sofa. "Tell me what you have been doing, Ada. Whom did you marry?" He looked at her now, looked right into her eyes.

It wasn't until she looked back into his eyes, and he said those words with such certainty, as if there was no doubt that she had married, it wasn't until then that she thought she might cry, or worse, she might find herself flying across the room in order to pummel him about the head. She might even yell at the man, right here, in the presence of her maid and her recent acquaintance.

Instead, she smiled, took two quick but deep breaths, and told him that she was now Mrs. Edward Pryce. "No. We have no children yet," she said in response to the inevitable follow-up question.

When Frederick learned that Katie was Ada's lady's maid, he turned all his attentions to her. "I would have guessed you for a mistress of some grand house yourself," he said to her, and Katie seemed, to Ada, to believe him.

"No. Just a poor Irish girl." Katie blushed as she spoke, causing Frederick to smile broadly.

"Never be ashamed of that. My father was a miner."

"No, never," Katie said.

"It's quite true. Ask Ada. She remembers, I imagine."

Ada had been spellbound by Frederick's brief exchange with Katie. She saw him, in his conversation with her maid, as he must have been with Ada so long ago. But now she watched him from outside the sphere of his attentions, and everything he said seemed premeditated and practiced, aimed only to seduce. It had nothing to do, really, with Katie's specialness. Any attractive young woman who looked at him that way would be fair game. She had sat, and listened, rapt as Katie was now. And she had believed there was something special about herself.

"Yes, it is indeed true. It is possible for any of us to alter our fortune, if we have the will and the education, I suppose."

Margery laughed at that. "Yes. Well, especially if you are a man. If you are a woman, I think marriage is the surest way to change your fortune. After all, how many women are professors here?"

Frederick stroked his face with the hand that had once explored Ada's own face, and her whole, fresh body. "We have to give the Woman Question more time, I'm afraid. It will come to you one day. Especially with women like you fighting for the cause. I have no doubt."

He believed that, Ada knew he did. But he didn't care enough about it to fight alongside women like Margery. Ada didn't care enough herself anymore. But maybe Katie would be different. Maybe she would surprise them all.

Soon another student came to consult Frederick, and they drew their meeting to a close. Frederick had spoken to Katie more during the time they were in his office than he had to Ada. In fact, he had treated Ada as he might have treated any student whom he barely remembered across the expanse of so many faces that filled the intervening years. Was he trying to obscure any feelings he might still have for her, or was he really so aloof? She felt shame now for the many times she had remembered and imagined his hands on her body. In the years since their affair, he had probably simply taken up with other students rather than waste his time reminiscing about Ada's romantic qualities. He had called her by name as soon as he saw her, but perhaps he only recalled her name because Margery had mentioned it to him recently. It was possible that Ada meant nothing to him at all.

THAT AFTERNOON, upon her return from Boston University, Ada closed herself up in her office, where she went over the meeting with Frederick in her mind again and again. Mary interrupted her agitated imaginings when she arrived with a message for Ada on the silver tray. Ada took the note, and Mary hurried away.

The message was from William:

I am writing to inform you that I will leave for Brazil at the end of next month. I wish to beseech you, if you find it in your heart, to continue the search you so bravely set out on earlier, and to contact me immediately if anything should arise. There is still time. You can send a message to me at the African Meeting House if you should discover anything that might enlighten me. Anything at all.

Yours,

W

Ada refused the image of Walter in the jungle that popped into her mind for a moment. She would not have it. It disturbed the sense of peace she was working so hard to cultivate, and that had been so rudely agitated by her visit to Frederick. It would be dangerous if she allowed herself even to think about the Brazilian jungle.

She sent a brief reply to William.

W—

Certainly no good can come of further inquiry into this matter. I wish you godspeed on your journey.

AP

As she watched the ink form itself into the words, she fought back the wide sense of guilt that encircled her. William had believed in her, and she had failed him. But still, it was preposterous to assume her husband had instigated the murder of a man who had dined in his own home. Grateful that William would soon be far from her, and thus unable to contact her so easily, she put her water-marked linen paper and her sealing wax away, swearing to herself that she would never think of Walter or William again.

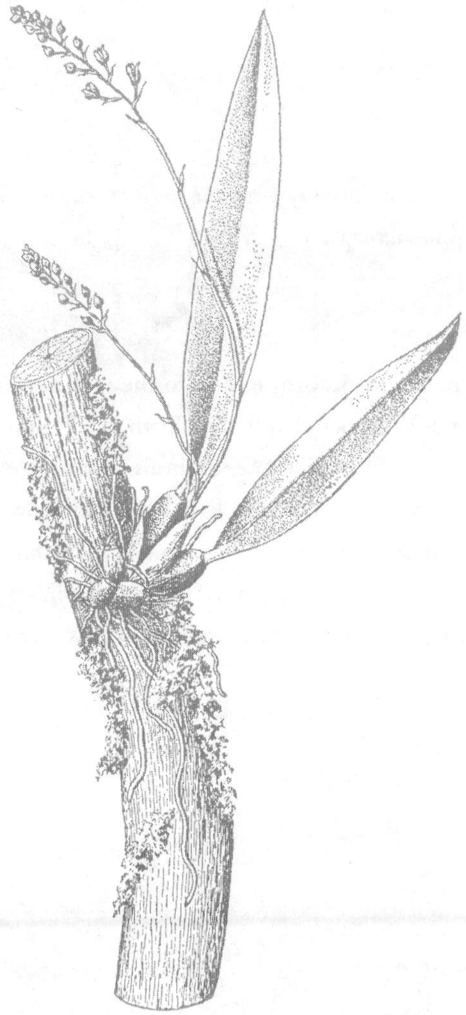

MORTIFICATION *and* DISHABILLE

After the abominable reunion with Frederick, Ada again set her mind to finally finding the right pieces for her still barren sunroom. Certainly it would make Edward proud to see her renewed commitment to the project. Following a long but fruitless day spent interviewing furniture makers, Ada sat in the dark, rocking in her Liberty chair. The movement of the chair was perfectly steady, and the rhythm transfixed her. She looked out her window at the half-moon as she rocked. Her arms rested on the chair arms, her legs were together. She alternated feet as she pushed the chair back, first left, then right, over and over. The sensation built up so gradually it was some time before she noticed that her movements were creating friction in her groin.

Simultaneous with her recognition of this interesting side effect, she saw a light in the barn. Perhaps Katie and Liam were in there again, loving each other in the hay. She stopped the rocker abruptly. As she stood, she noticed the dampness between her legs. It dripped onto her underwear and made the bit of her upper thighs that touched inside her undergarments feel sticky and hot.

They were almost finished when she got out to the

carriage house. She climbed onto a bucket and peeked into the window just as Katie, who sat astride Liam, threw back her head in anticipation of her final crisis. Her face moved out of the arc of light from the oil lamp, and in the darkness it seemed almost otherworldly.

Shame and disappointment in herself propelled Ada off the bucket and up the stairs, into her rocker with her copy of *Karezza* in hand. That's how Edward found her when he came home from the Club. He took her into the bed. She was still wet between the legs from the rocking when she climbed on top of him. At first, she was able to move slightly, carefully, in tempo with Edward's controlled movement. But the image of Katie's shadowed, moaning face insisted upon popping up. In an effort to banish the vision, Ada took hold of Edward's face, turning it toward her in order to look into his eyes. But as his face slowly rotated toward her, bit by bit it turned into Frederick's face.

Here, in bed with her husband, the image of Frederick's face that Ada saw was not the face that so calmly kissed her for the last time, or even the face that she had seen so recently in his office. It was the face that only minutes before that final goodbye had been loosened and misshapen by crisis. He had yelled out, just briefly, as he climaxed, his eyes rolling closed, his mouth twisting. The sight of that face had brought her to crisis. It wasn't love. She knew that. Something about it made her feel a sense of power over Frederick, and she was intoxicated by that. Yet ten minutes later he reclaimed that power and walked away with it.

As Edward made infinitesimal movements inside her, traces of her Shakespeare teacher's face, sloe-eyed with desire, superimposed themselves over Edward's even features. She pumped her hips, three, four, five times, pumped them hard, and she allowed her breath to speed up.

She stopped when she felt Edward's hand gripping her neck. "Ada." His voice was lacking emotion or ardor. "Ada. Slowly. Slowly." He stroked her neck in tempo with his speech. "There. There," he said. Wasn't that the way adults spoke to children when they were upset?

She tried to calm herself. But Frederick's face, the smell of him, his tensed muscles and quick grunts when he reached orgasm, all these memories assaulted her and refused to leave her in peace. She wanted Edward's performance in her bed to be urgent, to displace any other worries or desires he might have, and to erase the misleading memories of Frederick that she had nurtured for too long. In an effort to force him into this sense of urgency, she put her lips on Edward's shoulder and sucked it, hard. The sucking sensation was like a taking in of life, of all the things she had been denying herself, as if she were swallowing orgasms, chewing on desire. She sucked so hard she began to choke. As she coughed, the muscles in her vagina contracted, and she began to climax. Her coughing and the involuntary muscle contractions were in synchrony; it felt as if they worked, and could only exist, in tandem. She rode the waves of the choking and the coming, certain she would ride them to a kind of death.

Edward remained still, all his muscles tensed, throughout the raucous ordeal. Finally, when it was over, and she could breathe again, he abruptly pulled out of her, then rose to dress himself.

"I simply do not understand this." He spoke as he put on his long underwear and his trousers. "As I explore Karezza, and become more deeply in tune with the mysteries of it, you become more and more implacably childlike." He stopped dressing, and the room became suddenly perfectly still. "Not childlike. *Hysterical* is the word I am looking for. Your outbursts put me in fear for your very sanity. Something must be done." He continued to dress, his movements cool and unhurried. "I will think on it, and decide on a course of action. It cannot go on." He stopped dressing when his speech was finished, but he didn't make eye contact with her. He left her room bare-chested, carrying his shirt and shoes in his hand.

Ada had been making love to Frederick all the while she had been connected to Edward. The memory of Frederick had propelled her to this crisis. Edward's rejection of her was like a repetition of Frederick's long-ago dismissal of her, and his cool attitude toward her during their recent meeting. But what she felt was not hurt. It was anger.

She didn't see her husband the next day. She slept late, and did next to nothing around the house. The only time she left it was to visit the Orchid House for half an hour. She couldn't shake herself loose of sudden brief memories of Frederick, as he was in her arms, his face during intercourse, the sound of his laughter, and his passion when he lectured on Shakespeare. Ada had always remembered his favorite quotes from Shakespeare. He said them so often, toward the end of their time together, she began to recite them with him.

The last afternoon together, before she realized it would be the last, he had recited these words:

> O, how this spring of love resembleth
> The uncertain glory of an April day;
> Which now shows all the beauty of the sun,
> And by and by a cloud takes all away.

It was from *Two Gentlemen of Verona*. She said the words to herself now, softly. Would he be proud that she could recite them still, even though she had read so little Shakespeare in the intervening years?

Edward came into her room that night, just as she leaned over to blow out her lamp. As he moved into her room, shadows lay themselves across him in broad swaths. She couldn't make out the features of his face. When he pulled the rocker next to her bed and sat down, she stifled an urge to tell him the rocker was hers and that he should not be sitting in it. The chair rocked forward and his face slipped into the light. He was holding the damnable list in his hand again.

"It has come to my attention that there is more discord among the house staff. You have been taking Katie with you on your ramblings, thus increasing the workload of those left behind. And then, there was your loss of control, again, in the bedroom last night." He rustled the list as he spoke, and Ada knew that he had again added to its length. "I have thought about this all day, Ada. I have consulted with others who understand this . . . This problem we have. And I've come to a decision."

She wanted to put her hands around his throat and squeeze. She imagined his face turning purple, his tongue hanging out. The rocker tilted back, and his head dipped into shadow, but she did not move or speak, not even to ask him what his decision was.

"I want to send you to a doctor who has a great reputation for dealing with hysteria. I have taken the liberty of setting up an appointment, as this is something that just can't wait. You will see him tomorrow at one o'clock. Liam will take you there. No one, of course, knows why you're going to see Dr. Casey. I told them you are having female troubles."

Them? Who was "them"?

He got up from the rocker, set the list carefully on her table, and walked to the door. The chair rocked back and forth for some minutes after he had gone, the fine wood swooshing quietly across her Persian carpet. It wasn't until the chair was utterly still that Ada realized she had not said one word to Edward in her own defense.

DR. CASEY'S OFFICE occupied the lower floor of his brownstone. The rooms were expansive and decorated in a riot of Turkish and Egyptian artifacts. The walls were covered with tapestries embroidered with tiny mirrors, the sofas were of embroidered cottons of primary colors. Ada recognized an Egyptian ankh standing in the corner of the room.

She wasn't left in the waiting room any longer than two minutes. Gertrude, the nurse, an officious young woman who wore her own walking suit rather than a uniform, ushered Ada into the operating theater. It was a vast room, with the table in its very center, underneath a suspended turquoise tent. The flaps on one side were tied back, exposing the table to the front of the room. Dr. Casey appeared, suddenly, as if on a breeze, from behind the tent. He was small and wiry, but with a belly protruding from beneath his white coat. He was young, Ada thought, certainly no more than thirty-five.

"Come, come, Mrs. Pryce." He ushered her over to the table. She hopped onto it, still wearing her dress, even her shoes and hat. He smiled at her. Ada didn't speak. "Your husband tells me that you may have a tendency to hysteria and nymphomania."

Nymphomania? Hysteria? "I . . . I . . ." It was all she could manage.

"Let me ask you this," he said. "Does your desire for sexual intercourse cause friction in your marriage?"

"Well, I suppose it might seem that way," she ventured. "But it's not true."

"Do you lose control during intercourse? Do you scream when you reach crisis?"

"Do I what?" Her back was hurting. The table was uncomfortable to sit on. She wanted to lie down on it.

He shifted his weight, touching the table with his hip, causing it to rattle a bit. "Let me put it this way. We doctors believe that unfettered satisfaction of sexual urges leads some women to spend far too much time thinking about sex, desiring sex, so much so that they ultimately neglect their household duties, and their husbands."

"But I am not allowed satisfaction of my sexual urges. They are never satisfied." She couldn't look into his eyes as she said the words. She spoke them to the fabric of the tent walls.

"Aha. I see. Do you try to satisfy yourself, then?" His hip was close to her thigh now. She could feel the heat of it.

Ada felt herself growing hot. Was it shame or anger? "Dr. Casey."

"Please, Mrs. Pryce, understand that I am a doctor. You must feel safe enough to tell me whatever is on your mind. I'm here to help you."

"Help me with what?"

"The problem in your marriage, of course. If you resist my efforts, it will only make things more difficult for you. I have no idea what steps your husband will take then. I am here for you, no one else. But I must be successful if your husband is to be satisfied."

"So you are trying to satisfy my husband rather than me."

"I mean to help you, but I can't help you if your husband chooses to send you somewhere else." He reached out and patted her hand. She didn't pull her hand away.

"Somewhere else? What do you mean?"

He was still touching her hand; it grew clammy. "In this situation, some husbands send their wives away for residential treatments. Others confine their wives to their homes and don't allow them to go anywhere, or read or have visitors. We believe the lack of stimulation has a calming effect on the female nervous system."

"Is Edward thinking of this for me?" Ada pulled her hand out from under his.

"As I said, Mrs. Pryce, as long as we are successful here, perhaps not."

"Will it be just this one visit?"

Dr. Casey laughed till his small belly shook. "No. No. Depending on the results, I would need to see you one, possibly two, or even three times a week. But the treatment is painless. And it does not restrict you in any way. I have the names of two patients I can give to you, if you would care for testimonials. My patients are very pleased with their treatments."

Edward hadn't offered her the option of conferring with Dr. Casey's other patients. She knew she would just have to brace herself and take the treatment. Maybe it would even help. Maybe it would ease the restlessness that had been plaguing her. "That's all right, Dr. Casey," she said. "I trust my husband's judgment. Why don't we go ahead?"

"Let me get Gertrude. She'll bring you a gown."

Within minutes, Gertrude was at the table, holding out a blue linen sheath. Once she stripped down and donned the thing, Ada lay on the leather table, pulling the thin linen sheet that lined it up over her body. The overhead tent made her feel encased in some exotic shelter. She could sleep here, if only they would let her. She had just begun to drift off into a dream she was sure would have comforted her when Dr. Casey came breezing back into the room and stepped inside the tent.

"There you are, all ready to go! This will be pleasant, so don't worry." He reached behind the back part of the tent and pulled in a tall metal rod on a wheeled platform. The platform contained what looked like some sort of motor. Ada recalled her abortion and began to panic.

"Is this going to hurt me? Are you going to put something inside of me?"

Dr. Casey touched her forehead. "All you need to do is relax. It may be cold for a minute, but it won't hurt, and I won't put it inside you." He pulled the sheet aside and pushed up her gown. "Please, just relax." He touched her belly, and she winced. But he only patted it, trying to get her to calm down. Ada let out her breath and watched the doctor pull some sort of gadget off the metal pole. He turned a dial, and the gadget began to make a racket. Ada closed her eyes and concentrated on her Karezza breathing techniques. She felt the metal between her legs, pulsing and shaking.

Dr. Casey had to yell to be heard over the thing. "Now, relax. You can move and make as much noise as you like. You're free to do that whenever you are here inside the tent!"

The metal warmed up. What Ada felt then, after the initial shock, was a warmth and a vibration that aroused her sexually. She wanted to thrust her hips up against the thing. She wanted to imagine Frederick's head down there, doing this to her. But how could she with Dr. Casey there, encouraging her? The vibration sent a sudden shock from her clitoris up into her womb. She groaned.

"Ah, yes. There you go," he said to her. Suddenly, she felt his fingers inside her gown, groping across her breasts. "Does that feel good? Yes?" As he spoke, he flicked and rolled her nipples, and he glided the machine across her clitoris, back and forth, back and forth, slowly, then quickly, then slowly again. She thrust her hips up and reached her hands down to the machine, pushing it up against her pelvis harder. Dr. Casey continued to fondle her nipples.

"You take it," he said to her. "Do what you like with it." He moved up to the top of the table and pulled her gown away from her breasts. She pushed the machine, grinding it across her groin, while he stroked her nipples so rapidly it hurt. Finally, she reached crisis in one large wave. She called out as loudly as she ever had, comforted by the noise of the machine, sure that it would detract from her shouts. Her muscles contracted inside her. She rocked with the contractions. He held her breasts while she rocked. When she finally stopped and opened her eyes, he stepped away from the table.

"Okay," he said. "We're finished. I'll leave so you can get dressed. There's a basin of warm water and a cloth so you can clean up."

Ada was stunned. What had just happened? Was this the treatment Edward intended for her? He wanted her to come to a doctor for orgasms so that she wouldn't have to have them with him? She held her hands in between her legs. She wanted to leave here immediately.

The water in the basin was warm, as he had said it would be. That could only mean that Gertrude had brought it into the room while Ada was in the middle of her treatment. The girl must have heard everything. They must think her a fool, or worse, a madwoman. She dressed quickly.

Only Gertrude was in the waiting room. The doctor was nowhere to be seen. The nurse smiled at her. "I hope you enjoyed your treatment. Everyone does. Step over here and I'll make your next appointment for you. Is the day after tomorrow all right?"

Edward didn't come home until late that night. She heard him go into his room, move around for a bit, and finally settle into his bed. Did he know what Dr. Casey did in his operating theater? If he did, then she despised him. But if he didn't know, perhaps he needed to be told. Should she tell him? Or should she continue going to the doctor, assuming that his treatments would, in the end, improve her marriage, improve her mastery of Karezza, even?

Unable to sleep, her nerves on edge, Ada decided to practice her breathing. But in the dark, as she carefully took deep breaths and released them slowly, evenly, the memory of the sexual shame she had experienced in that blue tent would not leave her.

Behind the shame, though, was a thin ray of desire. The desire to be back on that table, holding the vibrating machine between her legs.

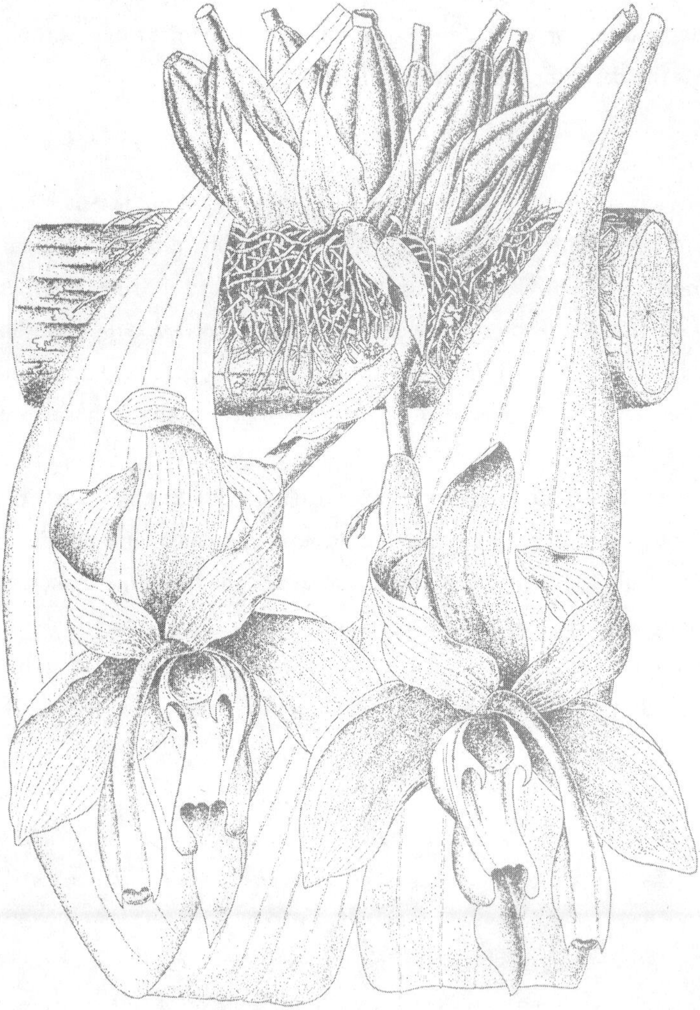

Mercurial Wanderings

It seemed too much to lift herself from her bed the next morning. She watched the light in her room change as the sun made its way toward its zenith, but still she could not move. The memory of the day before made her feel as if her body were made of lead, heavy and immobile. Finally, turning her head slowly toward her bedside table, she noticed Edward's list, still there, accusing her of all her sins. She picked it up and crumpled it, then opened the drawer to hide it away.

Suddenly, the thought of William, gone from Boston, seemed an absence that she could not bear. She wanted to be with him now, sitting in his office at the African Meeting House, discussing his trip to Brazil with him. If she were with William, she would not be here, and she would not be asked to return to Dr. Casey's office. But there, inside the drawer, was William's note, telling her that he would leave for Brazil next month. She pushed it to the back of the drawer, along with Edward's list, and closed it.

How could her own husband treat her with so little respect? A week ago, she might have dreamed of Frederick as a refuge, but now, after their brief meeting, those imaginings seemed absurd. He was not her ally, even in her fantasies. She took out William's note again. *I wish to beseech you,* he had written, *if you find it in your heart, to continue the search you so bravely set out on earlier, and to contact me immediately if anything should arise. There is still time.*

Ada was dressed and in Edward's office within a quarter of an hour. She didn't ask herself what had made her change her mind, but suddenly, she fervently believed there was something she didn't know about her husband, something she had yet to find out about him that he would never tell her. She locked the door to his office. If George came by and dared to turn the handle, she would tell him to go away. What else could Edward possibly do to her if she was discovered? She had suffered such humiliation already.

This time, Ada found Edward's appointment calendar. He kept another at his office. But this one contained more personal appointments. Flipping through the pages, she went back to the weeks around the time that Walter had been killed. Finally, she saw a scrap of paper wedged between two pages. Its message seemed ominous, portentous.

Whatever it takes, then? Please advise—JJ

Ada put the scrap of paper back where she found it and returned the appointment calendar to the bottom drawer of Edward's desk. Then she pulled his personal address book from the same drawer. She flipped through it with shaky fingers until she found what she needed—the address for John Jefferson. She copied it carefully onto a piece of paper, then replaced the pen and ink in the precise location from which they had come, and exited the office without, she believed, ever being seen.

Ada spent the rest of the day just waiting for what was to come next. When dinner was over, Edward was home and finally in bed, and the whole house creaked in protest against the inactivity of night, she crept out of her room and out to the stables. She had John Jefferson's address, and she had a fast horse.

THE CARRIAGE HOUSE was empty of any living thing other than horses. Still, Ada could hear the high pitch of Katie's sex voice. She lifted her head to listen, tilting her ears in the direction of the moaning. They were in Liam's room above the carriage house. Perhaps it had grown too cold in the carriage house for them. She admired their audacity, and at the same time was relieved she couldn't see them. Ada pushed the heavy door open. Inside, she walked past the other horses straight to Edward's prize black stallion, Mercury. He roused himself from a doze and looked into her eyes as she stroked his long nose. His eyes settled into hers, watching her as if he had known all along that she would end up here.

She lifted a man's saddle from the wall. It was heavy; she struggled to get it onto his back. But Mercury stood patiently, waiting for her to settle the thing onto him and buckle it in place. He remained still and solid as she boosted herself up into the stirrups. Her skirts were full enough that if she hiked them up, she could throw her legs around his back. The saddle and his coat brushed the skin of her thighs, at the small gap between where her stockings ended and her pantaloons began. It made her feel connected to the animal; it was a kind of closeness that was so unfamiliar to her it made her feel queasy.

The clap of his metal shoes against the cobblestones must have been heard in every house up and down the street. Ada kicked at the horse's sides, urging him to go faster. As Mercury picked up speed, Ada leaned her body forward, moving her face close enough to his neck to feel the heat rising off it. She steered him over to the river. The scenery went by her in a blur. If they passed a constable, he would probably suspect them of some illegal activity, their pace was so furious.

She smelled the Charles before she saw it. The briny scent filled her head and her lungs, the moist air slicked across her dress and settled on her hands, face, hair; Mercury's coat was dense with it. The moon was nearly full. It bleached the darkness, turning it to a wash of silver. The river reached up to the beams of light, rustling its surface, showing off in the luminescence. Mercury snorted, slowing his pace. Ada felt a thrill of danger. She was out, alone, in the dark riding a horse through town.

The horse raced along the river until they reached the New West Boston Bridge. They turned a hard right onto the bridge. Mercury's breathing was rough, but its distinct rhythm soothed Ada. A slip of fog moved in from the east, swallowing the sounds of Mercury's hooves. The fog cushioned everything, making Ada feel safe. Save for the sounds of Mercury's movement across the bridge, there was a heavy silence. They passed a single carriage traveling in the opposite direction. Suddenly, for an instant, the carriage sounded as if it were right on top of them, then just as quickly, it was gone and the silence returned.

They reached Cambridge and rode past Harvard Yard until they reached the address Ada had for John Jefferson, orchid collector. They pulled up in front of a small, wooden frame house. It was dark, as were the other houses on the street. Ada dismounted, and tied Mercury to a hitching post, then stood outside the house. What could she possibly do now? Call John Jefferson to his door and accuse him of murder? She sank down onto the stoop, her dress dragging in the detritus on the sidewalk. What had she believed she would accomplish here? The idea that she had the power to do something, to force a confession from Jefferson, to prove that someone had indeed murdered Walter, was almost as absurd as her onetime belief that she and Frederick might make a life together, or that women would win the vote.

The fog skulked in, growing denser. Ada sat on the stoop until she heard voices in the distance. They seemed to be coming near. Eager to avoid any sort of confrontation with strangers in the middle of the night, she climbed onto Mercury and headed back for the river. She felt as if she had attached the fog to a cord and was pulling it along, bringing it home with her. By the time they came to the Pryce house, they were enveloped in its plump mist. It was a piece of luck; the fog muffled the sounds of Mercury's hooves against the street as she took him back to the carriage house.

They picked their way carefully along the driveway. Mercury's belly swung back and forth beneath her, the movement exaggerated by his cautious steps. Ada pushed the carriage house door open slowly. Finally, inside, she congratulated herself on having pulled this adventure off without being found out, even though it had been a futile mission. She hung up the saddle by the thin strips of moonlight that made it into the windows, and kissed the horse on the forehead. Though her quest had been fruitless, she had felt a sense of freedom she had never known in her life as she rode through the city alone.

The next afternoon, Ada had an appointment with Dr. Casey. As Liam drove her to his office, her perambulations of the night before seemed never to have happened. This was her real life.

In the beginning, Ada had counted the number of times she went to Dr. Casey's office. She knew precisely when she made her third, her fourth, her fifth visits to him, and even on to the tenth and eleventh. But sometime soon after the twelfth or thirteenth time she climbed onto his table and opened her legs to him, she forgot to count. Although she didn't realize it at first, this failure to keep track of numbers coincided with her gradual acceptance of her visits to Dr. Casey, and what he did to her on his table, as normal and ineluctable. Edward, eager now to proclaim Ada's transformation complete, took Dr. Casey's advice and advised her to limit her activities outside the house, and her visitors to the house. He gave her a list of acceptable visitors. Emmy and Beatrice were among those people allowed; Margery and even Minnie were on the list of those who were forbidden.

"Margery and Minnie can't come see me? Why ever not?" She was unable to refrain from asking the question.

"Well, we both know that Minnie is a bit of a rabble-rouser, even for someone of her age; she talks incessantly." And, of course, Ada thought, Minnie was married to Anderson Lovell, who might be upset that his orchid hunter wound up at the bottom of a mountain. Ada hadn't seen Minnie since she borrowed *The Woman in White* from her. Now Edward was declaring her off-limits. Was he afraid Minnie might tell her something? Ada was angry with herself that she hadn't thought to somehow take Minnie into her confidence earlier. Now it was too late.

"And the house staff insists that Margery is behind much of the tension among them," Edward was saying. Ada wondered if Edward knew she had gone to the university with Margery. He probably did. But certainly he knew nothing about her history with Frederick. It wasn't possible. The first night she had spent with Edward, in the hotel after *Cleopatra*, Ada had been lucky enough to start her menstrual cycle, so there had been blood on the sheets. Edward no doubt thought it to be the detritus of her virginal cherry, and she had done nothing to set him straight. But still, she worried. He had never believed there was much value in her having gone to college, and he would certainly object to her return visit there with the forbidden Margery.

Her limited and carefully controlled movements, broken only rarely by trips to look at furniture for the sunroom—furniture that was never quite perfect, and so which she never chose to purchase—and visits to Dr. Casey, threatened to turn her into the hysteric Edward already believed her to be. Her escape on Mercury the night she rode to John Jefferson's was the most exciting thing she had done in weeks. It stood out in her memory when she went to bed at night, tired from inactivity, and it figured in her dreams. Soon, that balmy ride became a symbol of the freedom she had lost and so longed to reclaim.

As her world constricted, Ada found it more and more difficult to sleep. The next morning, after another long and restless night, Katie came into her room with the breakfast tray and a large brown envelope. "This came for you, Ada." She handed the package to Ada, then left her to open it in private.

The letter made her forget her exhaustion. Ada tore off the red seal and reached into the package like a starving woman might ravage her first meal. She pulled out a letter and a photograph. The picture was the one of Walter that William had showed her in the African Meeting House. She had to stand up to look at it; she couldn't take it lying down. She paced along all four sides of her room, gazing on the thing with an unfamiliar longing. She would be happy to die young, she thought, if she could just have the life Walter had for even one year.

Ada collapsed into her rocker and allowed her entire body to sink into the mire of her tears. She couldn't stop the crying. The tears came for so long, she wondered how she could produce so much moisture; she wondered that she didn't just dry up completely.

When her tears finally did recede, she went to her bed to read William's letter.

Dear Mrs. Pryce,

I am writing to tell you that I will be leaving for Brazil in two weeks' time. I wanted you to have this photograph, since I won't be able to take it with me. I am sorry we discovered nothing new about our friend. Perhaps I will come upon something in my travels. I wish you the best. I rest in the certainty that you are enjoying a good and happy life.

Yours,
William

Ada really hardly knew this man. But his note hit her like a message from a dear friend. It hurt almost as much as the letter she had received from Moira years earlier, just before her wedding. The letter had been brief, like this one, yet filled with a world of information. Moira wrote, in a simple paragraph, that she was leaving Boston.

Ada still remembered the exact words, though she hadn't looked at the letter in years.

Dear Ada,

I am writing with wonderful news. I know it is sudden, but it can't be helped. James has decided we shall get married abroad. Our ship leaves next week. I have no time to do anything other than prepare for the journey. I am distraught that I will miss your wedding. But it can't be helped. I will be with you in spirit, and wish you all my love.

Moira, who had sworn she would never marry, was running off to marry a man she hardly knew. Two months later, Ada received an expensive set of crystal vases from Paris for her belated wedding gift from her college friend. Moira came to visit Boston two years after, but Ada only heard about it; she wasn't invited to visit Moira. And Moira never wrote from London to give Ada her address.

Why did this note from William feel like the same sort of loss? There was no comparison. Yet the sickness in her stomach, the sudden chill in her palms, were all similar to what she had experienced then. But the meaning inherent in the two disparate messages was separated by class, by personal history, by matters of the heart. When she went to bed that night, she took the picture and William's letter with her and looked at them both, over and over, until she finally felt tired. She hid the letter and photograph under her pillow, reminding herself to put them into her trunk in the morning before Mary or Edith appeared in her room. But she felt a rage, and a desire to do something, and sleep did not come. Finally, she dressed herself and sneaked down to the carriage house.

She rode Mercury across the bridge and past John Jefferson's house, then she came back into Boston again and rode to Beacon Hill and past the African Meeting House. The movement of bodies through space, the moisture from the river, the heat of the horse's wide back, the thin light of the moon—all these things were brief inlets into the geography of freedom. As she rode, her hair trailing out behind her, the work of Mercury's muscles warming her thighs, she felt free, but she also felt as if her world had become as small as that of an animal caged in a zoo. She was riding but going nowhere, like an animal pacing in circles. When she arrived at the destinations she had set for herself, there was nothing for her to do but turn and keep riding. Finally, she headed for home as the sun began to edge up toward the horizon.

Just before she turned onto Marlborough, a cart pulled by two horses came racing around the corner and came close to running into Mercury and Ada. The near miss spooked Mercury, and he stopped suddenly, throwing Ada from his back. When she hit the ground, the wind was knocked out of her. She lay sprawled there, her skirts akimbo, unable to move for a moment. The driver of the cart pulled his horses over and came running to help.

"Madame. Madame. Are you all right?"

Ada looked up into the eyes of a very startled young man. He took off his porkpie hat and waved it across her face. She tried to move, but couldn't find the energy. Nonetheless, she refused to admit there was anything wrong. "I'm fine," she said. "I just need to get home. I'll be late. My horse?"

"He's fine. He's here waitin' like the fine beast he is. D'you need help gettin' up?"

Ada tried to sit up again, but still felt too stunned. "I think so." She reached out her hand to the man, and he pulled her to a sitting position. Ada was grateful it was still too early for a crowd to have gathered. The streets were quiet, and the light was still ashy. Her back hurt; she wasn't able to stand on her own. The man saw her struggle and reached his arms around her waist in order to pull her to her feet.

"I think you'll be needin' a doctor." The sun moved closer to the horizon, and in an instant the color of the man's hair and the features of his face became distinctive in the fuller light. His hair was a light brown, his face was burned by the sun. Ada was glad to be able to see him, but knew that the light signaled danger for her if she didn't get home soon.

"I assure you I have no need of a doctor. Would you just help me onto my horse?"

The man hesitated. He twisted his hat in his hands. "Are you sure, ma'am?"

"Absolutely. I must get home."

The man brought Mercury to stand right next to Ada, where she now waited on the sidewalk. He laced his hands together and held them out so Ada could use them as a step up. As she boosted herself onto her horse, the movement sent a pain up her back that seemed to her to be shattering her spine. She winced, but refused to cry out. She couldn't have this young fellow take up any more of her time with his worry.

"Thank you for your help." Ada rode away from the man without looking back, but she sensed him watching her, and fretting. By the time Mercury stepped into the drive leading to the carriage house, Ada could hardly sit up. Before she made it from the front of the house to the carriage house, George and Edward were at her side, lifting her from the horse.

"What happened? Ada, are you all right?" Edward spoke as George helped settle Ada into Edward's arms. Ada was relieved Edward hadn't allowed George to carry her.

"Yes," she managed to say. "It's just my back."

"Tell me what happened."

"I fell off the horse." She closed her eyes and said no more. Edward didn't ask her any further questions until he had settled her into her bed.

"I'm going to call the doctor," Edward told her, then left her alone with Katie.

Dr. Fentzling arrived in Ada's bedroom within the hour. As he leaned over her, peering into her eyes, she felt his hot and aged breath on her face. It surprised her to realize she had never quite forgiven him for telling Edward about the abortion, even after all this time. Now his presence in her room for such a trifle felt like an affront to her. She turned her head away from him. Her back hurt her less now.

"You seem fine," the doctor said. Ada felt a sweet sense of relief. "But you have had a shock to your system. You must stay in bed." He looked at Edward, who stood peering down at Ada from the other side of the bed. "She shouldn't leave her bed for two days."

Edward's brow creased as he listened to the doctor. "Only two days? Are you sure?"

"She'll be in the pink in no time, I assure you," the doctor said.

The instant the two men had gone, Ada called Mary and had her turn the water on in the tub. Ada had had the bathroom constructed soon after their honeymoon. A square tub lined with blue and white tiles was set inside a platform of wooden slats and marble slabs. The piped-in water was heated by a boiler below the tub. The far end of the room had floor-to-ceiling leaded windows, with steps leading up to them and culminating in a broad mahogany window seat. During the thirty minutes it took to fill the tub, Ada changed into her bathrobe, then came back into the bathroom. Mary was still there, laying out soap and towels for Ada. Finally, the girl curtsied to Ada. "Will there be anything else, ma'am?"

"No. That's wonderful, thank you, Mary." Mary curtsied and hurried away. Mary and Edith had never been comfortable with Ada since the day

George had caught them drinking and dining with her. George and Ettie must have frightened them with the threat of losing their jobs. Since that day, Ada never pushed them to be more friendly; she knew it might serve to harm them in the end. Mary's obvious discomfort made Ada feel relief when the girl finally left.

As she submerged herself in the water, she felt the ache in her back again. But it was certainly nothing to worry about. In fact, it was almost a comforting ache, the kind that reminds you you are alive. This is the way a body feels when it's used often and pushed hard, Ada thought. It must be the way orchid hunters felt when they went to bed after climbing mountains all day.

The water came up to her neck. Her auburn hair snaked out across the surface of the water, weaving back and forth, over her breasts, then away, then back again. The water on her skin was almost like the touch of a man's hands. But could it hold her as a man could? Ada had never learned to swim, so she didn't trust that she could float on the surface of the water while exerting little energy. People said it was possible, but were they right? She dipped her face under the surface for just an instant, opening her eyes in the water and looking down at her own body. The blue of the tiles reflected onto her skin, making her look almost fish-like.

Horses were good swimmers, weren't they? What would Mercury look like swimming across the Charles? Would he be graceful, or would he struggle to stay above water? When she surfaced, she sucked in the air. The sound echoed, bouncing against the tiles and up to the windows. It was as loud as the snorting and breathing of a winded horse. When she returned to her room, she sat in her Liberty rocker, wrapped in a heavy robe, and looked out at the carriage house, imagining Mercury in his stall, standing still, waiting for his next opportunity to run.

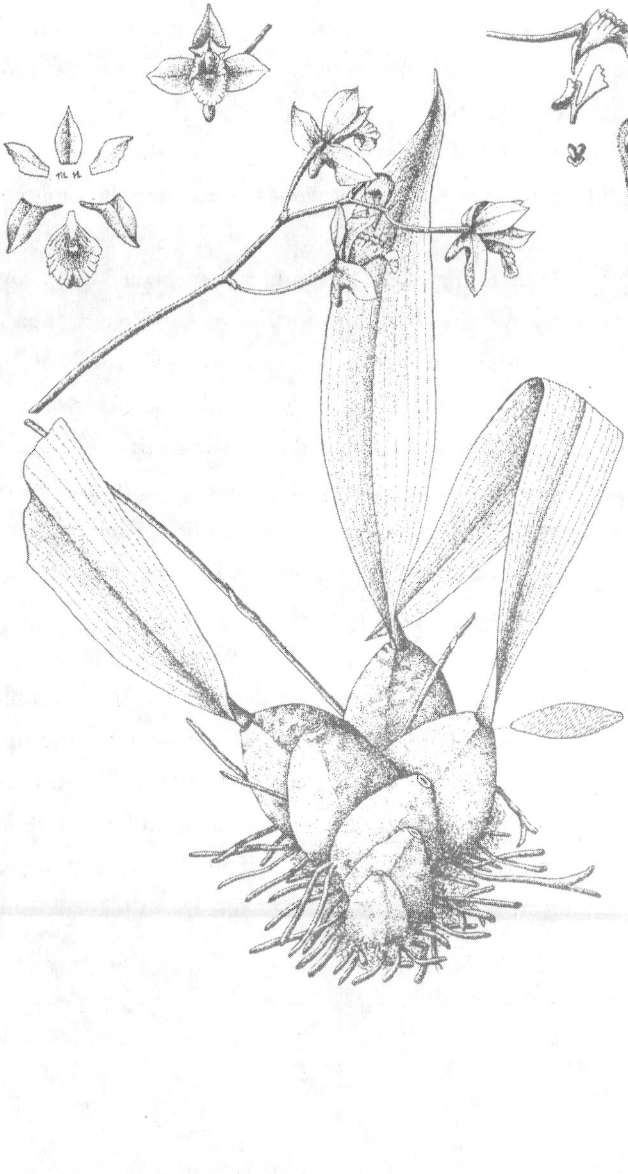

The Labyrinth

After her bath, Ada climbed into bed and fell asleep. She slept through the day and into the night. She woke suddenly to a house alive with the creaking and stretching of late night. She extricated herself from the linens that had twisted all about her from her thrashing, and went to the window. The moon was waning; the backyard was a labyrinth of shadows. The bushes looked like people, people who seemed to be creeping about. The idea caused her to pull the curtains across the window and return to her disheveled bed.

The next morning, she felt as if she had not slept at all, though she knew she must have been sleeping when Edward came into her room, waking her as his boots slapped the floor. When she opened her eyes to look, she saw two of them standing there—Edward and Dr. Casey. It bothered her that she hadn't sensed from the sounds of their feet that there were two of them. As she struggled, through her tiredness, to sit up, her back reminded her of her fall from the horse, but she managed to keep from wincing.

"Ada, I have brought Dr. Casey to examine you. I'll leave you alone with him now. I must be off to the office."

As Edward left her room, George arrived, carrying Dr. Casey's vibrating machine. He set the contraption next to the bed. "Good morning, ma'am," he said, then bowed slightly and left.

"Well, Ada," Dr. Casey said. "Edward tells me about your adventure. He's quite worried, as well he should be."

"So he's asked you to give me treatments at home? Why?" Ada gazed on the machine. Its presence in her room vexed her. She wanted to kick it over. What had George thought as he carried it to her room? What about the rest of the staff? Did they know what it was? If they did, surely they were appalled.

"We discussed it at length. He stopped by my offices this morning. He was very concerned about you. Edward isn't convinced that your hysteria is subsiding. We agreed that you should be confined to the house, but perhaps for a longer time than Dr. Fentzling prescribed. I think you should refrain from stimulus of any kind for at least a month. No visitors, no reading, no leaving the house for any reason. I will come to see you three times a week. I think you will notice a marked change after thirty days." As Dr. Casey spoke, he fiddled with the vibrator, setting it in the proper position, twirling its dials, testing the reach of the cord. Finally, he stopped talking, and he moved in close to her with the vibrating attachment. Ada slipped down into her bed as he threw her covers back and pushed at her gown.

As the doctor worked on her, she allowed herself the luxury of imagining it was Frederick—Frederick as she had believed him to be before that final afternoon when he left her alone in their rented room. Only this fantasy allowed her to slip into acquiescence, allowing Dr. Casey to do what he would with her body and her dignity.

THE SCHEDULE DR. CASEY had prescribed for her proceeded like this: Katie brought her food in the morning, Edith and Mary came to remove the dishes and empty her chamber pot, and once a week they changed her linens. If she wanted to take a bath, she had to ask George for permission, and then he would send Katie to escort her down the hall. On her way to the bathroom, she passed the library and her office, both rooms that were forbidden, and whose allure she was forced to resist throughout her lonely days.

Katie brought lunch and dinner as well, and Edith and Mary again cleaned up after her. George knocked on her door around nine at night to tell her she should get ready for bed, then Katie came to see if she needed anything. Ada was left alone after that, though she did hear George pass in front of her door every night around midnight. Between nine and midnight, she read from the books that she kept hidden in her old trunk. Her door was locked from the outside, so he wasn't worried about her escaping. He was just listening at the door, and probably trying to impress on her the fact that he was there. Whenever she sensed his presence, she put the book she was reading under her pillow, and used her Karezza breathing exercises to calm herself, to keep the anger and anguish at bay. Most of the time it worked well enough.

Dr. Casey came to see her three times a week, as he had promised, bringing his portable vibrating machine with him. Ada felt a sense of degradation in her own room that was beyond anything she had experienced in his office. She lay on her back, on the bed where she and Edward had made love, and then had practiced Karezza, and tried to force herself to climax so that Dr. Casey would be satisfied with her and leave. But she imagined her entire household staff outside her door, laughing at her, knowing what she was doing in here with the doctor and his contraption. Perhaps even the neighbors saw him bring it from his carriage, and whispered among themselves about the hysteric in the Pryce house. As the machine buzzed across her, Ada stared at the plaster leaves on her ceiling, and imagined herself in the jungles of the Amazon.

When Edward came home from his club early enough, he visited her in her room. Usually, he read to her from *Karezza,* but didn't allow her to read herself. Ada didn't hear the words he read, but she was good at nodding and making one-word comments at just the right time, so he believed she was listening attentively.

Sometimes Ada invested time in tracing the chronology of her descent into this strange captivity in her own home, trying to pinpoint the moment at which she made the fatal error, the one event that might have changed her destiny had she made a different choice. She found the exercise could eat up half a day, if she allowed herself to obsess over the minutiae. It was possible for her to slip into these ruminations while Edward read to her, and even to nod her head and speak at appropriate intervals without interrupting the thought patterns in her head. She worked backward in time, mining long-forgotten details of her life, but never managed to reach the one event that had changed their marriage so drastically, so irreparably.

But even without going over that one event, she knew it well enough. It lingered there, always hovering over the boundaries of every thought she entertained. Edward had been punishing her, for three long years, for having had an abortion without his permission. Ada knew this on a level that transcended conscious awareness.

Two weeks into her ordeal, Katie came into her room with the breakfast tray. As she set the tray down on the bed, she pulled an envelope out from underneath it. Evidently she had been hiding it there. "I'm not to give you messages of any kind. But I . . . well, I thought you would want this." She handed Ada the envelope. "I just couldn't see the harm in it." Katie was gone before Ada had a chance to thank her.

Ada expected it to be another note from William. His tenacity in contacting her was strangely satisfying to her. She opened it with a sense of anticipation, maybe even hope.

William leaves for New York in four days. Don't let him go away with nothing.

Minnie

Minnie, of all people. So she knew or suspected something as well. Perhaps she had known all along. She might have even purposely chosen *The Woman in White* when Ada came to her, hoping it would make her think about murders close to home.

But Ada had acted too slowly. She had been too careful. Now William was headed off for Brazil, to travel the foreign countryside in search of rare orchids, while she would remain locked away, unable to help him or even herself. The note from Minnie made her impotence seem total, her imprisonment, final. She had to get out of her room. Just an hour outside its walls would restore her vitality. When she heard Edward rummaging about in his room, getting ready for his workday, she knocked on the wall between their rooms until her knuckles ached. There was no response. She pulled a boot from her closet and pounded harder on the wall with it, then waited.

At last she heard the key in her door.

"What is it, Ada?" He asked the question with a certain note of impatience.

"Oh, Edward, darling. I needed to speak to you before you left." It was the first time in her marriage that she noticed calling her husband *darling* required a certain flexing of her will. She wanted to choke on the word. "I am sure you can't imagine what it is like sitting in your room day in and day out with no relief. I simply must have some stimulation."

"I don't know. The doctor says—"

"Call the doctor. Please. Ask him if I might just visit the Orchid House. Not even every day. Perhaps two or three times a week."

She went to him and took his hand. "Edward, it would mean ever so much to me."

"Fine. I'll telephone George later this morning with an answer."

He didn't kiss her when he left. Ada was glad of it.

George came to her room after ten, to tell her the doctor had approved two visits per week to the greenhouse. Ada was overjoyed, but kept a straight back and a calm face until George had left her doorway. When he was gone, she danced around her room. She covered her floor in the one-two-three tempo of a waltz, her bare feet barely touching the wood or the carpets. Her back was completely healed; there was no pain at all. There was no tangible reason for her imprisonment to continue, which made the idea of it more disturbing still to Ada.

George had agreed to send Katie to fetch her at half past twelve, after her lunch dishes were taken away. At half past eleven, Ada began to dress for her trip across her yard. She used the entire thirty minutes before her tray was due to attend to her dress and makeup and hair. Her hands shook as she dusted her cheeks with powder. Her hands went clammy and her underarms hot. How long had it been since she walked on the solid earth or felt the sun on her head? She wasn't quite sure.

The slick taffeta of her blue skirt reflected the sun back into her eyes as she strolled across the yard with Katie. "Please, let's walk slowly," Ada pleaded. "I have been locked inside for so long." When Katie's eyes moistened, Ada felt shame. How could Edward have put her into a position where she must beg like a child for simple allowances? She hated him, she hated Dr. Casey. She hated George. If she didn't love Katie so, she might even hate her for her everyday freedoms.

At the door to the greenhouse, Katie turned away and went back into the house. No one was watching her! Ada closed the door, and meant to move her feet forward, but suddenly she found herself on the floor, clawing at the planks, thrashing wildly. She wanted to scream, to cry out as loudly as possible, but she knew there was danger in that simple act, so she opened her mouth and pushed silent air out from her lungs in a noiseless scream. It hurt her chest and her gut, it hurt her jaw, but she couldn't stop. Rolling over onto her back, she kicked her heels against the floorboards and pounded her fists. The sun peeked through the glass ceiling, cutting across her eyes, blinding her for an instant. In that momentary whiteout, she imagined herself in the jungles of Brazil, hunting orchids with William. She even, then, imagined Walter with them, still alive, laughing and telling stories as he had at her dinner party. That image was the thing that pulled her off the floor and back to her feet.

Her head felt swollen, her mind could hardly identify the place where she stood. She looked around at the plants. They stood in ordered rows upon clean shelves, categorized by genus, and by color within genus. Each plant was labeled. Every container was identical in form and color, with variations only in size. The symmetry of it all seemed to mock the chaos of Ada's brain. She couldn't make sense of this rigid order.

There was no thought involved in her actions. They were inspired by a purely primal force. Tactile sensation and visual stimulus moved her. She wiped her arm along the first shelf, dropping half a dozen plants to the floor.

The sound of the clay pots shattering, the loam thumping onto the boards, sent a lovely chill through her arms and up into her neck and head. She wiped off the second row, then, the floor covered with orchids, she went to them and ground the heel of her boot into their pulpy petals. As she returned to the shelves, eager to launch another assault, she stepped on a shard of a pot. The jagged clay dug through her boot and into her foot; the pain made her pause. It was then that she stopped to view what she had done.

The plants looked right there, on the floor in a mess of earth and clay and moss, their battered heads stretched out parallel to the earth instead of upright. This was more like the great chain of being, she thought, with the plants down there at the foot of humans. The pink slipper lay next to her boot. Its neck was broken right in half. It was dead. It was beyond repair. Not even Edward could save it. Ada reached down to touch it. As she made contact with its cushiony sepal, she wondered what Edward would do when he saw it. The thought made her laugh. The laughter took off like a rolling ball of thread, unwinding, moving rapidly away from her, out of her control. She laughed until her sides hurt, and her head felt as if it would split.

She crunched the flower in between her fingers. The popping sound it made somehow brought her to an awareness of the position she was now in. She stepped back and looked at the havoc she had wreaked, and it registered for the first time that she had committed a sin that would never be forgiven. As she felt the fear creep through her veins, she dropped the pink slipper orchid to the ground.

The pot shards and bark and flower petals ground under her boots as she walked out of the greenhouse. The familiar, lovely scents filled the air, but she didn't note them. Ada was buoyed by the thrill of a new awareness. She was feeling the wholly unfamiliar sensation of the adrenaline of fear. The possibility of ever regaining her freedom was now seriously at risk, and she needed to move quickly.

Back in her room, she pulled out her carpetbag and packed it with the simplest dresses she owned, the books in her trunk, and the money she had failed to spend on the sunroom. She never had settled on what furniture to buy for her once favorite room, and then her imprisonment had interrupted her plans. So the personal kitty of money she had hidden in the trunk still contained more than seven hundred dollars. She thought it would be enough to support a modest lifestyle for a year. She threw in rags for her menses and a few toiletries, then she hid the bag in the trunk and pulled the cord that rang for Katie. Her maid was there within minutes.

Katie could see the look of fear on her mistress's face. "What is it? What's happened?"

"Katie, please don't question me. Please. I need your help."

"With what, miss?"

"Edward is going to keep me locked up forever, now. I need to get out of here." Her head suddenly felt about to burst as she spoke to Katie. "I can't live this way another minute. I simply cannot."

Katie's hands were twisting about in the folds of her dress, and a fine sweat popped out on her forehead. "What can I do?"

"I need you to get me some of Edward's old clothes from the laundry. Things he meant to throw out. Things I can wear on a horse."

"Oh, Ada. No!" Katie threw herself to her knees and wrapped her arms around Ada's waist. "Don't go. What will happen to me without you here?" Ada put her fingers in Katie's hair and pushed the tendrils away from her face as she pulled her up to her feet.

"If I stay, it will be bad for us all. I have to be gone before George goes to the Orchid House. Please, get me the clothes. Three sets of trousers, jackets, and shirts should do. A hat. And some food. I should have food. Quickly now." She pushed the girl out the door.

Ada found a blanket, rags for her menses, and some sturdy boots, and added those to her bag. Candles, lucifers, and pen and ink went in on top. Katie returned with the requested items, and Ada set about changing into a suit of Edward's. It was too big, of course, but Ada wasn't trying to impress anyone.

Katie helped Ada dress, crying and objecting all the while. "What will I tell Mr. Pryce?"

"Tell him you know nothing. Lock the door after I go. I'll leave my window open so he thinks I climbed out it." Ada looked at herself in the mirror. The image was too surprising; she turned away from it quickly. "Now, help me downstairs with my bag. Quietly. George mustn't hear."

"He's in town. He won't know," Katie said.

"Good. Then we have only to get past Ettie. She will tell him if she sees us."

"I'll carry your bag out to the carriage house, Ada. I'll say it's for Liam if anyone asks. Come down in five minutes."

Ada handed Katie the bag, then took the girl's worried face in her hands. "I'm sorry I'll miss your wedding." Katie began to cry. "I love you, Katie," Ada said. "I am going to miss you."

"Oh, miss." Katie choked the words out through her quiet sobs.

"Stay in touch with Margery. She'll help you if you need anything. And will you take care of my orchid?"

"Oh, of course. It'll remind me of you."

"Thank you," Ada said. "Now go."

She didn't watch Katie walk away. Instead, she went to work stuffing her long, thick hair into Edward's old hat. It took a large handful of pins to secure it so that it looked as though it might be a man's head of hair. She felt satisfied when she viewed herself in the mirror, looking so unlike herself, and so unlike a woman.

Dressed in her husband's old country suit, she managed to get out to the carriage house without anyone noticing her. When she went in, Liam was there, holding Mercury, saddled and ready to go.

"I will deny I ever did any of this," he said to her.

"Of course you will. You are innocent." She took hold of his hand and squeezed it. "Take good care of Katie."

"You look like a young boy, just starting out in the world," he told her. He reached out to help boost her up onto the horse.

Waving him away, Ada laughed and clapped him on the back. "I suppose I should get used to acting like one." She put her foot in the stirrup and threw her leg over Mercury.

"Godspeed, miss," Liam said just before she galloped away from the carriage house and into the lively streets.

PART TWO

A Lady an explorer? a traveller in skirts?
The notion's just a trifle too seraphic:
Let them stay and mind the babies, or hem our ragged shirts;
But they musn't, can't, and shan't be geographic.

—"To the Royal Geographical Society,"
Punch, 1893

The New Man

Riding through the busy daytime streets astride Mercury, Ada saw the life of the city all around her in a different aspect. This newfound place was like the story of a good book, and she was the reader, finding her way through this strange territory at the same time she surrendered to it and allowed it to lead her. Anything could happen here.

She rode with her back straight, her head high, and no one looked at her with contempt. Anyone who noticed her considered her with nonchalance, as if she belonged here. She forgot at first that she was dressed as a man. When she remembered, she felt herself swell up with a strange pride. I am a man, she thought. No one dares question me. Nonetheless, the veil between her disguise and the reality of her situation was thin. The fact that she belonged to a wealthy man, and was trying to escape him, made her position dangerous. She steered Mercury toward Beacon Hill without having considered any other possibility, and tied him to a hitching post outside the African Meeting House.

Esau opened the door to her. He didn't register recognition when he saw her, and Ada made no effort to enlighten him. "Hello," he said. "What can I do for you?"

Ada pushed her voice down to the lowest register she could manage. It made her throat feel rough. "I need to see William Parrish. It's urgent."

"He isn't here."

"Can you tell me where he is?

Esau kept silent. Why would he tell a strange white man where William was? It was highly likely that no good would come of it.

"Please. I'm a friend. Can I send him a note? It really is urgent."

"Go ahead, then. I'll take the note to him." He ushered her into the hall and offered her paper and a pen. She scribbled her note quickly, folded it, and asked for a seal.

"How long will it be?"

"Give me an hour," he said as he led her out the door.

There was nothing else to do but ride Mercury. With this piece of time stretching out before her, and everything in limbo until she reached the other side of the hour, Ada had the leisure to consider what she was doing for the first time since she had run out of the Orchid House. Mercury was comfortable with her on his back, even trusting. He had no reason to believe that she was leading him into any kind of danger. And now, with the fabric of the trousers around her legs, she felt she suddenly had the kind of control it took to establish order out of chaos. She could make a new life for herself, with just this horse and her trousers.

They sauntered along Joy Street together. Certainly without Mercury she would have felt more alone. The horse urged music out of the cobblestones as his hooves clopped against them in four-four time. Ada felt herself lightening. She let her body rest into the bounce of the horse's stride. This was better than Karezza, or that doctor's vibrating machine.

At that sudden memory, a hot rocket of shame shot up from her groin. How could Edward have allowed her to lie in her bed with the strange man's hands between her legs and on her breasts? How could she have married a man who would encourage such a ritual? Her shoulders shivered up, and she pulled her wool coat around her. Who would ever think to put a man on an operating table and stick a machine between his legs, forcing him to crisis so he wouldn't go out into the world to cheat and bully people? She felt an urge then to pull the dresses from her bag and throw them into the street. She would be happy never to see another corset or muttonchop sleeve for the rest of her time on earth.

When Ada returned to the meeting hall, William was there. His face made it apparent that he had certainly not expected to see her, and especially not dressed as a man. He couldn't choose the words he wanted to say, it seemed, so he remained speechless. "I'll explain," she told him as they hurried to the office together.

"Mrs. Pryce," he said to her once they were alone, "are you in some sort of danger?"

"Well, yes. I believe I am. My husband imprisoned me in my own house. I have escaped with his horse, and if he finds me I can't imagine what he'll do."

"How did you think I might be able to help you? I am a Negro with little money and no influence. I just don't know what I can do for you."

"I want to go with you to Brazil."

William laughed. He tried to stifle it, but his belly bounced with the joy of the idea.

"William, you think my husband killed Walter. What makes you think he won't kill me?"

"He was able to get away with killing Walter because there is no one to speak for Walter. But how would he do that with you?"

"I'm just a woman. He could say whatever he liked and the authorities would believe him. I need to get away from him. Please, help me." For the first time, Ada let herself consider the possibility that Edward indeed might think to kill her. The idea wasn't completely far-fetched. But even if he didn't physically kill her, there was no doubt that he would kill her soul, or whatever it was that made her human, were she ever to return to him.

"But what would you do in Brazil?"

She looked out the window, searching for the bird that had entertained her before, thinking it might serve as an omen if she found it. She continued to look out the window as she spoke. "I love orchids."

"That's fine, a fine thing, Mrs. Pryce. But how will you survive in Brazil? Where will you go?"

She turned back to him, abandoning her search for the bird. "I want to be an orchid hunter."

She saw the look in his eyes. It came close to the looks she got from the other men—Edward, George, the doctors, even Frederick—when they were about to dismiss her as just a woman, or worse, an hysteric. But then something shifted in William's eyes. Perhaps he recognized the desire in hers. He wiped his face with his hand. "But this life is a hard one. It takes a toll on the body. We sleep on the earth, and wash in rivers. We eat strange foods, insects feast on us, we carry heavy loads, we spend too many hours in the sun."

"I can do all those things."

"How do you know? You've lived a life of luxury and leisure. How do you know you could withstand the strain of this life?"

"Remember when you first came to me asking for my help? I asked you why you thought I would help. You said it was because you knew I wasn't the sort of person who would protect a murderer?"

"Yes, I remember."

"Well, if I continue here, the only choice I have is to protect this man who is my husband, to go along with whatever he says so that he doesn't lock me up again."

William never asked her why Edward had locked her up. Perhaps even he had heard the rumors of her sordid domestic life and he already knew the reason. Or perhaps he was simply too kind to meddle. But Ada was grateful in any case. She didn't want to explain that part of her story.

"I have money, William. I will back you with it."

William sat a little higher in the chair, opened his eyes a little wider. "Back me?"

"Do you want to go down there as your own agent, not beholden to the men who pay your way?"

"But if I take your money, I'm beholden to you."

Ada pulled off her hat and tugged at the hairpins, letting her hair fall down around her coat. She ran her hands through her hair, digging her fingernails into her scalp. Finally, she spoke it out loud. "No, you won't.

We'll be partners. In exchange for taking me on, I will back the expedition financially. You will owe me nothing. We'll split the profits."

William laughed again, but this time the laugh wasn't stifled. It rang out, with notes suggesting both joy and bewilderment. "You can't be serious?" He seemed to hold his breath then.

"I'm completely serious. I want you as my partner."

"Oh, if anyone ever found out they'd hang me."

"I'll never come back here." Her voice caught as she said the words. Was this true? "They won't know."

His eyes narrowed, and he gazed at her from behind the narrow spaces for some seconds before he spoke again. "All right. What do I have to lose? Let's see how you work out as my partner." He reached out to shake her hand, but Ada turned his hand and kissed it.

Did other women do things like this? she wondered. She wanted to believe that fictional women like Rosalind, who escaped to the forest disguised as a man in *As You Like It*, and Portia from *The Merchant of Venice*, who also took on a man's identity, could and did exist in the real world. She would like to know that she had company, that others had gone before her. Whether they succeeded or failed didn't even matter. She simply wanted to know that they had made the effort.

"We can't do this alone, though. We need another man," William said.

"Who?"

"Jao is the perfect third partner for us. He and I planned this trip together. We're going unsponsored. After what happened to Walter, we decided it was time." He rubbed his hands together, as if he might be getting excited about the idea of Ada's backing. "You remember Jao, don't you? He was at your dinner."

Of course she remembered Jao. The man who loved Shakespeare. "Do you trust him?" she asked. "What if he contacts my husband?"

"I trust him with my life, Mrs. Pryce."

Ada was willing to believe William. She had no other choice, really. "When do we leave?"

"In three days. But I have to figure out where to put you up until we do leave."

"Can't I stay with you?"

"Oh, I don't think that's a good idea. Not a good idea at all."

Of course it was impossible. Ada knew that. "I suppose it isn't." She ran her fingers through her hair again. "I should cut this off."

"All in good time." William got up from the table and walked to the window. He looked out in silence for a moment, then looked back at Ada. "I suppose I'll send you to my sister, Mrs. Pryce."

"I'm going to have to find myself a new name. Mrs. Pryce won't do. How about Adam?"

"Adam? That sounds fine."

"Adam Wilson. I like that."

"Adam Wilson it is, then. We'll have to get you some papers."

"Papers?"

"Sure. You'll be needing them." He stopped to think for an instant. "You aren't required to have a passport, but I think it will make things easier for you. It'll make people less likely to question you."

"And you know where to get them?"

He didn't answer. Instead, he winked at her. Of course, his parents had certainly known people in their time who needed papers in order to save them from angry white men. Perhaps they had needed them themselves. Maybe William understood her position better than any of her so-called peers ever could.

"What about my horse?"

"We'll leave him here for now. Esau likes horses, and we have a stable out back."

WILLIAM'S SISTER LIVED with her husband and two children in a third-story flat on Southac Street. A petite young African woman with a white scarf wrapped around her head opened the door to their knock.

"Why, Master William," she said, then turned to Ada and did a little dip of a curtsy.

"Hello, Felicity," he said. "May we come in?"

"Well, of course. I'm sorry." She stepped back to let them in, apparently surprised that Ada would want to enter the place. They walked into a long hallway, whose polished wood floors were graced with a Chinese wool runner. Felicity led them into the front parlor. That room was large, with the same polished floors, more Chinese carpets, dark wood tables, and two bright velvet sofas. The fireplace was a grand marble affair, and its fire washed the room in a burnt orange light. Ada was surprised by everything she saw. She didn't realize there were Negroes living such comfortable lives.

"Sit," William told Ada.

"Felicity, this is Adam Wilson. Though he's not really Adam. Take off your hat," he said to Ada.

She took it off, without hesitation, and pulled the pins from her hair again. Felicity drew in a quick breath.

"We won't bother with her real name. Just call her Adam." He turned to Ada. "Felicity is my sister's maid."

Ada reached her hand out to Felicity. "How do you do?"

Felicity took Ada's hand in her own, but she did so carefully, as if she might be corrected for her form if she didn't get it just right. "Charmed, I'm sure," she said, executing another small curtsy. "Oh, dear. May I take your coat? I'm so sorry I didn't ask before, when you first came in."

Ada peeled off her coat and handed it to Felicity. She sat in her oversized suit jacket and shirt, aware of the relative freedom of her body parts inside these clothes.

"I imagine this is a first for both of you," William said. "Adam here is visiting her first African home and meeting her first African maid, and Felicity is entertaining her first white guest at the same time she is meeting her first woman dressed as a man. Am I correct?"

The two women nodded their agreement with this assessment. William allowed himself a leisurely chuckle as he watched the two consider each other with timidity. "I'm enjoying this," he said. "But maybe we should get Harriet."

"Oh, my Lord, forgive me, Mr. William." Felicity hurried out of the room and returned with William's sister. Felicity lingered through the introductions, apparently reluctant to miss any of the excitement.

Harriet was tall and thin, with a long neck and the same dark skin William had. Ada was taken with the graceful set of her head on that neck. She enjoyed watching Harriet as she spoke.

"Harriet's my big sister," William told Ada. Harriet looked years younger than William.

"Yes, I'm five years older than him, so he has to listen to me when I tell him what to do." She patted his cheek, the way one would pat a child's face. Ada felt a sudden desire to just stay here. She would like to have Harriet for a sister, to be told what to do by her. Maybe that would be altogether wiser than going off to South America.

Harriet turned her attention to her maid. "Felicity, would you get us some tea?"

Felicity took her eyes off Ada and hurried out of the room.

"Adam's a fugitive," William explained to Harriet. "She's dressed like a man so no one will recognize her."

Ada was taken with Harriet's simple acceptance of this strange situation. She tried to imagine how Emmy would react if she appeared at her door dressed as a man. There might be a note of hysteria in her response, Ada suspected, and a great deal of confusion and embarrassment. And no doubt, in the end, she would feel compelled to tell Franz, who would immediately inform Edward of Ada's unacceptable behavior. But all that was behind her now.

"She's going to need some clothes that fit," said William.

Harriet sized up Ada as she spoke. "That won't be any problem."

"Harriet and her husband own a clothing store," William explained.

When Felicity brought in the tea, and Ada bit into a cake, she suddenly realized how hungry she was. It had been hours and hours since breakfast, her last meal. She savored every bite, and helped herself to another when Harriet offered the plate to her again.

"Harriet, I need you to keep Adam here for a few days."

Ada felt her heart sink. Why on earth would this woman agree to such an arrangement? Entertaining a complete stranger, all on her brother's whim? Her breath went shallow, in anticipation of Harriet's response.

Harriet smiled. "Well, William, you've made stranger requests over the years. Why not?" She set down her delicate china cup and leaned back on the sofa. "Tell me, though, what on earth are you two up to?"

William hesitated. But Ada wanted Harriet to know her story. It was really all she had left of herself, anyway. Just this strange story.

"My husband decided I am an hysteric, and the cure would be to prevent me from experiencing any sort of stimulation. He locked me up inside my own bedroom. I would rather he kill me than keep me locked away any longer, with no friends or family, without even a book, or a simple song, or a chore to perform. So I took his clothes and his horse and ran away." Ada sipped some tea to wet her throat. Other than when she spoke to Katie, she hadn't said so many words together in weeks. "And now I'm going to Brazil with William. I want to be an orchid hunter."

Harriet's eyes narrowed. "William, what sort of tall tales have you told her about South America?"

"None. I told her only the bad things."

"It's true. He tried to convince me not to go. But there's nothing for me here. In fact, I would be forced to live my life in hiding if I were to stay. And I love orchids. I have wanted to be an orchid hunter ever since my husband first started collecting the plants." Was this true? Perhaps. But if it was, Ada hadn't realized it until she spoke the words. Once she said them, though, the idea settled into her personal history as a simple fact, and she would repeat it many times.

"Oh, my stars. Well, I hope you have a good strong constitution, Adam. I really do." Ada was beginning to like the sound of her new name, to enjoy the sound of it on other people's lips. She liked it, too, that Harriet didn't fuss about it, or feel forced to conform to convention and call her Mr. This or Miss That. Just Adam. Ada wanted to tell this story to Katie. But she would never see Katie again, would she? This realization squeezed her chest, as if a metal band were being pulled tighter and tighter around her torso.

No Katie. She saw her freckled face, and her loose curls forever falling around that face. Katie would like Harriet, Ada was sure of that. Why hadn't she insisted that Katie come with her? If Katie hadn't fallen in love, who knows, perhaps Ada would have asked her to come. But now that she was a fugitive and Katie was at Edward's mercy, her friendship with her maid was over; she wouldn't even be able to write to her. There would never again be anyone in her life who knew Ada Pryce, wife of a prominent Boston lawyer, daughter of a powerful Brahman. All those pieces of her life were gone and existed now only in her memory, and in hers alone.

Harriet touched Ada's hand, and suddenly the band released its pressure. "You look tired. Would you like to rest?"

Harriet took Ada into her daughter's bedroom. "She's at the shop. She won't be home until later. Please feel free to just relax."

Alone in the room, Ada pulled off her wool pants and her shirt, keeping on her undershirt and men's long underwear. The bed stood near the window; it was a deep mattress upon a heavy four-poster, covered with thick blankets and topped with an intricate quilt depicting scenes from the Charles River and Beacon Hill done up in bright primary colors. The quilt was covered with bridges, trees, brownstones, and even ships. She crawled under the blankets and quilt. Pulling that picture story up over her shoulders was like enveloping herself in the history of the African people in Boston. She sensed a richness there that was completely missing from her own background. If she slept under this quilt long enough, could she make a place for herself in this complicated story?

Seconds after asking herself the question, she was asleep.

She dreamed she was in a large room, something like the open room at the African Meeting House, with Frederick and Harriet. The two were arguing some fine point of legal reform. Frederick seemed to be quoting Shakespeare in support of his arguments, while Harriet kept repeating, over and over, "You have to listen to the songs. Don't forget the songs."

When she woke, the dream lingered about her, a half-remembered hope. The sun had dropped itself down below the horizon, or the world had spun itself away from its light. The room was too dark for shadows to find their way there; and it was cold. But Ada felt safe. And in the moment when she recognized the quality of safety in which she was cocooned, she also understood that she had felt unsafe for a very long time, since long before Edward ever locked her in her room. She heard voices, and the occasional creak of a floorboard. These people hardly know me, and yet they are willing to protect me, she thought. The distant murmuring floated down the hall, under the door, and across the room to envelop her like a newborn baby in a receiving blanket.

But then the timbre of the voices changed. They became high-pitched, louder, more strident; they sent a buzz out into the hallway. Ada jumped out of bed and groped for her pants and shirt. She dressed quickly, then sat on the edge of the bed in the dark, waiting. Someone would come to tell her this wasn't going to work, she would have to leave now. The voices continued to bump up against one another, rising and falling too rapidly. Perhaps Edward would show up at the door, ready to take her home.

Footsteps hurried down the hall, two sets. They stopped outside her door, then moved away, not as quickly. Ada felt her breath thin out and hold itself, hovering just outside her lungs. She waited for the footsteps to come back to her door again, but they never did. The voices started up again, calmer this time.

She had to know what they were saying. She tiptoed down the hallway in her stockinged feet, stopped at the parlor door, and looked in. William and Harriet were there with an elegant young woman, all done up in a black-and-white suit that was the latest fashion, with huge muttonchop sleeves and a wide silver belt at the tiny waistline.

"It won't be for long," William was saying to her.

"All right. All right, then. But do I have to give her my room?" the young woman asked.

At that moment Harriet saw Ada standing in the doorway. "Hush up, Juliet," she snapped. "Come in, Adam." She said the name so naturally, as if she had no concern at all with calling a runaway woman by a man's name. Ada walked into the room, aware as she went of every nerve ending in her body, of every muscle and tendon, every bone. It was a wonder she could make them all work in synchrony to get herself across that floor. The sense of shame that had become as much a part of herself as her awareness of her own name returned in a comforting rush. All these people were troubled by, brought together by, preoccupied with, her. It was a burden.

"Adam, this is my daughter, Juliet. She was just about to tell me that she would be happy to give up her room to you. She can sleep in her brother's room."

"Oh, but I could sleep there if she wants to stay where she is."

"I insist that you stay in her room. It's more appropriate for you."

Ada turned to Juliet, anticipating the anger in her eyes. But the young woman smiled at her, and the smile reached her eyes. "I'm sorry. I didn't mean to be rude." She held out her hand, and she and Ada shook just like men.

William left soon after. Ada had dinner with mother and daughter and Felicity. The maid served the food, and sat down in time to eat it along with everyone else. Wouldn't it have been nicer if Katie and Liam had joined Ada and Edward at dinner every night? The Pryce house would have felt more alive. She imagined their Irish brogues reaching out into the ethers of the room, warming it and enlivening it.

"My husband and son are on a buying trip to New York. For the store," Harriet said. "They won't be back for four more days."

"I'm sorry I'll miss them."

"When are you leaving?" Juliet asked. Ada saw Harriet shoot a look at her daughter. That glance was the only indication that Juliet might still be angry about her room; there had been nothing in Juliet's tone to suggest it. But Ada again felt the hovering shame.

"I don't really know when. It's all up to William."

"Yes, I imagine my brother is full of all sorts of wild plans."

Ada looked down at her etched china plate, and spoke toward it. "It takes a wild nature, I think, to accomplish what William has accomplished."

"But what is that, exactly?" Ada lifted her head and saw Harriet staring straight into her eyes.

It wasn't hard for Ada to answer the question. She had been thinking about all these things ever since she decided to leave her home and her husband. "He has succeeded in making a life for himself that doesn't require that he follow someone else's rules. He has created a kind of freedom."

"He is able to get out of the cities. But he's still at the mercy of rich white men's whims."

"Perhaps not anymore," Ada said. She was grateful to Harriet when she smiled.

"Well, I look forward to the realization of your dreams. Both of you."

Juliet had continued to eat quietly throughout this exchange, without ever looking at the other women. But Ada was certain she was taking in every word. The silence now stretched a little longer than was easy on any of them. Finally, it was Juliet who interrupted it. "Things went quite well at the store today, Mother. We sold ten suits, and placed orders for another four."

"I'm proud of you. I knew you could do it!" Harriet leaned across the corner of the table toward her daughter, encircling her in her arms. Juliet laughed, kissing her mother's cheeks and forehead.

"Now what will Papa say about me going into the business?"

"We'll keep working on him, baby. He'll come around."

Ada was surprised by their open affection. They paid no attention to the china and silver around them. They both simply leaned over the table to embrace. Their kissing and hugging was noisy, it rattled the table slightly, causing Ada's crystal goblet to hum. Her mother had never demonstrated her affection for Ada in such an overtly physical way. She imagined this must be what heaven really was, this sort of comfort. She wanted to stand up and step right into the center of the circle of their embrace. Instead, she held her goblet. Felicity leaned toward her, putting her hand on Ada's arm. "Ain't they a pair? Ain't they somethin'?" Ada contented herself with the soft touch of Felicity's hand.

Juliet forgave Ada for taking her room. She brought Ada three suits from their store—suits that fit. They were all casual, meant for an adventurer and traveler, but they were good clothes. Ada tried them on and showed them to the women. Harriet, Juliet, and Felicity applauded her each time she entered the parlor in a new suit.

"Now, sister," Felicity said, "all you have to do is learn to walk like a man." The other women laughed louder than Ada had ever heard any woman laugh. The laughter was so thick it subsumed Ada, and soon she was laughing as if her own laugh was a part of the greater laughter that filled the room. She laughed so hard her stomach began to hurt and she wanted to stop, but she wanted never to stop.

She walked for them, with her feet below her hips, her head leading, her arms swinging loosely.

"No, no!" Juliet took Ada by the shoulders and pushed them down. "Relax your shoulders." Ada tried again. There was more laughter, but it was softer. "Women put their walk in their feet and hips and legs. Men put it in their shoulders and chests."

"My Lord," Harriet said, "when did you take it upon yourself to study men's gaits so closely?"

"Oh, Mama, you know I have a keen eye."

"Indeed she do," Felicity said. They all laughed at Felicity now.

Ada collapsed onto the sofa. "I can't go on," she moaned. "You make me laugh too much." She spent two more evenings in the parlor, entertaining her hostesses with her manly glide. Finally, with the help of her hostesses, she adopted a walk that at least wouldn't call undue attention to herself, and she was happy with that. By the time William came to take Ada away, three days after she had arrived, she felt as if she were taking leave of her long-lost sister and her real mother. All four women cried when Ada walked out the door for the last time, dressed as a man and accompanied by William.

Someone, Esau no doubt, had brought Mercury and tied him to the hitching post in front of the house. Early morning dew still clung to the surfaces of everything. The sun, even though it was lifting itself above the horizon, didn't offer warmth. Ada touched Mercury's cold coat. His muscles quivered under her touch. He evoked in Ada a combination of joy and dread. He had served as the conduit to her current freedom, and yet he was a holdover from her life as the wife of Edward Pryce. The fact that she no longer considered herself his wife was the foundation of her current sense of awareness. And here was Mercury, his prize horse.

"What should I do with him?" she asked William, hoping he would have the answer.

"If you want to take him, we could put him on the train and the boat. But that would be expensive. And difficult for him."

"Would he be valuable to us in Brazil?"

"It would be cheaper to buy a horse there."

She stroked Mercury's nose; he nuzzled her and stomped his front hoof. "I can't give him to anyone here. He might be recognized. Do you know someone who can take him back to Edward? Someone who won't be identified?"

"We can find someone."

"I'd better let him go, then, hadn't I?"

"I think that's the best choice, Adam."

They took him back to the meeting hall, where William had gathered his supplies for the journey. "I'd give him to you," Ada told Esau, "but you might be accused of stealing him."

She was surprised by how difficult it was to say goodbye to the horse. There was an instant in which she felt she would fall into the abyss of her guilt and would be unable to walk away from him. She had suffered no such pang over leaving her husband. Why was that? Perhaps the accusations were true: she was an hysteric, and this ridiculous fondness she felt for Mercury was more proof of the fact. Finally, she kissed his nose, then hurried back into the hall. He whinnied softly, but she didn't turn to look at him again. The final remnant of her former life was behind her now. And she and William had a train to catch.

Esau and William loaded his steamer trunk and Ada's carpetbag into the back of the carriage, and Esau drove them to the station.

WILLIAM WASN'T ALLOWED to sit with Ada on the train. Ada saw no reason to sit alone in the whites-only section of the train. She had just lived with an African family for three days. That real-life experience had made these artificial barriers between the races seem even more absurd than they had when she considered them in the abstract. "I want to go with you, William," she said.

"Now, why stir up notice, Adam? Just go sit with the white folks, please."

"I don't want to."

"But you should. If you come with me, people will notice us. Someone may start thinking, and put two and two together when they hear you're missing. It's dangerous."

The thought of sitting alone, pretending to be a man, all the way to New York filled her with dread. She couldn't even take off her hat. She promised herself she would cut her hair the minute she had a room and a pair of scissors.

The train wasn't crowded. No one sat in the seat next to her. She set down her bag in the empty seat and stretched her legs. The sensation of moving her legs freely was still new to Ada. It thrilled her to be able to cross her right calf up and over her left knee. The position was so easy on the spine. But the most stunning thing about it was the sensation of openness around her groin. With all the petticoats and layers of underwear gone, with just the long underwear and the trousers between her private womanly parts and the outside world, she felt oddly in control of her own body. She crossed and uncrossed her legs, stretched them out in a V in front of her, even threw one over the arm of the seat at one point. This was bliss.

When she finally tired of playing with her legs, she spent the remaining hours on the train reading *Moby-Dick*. She had never read the book, but she had heard the first line repeated often enough. Who hadn't? She read it now. "Call me Ishmael," it commanded the reader. Why not "My name is Ishmael"? she wondered. I shall call you Ishmael, she thought, but what is your name really? Was he in hiding, like her? The book was dense; when she tired of it she looked out the window. As the bits of landscape flew past her, she felt an inexplicable desire to examine and make herself part of each of those locales they passed over so quickly. She wanted to bring a piece of those places with her. She hadn't considered any such thing when she was on her European tour. But now she couldn't say whether the difference was in the places, or in the fact that Edward had been at her side everywhere she visited in Europe. Her experience of movement across geographical boundaries was altered by the fact that she was on her own. She felt the power of the steel machine she rode in, and listened to the rhythm of its glide across the land. This slipping from one place to the next, from one gender to the next, from one way of living to the next, was a rearrangement of her self. But it was a realignment that was still in process, so she had no idea who she would become in the end.

They arrived at New York's Grand Central Depot that evening. Ada hadn't been here since her honeymoon. The crush of people surprised her; just standing there shot her through with energy, as if she had devoured the strongest of the famous elixirs hawked in every newspaper and magazine across the Eastern seaboard. She stared up at the high ceiling, and the light coming through the hundreds of windowpanes. She almost forgot to look for William. But as the sun began to slip down and the light in the depot dimmed, she panicked when she remembered she was alone here except for William, and that she had no idea where she was going.

She found him walking up and down the platform, searching for her. She hurried toward him. "Where do we go now?"

"You have placed a great deal of faith in me, haven't you?"

"Well, I've never done this before, as you may know." For an instant it occurred to her that, despite his position in society, between them William's life had been lived with greater access to variety and choice than had hers. At least until now.

"Jao is meeting us in front of the station."

He was there, with a rented carriage. Ada had not seen this man since the evening of her dinner party. Now he stood, in the early winter twilight, his dark face reflecting a bit of the lingering orange of the sun. Evidently he knew the young man traveling with William was really the Mrs. Pryce of the dinner party. He took her hand when he saw her as he would a woman's, not shaking it, but holding her gloved fingertips and looking at her hand as though he might kiss it. Suddenly uncomfortable, she pulled her hand away from his.

After the two men had thrown the luggage into the carriage, Ada asked again, "Where are we going?"

"Please, get in. It's cold," Jao said. His voice had soothed her at the party, she remembered. But now it seemed somehow ominous. She realized she knew nothing about this man whom she had agreed to join forces with, to whom she would be entrusting the only money she had on earth.

Ada climbed up into the seat of the open carriage. Her hands were cold, in spite of the gloves, and her face felt numb. There was no snow on the ground yet, but the air felt thick with its potential. No one spoke during the ride along Fifth Avenue. The carriage wheels were too loud against the bricks, the air too chilly, Ada and William too tired. Ada didn't worry about the silence; instead, she watched the New York streets and the people who filled them. Could there really be so many people in one place, or was she suffering from exhaustion and imagining them all? They hurried across the street in front of the carriage, behind it, alongside. Children played on the sidewalks, unmindful of the cold; people hawked linens and meats, hats and boots; Ada thought she even saw a prostitute or two. Horses, carriages, and streetcars battled on the streets. The place stank of horse shit.

Jao steered the carriage off Fifth Avenue, down a side street, and then into a narrow alley, barely wide enough for the carriage to fit through. Dirty brick buildings lined both sides of the street. Overhead, running across the alley between the buildings, hung line after line of laundry, like a strange gathering of tired spirits, hovering over the unfortunate, too spent to take action. They pulled up in front of one of the blackened buildings.

An African mother and child stopped to observe the newcomers. They watched the carriage without any sense of curiosity. Their sadness seemed to hold them in place as they gazed at the activity listlessly. "We have rooms here," Jao said as he unloaded the bags. "For five days."

Ada picked up her bag and followed the men into the building. Five days, she thought. Would she be able to bear this place for five days? She longed to be back in the parlor with Harriet, Juliet, and Felicity, practicing her walk, listening to Juliet play the piano, even listening to the women argue.

They walked up a narrow and tilting staircase to the third floor. William and Jao would share a room, Ada had her own room across the hall. Jao left them in order to return the carriage. Ada watched William disappear inside his room before she opened her own door. She almost wished she could sleep with the men. She would feel safer in their company. Her room was small, low-ceilinged, and cold. The bed was narrow. Next to it was a rickety wooden table and a straight-backed chair. The floor was stained and without even a single rug to warm it. A wood-burning stove stood in the corner, but there were only half a dozen logs in the bin. Would they give her more in the morning, or would she have to ration these?

She picked up a log and put it into the stove. In that instant she became aware that she had never, not once in her entire life, actually built a fire. But she had watched servants do it thousands of times, hadn't she? She knew she needed kindling. There were rolls of brown paper in the bin, and a box of lucifers. She stuffed some of the paper under the log, struck the lucifer, and held it to the paper. A rush of wind shot from the window and aimed directly for the light, blowing it out.

Ada struggled with the fire for ten minutes before it was finally lit. Her hands were so cold she could hardly bend her fingers. The bed was far from the stove, and too close to the window; she couldn't imagine sleeping in it. The heat her fire gave off was thin. Ada pulled the blanket off the bed. Wrapping it around herself, she settled down for a night on the floor. With Ada's money, they could have afforded a nicer room, but a better establishment wouldn't take in William and Jao.

In the middle of the night, she woke. The fire was out, her face and ears were stinging with the cold. Her body hurt from the pressure of the floor, and it vibrated with shivers. She got her overcoat from the chair and put it over her blanket, then tried to sleep again. But the shivering did not stop. It made her angry. How would she survive sleeping out in the jungle if she couldn't brave a single night in a room without a fire? At last, she got up and struggled until she had lit another log. The crackling of the fire lulled her to sleep quickly. She dreamed of Mercury, and of Harriet, Juliet, and Felicity. She even dreamed of an orchid or two. But there was nothing in her dreams to remind her of Edward.

The cold woke her yet again just before sunrise. Her bladder was full; she relieved herself in the chamber pot. The odor of urine filled the room. Huddled in her overcoat, shivering still, she waited almost an hour to walk across the hall and knock on the men's door.

"Who's there?" Jao shouted through the door.

Ada dropped her voice as low as she could manage. "Me, Adam," she said.

A bit of quick shuffling about preceded the opening of the door. William stood there, in his pants and undershirt. "Is something wrong?"

"No. Just . . . It's just that, well, my room is like an icebox, and I don't have much firewood."

"Meu Deus," she heard from the bed by the window. Jao's hand reached out, pulling the covers up tightly over his head.

"I just wondered if you had extra firewood?"

"Adam," William said. It was obvious he was trying not to be impatient with her. "We can get more wood from the landlord. Twenty-five cents."

"Oh, thank you." Ada stood there for a moment. She half expected William to pull on his shirt and go down to get her the wood. She had been waited on her entire life, after all. But she only entertained the thought for an instant. She could read his face well enough by now to know that he expected her to take care of herself. "Where is the landlord at this time of morning?"

"His room is on the first floor. Right by the front door. He won't be happy to see you this early, though."

Ada went back to her room and lit a fire using all of the remaining logs. She sat on her bed reading until the fire burned low, then she put on her hat and took herself down to the landlord's room.

There was no answer to her knock. She knocked again, but still no response.

"Hello!" Still nothing. She reached her fingers inside her hat and scratched at her scalp. Her head warmed the tips of her fingers, making her aware of their stiffness, of the slow circulation of blood to her extremities. Why had she listened to William and waited to come down? Her head tilted toward the floor, and she was overwhelmed by a sensation of falling. She leaned into the wall, waiting for the strange vertigo to pass, then she took herself back upstairs.

Her fist on the door roused William again. "Adam. Would you like to come in?" He opened the door wide, but he remained standing in the center of it, blocking her entry. He didn't really want her to come in.

"Yes," Ada answered, pushing past him, forcing him to step aside for her. Jao sat on the edge of his bed. Both men wore long undershirts and trousers, but they didn't seem embarrassed that she should see them this way. Refusing to be embarrassed herself, she took the chair next to the small table, crossing her legs like a man as she settled into it. Her legs were colder than they had been when they were surrounded by so many yards of fabric, but she still preferred the freedom of movement to the warmth. "I'd like to help plan. I expect to be included in the planning of this venture."

"See?" said Jao. "This is exactly what I was afraid of."

Ada felt the blood rise into her eyes, clouding her vision. "What is he talking about?" she asked William.

"He won't tell you. I will," Jao said. Ada tried to ignore the rhythm of his speech, to ward off the soothing quality of its tones. "We can't have a novice telling us what to do. This is difficult work. William and I have been doing it for a long time, and we know what we need to do to succeed. Your money doesn't make you an equal partner." He slapped his knee, then jumped up and began to pace the small room.

Ada stood, stepping right in front of him, blocking his path, forcing him to look at her. "I never said I would try to override your decisions. You two have veto power over me. I simply want to be included; I want my ideas to be considered."

"It's a reasonable position, Jao," said William.

"We've been arguing about this since we woke. We've nearly come to fisticuffs over you, Mrs. Pryce," Jao said.

"Adam," William corrected him.

"Adam, then. Adam! Whoever you are, you're not a professional orchid hunter."

Ada leaned in toward his face, taking a stance she'd seen many men take, but which she herself had never even attempted until this moment. "You had to start sometime, didn't you? Were you a professional the first time you went out?"

"All right, then, of course I wasn't. But tell me what you bring to this enterprise other than your money?"

"I bring a love of orchids. And a knowledge of them. I know how to identify them, how to care for them."

William stepped toward them both, forcing Ada to move back, cede space to Jao. "Listen, Jao," William said. "For now that's enough. It's more than we have a right to ask for. We'll reassess later, but now we need to press on. We can't afford to get caught up in petty differences."

"But the woman is a liability, William. She has run away from a powerful man in our business. A powerful man who is also a party to murder. What's to happen to us if he finds out she's with us?"

Again the sense of responsibility and guilt settled over her like a heavy blanket. Perhaps the familiar sensation even comforted her in the same way a blanket did. She felt safe, at home, well rested, when she accepted guilt. Pulling it even tighter around her, she turned to Jao, daring him to come into the warmth with her.

"You've already gone too far. If I were to go back now, what would stop me from claiming you kidnapped me?"

William melted down onto his bed, put his face into his hands. "Just as I feared," Jao said to William. "Didn't I tell you it would come to something like this?"

"You must understand, I am desperate." She felt cornered. "I can't go back to my husband. If you send me back to him, I can't be responsible for what will happen, for what I will say. But if you take me with you, I will do anything to keep all three of us out of harm's way."

William lifted his face from his hands. "Let's just stop this nonsense and talk business."

"Fine. But mark my words, we shall reassess. If anything goes awry due to this woman, all agreements are off." Jao dropped himself onto his hard bed. He studied her for a moment, then said, "And you won't convince anyone that you're a man."

A surge of anger lifted itself from her gut. His lack of confidence in her ability to perform made her angrier than anything else he had said to her. It would satisfy her to pull rank on him now, to call him what he was, an adventurer whose very existence depended on those who were more successful than he. She could taste the words; they were bitter and she wanted to spit them out at him. But instead, she spoke in a steady voice. "I'll work on that. And in the meantime, you should tell me what we need to do to prepare, and what investments we need to make while we're here."

The two men looked at each other. Both their faces wore that I-told-you-so expression, but each had a different story behind it. Jao believed she would be a liability, and William, perhaps, had already determined that she was stubborn. Perhaps he even believed in her worth. Ada didn't ask, nor did she comment on their coded communication. Instead, she requested paper and pen and set out to help organize the endeavor.

"I've kept books for a large household. Certainly I can do it for us. Tell me what we need, and what you think it will cost."

William brought her the writing supplies, then reeled off the list to her.

"We need a good medical kit. We need a couple of machetes, burlap bags for collecting the plants, packs to carry our supplies on a mule, sleeping bags, lamps, a camp stove. We already have a good tent, good, thick canvas. And we have the best maps around, don't we, Jao?" Jao nodded and shrugged at the same time. "Most of the other supplies we'll get there."

As Ada wrote up the list, Jao tried to estimate the expense of each item. "I'd think we need at least seventy-five dollars," he said.

"And seventy-five dollars we have," she said.

"The other thing we have to do while we're here," Jao said, "is try to get some orders before we go."

It was a simple idea, an obvious one, but somehow Ada had never thought about the concept of pre-selling the plants. That one detail made the whole prospect seem out of her reach. It sent a small bubble of panic rising up in her chest. "Is that the way you always do it?"

"That's the way the people who are in the business of selling orchids do it," Jao said. "The difference between what we did before and what we're about to do is that we're not just going down there to look for some rare specimens for a few rich collectors. Those collectors could afford to make it worth our while to find plants just for them. But now we're on our own."

"That's right," William said. "We have to make it worth our while."

The bubble in her chest grew bigger, threatening to cut off her air supply. "So how do we find people to place orders?"

"We knock on doors of likely buyers. That's why we're here for five days," William told her.

"Oh. I see." It wasn't that she assumed the buyers for their orchids would appear like apparitions and make away with the plants, leaving trails of money behind them. The problem was, she had never thought about it at all before this morning, sitting in this cold rooming house with two men who were really strangers to her.

"You'll come with us, learn the ropes," said William.

Jao's eyes widened, but he kept his mouth closed.

The three of them put on their best clothes. Ada wore her only wool sack suit, with overcoat, both from William's sister's shop. But as she stuffed her hair up under her hat, she remembered Jao's doubts about her ability to pull off this charade. She went back to William and Jao's room, to borrow a pair of scissors from them. William managed to find a pair in his trunk, but just as Ada was ready to go back to her own room with them, William offered to cut her hair for her. Ada removed her coat, and William draped a towel around her shoulders. First, he cut off most of the length of her hair in large clumps. Jao watched from his bed, as if the process were somehow important and required an observer, but he never spoke.

Ada felt a lightening in her shoulders and neck as the hair came off. One more thing that made it easier for men to be in their bodies, she thought. Once her hair was above her shoulders, William set to work cutting her hair the way he cut the hair of men in the jungle who had grown tired of wearing it long. There was no mirror, so Ada couldn't scrutinize his work, but her head felt free the instant her hair was gone. The haircut seemed to be yet another unsettling of her sense of self. First, she had divested herself of the familiar corset. Then she had traded yards of skirt for the simplicity of trousers. Now she had freed herself from the weight of her hair. All these things together had been essential to her physical identity. Their loss, in this continuous thread between Boston and New York, made her feel at once more autonomous and more anonymous.

When William finished his work, he stepped back and looked at her. "I'll be damned," he said, and then he whistled.

"What is it?" Ada asked, touching her hair.

"I never would have thought it possible, but you do look like a boy." William looked over to Jao for his approval. Jao nodded his head so subtly, Ada wasn't sure he had responded at all.

She jumped up and went to the window. The brick building directly across the alley made the window dark enough for her to see a washed-out rendering of her head. It did look boyish, with the hair ending below her ears, and low on her neck. The shape was passable. Now she was free to remove her hat in public. That was something, wasn't it? She took no time to mourn the loss of her beautiful hair. She turned to the two men, smiling, and she was certain Jao even smiled back for the briefest moment.

They went together to a posh building on Fifth Avenue, where they were ushered into the third-floor office of a Mr. Hiram Robinson. Ada never did learn what his business was, but if the décor in his offices was any indication, he was a man with a great deal of money. She recognized the furniture and the objets d'art. They were of a quality that every one of her female acquaintances in Boston would have lusted after. But as Ada sat in the Chinese bentwood chair, she felt herself physically separating from the world in which this mattered. She sat in it lightly, as if she was struggling to leave no mark on it, or to keep it from marking her. This chair was the signifier of the things that could cut into her, flay her even, leaving her too exposed to survive.

William and Jao did all the talking. Ada observed them closely, determined to learn enough to make a valuable contribution in the next meeting. Hiram Robinson was big, with a voice to match his size. It boomed out into the room and bounced off the walls. "Well, well, tell me, boys, how can you guarantee me that you'll bring back the plants I order?"

"We have a special offer, just for you, as we know you to be a connoisseur of orchids."

"Well, go on, then, don't leave me hanging," Robinson bellowed at them.

William took over now. The two men spoke as a tag team, first one, then the other, throughout the rest of the meeting. Ada's head moved from one to the other as she listened. "Instead of the usual fifty percent advance, we ask only twenty-five percent. We can do this because we have financial backing for most of the trip. We promise we'll bring you orchids that you will be proud to sell, or keep for your collection."

Robinson leaned across his desk toward them. He included Ada in his gaze, making her feel as if she had a right to be in his office. She wondered how they looked to him, this African man, the dark-skinned South

American, and the skinny green-looking boy who seemed unable to speak. Certainly they didn't present the image of a high-powered business triumvirate. "I know you boys. Well, at least I know the two of you," he said to William and Jao. "I know you know what you're doing. But twenty-five percent, if you fail, is a one-hundred-percent loss for me of whatever I might advance to you."

"How could we fail completely? Why would that happen?" asked Jao.

"I can think of lots of ways. An earthquake down there. An outbreak of cholera. A fall down a mountain." Ada watched Jao and William, wondering if they would react to this. But both remained silent, fixed in their chairs. "Why, hell, you could meet pirates on the high seas. These things are always risky. I want to think about it. Come back tomorrow."

There was a thin but chilly wind cutting down Fifth Avenue. Ada's overcoat wasn't warm enough. She wanted to go back to her room. But she didn't have any wood for her stove. What if she couldn't get any?

"Okay," said William. "Next one is on Twentieth. We can walk."

"Why don't we just take a trolley?" Ada asked. She knew the instant the words were out of her mouth how ridiculous she sounded.

William seemed tired when he answered her, as if her question had drained all the energy from him. "They might not let us on, Adam."

The rest of the way to the meeting Ada just listened as Jao and William strategized. The second office was in a brownstone. It wasn't as grand or richly appointed as Mr. Robinson's, but it did, nonetheless, exemplify success and wealth. The man who met them there, an older, narrow gentleman with wisps of white hair on his mottled head, dismissed them inside of five minutes. Ada regretted only that she couldn't stay in front of the undulating, licking flames in his fireplace.

Outside again, Ada's feet hurt; there were blisters forming on her heels. Now, in addition to being cold, she was hungry as well. "I'm famished," she said. "Can't we stop to eat?"

"Not here," Jao said. "We'll have to go back down near the rooming house."

Of course. They wouldn't be able to sit down in a tea shop, either. "It's not like this in South America. If you have money, you can go anywhere,"

William told her. He didn't seem angry at her naivete. Perhaps he understood that it wasn't her fault that she didn't understand. But Ada was irritated with herself. How could she have been so stupid two times in a row? She knew Africans weren't allowed to mingle with white society, that they weren't able to patronize the places she could walk into without a second thought. How could she forget so easily? Maybe if she had been more committed to suffrage, she would have been more thoughtful now.

She found herself thinking of Margery and the Blackwell sisters. What would they think if they saw her dressed as a man, heading for the jungles of another continent? The very idea of their learning about her subversive behavior warmed her a bit.

They stopped for tea in a basement shop off Fifth Avenue. The room was warm, its small windows opaqued with the steam rising off the bodies inside. The place was crowded, the clientele mostly African or poor European immigrants. The three found a small table in the back and ordered beef stew and bread. "And please, make my tea strong," Ada said to the waitress.

The waitress was young but tired-looking; the hair that had escaped her white cap was damp and clung to her pale cheeks. But when Ada spoke, suddenly the waitress's head lifted and her eyes widened. "Of course. Sir?" She raised her eyebrows as she stretched out the word *sir*, turning it into a question, and the corners of her mouth lifted into a sort of smirk. Ada looked across the table to William for help. William just shrugged his shoulders at her. She felt utterly dejected.

The waitress left, and William and Jao spoke to each other, but Ada didn't hear what they said. Instead, she fretted silently over her failure. But conversation ceased between the men when their food was dropped onto their table. When the waitress set her bowl down, she whispered so that only Ada could hear. "There you are, ma'am." She seemed to get some sort of satisfaction from letting Ada know that she was on to her scheme. The waitress sauntered away, pleased with herself. Ada looked out the window and watched the feet of the many passersby. What was she doing here? She had been mad to believe she could ever pull this thing off.

The stew's aroma reached her then, and her hunger poked at her. She dug her spoon into the brown mess. The first bite of food caused Ada to forget about the incident with the waitress. This was the most sublime meal she had experienced in her life. No one could have told her that it was simply her hunger and exhaustion that infused the food with textures and tastes that surpassed those of the finest restaurants in Europe and America.

She remembered the stew that night when she lay in her bed, her stomach starting to make its emptiness known to her again. When they returned, Ada had stopped by the landlord's and bought a bundle of wood. Her room was warm now, so there was no need to make her bed on the floor. Her trousers and jacket were draped over the back of the chair at the foot of her bed. As she gazed on them, she suddenly wondered what Frederick would think if he saw her now, dressed as a man and living in this barren room. Forgetting the dismal reunion she had had with him at his offices, she imagined now the skim of his soft fingers across her thigh, like an artist's brush, filling in the shape and color that made her real as he touched her surfaces. During their months together, when she didn't see him—sometimes for days at a stretch—she felt insubstantial, and the life that she lived without him seemed no more than a charade. And Moira's intense reaction to the affair had made Ada's life away from Frederick seem even more unreal.

MOIRA HAD BEEN ANGRY about Ada's relationship with Frederick. She insisted, for as long as the affair lasted, that her anger was only because the affair had changed the dynamic within the group of students. "We can't see you as our equal now," Moira had said. "Not really. You are in league with the professor. And in some way, he is the enemy. Just as parents are the enemy to groups of children."

"Oh, Moira, please, don't be absurd. I am still the same Ada."

But she knew she wasn't. It was necessary for her, if she was to see Frederick, to alter her schedule on short notice. During the times when she and Moira used to walk through the Common and stop for tea, Ada would now rush home and wait for a message from her lover, asking her to meet him. Eventually, their friends stopped referring to them as Moida. Whenever Frederick came up in conversation, the talk of him was stilted, dead-ending before it gained any momentum. They couldn't complain about their professor; his lover was their pal.

Over the Easter holidays, Moira invited the crew to Redruth again. Not knowing whether Frederick would be able to get away, Ada didn't respond to her invitation immediately. Moira pushed her to give an answer. Finally, Frederick agreed to go for one night only, and Moira convinced Ada that she should stay the entire five days.

"It doesn't help his image of you if you are forever dropping everything to be with him. Men don't like that in a woman," Moira told her.

Maybe her friend was right; perhaps she would make Frederick run from her if she continued chasing him. But she was happy at Redruth when he was there with her, and as soon as he left she felt like a ghost of herself. Her body was simply an apparition, left behind, waiting to catch up with the animating force supplied to her when her lover was in the vicinity.

Interactions with her friends were listless. She forgot to listen when they were talking, she lost the thread of conversations, the point of games, the order of the days. At night, she couldn't sleep. Redruth was alive with memory triggers. Outside her door (the same room she had slept in last time) was the spot where Frederick told her good night that first time they were alone together. The patio beneath her window was where she discovered him; from there they walked to the beach together and made love for the first time. There were traces of him everywhere, in every room, on every surface, on every bit of ground.

One night she lifted herself from her sleepless bed and went outside to be in the place where they had first talked. She heard voices coming from the patio before she saw the narrow light. Something urged her forward. Perhaps it was simply because she was nervy from lack of sleep and didn't know what else to do with herself. But she sneaked up on the voices, wanting to see who was out here, wanting to hear what they talked about. At the edge of the stone patio, she stood behind a small tree, peeking out from behind it. The lantern's glow reached out to caress the two faces hovering over it. Ada recognized Bayley and Ralph. Deciding to reveal herself, so that she would have someone to talk to, she stepped out from her hiding place.

But as she walked forward, they moved off the patio, toward the path to the ocean. As they walked, the lantern swinging its light up and down their bodies, Bayley slipped his arm into Ralph's, and Ralph rested his head on Bayley's shoulder. Their gestures were uncomplicated, familiar. Ada knew instantly that they were lovers, and that they had been for long enough to reach this level of comfort with each other. She turned back to the house, uncomfortable with the idea of disturbing their close orbit around each other.

Ada thought about the two men as she continued to struggle with wakefulness. Why had they always hidden their relationship from everyone? Ada was in an illicit relationship, and yet all her friends knew. Was it really so subversive to love another man? She understood that society didn't acknowledge this sort of coupling, but her own reaction to seeing it was not one of revulsion or judgment, so why would anyone else respond that way? Of course, she was younger then. Since, she had been married to a prominent member of society for four years. Edward never would have tolerated what Ada accepted so easily.

Hunger pangs woke her early the next morning; she went scrounging for food in the kitchen. Ralph and Bayley were there, at the table, their heads close together. The sun wrapped a halo around their hair, making their heads appear conjoined. When they sensed Ada watching them, they abruptly, guiltily, pulled apart.

"Oh, you two, you don't need to do that for my sake. Go right ahead."

"What ever are you on about?" Bayley asked her.

"I know what's going on between you two. And I don't care, so don't worry about me."

Ralph leveled his gaze at her. "What's going on between us, then?"

"Same thing that's going on between Frederick and me. Illicit romance."

The two young men stiffened, failing to see the lightness of Ada's intentions. She sat down with them and put a hand on each of them, caressing their arms as she spoke. "I think you make a lovely pair."

"We just came down to eat. Happened to be up at the same time," Bayley said. "I almost tripped on him on the stairs, I was so groggy."

"Would you like some bread pudding?" Ralph held up his bowl to her. "It's delicious."

"I'm just going to make some tea." Ada went to the stove. She felt relaxed in this house without servants. Even though it meant extra work, it also meant a sort of freedom to say and do whatever she wanted without fear of word getting back to anyone through the household help grapevine. Taking care of her own needs the times she did stay at Redruth gave her the false sense that she actually understood what it was to take care of herself in the world.

SHE COULD SEE clearly now, from her thin, hard bed in Manhattan, how naive she had been. And how she had created a sense of self grounded in her sense of sexuality. Even with Bayley and Ralph, she exuded an awareness, a tolerance, a hunger that centered on sex. Now there was no object for her desire, and there were no couples she could involve herself with as a stand-in for her own sexual activity. Most of all, there was no one to take care of her. There was nothing. Just the running from an old Ada, and toward an unknown and untried Ada.

They were to visit three more offices. Alone in her room, before leaving for the first meeting that morning, Ada practiced speaking in a deep voice. "Pleased to meet you," or "It's been a pleasure," or "Good to do business with you, sir." She held her stomach and laughed a man's laugh. She said the lines and laughed over and over until her throat was tight and her voice hoarse. By the time they set out for their appointments, Ada looked forward to speaking, as a man, in the meetings. But they were ushered out of the first office before she got her chance. The second stop was in the office of Hans Jansson, on Twenty-sixth Street. His office was opulent, even compared to Robinson's. It seemed to take forever to walk from his doorway across the Chinese silk rugs to sit in the chairs in front of his desk. The desk itself was a good ten feet long and five feet wide, of a highly polished, inlaid teak. The fireplace took up one entire wall; its mantel was ornate marble with carved dragons climbing up the sides.

The three partners sat before the great man, who was of medium height and build, with thick black hair. Ada was surprised to look into a face that wasn't much older than her own. He seemed imperious beyond his years.

"Describe your enterprise, and tell me how I can profit from it," he ordered. Jao launched into the speech that Ada had memorized by now. There was little variation. She noticed Jansson's eyes glazing over. He was no longer listening. Ada suddenly imagined herself, a year from now, her money gone, living in the rooming house off Fifth Avenue. She was out of her chair, pacing the rug in front of Jansson, before she had given herself a chance to plan what she would say.

She pushed her voice down so that it came from deep in her belly. She felt it rumble up and out of her throat. "The thing is, Mr. Jansson"—she imagined that her voice must be definite enough to cut through solid obstructions in order to be heard—"orchids have a unique ability to inspire something in all of us. They offer us insight into the ancient ways of the earth, they suggest intelligence, and they hint at romance and even sexuality." Her voice began to lift in her excitement; she stopped to breathe, pushing it down again. "What man of means cannot understand the thrill of collecting a rare genus of orchid? And what woman doesn't desire to be given a rare orchid by her lover? The difference between us and many of the other hunters is that we love and understand orchids. We involve our hearts in the hunt." When she stopped to look around her, pulling her focus away from whatever had driven her to jump up and start talking, she saw three silent, dumbfounded men staring at her, immobile.

Ada sat. And waited.

William and Jao were waiting, too, evidently unsure of whether their ersatz client would be pleased or displeased with Ada's performance, whether or not he would see through her disguise.

"Well, Mr. Wilson," Jansson finally said. There was no note of irony in his pronunciation of the word *mister.* Ada let out the breath she had been holding. She had done it! "I have a mind to place an order with you and your fellows here."

They walked out with an order for one thousand and one of the best orchids they might find.

"Why the extra orchid?" Jao had asked him.

"After the one thousand and one Arabian nights, of course. We might as well add a bit of romance to the deal."

This was the last man Ada would have thought to be romantic. But she had sensed something in him, something that made her stand up and speak as a businessman for the first time. When they reached the street, William and Jao clapped her on the back and exclaimed over her performance.

"You were superb, Mr. Wilson," William told her. Jao nodded his head in agreement, and Ada felt a sense of accomplishment that was unfamiliar to her.

They returned to Hiram Robinson's office the next day. He seemed surprised to see them, as if he didn't remember their ever having been there. When they reminded him, he invited them to sit at his desk. He was on the edge of his chair, as if he expected to stand up again at any moment. His big voice took over the room. "Well, what do you have to say for yourselves?"

William spoke. "Hans Jansson ordered one thousand and one plants from us. He gave us twenty-five percent in advance."

Robinson leaned back in his chair and sighed as he looked up at the high ceiling. "That son of a bitch!" He opened a drawer, rifled through some papers. Finally, he came out with a bank check. "All right. Two thousand, then. Two thousand plants that are better that Jansson's!" He handed the check to William. "And that's a fifty percent deposit. So you'll give me preference over your other clients. Remember that. I gave you fifty percent!"

They now had more than enough money to travel through South America, find the plants for Jansson and Robinson, and stay to gather plants they would barter to other dealers. They could go on for a full year with what they had. But of course, they would have to deliver the flowers, or they would be out of business.

"The funny thing about it," William said as they ate dinner together near the rooming house, "is that neither of those men is an orchid dealer. They're both collectors, indeed. But they have never tried to turn a profit off the plants before."

"Well, they both have a nose for money," said Jao.

"Neither one of them would have backed us if Adam hadn't convinced Jansson, though. That was a work of art, young man." William clapped Ada's back again, just the way he would with any man. She was starting to believe that he actually saw her as a man now, somehow. It made her feel unsettled, sexless. Since the age of fifteen or so, she had been preening and priming herself for the attentions of men. But now she was one of them, and the men around her saw her as one of them.

Jao looked at her now, nodded his head slightly, and even smiled. "Nice work."

All in a moment, the shifting secret world of men had opened up to her, and the life of skirts and corsets, of babies, of melting under the heat of a man's touch, and of static domestic spaces was now a jumbled memory.

WRITTEN *in* WATER

They were on board the steamship *Voltaire*, bound for Southampton, England, early the next morning. There was a direct sailing, but they would have had to wait another ten days for that one. The *Voltaire* would get them there sooner. Ada purchased second-class passage for herself, so that she wouldn't be thrown into a room with a half dozen other men, and steerage for William and Jao, because William wasn't allowed to travel second class, and although Jao could have, his dark skin would have drawn undue attention anywhere other than steerage. The trip was uncomfortable, they were cramped and not well served, the food was inferior. But the company was raucous. Not even in her college days had Ada experienced the sorts of abandoned pleasure-seeking that was common during the six days of their Atlantic crossing.

William and Jao's shared room was narrow, with no windows. The bunks, slim wooden platforms attached to the walls, were hard. Ada's own bed was hard; she woke every morning with sore hip bones and a stiff neck. But she had her own room, and it was clean enough, with a lock on the door. It was more than could be claimed by many of the passengers in third class. She was lucky, she knew.

Her small cabin was in the fore of the ship, the section reserved for single men. The ship maintained a strict separation between the sexes in first and second class. This separation was more difficult to control in steerage. In these close quarters, Ada's presentation of herself as male became crucial. But it was pure performance. And in the act, she found all of the socially accepted definitions of gender became slippery. It was difficult at times for her to grasp who she was outside the trousers and the shorn hair, the falsely lowered voice and the manufactured swagger. At all times, no matter what the setting, she was beyond the male sexual gaze.

On her bed the first night, under the thin blanket, wearing only her cotton drawers, she reached to her groin to relieve an itch. She half expected to find something there, a new appendage in place, as her fingers dug into the space between her legs. Instead, she discovered her monthly had begun. She rummaged in her bag for a rag, wishing she could discard this curse along with her corsets and gowns.

Ada spent afternoons in the third-class smoking lounge. She learned to smoke cigars only so no one would notice she didn't smoke. And as she smoked, she listened. The conversations were offensive, thrilling, sometimes even boring. But she wanted to hear every word, to make up for a lifetime of having been denied the company of men.

Jeffrey Stipes, a young man from New York who was on his way to South America as well, befriended Ada, believing her to be, apparently, a man of his age and class. His eyes and hair reflected the dark moods of the sea. His hands were big and rough. She realized, the night she met him, that she was watching his face too intently, and that he might think her odd. Did men look at one another this way? She gazed around the smoky room, at all the small hoverings of men, and at the larger groups. They talked and joked, boasted, even sang songs. But their eyes never lingered on another man's eyes for very long; they jumped from one to another, each checking to make sure every other man was hearing him out. They demanded, with their eyes, the audience they were certain they deserved. Why didn't women know how to look at others with such determination?

She practiced the look herself, trying it first on Jeffrey, then on William and Jao. Jutting her chin out, puffing up her chest, she swept her eyes from man to man, resting on each of them for two heartbeats, then she spoke.

While Jeffrey sat with them at their table in the smoking room, she was nearly silent, afraid that her voice might reveal her femininity. But as soon as he left, she wanted to talk. "I'm going to shoot myself an alligator. That's the first thing I intend to do when we set foot on South American soil." She had never considered doing any such thing until this very moment. But she was proud of herself for having come out with such a manly remark. "I hear alligator meat is good eating."

William snorted. "Last time I checked, you didn't even know how to hold a gun."

"I'm eager to learn, though. That's what's important." Jeffrey reappeared then, and her voice threatened to rise to its most feminine register, but she fought it down with the surfaces of her manhood—her wide-positioned feet on the floor, her slim trousers, the flat heel of her boot.

"Hell, I'll give you a lesson when we get to the jungle," Jeffrey said. He sucked on his cigar, then blew out a perfect ring of smoke. Ada watched the circle as it floated up and spread out, finally thinning into a line and stretching toward the other side of the room. She pointed her chin at him in response, in recognition of his offer. She would practice blowing smoke rings tonight in her berth.

But later, when she went to her berth at last, she decided against the cigar. There had been too much smoking and drinking; another cigar would be out of the question. Smoke rings could wait for another day. She slipped under the covers in her long underwear. The linens dragged across her nipples; the sweet incision stalled her in her purpose. As she bundled the bedclothes tightly around her for warmth, she tried to remember the touch of a man's hand on her skin. When a quick slip of a memory brought a patch of heat out on her thigh, she was certain the imprint was Frederick's, not her husband's. As she drifted into sleep, she thought she could smell him in the bed with her.

The ship tilted, leaned toward the surface of the sea in the middle of the night, sending Ada into the wall. When she opened her eyes she saw nothing. Her window was small, and the moon, she knew, was narrow tonight.

The absence of any sort of light made her claustrophobic. She needed to get out into the open air, to see a sliver of moon. She lay in her berth, immobile, angry at the dark, for quite some time before it occurred to her that she could get up and walk the decks without fear; she was a man now. Her legs were inside her trousers, her arms secure in her jacket, in seconds. Out on the lower deck, a smattering of lamps still burned, and a few men strolled about, alone and in groups of two or three.

The water was as smooth as a freshly made bed now, crisp and unruffled. The new moon shot a slant of light out across a section of the black water. Ada nodded at the men who passed her, but didn't trust herself to speak. Her voice would come out too high, she was sure. She leaned over the railing and looked into the dark waters as they slipped around the hull of the ship. Mesmer might have done as well with this as a means to hypnotize hysterical women as he did with his glass harmonica.

Ada heard her name then, her new name, as if from deep inside a trance.

"I say, Adam."

She turned to face Jeffrey. The extra thumping of her heart that was so strangely out of time was surely just a symptom of her sleeplessness.

"Did the bump in the night wake you, too?"

"Well, old chap," Ada said, in her deepest voice, clapping Jeffrey's back as she spoke, "it did at that. I thought a spin around the deck might help me get back to sleep."

"Oh, why bother with sleep? It's a splendid night. Look at the stars."

Ada checked her speech, delaying her responses in an effort to choose the kinds of words men preferred. Would a man look up at the stars and gush over their loveliness, or would he pronounce them jolly or even sporting? She settled on some good manly words, she thought. "There are quite a few more of them out here, aren't there?"

"I'll say. It's as if some scalawag of a god made off with the entire lot of them, from every last corner of the universe, and tossed them all here. Just for us to see," Jeffrey said.

Ada had to catch herself as she leaned in toward him. She wanted nothing more than to touch her sleeve to his, to feel the warmth emanating from inside his jacket, out into the ethers that lingered between the two of them. A star shot across the sky, its tail extending out behind it for long seconds, silencing them.

As Jeffrey gazed up, Ada marveled that he could be so unaware of the charge he gave off. Finally, he disturbed the silence between them. "The Dog Star is fine tonight."

"Dog Star?"

"Sirius. The brightest star in the sky. Sirius was one of Orion's dogs." Jeffrey filled his lungs. Ada watched his face change as he did so. She thought she might be looking into the face of a contented man, a quality Jeffrey had not displayed until this moment. "The Dog Star guides the traveler. Wherever you go, there he is. Faithful, ever present."

Hoping to keep him talking, she nodded her head and mumbled a low "Mmm-hmm" as she continued to watch his face. Her voice floated past him and out over the water, merging there with the utterances of the sea, the noisy machinations of the ship.

"It's part of the constellation Canus Major. See there, just above it?" He pointed to the place he wanted her to see. But the sky was so big, and they were so laughably minute, his finger might have been pointing anywhere. She looked up, searching vainly for the spot.

"No, not there," he said. He took her face in between his hands and pointed it in the direction she needed to look. He lifted his finger again. "There."

"Oh, yes." Ada spoke slowly, keeping her voice trained down.

"That's Orion. See Orion's belt?"

"Yes. Yes."

"You'll get to know the constellations if you spend many nights sleeping out under them, mark my words, Adam."

Ada imagined herself sleeping under the stars, on the boundaries of a field of orchids. She would feel safe and perfectly contented with these two things—stars and orchids—if this man was there with her. Could she tell him now that she was a woman? What was the point in continuing the charade? No one here would recognize her, report back to her husband. They were out on the high seas now, out of harm's reach. She longed to tell him her name, to tell him to stop calling her Adam.

Allowing her voice to slip up a little, she spoke, testing him. "Will you come with us for a while, then, when we get to South America?"

He seemed not to notice the shifting tonality of her voice. "I may do that. For a few days, anyway. Depending on what happens between now and then."

Ada ventured a question, framing it not with her knowledge of how men talked about these things, but rather with the sense of vastness the universe offered to them now, as they stood at the ridge of it. Certainly the infinite nature of it would make her question seem small and easy to answer. "What are you looking for in South America?"

"Anything that's there."

"Well, what have you found there in the past?" Perhaps he refused to answer for the same reason that William and Jao ordered her to keep their mission vague. Orchid hunters never revealed their purpose, so that they would leave no trail for others who might be after the next big discovery.

But he answered this question. "I've gone after pearls. After rubber. Rubber's good. I've even been sent down to make astronomical observations. This time, I just don't know yet."

Maybe he was telling the truth. Ada felt suddenly tired. How was that possible, when she wanted nothing more than to be out here, standing next to Jeffrey?

He looked at her, and seemed to sense that she was tired. "I think I'll try to get back to sleep now. Have a good night, old chap."

Ada waited until she could no longer see his form in the dim light of the lamps, until she could no longer hear the clip of his boot heels against the deck, and then she returned to her cabin. She hardly remembered climbing back into her bed. She woke early the next morning, feeling strangely well rested.

But Jeffrey seemed to have disappeared from the ship. Ada didn't see him for the next two days. His absence allowed her time to consider her conversation with him on the deck. Why had she been so eager to declare her womanhood to him? What could she hope to have accomplished if she did such a thing? They needed to continue to be cautious. Edward knew many people; there was little doubt that he was searching for her, and she didn't want to be found.

Jeffrey next appeared one evening in the third-class smoking lounge. Jao and William were playing cards, gambling small amounts of money in a game that had grown fevered. Jao, Ada thought, was good at bluffing, his face never altering expression until the hand had been played out. She sat by, watching, smoking and drinking a thick ale. Ada was surprised by how easily she had taken to these masculine pastimes. She had never desired alcohol or cigars before, thinking they wouldn't agree with her constitution. Now she thought she understood why men were forever disappearing to their clubs and private rooms—so that they could indulge themselves in these blissful vices, unmolested by protesting women.

Jao lost a hand. As the winner pulled the coins across the table, Jao slammed his cards down and let out a guttural moan. All of his contained emotions flushed into his face, filling it with the markings of anxiety, anticipation, dread, hope. "Damnation! I'm down ten dollars!"

But William began to win. His face remained impassive, even though the stack of coins in front of him was growing, and everyone could see it.

Five men anted up for the next hand. Jao threw his cards down before drawing new ones. "I'm out." The words came with a metallic hardness to them, clanging about above the surface of the table. Ada looked away from him, tired, suddenly, of watching the men play. Her eyes drifted across the room at the precise moment that Jeffrey appeared in the doorway. The sudden unstable ticking of her heart infuriated her. She got up from her chair to pace the room, heading away from Jeffrey. With her back toward him, she imagined his eyes following her, his gaze searing itself into her neck, her shoulders and spine.

In that instant she forgot that the image she presented to Jeffrey was that of a man. She imagined that he saw her as a woman, wearing a dress, her long hair piled atop her head, her delicate nature on display. That was what he was seeing now, surely, and he was drawn to what he saw. Her hands grew moist. Reaching down to wipe them surreptitiously on her dress, she made contact with the rough linen of her trousers instead. It was this brief contact, the touch of her fingers on the gray fabric, that reminded her of how Jeffrey must really see her. She was a thin, somewhat short, too delicate young man who had little knowledge of the world. If Jeffrey did desire her, then he wanted to be with a man who wasn't quite a man, not with her.

Ada turned back toward the game table then. Jeffrey was sitting in her chair now. William was drawing in the coins from the center of the table, obviously having won again. Her spine stiffened, her chin jutted forward as she strode her roughest, longest stride back to join them. Standing behind William, she nodded her head at Jeffrey, doing her best representation of restrained interest. There was some commotion at the table now, but Ada saw only Jeffrey, who touched the brim of his hat in a salute to Ada. "Adam. Good to see you," he chirped. Like a bird that had just gorged on worms, she thought. Too contented. Had he found a woman to pass the time with? Is that why he had disappeared for two whole days?

A scraping of chair against floor and a shaking of the table forced Ada to finally take her attention from Jeffrey and look at the source of the noise. A small man in a cheap fancy suit stood in front of his chair, leaning over the table. "Who ever said a darkie could sit at this game?" He looked around the table, his eyes snapping at the other players. No one answered him. He pushed his chair till it fell to the floor, and walked around the table to face William.

"You shouldn't be playing this game. That means you shouldn't have my money there in front of you." He reached out and grabbed at William's coins. "Who wants their money back?" He held his full hand out to the others. The coins glinted there, mocking the losers at the table. "This nigger shouldn't even be on the ship. Who the hell let him on board?"

Ada wanted to jump up and hit the man, but she had never been in a physical fight in her life. He'd probably kill her. She looked toward Jeffrey, who sat silent, staring at the small man.

Jao leaned forward in his chair, settled his dark eyes on the man. "I think I lost fair and square. Maybe I'll just quit the game. Maybe you should, too, if you can't afford to lose any more."

"I can afford to play. Now that I have my money back. Soon as this low fellow leaves, we can all get back to the game." He peered at Jao then. "You look half nigger yourself. Maybe you both should leave."

Jeffrey picked up the deck of cards. "How about we all just settle down? I'll deal a hand."

Jao reached out and grabbed Jeffrey's wrist. "Not until this gallnipper returns the money he rightfully lost."

The small man pulled his right arm back and then let it fly straight into Jao's face so quickly, there was no time for Jao to duck or block him. William was out of his seat and had the man's arms twisted behind his back before Jao had a chance to take his hand from his jaw. At that instant, every man at the table was on his feet, helping either Jao and William or the angry little man. Two or three men from the game, and others from elsewhere in the parlor, came to help the small man, egging him on with shouts of "Go, Thomas," and "You can take him, Thomas." Ada watched the men brawl for a moment, her heart racing and her palms sweating.

But she found she could only watch for so long. Finally, the itch to join overcame her fear of getting hurt. She elbowed her way into the melee and jumped right onto Thomas's back as he swung at Jeffrey. She kicked and swung her fists, pulled at his hair, even bit his ear. She knew she was fighting like a woman, but she also knew this was how she could inflict the most harm on this horrid little man. In the end, he was subdued, and the rest of the men, seeing this, settled down.

"Now," Jao said to Thomas, "give the gentleman his winnings."

Ada stood over the instigator, her fists ready, threatening, as he released the coins onto the table in front of William.

Jeffrey took the cards up again. "Who wants a hand?" All of the men save the small one and Jao returned to their seats. "I think it's time for me to fold," Jao said.

"We have an open seat," Jeffrey said. "Anyone want to take it?" He looked around the room. Thomas walked away, muttering, surrounded by a handful of his defenders. Jeffrey's gaze settled on Ada. "What about you, Adam?" Jeffrey asked. "Are you a card player?"

Ada knew how to play whist and a few of the card games women played at dinner parties. She had never played a hand of poker, couldn't even remember whether Edward ever played it. All she knew about it was what she had gleaned from watching Jao. "Not much of one, no."

"Oh, come on, Adam. Give it a go," Jao said. He held out his seat for her. Ada's vision went blurry with anger. He knew she couldn't possibly know how to play poker. Why was he doing this to her?

"I'll pass." She managed to say it without raising her voice, without allowing a quiver of anger to enter.

Suddenly overtaken by claustrophobia, Ada walked away from the table. The air was too close, the cigar smoke floated around their heads, and the scent of men's bodies hung everywhere. She was already feeling sore from the fight, and her head began to pound. How could these men have a fight like the one they just had, and then simply return to their game? She wondered if, now that she was a man, she was expected to enjoy a good fight on a recurring basis.

The instant she pushed the doors open and smelled the sea air, she felt lighter. Her boot heels clicked across the wooden passageway, echoing. The vibrating hum of the steamer's engines rose through her feet and into her calves. She climbed the stairs to the deck, ignoring the ache in her shoulders as she pulled on the stair rail.

She was sick of men.

Out on the deck, groups of women walked together, or tended children together. These were working-class women, not the same kind of women Ada had known in Boston. As she watched them together, she imagined that their conversation would be more interesting than Emmy's or any of the other wives of Edward's friends and associates. These women might talk to her about their desires. They would probably think Karezza to be absurd.

Two young women walking toward Ada smiled and nodded at her. After they passed her, she heard them giggling. Were they making fun of her now, so soon after smiling at her so sweetly? Did they think her a silly specimen of a man? She turned to look at them and saw that one of them, the younger one, was looking back at her, too. She smiled at Ada again, and blushed.

One might suspect that it shamed Ada, or even distressed her, to realize that this young woman was flirting with her. But the truth of it was, it gave her an increased sense of power, and at the same time, it reminded her of Moira.

ONE WEEKEND, Frederick had promised Ada he would take her away for two full nights. He had reserved a room in a hotel in Salem—a place where they were unlikely to encounter anyone who knew them. She looked forward to the time with Frederick to the exclusion of anything else. It was as if there were nothing for her beyond that weekend. They would linger together in bed as long as they wished. They would stroll the town holding hands if they so desired. She could throw her arms around him without his having to reach up and remove them quickly, admonishing her for her show of affection. She would have two and a half days in which to share with him the thoughts that she now had to save up, the things she said to herself because she so rarely got to be with him for any extended period.

When she received the message, delivered to her at her mother's home, that he had to cancel the weekend, Ada's body turned to lead. She could hardly drag herself from one room to the other, she couldn't lift her head, her eyes were too heavy to keep open for any length of time. Her mother began to pester her.

"What's wrong with you? Should I send for the doctor?" Beatrice leaned over Ada, where she was sprawled on the sofa in her bedroom.

Ada spoke to the back of the sofa. "Please don't." The words weighed down her mouth as they passed through it. "I'm fine."

"If you're fine, then you need to get up. Do something. This just isn't acceptable."

Ada finally dressed herself to leave just to get away from her mother's concerns. It took so long to dress properly, she was exhausted when she made it out the door. She took a streetcar to Moira's home.

There, after the briefest conversation with Moira's mother, she sprawled herself out on her friend's bed.

"How could he have done this to me? He didn't even say why. He didn't even say he was sorry."

Moira sat in the straight-backed chair next to the bed. She had a comfortable overstuffed chair on the other side of the bed, but didn't choose to sit in it. "You have got to get over this man, Ada."

"How can I get over him? I love him too much."

"You love him? Do you really think that is what you suffer from?"

Ada sat up in the bed and looked into Moira's eyes. "How could you even ask me that question? Of course this is love." She threw herself face-down into the bed now.

Moira shook her shoulders. "Get up and straighten yourself up. I'm due to meet Bayley and Ralph for tea. You're coming with me."

AT THE HOTEL, Moira moved quickly through the lobby and into the restaurant. Ada's feet were like leaden weights. She had to work herself hard to keep up with her friend. When they saw the boys, Ada wished she had someone with her to push the corners of her mouth up into a smile, to lift out her hand for her as she offered it first to Bayley, then to Ralph, to be kissed and petted.

All their circle of friends knew about the boys now, and accepted their relationship, even protected them from the gossip of outsiders. But out in public, they put on a show. Today, Bayley led Ada to their table, while Ralph became Moira's escort. They talked about school, complained about the pressures of their studies, pontificated about philosophies of life. Ada half listened, barely responding to their pronouncements, not really following the progress of the conversation. She ached to be with Frederick. All this noise was an intrusion on her ability to nurture her pain.

"But who is this Freud person, anyway?" Moira was saying. "What has he published?"

"Nothing, at least not in English. But I have friends with friends who have studied with him. He claims that we push things that are too painful to remember into our unconscious. He is developing a treatment for hysteria."

Moira laughed. "Maybe we should send you to him, Ada."

Ada looked across the table at her friend. "Are you calling me an hysteric?"

"Well, isn't that what this absurd behavior of yours is all about? It certainly isn't love."

Ada wanted nothing more than to reach out and slap Moira. Only twenty years of training in social etiquette stopped her. In fact, she imagined leaping at her friend, throwing her to the floor, and tearing her hair out in large clumps. Instead, she narrowed her eyes and hissed as she spoke. "You're just jealous because you don't have someone to love. You're small-minded."

Moira stood abruptly. "Excuse me. I'm going to the Ladies."

They watched her walk away, silent until Moira disappeared from view. Then Ada settled into her chair. "Well, am I right? She's jealous, isn't she?"

Bayley and Ralph looked at each other, telegraphing some hidden message. "What?" she asked.

"What do you mean, what?" asked Ralph.

"You two are talking to each other with your eyes. What did you say?"

This question inspired yet another wordless interchange between the men. Then: "Ada, don't get hysterical with us, now," Bayley said.

"I will not have you accuse me of being hysterical."

Ralph finally broke, and fell in with Ada. "She's right, Bayley. That's hardly fair when we know what's going on here."

Ada leaned forward. "You've said that much. Now you must explain yourself. And quickly. Before she returns."

"You're right," Ralph said. "She is jealous. But not in the way you think." He stopped talking then, giving Ada the opportunity to try to guess at what he meant.

She refused to play the game. "Go on. Quickly."

Bayley took his napkin from his lap and slapped it onto the table. "All right, all right. Enough of this. She's jealous of your love for Frederick because she wants you to love her instead."

"She's madly in love with you, Ada," Ralph chimed in. "Can't you see that?"

Ada might have obsessed over this new information if she hadn't been so forlorn about Frederick. When he finally did end their affair, Ada slipped comfortably into her grief, and there was little room there to think about Moira's loving her. The two women remained friends throughout the rest of their time in college, but they were no longer "Moida." By the time Moira disappeared from Ada's life, and moved away with her new husband, Ada hardly noticed her absence. The shift had been gradual, and eclipsed by her affair with Frederick, so the pain was brief and shallow.

THE FLIRTATIOUSNESS OF the young woman on board the *Voltaire* reminded Ada of Moira for a complicated set of reasons. First, when the woman looked at her, and she realized the glance was inspired by attraction rather than ridicule, Ada felt a small stab of desire in her lower gut. The desire was tangled up with the sense of power inherent in her very maleness. Perhaps men sought women purely because of the control it gave them over another person. The woman's glance was one of acquiescence, of supplication. Had Ada looked this way at Frederick, or Edward? If she had, no wonder they wanted to possess her. Finally, Ada experienced for an instant what she imagined Moira wanted from her.

She had been able to continue her friendship with Moira because she had no understanding of what it was Moira really wanted from her. Ada had never even contemplated the idea of sex between two women. But just now, as the young woman had looked at her, an image of two female bodies, entwined, slick with sweat, flashed across her mind. This is what Moira imagined for the two of them, no doubt. Ada looked back again, to get another glimpse of the young woman. Just then, the woman turned, and their eyes met again. Ada snapped her head back, feeling suddenly guilty.

There was nothing to do but continue on her walk around the deck. The seas became choppy, though, and walking grew difficult. She moved to the rail in order to hold on as she walked. Her cramped cabin would make her sick, and she had no desire to return to the smoking room. It wasn't possible for her to seek the comfort of women, she saw that now. So she pulled herself along the rail, watching the sea as it rose up in response to the wind.

William and Jao knew she was a woman. Why did they insist upon treating her like a man? Why didn't one of them come to her rescue? There was nothing they could do, though. Ada knew this. If Edward were here with her, the only thing he might have done is sit with her, hold her hand, and tell her not to worry. He couldn't have stopped the wind for her, any more than William or Jao, or even Jeffrey, could.

The skies grew dark, and the ship began to roll. Stewards came around to warn passengers of the storm they were headed for. Ada held the railings, continuing to watch the sea. At first the swells were small, and the ship rolled over them gently. But they increased in size, and the *Voltaire*'s pitch and roll became more pronounced. Ada lost her footing and was forced to scramble to stay standing. Finally, the bow of the ship cut headlong across a swell, and water sprayed onto the decks. The chill wind on her wet clothes was like diving into a bucket of ice. Ada retired to her cabin.

But the raucous seas continued. Unable to stand in her room, she changed clothes prone in her berth. Sleep was out of the question. Soon after she climbed into her bed, Ada's stomach began to churn, her head was on fire, and her sense of up and down was obliterated. She vomited on the floor, but was too sick to get up and clean it. She lay awake in her dark bed throughout the night, smelling the stench of her own vomit and thinking perhaps death would be preferable to this. The ship, as it crashed its way through the uneven seas, shook and creaked, sounding as if it would certainly split in two. The thunderous noise expanded the ache in Ada's head until she thought it would cleave it in two.

If Edward were with her on this trip, Ada thought, she would at least have had a cabin with a window rather than the peephole she had in this room, and a steward would have come right away to clean up after her, perhaps even given her a wet towel for her head and a cup of tea.

THE NEXT MORNING, the seas had calmed. She must have slept at least a little. Ada went to the washroom and stood over the basin. She was the only one in the room, but someone could enter at any moment. Using her own cloth, she washed under her arms without removing her shirt, then quickly put the rag down her trousers to wash her crotch. It wasn't much of a cleansing, but it would have to do for the time being.

In the steerage dining hall, Ada found William and Jao, both looking as if they had spent a night as difficult as hers. They drank coffee together, silently. Without uttering more than a dozen words to her companions, Ada returned to her berth and slept the afternoon away. Someone, blessed soul, had come in and shampooed the floor during her absence.

WATERLOGGED

They arrived in Southampton the evening before the *Sea Witch* was due to leave for South America, so they simply moved their luggage from one ship to the other. The *Sea Witch* was a smaller vessel, and served as both a mail and a passenger ship. There were fewer passengers but there was more room. In spite of this fact, Ada wasn't certain she could tolerate another long week at sea. But she had little choice in the matter.

Her cabin, even though it was still a second-class cabin, was a bit bigger than the one she'd had on the *Voltaire* and had a decent-sized window. The first thing she did was open the window, filling her cabin with the salt air of the harbor.

As the ship set sail, the sea was calm and the winter weather mild. Ada prepared herself to spend ten stultifying days at sea. Once the continent was out of sight, there would be nothing but ocean and sky, and the rumble of the engines beneath their feet. The sea was beautiful from the shore, but from out in its far reaches, it was too big, too gray, and too constant. It could drive a person mad.

Each day was like the next for long enough to cause Ada to lose track of the date and the day of the week. Standing out on the deck, looking into the water as it churned away below, she felt too small to be substantial. Even the two-hundred-foot-long ship seemed minute against the flat, wide reach of ocean.

Ada fought her boredom with meditative strolls around the ship. On one of these jaunts, she saw Jeffrey with a beautiful young woman. They were strolling together, laughing. The woman touched her hair and her bonnet, fiddled with her sleeves and her earrings. Evidently Jeffrey made her nervous, made her heart beat too quickly. It was too easy for Ada to imagine exactly how the woman was feeling at the moment. As they neared, it became apparent that the woman's clothes were expensive, her walk restrained, like a member of the upper class. How had Jeffrey made her acquaintance? Ada wondered. Her face heated with anger as she watched them gaze at each other. Jeffrey noticed Ada when the couple had almost passed her.

"I say, Adam," he called out. Ada thought she saw Jeffrey wink at her, as if he were sharing some coded message meant only for other males of the species. She was quite certain that he meant to show off his prowess in having attracted this woman. She nodded at Jeffrey without speaking, then hurried to her cabin, where she flounced onto her narrow bed. She pummeled her mattress with her fists, and kicked her feet against the wall until her legs grew tired and her muscles seized up. When she stopped, her legs were flung out in front of her, spread wide, one toward the wall, the other hanging off the bunk. The position strained her trousers. Ada tugged at them to release the pressure on her crotch. But she didn't really notice these things about her trousers, or her legs, or her pummeling fists. These things were becoming ordinary and natural to her. It happened quickly, but not suddenly, so there was no tracking the moment when the shift occurred. There was no moment.

To console herself, she went to the smoking lounge for a cigarette and brandy. Jao was there, playing cards. Ada sat in a chair behind him, not because she was interested in his game, but because she didn't want to speak, and she knew Jao would have little to say to her while he was in the heat of a game. Or any other time. He rarely said much to her. His interactions with her were all restrained; she knew he still felt she would be a hindrance to their project, in spite of her success in obtaining a contract. But she couldn't prove him wrong until they were in Brazil, hunting orchids.

She smoked and drank, and listened to the men's voices honking and barking and bellowing. The room thickened with their utterances. How different from a room full of women's voices. Men's voices were free of the variations, the gradations that were the result of so many considerations. Ada let the timbre, the freedom of their speech wash over her without trying to make out the meaning. Jeffrey entered the room some time later, but she didn't even notice his voice, couldn't have picked its particular melody from the chorus of male sounds in the room. When she finally did see him, she congratulated herself for not having heard him immediately.

She went to bed early, but woke in the middle of the night, disturbed by a dream in which a large group of men sat at the foot of her bed, talking and arguing, instructing her in loud voices, giving her crucial advice that she couldn't decipher. Unable to get back to sleep, she dressed and went out to the deck. The moon was black, the water around the boat a void. She leaned over the rail for a moment and caught herself hoping that Jeffrey would appear again, as he had that night on the *Voltaire.* But she never saw him. He was probably entertaining the beautiful woman in his cabin.

Back in her bunk, Ada found herself suddenly thinking of Edward, and the touch of his body when they were performing Karezza. Perhaps even this restrictive practice was better than no sex at all. Or maybe she just wanted to be back in her bed, in her room, in her house. Maybe the certainty of what she had there was better than this journey into the void. She put her hand between her legs, stroking herself as she tried to remember sex with Edward during their first year of marriage. But she wasn't able to replace images of Karezza with the memories of the real sex they had once had. Using Karezza techniques, she steadied her breathing until it moved in and out of her lungs with perfect stillness, like the surface of a lake on a windless day, and she finally fell asleep.

• • •

A FINGER OF the sun reached through her cabin window, poking her in the eye. She was surprised, as she jolted awake, that she felt so rested. It was the Karezza, she decided. It had relaxed her, made her stop thinking about Jeffrey. Ada began to wonder if perhaps Edward had been right all along. It was possible that sex and crisis and desire were distractions that led one away from spiritual fulfillment. At any rate, Ada believed that she had gained control over her desire for Jeffrey, and she was eager to get up and live the day.

As she threw the covers off, she was overwhelmed by her own stench; it came at her from her crotch, from under her arms, even from her hair. When was the last time she had bathed? There were clean clothes in her bag, but she didn't want to wear them until she was able to wash herself properly. Afraid to strip down in the communal shower room, she gave herself a quick, guarded sponge bath in the washroom, but it wasn't satisfying. She walked through the day disgusted by her own scent.

As they traveled south and west, the weather grew warmer. One afternoon, leaving Jao and William to the smoking room and the raucous conversation of the men, Ada went to sit in a deck chair and read *Moby-Dick.* She felt like Ishmael, out here in the center of this vast sea, headed, like him, for the belly of the universe, to the vortex that might suck her into the center of the earth. It occurred to Ada that she had no idea of the date. She set the book aside and asked a steward as he passed, "Excuse me, what is the date?"

"Why, it's December twenty-third, sir. Two days until Christmas." The steward tipped his hat and hurried on. Ada had entirely forgotten about the impending holiday. Edward had given her permission to spend it with her mother. The idea that he had believed he could define her life so narrowly made her want to have him in front of her now, so she could show him just how little regard she had for his plans for her. Edward and Beatrice would probably spend the holiday together, commiserating about their shared rage toward Ada.

But how much did a thing such as Christmas really matter? What was

Christmas? A time to spend with family? A celebration of the birth of Jesus? Ada didn't understand family any more than she understood fervent belief in the myth of Christ.

THAT EVENING, Ada ran into Jeffrey in the smoking room after a dinner of watery meat and biscuits in the dining hall. She gulped sherry to wash down the aftertaste of her meal. Jeffrey sat next to her and put his arm around her shoulder for an instant. The pressure of his body on hers, even at this nonsexual point of contact, was like the buzz of Dr. Casey's vibrator. In and of itself, it had little to do with sex, but the end result was crisis. Ada felt she would dissolve into an hysterical paroxysm if Jeffrey didn't move away from her.

"We'll have smooth sailing all the way there this time," he said to her. "I plan to take advantage and find myself someone to keep me company. How about you, old man?"

Ada was proud of her quick response, in spite of how shocked she was by Jeffrey's comment. "I think I'll wait till we get there. I like to take my time with these things," she said.

"Not me. I fall in love easily and often."

If she could get over her disappointment, Ada knew, this was an opportunity for her to learn more about the way men operated with women. Not wanting to know the answer, but filled with a need to understand, to peek inside, Ada asked, "Have you seen a likely victim yet?"

"Victim you call it? Don't tell me you're one of those insufferable romantics?"

"Have you or haven't you? Seen someone?" She waited for the answer without being able to look at him. It took him a long time to respond.

When he did speak, she suddenly felt cold. "There is a woman. I met her on the *Voltaire*. She's lovely, and I think she may be just lonely enough, or sexual enough, to allow me to lure her to my cabin."

"What you mean is that you simply want to have sex with her? You don't care for her other than that?"

"Oh, my dear boy. You are young, aren't you? Do I seem like the marrying kind to you? We bachelors need sex, too, now don't we? How else are we supposed to get it?" Ada didn't answer him, so he answered himself. "Oh, of course I could go to prostitutes, but they are quite a squirrelly bunch, aren't they? They leave you longing for a wholesome woman. No, I think this girl, Hannah, is just my cup of tea."

Ada tugged at her trousers, ground her heels into the floor. She still couldn't look at him.

"You need to find yourself a girl. There's going to be a Christmas dance. I'll see if Hannah has a friend who would like to dance with you."

The panic must have shown on her face. Jeffrey laughed and punched her arm. "Don't tell me you're afraid of girls. Listen, old chum, we'll get you past that before this ship docks. Trust yourself to me."

CHRISTMAS CAME, even though Ada willed it to stay away. The third-class saloon was decorated with a tree, and the food was much improved from the usual fare. They ate roast beef and plum pudding, and everyone drank freely.

There were many musicians on board. The music and singing started out sedately, with everyone joining in to sing "God Rest Ye Merry Gentlemen," "We Three Kings," and other standard songs. But the crowd grew restive as they continued to drink, and soon enough the music became more popular, and people began to dance. Finally, an African man went to the piano. The crowd grew silent, holding their breath, waiting to see what sort of music he would play for them. The piano exploded with the fractious energies of early ragtime. Ada felt as if she recognized the syncopated rhythms, though she was certain she had never actually heard such music. It was impossible to listen to it without wanting to move. Her toes tapped, then her head began to bob. The dancers turned frantic circles around the floor, and the crowd whooped in encouragement. Or perhaps it was a form of possession. Ada's hand went to her neck in an old feminine gesture that she had forgotten to use in the last couple of weeks.

Her entire life had been a continuous lesson in self-control. She had learned first in her mother's house, and then in Edward's, that physical excitement and its expression were to be avoided, even if the denial of it caused illness. A woman who takes to her bed from nervous exhaustion is respectable. A woman who lifts her skirts and submits to the rhythms of music or sex should be feared.

The striking of the hammers on the piano strings sent a vibration through the floor and right up her legs. She had no idea how to dance to this music, but she wanted to try nonetheless. She wanted this almost as much as she had ever wanted the experience of crisis. Her desire to dance filled her with the same sense of shame and excitement she had battled during the last year of her marriage. Her hands became clammy. She stuffed them into her pockets. But her toes continued to tap. The stress of her longing to dance settled itself in her back, which she held perfectly still except for the minute vibrations from her tapping toes.

Jeffrey danced with Hannah, the girl he had been pursuing. Ada forgot to be jealous of her. She was simply jealous that they were dancing and she was not. She could grab a girl and twirl her onto the floor, but she wasn't confident enough in her maleness to dare such a thing.

Jao had found a dance partner, too. Ada watched them as they danced from one side of the room to the other, laughing and allowing their bodies to submit without shame to the manic tempo. Jao was smooth, sensuous. The girl, tall and South American–looking, was obviously taken with him, happy to be held by his strong hands. Jao's dance steps became an amalgam of ragtime and Brazilian, and his hips rolled up against his partner's. She blushed, but rolled her hips back at his nonetheless.

Ada took a glass of lager, hoping it would help numb her to the pain of listening to this music, of watching these dancers. The upper classes had no idea what was going on under their noses. They prided themselves in their superiority, and yet, at least in Ada's experience, they seemed to have forgotten the art of joy and love of the body.

Jeffrey approached her, dragging his girl by the hand. "Adam, old chap," he said. "I want to introduce you to Hannah. Isn't she beautiful?"

Hannah was small, dark, and quite pretty. She held her hand out to Ada. "Pleased to meet you, Adam." She spoke with an English accent.

Ada pushed her voice down to its bottom and greeted the girl. It wasn't until then that she noticed the woman standing behind Hannah. Hannah pulled her friend forward, practically setting her in front of Ada. "This is my friend Elizabeth."

Elizabeth giggled and held out her hand. She was as tall as Ada, blond, with direct blue eyes. "How d'you do?" She was English, too.

"Lovely to meet you," Ada managed.

The music continued, its energy expanding, speeding up the level of activity in the room. Jeffrey put his elbow into Ada's side and leaned toward her ear. "Ask her to dance," he said.

Ada looked at him and shook her head. "Don't know how," she said into his ear.

Elizabeth had heard her. "Come along with me. I'll lead," she said, and then laughed a tinkling sort of laugh. The kind of laugh one might expect from a woman who is comfortable enjoying herself, comfortable with men, and comfortable getting her way. Her first giggle hadn't given any such indication.

Elizabeth took Ada's hand and pulled her to the center of the room, the locus of the frenetic physical activity. Ada's thoughts raced over the surfaces of everything she had tried to teach herself about behaving like a man. Dancing had never come up. Her fear of misstepping made her even more awkward than she might have been. But Elizabeth gripped her hands and pulled her along with the kind of assurance a mother has when teaching her baby to walk. Ada suddenly forgot to feel fear, and soon enough she was reveling in the sheer physicality of dancing wildly to ragtime.

Her body was gorged with rivers of blood, gushing everywhere in response to the storm of activity. This could go on forever. There was no need for anything else. But the song ended and the piano player stopped. The dancers stood on the floor, stunned, lost. They called out to the piano player. The man stood at the piano and called out to the crowd, "Just five minutes, folks. I need a drink!" The crowd roared their approval.

Ada caught sight of William, by himself, near the piano. Ada realized that he was probably afraid to offend any woman there by asking her to dance. She touched Elizabeth's shoulder. "See the African man by the piano?" Elizabeth nodded. "He's a friend of mine. I think he would be happy to dance with you for a few songs." Elizabeth understood the situation immediately. When the piano player returned, she moved across the floor, flashing her smile for William as she went. William looked at Ada and nodded. He understood, too, and he seemed happy to accept Ada's and Elizabeth's mercies. The music resumed, to much applause, and Ada stood back to watch William and Elizabeth dance.

William knew what he was doing. Elizabeth relinquished her role as leader easily, allowing herself to be steered around the floor by an experienced practitioner of the art. Ada was surprised by William. He was always so aristocratic in his mannerisms. Now he was like a man transformed. He kicked up his heels, threw his head back in laughter that spread out all around him and settled onto the rest of the laughter in the room, underpinning it with the full, low tones of his voice. The sound of it comforted Ada. William was a good half foot taller than Elizabeth. He looked so manly next to her. She was surprised that Elizabeth eventually chose to leave William and return to her side. Why would any woman choose the boyish, weak Adam over someone as dashing as William?

"Aren't you tired?" Ada asked her. Elizabeth shook her head and pulled Ada back to the dance floor. But this time, the ecstasy of dancing didn't overshadow Ada's discomfort at pretending to be a man with a woman who might find her, well, appealing. Having no desire to hurt her, Ada was hesitant to reject Elizabeth outright. And she knew, even then, in the heat that was generated by their dancing bodies, she was feeling a certain sense of satisfaction as a result of Elizabeth's interest. A certain sense of power. It was good, this man thing, the ease of it, the ability to create your own plan and then set to work realizing it.

They danced until their feet ached, and in between dances they drank. Finally, Ada attempted to do what any gentleman would do.

"It's late, Elizabeth. And we're drunk. Let me walk you to your cabin." Her body swayed as she struggled to wrap her tongue around each syllable.

Elizabeth put her hand inside the button placket of Ada's jacket. Her hand came close to touching Ada's breast. "I don't want to sleep alone tonight, Adam. Take me with you." Her head dropped onto Ada's shoulder. "Come now, take me with you."

"I can't do that. Let me walk you to your room."

"They'll stop you. I'm in the single ladies' wing." With her head still attached to Ada, she staggered. Ada skipped in order to keep her balance. "They won't even allow you to walk into the hallway."

"Let me escort you as far as the main door, then."

"Oh, all right."

But as they walked through the saloon and down the hallway, Ada had to support Elizabeth. Finally, the girl stumbled and fell onto Ada. She was near passing out. They hadn't even reached the stairs to the second-class deck when Ada realized Elizabeth wouldn't make it to her room on her own feet.

Elizabeth rallied momentarily, raising her voice. "You simply must take me to your bed, Adam. Don't refuse me."

"Shhh. Quiet, Elizabeth. You're making a scene." As she said the words, Ada felt a sudden sympathy for her husband. This is what he must have felt like when he was dealing with her hysteria. Elizabeth was becoming unmanageable, and Ada had to find the solution.

The only thing to do, really, was to take her back to Ada's room. She was too drunk to last long. Ada would let her sleep it off, then early in the morning, she would take Elizabeth back to her own room.

Elizabeth remained ambulatory long enough to make it to Ada's narrow bed. She passed out the instant she saw it. Ada climbed in with her, still wearing her trousers and shirt. If Ada took them off, and Elizabeth woke before Ada in the morning, she'd see Ada's breasts, their shape outlined by the long underwear she usually wore to bed.

In order to fit into the bed, Ada had to lie on her side. The small space left to her made her body go stiff. Her tight trousers and the alcohol in her bloodstream disrupted her sleep throughout the night. Her dreams were loud and chaotic. She woke once thinking there were people in her cabin, drinking and singing. In another dream, Edward chastised her for not loving the orchids as much as she loved sex. She dreamed Frederick was kissing her, but the alcohol interrupted the kiss, rousing her from her sleep. Though she was sure she was awake, she still felt the pressure of lips against her own.

It took her a moment to realize Elizabeth was awake, and kissing her with her beer-thickened tongue.

Ada felt as if she were suffocating. She wanted to scream, but no sound came from her mouth. Finally, she pushed Elizabeth away from her, and Elizabeth fell back, dead to the world again in an instant. Ada fell back into her active dreaming. The night filled with further wild romps and incoherent messages. Somewhere in the midst of all of it, Elizabeth put her arm around Ada, but Ada was dreaming, and thought she was with Frederick again. She took Elizabeth's arm and pulled it tighter across her chest, holding it in both her hands as she fell back into fitful sleep.

When she woke in the morning, Elizabeth was wrapped around her, breathing hot breath into the back of her neck. Ada's head hurt, her neck was pinched, and the stench of stale ale filled the room. If she didn't get out of the cabin, she would surely be sick. Even after Ada threw Elizabeth's arms and legs off her, the girl remained asleep. Ada walked out the door of her berth as she was, clothes rumpled, hair matted to her skull. She didn't care. She felt death hovering; the urge to escape was primal.

Leaning over the rail and holding her head out parallel to the sea seemed the best treatment for her condition. Her head felt better if she kept it just that way. Elizabeth would be aggravated to find herself alone in Ada's bed, but she would just have to live with it. In fact, Ada intended to stay out on deck until she was sure Elizabeth was gone from her bed. What good could come of an encounter with the woman?

"I say, Adam!" The voice was loud enough to make Ada's head reverberate. It felt as if the inside of her brain was struggling to escape her skull. She knew it was Jeffrey without looking up. She braced herself for the clap on the back that always accompanied a greeting from him, and managed not to vomit when his hand landed, disturbing her delicate equilibrium.

"What are you doing out here? I just saw that lovely lady come from your room. Why aren't you there with her?"

Ada couldn't answer. She groaned and moved her head farther out over the water.

"Oh, too much to drink, eh? Shame, when a girl like that is in your bed."

Jeffrey stopped talking for a moment. Ada didn't lift her head, but she sensed that he was looking out to sea. "You fared better than I did," he said finally. "My girl wouldn't succumb."

Ada moaned, trying to enunciate the word *sorry*, but failing.

"Ah well, sometimes you win, then again, sometimes you fail miserably. I'll have another go at her, though."

Jeffrey smacked Ada again before he left. It was at the instant when his hand knocked against her back, pushing her chest down against the rail, that she had a brief but clear vision of her bedroom in Boston. It came to her like some mystical sign, like the spiritual perfection she had tried but failed to gain through Karezza. It had been there for her all along, in that room in Boston. The thought of climbing into her bed there right now made her legs go wobbly underneath her, made her head spin, caused her to confuse the sea with the sky. Could a person miss a room and a bed more than a husband or a life? Was it possible that longing for a place could cut deeper than longing for a love?

She walked carefully back to her shipboard room, her gait slowed by her hangover and by that vision of her lost bedroom. It didn't even occur to her to try to walk like a man.

Her cabin still stank, and her head still hurt, but she managed to sleep. After the night spent with Elizabeth, being alone in the bed felt sweet. The berth held her inside its borders as if it had been made to fit her angles, her dimensions. She slept through breakfast and lunch, and by the time dinner came around, she was finally in shape to eat a bite or two.

She found William and Jao in the dining hall. They both watched her in silence as she sat.

"Hello," she said. They nodded, stiffly, in response.

"They're serving the Christmas leftovers, I see," she said. The two men shrugged and looked at each other.

"Well, I guess we didn't eat that much, did we? We drank instead?" Ada laughed at her own observation. Their response was weak, insincere laughter.

"What is wrong with you two?" They didn't answer.

Ada gazed at them and they dropped their eyes. "All right," she said. "I've had enough. Tell me what is wrong."

William squirmed for a moment before speaking. "All right. Here it is. It seems you've wronged a lady."

Jao put his face close to hers. "I think you're taking this game of dress-up you're playing a little too far, don't you?"

"I've wronged a lady? Elizabeth? What on earth are you talking about?"

William pushed his plate away and spread his hands out on the table in front of him. "She had breakfast and lunch with us. Cried all the way through both meals."

"But whatever for? I didn't do anything."

Jao watched as William spoke, his face pinched, his eyes narrow. "She says you took advantage of her."

"Be serious, please. How would I have done that? I don't quite have what it takes to wreak the havoc you men do, now do I?"

Jao remained silent, still allowing William to guide the conversation. "She said you had your way with her, then disappeared, leaving her alone in your room."

Ada looked at Jao as she spoke. She felt he was the one she needed to convince. "I brought her to my room because she was drunk. I didn't want to leave her on her own. But we slept. That's all. I left in the morning to give her some privacy."

Jao shook his head. "By the time she left us, she swore she would charge you with rape."

"That's simply preposterous," Ada said. "How could I rape someone?" Her face flushed with anger. She ran her hands through her dirty hair.

"There are ways," Jao said, his eyes narrowing.

William picked up his narrative again. "Elizabeth said she woke up in the middle of the night to find you molesting her."

How much more ridiculous would this story get? Ada wondered. "She woke me up in the middle of the night. I pushed her away, and she passed out. That's the true story."

William laughed at her. She puffed up her chest and glared at him with her best masculine glare. "Obviously, this is a case of a woman scorned trying to save face. Don't you recognize it?"

"Why would I be able to recognize it?" Jao asked.

Ada's response was immediate. "Because it's a tactic also employed by your sex, isn't it?"

Jao and William laughed together; their laugh was almost infectious enough to cause Ada to catch it. But she was just angry enough to resist. "This is a disaster, and you two find it amusing."

William patted Ada's back. "She'll get over you, Adam. You're not that devastating."

Jao glared at her. "I honestly don't find it amusing. No matter what happened between you in your bunk, she never should have been there with you. You should have come to one of us for help. That kind of bad judgment in the jungle can be fatal."

"But I don't know what to do. You must understand." She decided she had to use her feminine wiles with them. They seemed to have come to think of her as a young, badly behaved man. "I've never had a woman in love with me." As she said it, she imagined Moira standing behind her, clucking her tongue at Ada's bald lie. "What do I do to make her lose interest in me?"

Jao turned away from Ada. "William, I think it's time to reassess this partnership. You swore if she became a liability, we would ask her to leave." Deep lines etched themselves across Jao's forehead as he spoke.

William shook his head violently. "We're in the middle of the sea, man. How do you suppose she would get home?" Ada might have hoped for a more vehement defense than this one. But it was practical. "Maybe I can help, though," William said. "I will invite Elizabeth to go to the New Year's Eve dance with me. Maybe I can help her to get over you."

As he spoke, Ada watched his face. His eyes looked away from her, even though he addressed her. He was embarrassed, she was sure. He hadn't been angry with her for behaving like a fool, he had been angry because he thought Ada had spirited away the woman he was interested in. A man, jealous of her because of her effect on a woman. Again, she found herself wishing she could share this moment with Katie, who would no doubt appreciate its strangeness, the irony of it.

What was Katie doing now without her? Had Edward kept her on? Did he blame her for Ada's disappearance? Was she a married woman now, allowed to live above the carriage house with Liam? There was so much she didn't know. She wished she could contact her somehow, just once, to find out if she was all right, and perhaps pass an hour talking and laughing with her.

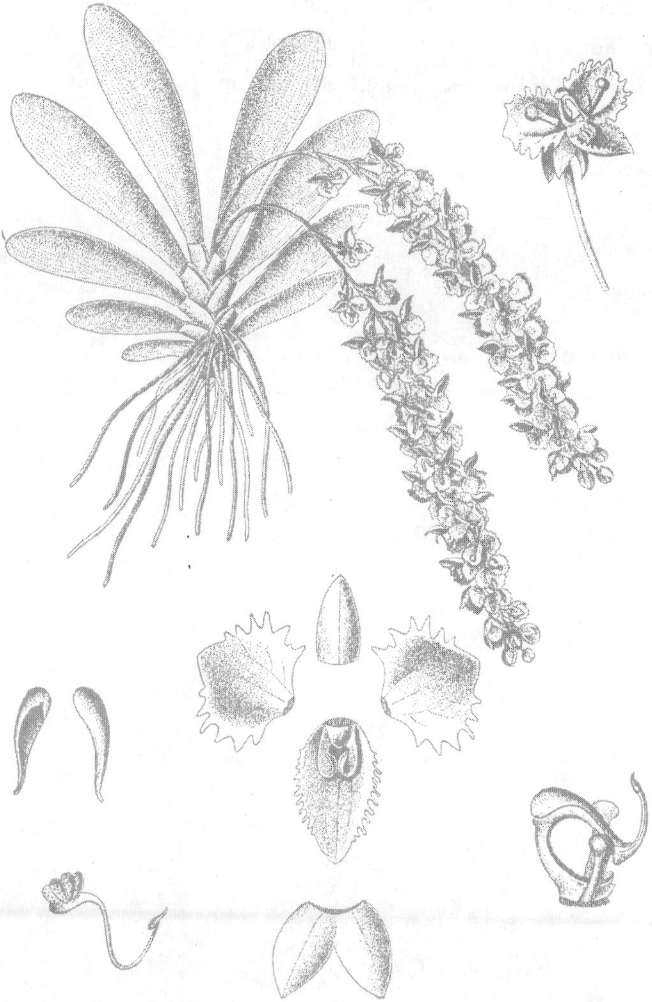

Southern Skies

After dinner, Ada walked around the deck with William. They enjoyed a calm sea and clear skies. By now, they were farther south than Ada had ever been. The sea was different here. Its color was the blue of maps and globes. The men who drew those maps must have traveled on these seas. If they had seen only the North Atlantic, they would have used a grayer blue, a darker blue. Here, the blue suggested an ease, a sense of peace the North Atlantic could never hope to obtain.

"It's lovely," she said to William.

"Oh, that's right. You haven't seen this before, have you?"

"No. Never."

As they strolled together in a comfortable quiet, the sea below them turned into a chaotic patchwork of flying fish. "Would you look at that?" Ada pulled at William, leading him to the rail, where they leaned over together to watch the spectacle. They were jumping and soaring by the hundreds, frightened, it seemed, by the ship.

"Imagine," she said. "Swimming and flying. Water and sky, with no ground to slow you down, to make you heavy."

"Well, sure, but they miss out on intelligent thought and creativity, don't they?"

Ada wondered if it was unusual for a black man who faced so many obstacles in white society to nonetheless appreciate human intelligence and creativity. But she didn't ask William. They stood together and watched the small spectacle on the water. "When will you speak to Elizabeth?" she asked.

"Tomorrow. At breakfast."

"I don't suppose I should have breakfast with you, then," Ada said.

Their wordless camaraderie was interrupted by a man's voice. "William," it called. "I say, William." They turned to see a man in expensive clothes, obviously a first-class passenger, hurrying toward them.

William took off his hat and extended his hand. "Mr. Wirt," he said. "Imagine seeing you here." Then he turned to Ada. "Mr. Wirt, this is Adam Wilson. He's traveling to Brazil, too."

Ada felt her voice drop down to her belly before moving up to her throat. "How do you do, sir," she said, trying to sound lower class and male all at once. This Mr. Wirt was someone Edward had spoken of. This man knew Edward. But if he was on this ship, there was no way he had heard yet that Ada was missing, was there?

"You're going orchid hunting, no doubt?" Mr. Wirt asked.

William smiled. "I may be expanding my horizons. I think it's high time for me to branch out."

"Oh. Do Pryce and Locke know anything of your new interests?" The question didn't sound entirely benign. Ada felt her back stiffen.

"My plans are far too modest to interest anyone other than myself, I'm sure," William said. Ada saw something in William's eyes change. When the eyes shifted, his entire physiognomy transformed. He was protective, inscrutable, his posture defensive but without retreating. He stood his ground in front of the man, but he wasn't about to let this Wirt fellow know anything about him.

"Well, then," said Wirt. "I hope your journey is fruitful. I'd best be on my way." He bowed his head slightly at Ada. She nodded to him, but didn't speak for fear her voice would crack.

"Nice to see you, sir," William said.

Ada and William turned back to look down at the sea again. The flying fish were gone. Neither one of them spoke. Ada listened to the sound of the water, and the ship cutting through it. The occasional call of a gull disrupted the rhythms of water and ship.

Finally, though, Ada had to ask the question. "What is that man doing on this ship?"

"He's a businessman. He has business in South America. Not orchids. Something that makes him very rich. What, exactly, is a mystery to me."

"How does he know you?"

"He buys orchids now and then. He's not an avid collector. But he does buy a few very expensive, rare plants. He buys them simply because he's rich enough to buy the best and make all the real collectors envy him. Your husband included."

Ada didn't mention what she knew they were both thinking. Did the man know she was missing, and had he suspected anything when he saw her? And if he did suspect, would he blame William? "I need to go to my cabin," she said. William nodded, as if he understood completely how much this Wirt's appearance had unnerved her.

As she walked away, she was careful to use a manly stride. Wirt might be watching her from the upper deck. Up till now, this disguise had been a matter of convenience to her. It was easier to travel as a man, especially since her companions were dark-skinned men, and a white woman traveling with them would be problematic. But now she realized the possibility of being recognized by someone who knew Edward, even this far from home, and the ramifications of that recognition.

She missed her bedroom, her chair and her comfortable bed in Boston, yes. But she had no intention of living as Edward's, or any man's, wife, ever again. Wirt's appearance had given her perfect clarity. She pushed her heels into the wooden deck and swung her arms freely. Wirt would never take her for a woman if he was watching her now.

After the encounter with Wirt, Ada became anxious in a way she hadn't experienced since she rode away from Edward. She looked over her shoulder, was conscious of her walk and her voice, her muscles were tense even at night when she tried to sleep. Wirt or Elizabeth might appear at any moment, and she wanted no interaction with either of them.

THE SHIP PASSED Teneriffe at some distance, and as they did so, the steamship *Ariadne*, headed for New York, crossed their path. Ada's ship sounded the *Ariadne*, spending some two hours alongside the other ship. Passengers were able to pass letters across, for the other steamer to carry home. Jao and William had written letters, and gave them to the ship's steward, who went aboard the *Ariadne* with the mailbag. Ada wished, as she watched her companions hand over their letters, that she she had been free to write to Katie. She would have been happy to write to her about the stars, and the flying fish.

William sat next to Ada on the deck after he had delivered his letters. "I'm sorry you can't write to anyone," he said. Ada appreciated his concern for her position. But instead of thanking him, which might have precipitated tears, she shrugged and said, "Bugger it." She reached her hand under her hat and scratched at her scalp. "Just bugger it, I say."

William laughed and slapped his knee. "You sound more like one of us every day."

ELIZABETH AGREED TO William's invitation to the New Year's celebration, but Ada made it a point to avoid the young woman nonetheless. New Year's Eve fell on the night before they were scheduled to arrive in Brazil. There was plenty to drink in the third-class saloon, and there was ragtime again, but this time she didn't feel like dancing. She watched Jao and even Jeffrey dance with other women, while she sat at a table alone, smoking a cigar. Jeffrey had given up on Hannah and moved on to another woman, this one dark and small as well. As he spun her around the floor, he held his hand on her lower back, almost touching her buttocks. Ada imagined his hand in the same place on her own back. He wasn't a trustworthy man, she knew that. But it didn't matter. His hand on her back would set something in motion, like the fall of the first domino tile in a complicated network of tiles, the energy would branch out and reach to every area of her body. Jeffrey would encourage her to come to crisis. He would urge her on, and he would be happy when the final impact moved her. He would laugh at Karezza.

The woman put her head on Jeffrey's shoulder. Ada looked away. She found William, in the center of the dance floor, dancing with Elizabeth. The sight of her made Ada feel sick to her stomach, as if she had another hangover. Elizabeth looked over just then, catching Ada's eye. There was something disturbing in her glance, even though she turned back to William quickly.

Elizabeth looked at Ada again, though, as if she knew Ada was still watching her. She was checking, it seemed, to see if Ada was jealous, if she intended to cut in on William. But Ada shrugged her shoulders at Elizabeth and motioned for her to keep dancing with William. The two disappeared behind another dancing couple. Ada got up and left the saloon.

The night was clear, and there wasn't a square inch of sky that was free of stars. Soon it would be a new year, but Ada was out in the middle of the ocean, far from home, and from her former life, in which dates and even days of the week mattered. The sky was what mattered out here. She looked for the Dog Star in the milky chaos above her, not sure where it was in the Southern skies. The night was so busy with lights, for the first time in her life, Ada had a sense of the infinite. It was as if she could see into new layers, into dimensions behind dimensions, beyond the end of the heavens, and it was all a conflagration of deep-space black and the burning white of star matter. The deck of the boat, perched high above the sea, seemed to be of a piece with the sky, and Ada felt as if she were standing among the stars. If Jeffrey were here, he would point everything out to her, tell her the names of the constellations and where they were in relation to their position on earth. Under his tutelage, she would feel rooted again on the surface of the earth.

What Ada didn't know was that as she stood watching the stars, Jeffrey was in the saloon, being rejected by another girl. And by the time she turned to leave the deck to retire, Jeffrey was alone, himself headed for the deck.

"Look at this sky," he said as he came up behind her.

"What happened to your lady friend?" she asked.

"This is striking." He put his back to the rail and leaned out so that his torso was almost parallel to the water. "I feel as if I'm swimming in it."

"She rejected you?"

Jeffrey pulled himself up so he could look at Ada. "She did, Adam. That she did. But never fear, I'll find a girl in Brazil."

"It may be that your technique is wrong," Ada suggested.

"So are you going to give me advice? You're hardly a man yet."

Perhaps Ada wanted to make him feel bad for not seeing that the perfect woman was right in front of him. Or perhaps she really did object to his shabby treatment of the other women. But in any case, she couldn't help herself when she said, "I did already have one woman practically force her way into my bed."

Jeffrey laughed at himself. "I must grant you that. So what would your advice to me be, oh wise one?"

"Let them come to you. If you don't invite them into your bed, they're more likely to think of it themselves."

"So when I do invite them into my bed, it changes everything?"

"It makes them feel as if you think little of them." The realization was coming to her only as she spoke. But as she spoke, she felt she was saying something that was true, at least of herself.

"Why have I been successful so many times, then, my boy?"

"Because you have managed to find women who think little of themselves."

"Listen to yourself. A week ago you were afraid to dance with a woman, and now you're giving advice to the likes of me?"

It was absurd. She'd never seduced a woman, had she? She only knew what one woman wanted from a man. The rest of them, they were a mystery to her as much as they were to any man. "Don't mind me. I really don't know what I'm talking about."

"Well, there may be some truth to your advice. For some women anyway." He looked into the stars again. "There's the Phoenix." He pointed as he spoke. "You can't see that in the Northern skies."

"When you look at the stars long enough, you can actually see the earth turning, have you noticed?" she asked him. Jeffrey nodded, without taking his eyes off the sky. "Maybe you should talk to your women about the stars," Ada said. "I imagine they'd like that."

Her comment was followed by an uncomfortable silence. Then there was a moment of small talk, and finally Jeffrey took himself off to bed. Ada stayed, looking into the circularity of the world around her, awed that it had at last become navigable for her.

Others passed behind her, taking late strolls around the decks. Some of them were clearly inebriated. There was singing, joking, and drunken roughhousing in fits and spurts, but none of it distracted her from her reverie. But then she heard hurried footsteps behind her, and a hushed man's voice, then a shrill hissing. The footsteps came right up behind her, and someone grabbed her collar.

"You. How dare you!" Elizabeth's face was so close, Ada could make out only one feature at a time. The one she landed on was Elizabeth's strained mouth, the lips pursing and spitting. "I've told William what you did, and since he refuses to take action, I shall tell the captain. You will be arrested."

Ada grabbed at her collar, swatting at Elizabeth's hand at the same time. "Arrested?" There was too much going on for her to sort out Elizabeth's intent. The woman's face was too close; her hot breath singed Ada's nostrils. At the same time, she pulled on Ada's collar, forcing her to deal with both her balance and the irritation of having Elizabeth's hand at her neck. The words were an additional stimulus that Ada's brain filed away without comprehending them.

"You have offended my honor."

William stepped into Ada's eyeline. He attempted to put himself between the two women, but there was no room, and Elizabeth refused to give ground. "Elizabeth. We need to discuss this calmly, like you promised," he said.

"I promised nothing. Adam took advantage of me. He encouraged me to drink, then took me to his room when I was in no position to fend for myself. I hate to remember what he did to me during the night."

Ada put her hands around the front of Elizabeth's throat and squeezed. There was no logical thought process involved in this action. It was pure instinct. She wanted the woman to shut up. Elizabeth stopped talking immediately. She made small gurgling sounds as Ada spoke. "I did nothing to you. You were too drunk to walk to your room. I let you sleep in my bed, but I never touched you. If you remember otherwise, you simply remember your dreams, not reality."

Elizabeth's arms were flailing now, slapping at Ada, trying to get her to take her hands off her throat. William grabbed at Ada. "Stop," he said. "You're going to strangle her. There will be no defense against that."

Ada removed her hands from Elizabeth's throat and stared at them, as if she only just then realized what she had been doing with them. She kept her eyes on her hands as she spoke. "I can prove to you I didn't do what you claim."

"How can you do that?" Elizabeth sputtered. "How?"

"Come with me. I want to show you something."

Elizabeth looked to William. He raised his shoulders, signifying his lack of knowledge of Ada's intentions. Ada stamped her foot, realizing as she did it what a feminine gesture it was. "You will be fine. Just come to my cabin for a moment."

"What, are you going to molest me again?" Elizabeth shivered, and her curls bounced under her hat.

"Bring William. Let him make sure I do nothing inappropriate." William nodded his assent at both of them, and they turned as a group to go to Ada's room.

Inside her room, Ada positioned them so that William was standing behind her, and Elizabeth was facing her. Without any discussion, she took off her jacket, unbuttoned her shirt, and pulled up her undershirt, revealing her breasts to Elizabeth, while William observed from behind.

"Now, tell me how I could have done what you claim," she demanded.

Elizabeth dropped down into the chair and waved her hand across her face. "Oh my Lord," she said, again and again.

Ada put her clothes back in order and shook Elizabeth's shoulder. "You need to calm yourself. Just calm down. It's not all that shocking."

"But you deceived me, then, into believing that you were . . . That I could . . . Oh, you are horrid." Elizabeth pointed her finger at Ada, then dropped her face into her hand. "Simply horrid."

Ada felt spent. She didn't know what to say in her defense.

"Elizabeth. Please understand," William said. "There was good reason for Adam to conceal his identity. She's running from a husband who means her harm. We must keep her identity secret. We need your help in this." William leaned over Elizabeth, taking her hands in his.

But Elizabeth was clearly humiliated. "But you let me dance with you. You flirted with me," she moaned.

"I truly didn't mean to," Ada said.

"Let me take you out for air," William said. "We'll walk around the deck, then I'll take you back to your cabin."

Elizabeth finally rose, and left the cabin without another word to Ada.

IT WAS A sunny early morning when the ship reached Pernambuco, their first stop in Brazil. The coral reef running along the coastline made it necessary for the *Sea Witch* to anchor off the coast, and the passengers to take small boats to get ashore. There was no need to leave the boat, but Ada felt, with land this close, if she didn't put foot on it, she might go mad. When she stepped off the dock and onto the solid ground of Pernambuco, though, the liquids contained inside her body continued to surge and recede as if they were still responding to the movement of water. Her feet didn't seem to make contact with the ground as she walked. It was as if the entire continent of South America were nothing more than a floating vessel.

The three orchid hunters walked from the docks to the main road together. Ada looked around for Mr. Wirt, but he was lost somewhere among the rest of the crowd of debarking travelers. Still, she stepped firmly and held her chin out, remaining conscientious about her manly qualities, in case he observed her from some hidden vantage point. Ada and her group, this band of men, went to a small cafe where they feasted on Pernambuco's giant pineapples and thick coffee.

The population here was largely Negro. The roads were small and unpaved. Mules laden with bananas, oranges, and other fruits passed by them on the dirt road, carrying their burdens to the ships. In front of them, in the rough sea, fishermen came and went in small boats with three-cornered sails. Children ran through the streets, many of them naked.

Passengers from the *Sea Witch* who were remaining in Pernambuco hitched rides in sedan chairs. These seats, carried on the shoulders of two strong Negro men, would bear them up the hill to the rooms they had reserved in local inns. Ada watched the men struggle up the trail with their burdens as the musical sounds of the Portuguese language drifted on the warm sea breezes. Her dark suit held the heat from the sun. It warmed her to her bones. In Boston, it seemed she was forever trying, and failing, just to get warm. Her long pursuit of the sun had finally brought her here, to a country made of sun.

Tonight she would take a bath, somehow, and would change into her light linen suit for their arrival in Salvador de Bahia. They returned to the ship just about the time Ada's body was regaining its earthbound stability. As she set foot on the deck of the ship, she felt the jungle at her back. That was where she wanted to be, out in the sun, the earth under her toes. She couldn't wait to get to Bahia and leave the ship behind for good.

After dinner, she strolled the decks with Jeffrey. The waters were smooth, the steamer cut through it like silk on bare skin. But Ada felt unsteady on her feet. She would have liked to just lean against his arm without hesitation, but such a simple act would set in motion a complicated network of events. None of the possible outcomes would be happy ones, she was sure. If he started talking about the stars again, she would have to stop him. How could she stand here, their last night on the ship together, looking into the million eyes of heaven with him, and continue to pretend she was a man?

Her breathing became shallow, making her light-headed. She had to gulp at the air. As she gulped, her chest and belly heaved. If she were standing here in a corset, she would surely faint from lack of air. Of course, if she had been wearing a dress and corset all this time, undoubtedly Jeffrey would have tried to lure her into his bed, and perhaps she would be there with him now, her corset on the floor beneath them.

"Damn!" The word escaped her mouth before she could censor it.

"Damn what, old man?"

"Oh, I don't know." Ada tried to think of something to say that a man would say after such an outburst. Everything that came to mind had the stamp of woman all over it. Damn, I miss my room back home. Damn, I want you to kiss me. Damn, I have no idea what I am doing here. Damn, I'm scared. "Damn this place for being so different from anything I've ever known," she said.

Jeffrey looked up then, out across the sea toward the shores they skirted. "I'm glad you said that. It just gave me new eyes. I've been here too many times. I've forgotten how truly fantastic it is."

Ada left Jeffrey early. She tipped a steward to bring a hip bath to her room, so she was finally able to enjoy a bath after a fashion.

The next morning, in honor of their arrival in Bahia, she donned her linen suit.

The Bay of All Saints

The ship anchored in the bay called Baía de Todos os Santos. Ada, her two business partners, and Jeffrey took the mail boat ashore, along with other passengers. This time they brought their luggage with them, all of them except Jeffrey. He would continue on to Rio de Janeiro. Ada was certain these were the last few hours she would ever spend with the man.

William hired a boy to guard their luggage, and the four found a cafe near the beach. They drank coffee and ate fruit and bread on the patio, the large bay and its sandy beach stretching out before them. Men with fishing nets stood in the gentle surf, casting them into the water again and again. The nets lifted and floated open against the sky for an instant before settling down onto the surface of the water and then sinking. The town of Bahia smelled of fresh fruit, fish, salt, earth, and heat. Behind them, blue, green, yellow, pink, and white houses painted the streets and hillsides. The entire landscape of the shore above the beach was blanketed with fruit trees and flowers of every color. In her memory, Boston seemed gray and motionless now.

It was hot. The sweat gathered under Ada's unbound breasts. She wouldn't have been able to bear the heat if she were in a corset and petticoats, but the thin linen of her trousers was freeing, and she welcomed the heat. She stretched her legs out in front of her and let them drop open, enjoying the expansion of the space between her legs.

After breakfast, William and Jao went to find rooms. They left Ada with Jeffrey. Ada suspected that William had done so purposely. But why? What could she possibly do with him in the hour or so they would be gone?

What she wanted to do was unbutton her shirt and show him her breasts, ask him if he liked them, let him put his hands inside her shirt. But instead of doing what she wanted to do, she questioned him.

"What will you do in Rio?"

"Oh, I have business there." Jeffrey looked away from her as he answered.

"What sort of business?"

He found something on the beach to feign interest in. Fishermen coming in with their catch, a boatload of travelers returning to an anchored ship, a wave crashing. Ada couldn't tell what he was looking at, but she suspected he didn't really see it anyway. "Why won't you say what your business is? Are you afraid I'll try to compete with you, or cheat you somehow?"

"You really are green, aren't you?" He took off his hat to wipe the sweat from his forehead. She imagined the taste of that sweat; it made her lightheaded. "In business, you play your cards close to the vest. Especially down here. There are a lot of men working on the fringes down here, making their own rules as they go. No one ever tells anyone the true nature of their exploits. You would do well to heed that advice yourself."

"But I wasn't asking you as one businessman to another. I was asking you as one friend to another."

"Ah, well, that's a decent gesture. But it's best to be wary of everyone."

"Isn't that a lonely way to live?" She felt her voice rising, becoming womanly. Perhaps her concerns were womanly as well. But Jeffrey didn't answer her. He turned back to the ocean, and this time his attention really did settle there. Ada was no longer in his awareness. She was certain of that. He had forgotten her as easily as one forgets a brief encounter with any stranger.

"I think I'll get a boat back to the ship now," he said.

Ada felt her pulse race at the thought of his leaving. "But you haven't said goodbye to William and Jao."

"They won't be crushed." He stood up, reaching out to shake her hand.

"I'll walk with you to the water," she said. He shrugged, and they set out together, strolling slowly to the sand. It was at the water's edge that she had first let her desire for Frederick transform itself from solitary to shared. Was she bewitched by the sea, was it the water that made her helpless in the face of a man's sex?

The sand crept into her boots and made walking uncomfortable. "Wait," she said to him. "I want to walk in the sand barefoot. I want my feet to literally touch South American soil." She flopped down into the sand and unlaced her boots. He watched her hands as they worked. It wasn't until she slipped off her cotton socks that Ada thought about how feminine her feet were. How could he possibly think even a nineteen-year-old boy's feet could be so small and smooth?

He seemed dumbstruck by her feet. She opened her mouth to speak, but she couldn't think of a word to say. She pointed her toes and pushed them into the sand. He looked up at her when her feet disappeared.

His face was like the map of the world, she thought. Tributaries and valleys, mountains and vast oceans moved across it. There was so much there to discover, it made her hungry for that adventure, and none other. All of a sudden, like the release of tightly packed snow in an avalanche, she let her true, woman's voice take control, gush forth. "All right," she said. "You must be thinking that my feet look ridiculously feminine. You must have wondered all along about me. I'm not very manly, am I? I don't think I'm even very boyish."

"What?" He looked simply dazed as he said the word.

"I'm a woman, Jeffrey. A twenty-six-year-old woman. Not a boy at all. Can't you see that?"

"But surely you're joking."

She threw open her jacket and gathered the fabric of her cotton shirt at the waist so that it pulled tightly against her breasts. So that he could see the shape of her breasts clearly. "I'm not a man. My name is Ada."

He stood abruptly. His balance was off, he had to shuffle to maintain his footing. "Really. Why are you telling me this now? This is a bit much, don't you think?"

"I think about you the way a woman thinks about a man, Jeffrey."

"But I have spent the past weeks thinking of you as a boy. This is too shocking. I need to go." He pushed himself up from the sand and began to walk toward the water. She hurried after him. Just before she reached him, he turned back to look at her. "I wish you the best of luck with whatever it is you are after. Ada." He held out his hand to shake hers, then he walked away, and this time she didn't try to follow.

Ada returned to her table at the cafe without dissolving into tears. As she waited for William and Jao to come for her, she drank coconut juice and watched the fishermen, and certainly no one around had any idea that she was distraught. When her partners arrived, Jao paid a young black man to load their luggage into a cart and follow them to the rooms they had found.

They walked across the plaza together. Black women in white hoop-skirted dresses sold fruits and many unfamiliar foods.

"Consecrated food," Jao said. "For Candomblé, the hidden Brazilian religion."

Consecrated food. Hidden religion. The idea made Ada wonder if she had lived a life that was too devoid of spiritual purpose. She never thought about food as anything more than something to satisfy hunger, and something that should taste pleasing. Jao pointed out acarajé, a black-eyed pea fritter fried in red palm oil, which was to be eaten in honor of Iansa, the goddess of wind, and Shango, the god of thunder and lightning. Small breezes lifted and dropped the branches of the palms and banana trees, people sang and talked, the melody of Portuguese fluttered all around them. She was here, here in Brazil, away from the cage that had kept her from knowing herself. There was really no time for mourning Jeffrey, nor was there purpose in it.

"Why is the religion hidden?" she asked Jao.

"The African people here were slaves until just a few years ago. Their masters insisted that they become Catholic. They had to hide their African religion from their masters. They wrapped it up inside the rituals of Catholicism, and no one noticed it there."

Later, alone in her small whitewashed room, Ada would allow herself a brief moment to grieve over the loss of Jeffrey, and then she would refuse to think about this man again. But now was for taking the time to see what was right in front of her. She had spent two weeks on the high seas, living as a man, in order to come here—the place from the photograph. This was the place that had called her, like a voice in the night.

After they had settled into their rooms and rested for an hour or two, the three adventurers met for dinner in a restaurant directly under their pension, or *pensão*. Neither Jao nor William mentioned Jeffrey to her. Ada felt grateful to them, and surprised by their consideration. She wondered if Edward would have had the sensitivity to even notice if a woman of his acquaintance was suffering for love.

In the cafe, she sat facing the street, watching the people go about their business. Again, she wanted to talk to Katie, to show her the man's suit she wore, to take her through the streets of Salvador de Bahia, strutting her maleness for Katie. Katie, she was sure, would fall easily into the South American rhythm. She would love it here. An idea came to her as she sat sipping her thick coffee.

"William," she said. "Do you know someone who could check in at Mr. Pryce's house for me? To find out about my lady's maid?"

He took his gaze off the people in the cafe, drawing himself back into the table. "I might. I would have to think about who could safely go there." He set to silent ruminations. Ada watched him, eager to hear a positive response. He rubbed his jaw, closed his eyes. Ada leaned forward, her desire to communicate with Katie growing with each silent second.

Jao suddenly spoke. "I know someone." Ada almost jumped out of her seat.

"Oh, Jao, do you really?"

"Yes. I know a secretary at the Orchid Society. He might go around to leave a message for Mr. Pryce, and ask a few questions while he's there. He could say he has a friend who knows your Katie."

"What sort of message could he give to Edward that wouldn't arouse his suspicion?" Ada held her throat. It struck her the instant she did it as an overly feminine gesture, but she was too tense to replace that instinctive action with another, more masculine gesture. Self-conscious of her hand now, she left it frozen there on her neck.

Jao and William both looked up at the ceiling, where a fan of palm fronds rotated, propelled by a wire contraption hooked up to some sort of winding device on the wall. The slight breeze it made ruffled across their heads at regular intervals. William's voice lifted across the puffs of air. "How about sending him a message from Walter's lady here, asking him what he knows about Walter's death?"

"Oh, William, I don't think that's a good idea," Ada said. The thought of it panicked her, made her feel suddenly vulnerable, even all these thousands of miles from Boston. It made her feel as if Edward were breathing down her neck.

William hadn't mentioned Walter since they left the United States. But now, in the tightness of William's voice, she could hear his hurt; it was clear William still resented the fact that Edward had not been charged and punished for Walter's death. "Why isn't it a good idea?" he asked her.

Wasn't it obvious? Couldn't William see that it would put her in danger? But she couldn't bring herself to say it. They had changed their plans, allowing her, a woman, to come with them on the journey that would soon get more difficult, and they hadn't complained. Or, at least, William hadn't complained. It was probably true that she should do something for them in return. But they had to understand that it would be impossible to prove Edward had anything to do with Walter's death. "He's a rich man. No one will believe it. And what would a message like that accomplish? What do you think he would do about it?"

"It would frighten him," William said. "He deserves every bit of discomfort that happens upon him. Or that we can visit upon him."

Ada felt an irrational urge to defend Edward. Even now, she hadn't fully considered the fact that Edward had abused her, had diminished her, had prevented her from being herself, and had made her feel ashamed of that self. Her experiences since she left him were rapid, alive with sensation; she had spent little time contemplating her marriage. But somehow, still, even though she was shedding so much of her former self so rapidly, William's attacks on Edward felt strangely like a criticism of her. And she had to defend herself against them.

"I can't see what good could possibly come of it. You should let it alone."

Jao held up his hand, signaling them to stop. "I know what I'll tell him to say. He'll simply tell your husband that he heard someone had found the *Cattleya labiata vera*."

Ada felt herself take in a sharp breath. What would Edward do if he thought the *Cattleya* was obtainable? Ada didn't want to know. "But, Jao," she began.

"No, no 'But, Jao,'" William said. "You have no reason to object to that. It will work. It's perfect, Jao." William's bearing changed then. His shoulders relaxed and his head lifted. He began to eat the food that had gone untouched until now. He even smiled at Ada. "That's all settled," he said. "You will find out about your maid, and we'll open up communications with Mr. Pryce."

In her struggle against this remembered fear of her husband, Ada had almost forgotten about Katie. Now, though, the mention of her maid was a mere distraction from the more pressing issue. "But don't you think it's possible that Edward will guess I'm with you?" Ada felt fear closing her throat as she spoke.

"Why would he think that?" Jao asked her. "It seems to me to be the last thing he would imagine of you. He probably thinks you ran off with some man."

"You don't know what he's like. He is very determined. He might guess." William was laughing as she spoke. He laughed silently, but his whole body was caught in the vibration of the laughter. His shoulders and head bounced, his hands clapped his knees. "What is so funny?" Ada demanded.

William shook his head. "I'm laughing at Jao. Saying Mr. Pryce thinks you ran off with some man. If only he knew you had run off with two men, and you yourself have become a man. If he were here, he would see nothing but men everywhere he looked."

Jao joined William. They laughed together until the table rattled. But Ada couldn't see beyond her fear. She was unable even to smile. Still, the sounds of these two men's laughter soothed her. Especially Jao's. She had worried things would be difficult with him. Now, though, his surliness seemed to be sloughing off just a bit.

"I'll go to the post office before we leave Bahia," Jao told them. "We'll find out the things each of us wants to know. In time." Ada relaxed into the awareness that it would take weeks for a message to get to Boston, and more weeks for Edward to respond, if he did have a response at all. Distance did offer a form of protection.

During their three days in Bahia, they ate in cafes, bought fruit from the women in the plaza, drank with people they met, and worked gradually toward acquiring all the supplies they would need for their venture into the mountains. Ada wondered if Jao and William were more casual because she was their partner. Would they have worked more resolutely on the trips financed by Edward and the other men from the Orchid Society? Did the simple fact that she was a woman remove the sense of urgency from their intentions? She didn't push the matter, though; she meant to store up her energies before heading out into the jungles. The imagined hardships were beginning to frighten her. Now that she was here, at the very edge of civilization, she felt the unknown tugging at her sleeve, breathing down her neck, whispering to her in her dreams. Anything could happen now.

THEIR LAST TRANSACTION in Bahia was the purchase of three horses to ride and three donkeys for carrying supplies and, eventually, orchids. The horses they bought were sturdy and healthy, but they lacked Mercury's sleek lines and aesthetic appeal. They were work horses. Ada paid seventy-five dollars for the three of them.

"It's better we own them, rather than rent them," William said. "Who knows where we'll end up? We may not be in a position to return the horses." They tied the beasts to a hitching post and had a final sit-down in a cafe on the plaza.

"Remember Snow?" Jao asked.

Ada thought he was yearning for cooler weather. William laughed. "He was a piece of work."

"He's buried not far from here," Jao said.

William removed his hat. "Hats off to the man." Jao took his hat off. The two held their hats and looked at Ada. She removed hers as well, her thick hair springing out around her head. They held their hats for three seconds, then replaced them on their sweaty heads.

So what had happened to this man? She looked around her, at the lush and alien environment, at her companions. No one in the world, other than these two men, knew where she was at this moment. Who would look for her if she vanished from the earth? "Was he an orchid hunter?" she asked.

"One of the best," said Jao.

Ada didn't want to know, but she asked nonetheless. "What happened to him?"

"Knife fight." William said it, and Jao nodded, as if it were nothing unusual.

Ada's head felt tight around her skull. The heat pressed in from every angle. Mosquitoes buzzed around her ears and eyes. She put her foot up on the rung of Jao's chair, causing her legs to spread wide. Resting her elbow on her knee, she dropped her head into her hand. William and Jao laughed at her.

"Did you think this adventure would be safe? Easy?" Jao asked. "I hope not. After all, you've always known what happened to Walter."

They settled their bill and climbed onto their laden animals. Ada didn't speak as they rode out of town and toward the ridges of the world. Memories of her bedroom in Boston bothered her again now. But she left the noise of her doubts unspoken. Inside her head only she battled with the strange desire to return to the comfort of a life that had almost annihilated her, to retreat from her fear of what was beyond the edges of this city, on the far side of comfort. Holding her back straight, her head high, she kicked her horse in the side, keeping pace with the experienced travelers who guided her farther and farther distant from the familiar.

The orchids, William and Jao had told her, were found in valleys of the mountains between Pernambuco and Bahia, at elevations between two and five thousand feet. They grew in tree branches and on their trunks, or on the bare rocks of mountain gorges. Brazilian orchids included Edward's beloved *Cattleya*, and the *Sophronitis*.

"I haven't heard of that one," Ada told them.

"The *Sophronitis* will stop you where you stand. It beckons you," Jao told her. "You could fall in love with the thing." The resonant baritone of Jao's voice radiated, surrounded her like an orb of sound. Even when he had been irritated with her, the sound of his voice soothed the impact of his scorn.

They would travel most of the way on their own, hiring men to help them only when they had found what they were looking for. "The fewer people who know what we're doing and where we're doing it, the better for us," William had told her on board the *Sea Witch*. At the time, she thought he was being cautious about competitors, but since their conversation at breakfast, and the mention of the dead man, Snow, she thought his warning might be more ominous. Perhaps he was worried about violence as well as competition.

It wasn't until they had ridden away from the city for over an hour that William finally took out his map for the first time. They stopped under a tree, a lush tropical tree that reached over them like a canopy, protecting them from the sun. William unfolded his map carefully, with a tenderness that was startling to Ada. She wondered then if William had ever really loved a woman. If he touched any woman the way he touched his map, surely she would never want him to leave her bed.

"I've made notations in code," he said, pointing to symbols and letters on the map. "The symbols represent different species of orchid. The letters indicate where they've been found. But not quite. I don't mark the exact spot. I have a system for marking based on a compass. All the marks are off by varying degrees, depending on what quadrant of the map the markings are in."

Jao laughed. "No one knows how to read William's maps. Not even me. If he died tomorrow, you and I would be out of luck, Adam."

William consulted the map just long enough to determine their next move. "We should head off over this hill, and toward that small valley there, to the northwest." No one was about to argue with him. By now, it was evident to Ada that Jao knew his way around the Brazilian jungle, but he followed his instincts. William's map was a scientific device, a technological tool, and Jao didn't consider himself in a position to question its superiority.

They rode their horses till Ada was hungry, and her back and buttocks hurt. She had never spent so many hours on a horse, had never imagined it could be so hard on a body. She wanted to stop, spread out a blanket, and enjoy food and laughter with friends. What had she been thinking when she suspected Jao and William didn't push themselves hard enough? If only they would take breaks more frequently, life might be bearable. Finally, just as she began to think she might expire quietly in her saddle, they stopped long enough to eat bread, fruits, and boiled eggs, to drink water from their canteens. Then they were off again, slowly climbing up into higher altitudes.

The first time Ada had to urinate, she simply couldn't bring herself to tell her companions. She denied her need until it was on the verge of spilling out of her. "William," she called. "I need to stop."

He slowed his horse, turning to look at her. She could see he was about to ask what she needed, but when he saw the look on her face, he nodded. He and Jao rode a hundred feet past her. She hid herself behind a tree and dropped her trousers, but as she squatted there, her rear exposed to the air, she imagined all manner of creatures finding their way into her orifices, and biting her, or worse, simply resting there, colonizing her most contained spaces. Without Jao and William within sight, she felt helpless.

But that was her first time relieving herself in the open air. The second and third times were easier, and soon enough, urination in open spaces, even changing her monthly rags out here, seemed perfectly natural. She even forgot to worry about hiding herself from William and Jao. After all, they didn't make much of relieving themselves in front of her if they had to. At one point, Jao jumped off his horse, stood at the edge of the narrow pathway they were on, and peed over the side, down the steep slope. He was finished in under a minute. When he came back to his horse, Ada called to him.

"Do you do that in front of all women, or am I privileged?"

The narrow trail didn't allow him to turn his horse around to face her, so he craned his neck around. "You're one of us, aren't you?"

"You mean I'm a man?"

"Yes, that's what I mean. You live as a man, you act like a man. So, to me, you are a man. Or at least a boy. It would make me too uneasy to start thinking of you as a woman."

"Let's move along," William said. "We need to maintain our progress."

The horses and the donkeys commenced their lumbering trek up the mountain, and the three partners fell into silence. Ada thought about this idea of her manhood. Never in her life had she wanted to be a man. She would have loved to do something with her education, and she believed it should be her right to vote, and she wanted the freedom a man has, but that had nothing to do with wanting to *be* a man. Strident opponents of women's suffrage claimed making decisions about the country's welfare was a man's game, and the women who wanted to participate in it had abandoned their femininity. They were not real women, they claimed. Ada had always felt womanly, though. Still, maybe Jao was right. This tendency to masculinity might explain why she hadn't wanted children, and why she enjoyed sex, and even college. And it would certainly explain why she had a sudden desire to take off on such an uncomfortable adventure. Few women, she knew, would even consider doing what Ada was attempting to accomplish.

THEY SPENT THEIR first night on the road in a thatched hut with dirt floors. It was late when they arrived, and Ada was exhausted. William would pay the owners of the hut, an Indian family who slept in another hut next door, the equivalent of one dollar for the room and breakfast for the three of them.

They all three slept in the one room together, on hammocks made of hemp. Ada threw her sleeping bag over the hammock and began to climb in. Even with an oil lamp burning and William and Jao talking, she was sure she would sleep instantly.

"Whoa. Slow down, there," Jao said. "You're missing a vital piece of equipment." He pulled something out of his pack and carried it over to her. "You'll get eaten alive without this. He shook out the mosquito net and hung it from the hooks holding the hammock in place, then spread it out all around Ada. "You can't live without these in the tropics."

"Thank you, Jao," Ada said. She fell asleep so quickly, in the morning she had no memory of anything after that instant.

She woke up, with the first sun, to a face leaning over her. Her instincts moved her to sit up, but the hammock started to swing as she struggled to find purchase somewhere on its soft surfaces. Finally, she simply leaned back and looked up into the face. It was that of a young girl. She had poked her torso inside the mosquito net, just to stare at Ada, it seemed.

"Bom dia," Ada said to her. The girl jumped back, tangling herself in the net. Ada imagined she was thirteen or fourteen years old. The white net was a foil for her long black hair and smooth dark skin. Ada was sorry she didn't know enough Portuguese to talk to the girl. She pushed the netting aside and looked across the room at Jao. He was still sleeping in his own hammock. She struggled to find something she could say to the embarrassed girl that would calm her.

"O que é teu nome?" She suddenly remembered, What is your name?

The girl had finally stepped outside the netting. Ada scooped it away so she could look at the girl, and wait for her answer.

"Gisela," the girl said, barely whispering her name. Her big black eyes widened, and her small face pulled back a bit.

Ada had slept in her cotton undershirt and underwear. She had no idea now whether the girl thought she was a man or a woman. Certainly she could see the shape of Ada's breasts through the thin shirt. But how could it matter? Surely no acquaintance of Edward's would find their way to this hut in the jungle and learn that Ada had been here. She put her hand to her chest and said her name. "Ada." She tapped her chest and said it again. "Ada."

"*Bom dia,* Ada," Gisela said. The girl's mouth spread into a smile that exposed her straight white teeth and creased dimples into her cheeks. The sound of her real name startled her. Ada and Gisela looked at each other, neither knowing what else could be said that the other would understand.

Suddenly, the girl dipped her head and covered her mouth. She chattered away in Portuguese, then turned and ran out of the hut. Fifteen minutes later she returned with a woman who must have been her mother. They carried trays laden with tea, a platter of an egg and meat dish, and mangoes. William and Jao stirred, awakened by the smell of the food, no doubt. Ada pulled a jacket over her long underwear while her companions distracted Gisela and her mother.

The three orchidists sat on the dirt floor to eat on a cloth spread in front of them. Jao spoke to the girl and her mother in Portuguese, offering to share the food with them, apparently. They refused, but they seemed unable to tear themselves away from the visitors as they ate. They watched their guests as if they were a rare entertainment, and not a move was to be missed. Ada wondered how they saw Jao. He spoke Portuguese, he had the same dark skin as they did, yet he dressed like a foreigner, and he brought with him these two strange Americans. Their curiosity was intense, but was it directed toward Jao as much as toward the Americans?

As he spoke to them, Jao was more animated and relaxed than Ada had ever seen him. His smile came easily, and often. Ada realized that she had rarely seen that smile. It creased his angular face and lifted his eyes as it showed off his white teeth. The mood in the room was so light, it made all the rest of the time Ada had spent in Jao's company seem formal and dismal in comparison. Portuguese filled the space around them. Occasionally, even William uttered a simple sentence or two in Portuguese. Ada felt banished by her ignorance of the language. She wanted to know what was making Jao smile so beautifully, what words made his shoulders lift and fall, what meaning inhered in the lush syllables that floated between the people in the room.

Her ignorance made her angry. When Gisela and her mother finally left, taking away the empty bowls and platters with them, and the language shifted immediately from Portuguese to English, Ada found herself snapping at her companions.

"What were you talking about?" She knew it came out more a demand than a question.

"Just the food, and the weather, and bits of nonsense," Jao said.

"It was rude of you to go on and on without telling me what was being said. Without saying anything to me at all." Ada felt the pulsing of her blood quicken. It was difficult to catch her breath. Hadn't she felt this same sensation, this doubling of the pressures in her body, so many times in Edward's company?

Jao's eyes narrowed as he looked into hers. "I was simply being polite to our hostess." He turned away from her, without further explanation, without waiting for a response from her.

William regarded her. His face registered surprise. Or was it disgust? But wasn't she correct in believing they had been rude? Jao might at least have translated a word here and there, just so that she would feel included. William went to assist Jao. Ada ran her hand through her short hair, and suddenly felt the loss of its length. Her fingers ached to complete the movement through the hairs, down past her neck and along her shoulder. How could they be stopped so abruptly, there beneath her ear? Would Jao treat her with more consideration if she were to grow it back and don a skirt? Ada went to do her part in helping her partners to pack the horses and the donkeys with fresh provisions. The three of them worked together without speaking. When the men went into the main hut without her, to negotiate and settle the bill, Ada found Gisela's mother, heading off into the jungle carrying a basket.

"Desculpe-me," she called out to the woman, whose name she never did learn. The woman stopped and smiled at Ada.

Ada remembered the word for dress. *"Vestido?"* Suddenly, she felt she had to have a dress, a colorful cotton dress like the ones Brazilian women wore. *"Comprar?"*

The woman smiled and spoke too quickly for Ada to understand a word. But she beckoned to Ada to follow her into the main house. There, the woman spread out three dresses on the floor and pointed to each of them in turn as she talked. From the inflection of her words, Ada guessed she was extolling the virtues of each dress in turn. The turquoise dress with green sashes caught Ada's eye. She touched it, and was surprised by how soft the cotton was against her fingertips. *"Quanto?"* she asked. The woman answered, but Ada couldn't understand. Finally, she took her purse from her pocket and held out a number of coins. The woman fingered them, finally picking out two twenty-*reis* coins. Ada picked up the dress and rolled it as tight as she could, then stuffed it inside her jacket. The woman laughed. Ada hoped she imagined that the dress was for a sweetheart, and not that Ada was in fact a woman.

"Obrigada," she said to the woman.

Neither William nor Jao was near the horses when she stepped outside. She managed to hide the dress in her pack before they appeared. She couldn't know then how much time would pass before she would have the opportunity to feel the soft cotton against her skin, or to present herself to the world as a woman.

PEREGRINATIONS

The night after leaving their hosts in the jungle, Ada had her first experience of sleeping on the ground. She was surprised by the realization that she had never even slept out of doors.

They threw the mosquito nets over tree branches and put the sleeping sacks underneath them each night. Once she was inside the net and the sack, the ragged crust of the earth under her body confounded her. There was no give there, and as the night air cooled, the ground seemed to freeze up in anticipation. Tropical birds squawked throughout the night, intermittent breezes ruffled the trees, Jao or William coughed or groaned occasionally, she heard animals rustling about nearby. All of these things in concert made her sleep scattered. Her bones felt wet when she woke in the morning, as if they had absorbed the earth's moisture during the night. Her muscles ached from the hardness of her bed.

Every bump and sway of the horse reminded her of her discomfort, and her linen suit absorbed the heat the earth reflected during the day, making her feel as if she were dressed in a small greenhouse. Her buttocks were sore from the hard leather saddle, and she was hungry and thirsty all the time. When they did stop to eat and drink, it seemed as if there never was enough. But she followed William's route, marked out on his precious map, without complaining. Though she was sure they heard her agony in the tone of her voice, and saw it in the set of her jaw, she was careful not to allow her words to reveal her discomfort.

After three or four nights on the ground, her body seemed to adjust to the rough edges. She forgot about the hardness, or the hardness began to accept her and conform to her own smooth and soft surfaces. It stopped hurting to lie down on the ground, and her sleep shifted from an amorphous, watery thing to a solid respite from the drudgery of travel.

The first night of deep sleep, she dreamed she was back in Boston. When she woke in the morning, she expected to find herself in the greenhouse there, surrounded by Edward's precious flowers. She was surprised when she opened her eyes and saw the clay so close to her face. Why had she dreamed of Boston? Did she miss home? Even the word *home* surprised her now. Was Boston home? Did she have a home?

The morning sun struck a cold beam across her face. The earth and the air were still too chilly for the sun to insinuate its warmth. She lay in her sleeping sack, too cold to get out and start to move. A sudden sting on her calf made her nearly jump out of her sack. Then there was another, and another. She threw the covers off and examined her legs. Fierce red welts slashed across her thighs and calves. She rubbed at her skin, trying to soothe it, but the burning intensified with the friction. Another biting sting brought her to her feet. Just as she stood, she heard William cry out.

"Ouch. Ow. Damnation." He was on his feet in an instant, hopping from one to the other and swatting at himself. Ada looked at his feet. It was then she spotted the columns of red ants: three of them, each headed toward a sleeping sack. By now, Jao was on his feet, too, shouting in Portuguese, kicking at his bedding. Then he ran.

"The river," William said, and ran after Jao. Ada followed. She jumped into the water right along with the two men.

The river was perhaps one hundred feet across. The water was a calm green, shallow enough near the banks for them to stand with their heads above water. William spit water from his mouth. "That was stupid," he said. "We should have been prepared for that." As he shook his head, Ada watched the water spin out from his hair in tiny droplets that caught the sun, refracting it. The denseness of the jungle around them seemed to cushion his voice and the sounds the three of them made in the water.

William waded out of the river and went to his pack. "I have remedies," he told them.

Ada and Jao sat side by side in the clay dirt while William applied moistened chewing tobacco to their bites. He topped the tobacco with a mud poultice. The stinging of the bites was so intense, Ada didn't think to be modest when William's fingers touched her bare skin. It would occur to her only later that it was fortunate she had no bites on her breasts, and thus was saved the embarrassment of exposing them in front of the two men. Jao and Ada together applied the poultices to William. The tobacco and mud were soothing, cooling. But they didn't prevent the fevers that struck all three of them.

William sprinkled kerosene in the dirt around their sacks to deter ants. "I should have done this last night. I should have known," he said.

"Never mind," said Ada as she climbed back into her bed. "Never mind." That was the last any of them spoke until, well into the evening, their fevers finally subsided. She drifted in and out of sleep. She dreamed of Boston again, of the activities and people in her house. She dreamed of Edward's orchids. As she woke, Katie's voice seemed to linger in her ear.

It was near dusk. The sun was bigger than the sky as it dropped below the forest canopy. It seemed as if they were somehow millions of miles closer to the burning orb than anyone had ever been. It cast a purple glow over the landscape that was visible through the lush vegetation.

They ate dinner, and afterward Jao talked about African-Brazilian mythologies, telling them the stories of some of the pantheon of Candomblé gods.

"Iansã is the goddess of storms, tempests, and rains. She was one of the Orixa gods who traveled from Africa to Brazil with the slave trade." Jao seemed to have let down his guard with her as he told these stories. Perhaps the remnants of his fever made him forget his wariness. "Her husband, Shango, is the god of thunder and fertility. Together they create storms, wreaking havoc and destruction." He leaned back against a tree and looked up into the canopy of branches above them. "For some reason, when I think of her, it brings to mind my favorite Shakespeare play, *The Tempest*," he said. "Wonderful story. I imagine Iansã as the force behind that storm Prospero conjured up."

Ada had forgotten that Jao read Shakespeare. If she had thought of it while they were sailing, she might have wanted to discuss his works with Jao. But now everything seemed different. Her ideas about Shakespeare might even be different. "What would that play have been like if Shakespeare had written it about a magical woman rather than a man? What if Prospero were a woman?" Ada asked.

Jao and William both fell silent. Even out here, when the Woman Question came up, men fell silent. In the silence, Ada's thoughts slipped to Frederick, and she wondered then what he would say if he were here beside her, riding through the Brazilian jungle on horseback, sleeping in the dirt, discussing African goddesses in light of Shakespeare. She laughed out loud, imagining him here with her, unwashed and dressed in simple clothes. He had always been so clean and nicely dressed.

Would he be drawn to Iansã? Jao told them that she is also, strangely, the goddess of the marketplace, and of funeral processions and cemeteries. This deity, who causes upheaval and guides the dead, also presides over creativity and commerce.

"What we believe," Jao said, "is stronger than what we experience. That is why African slaves were able to survive the horrors they lived. What we believe, we often have to keep secret. Because Candomblé has been hidden, it celebrates the secret side of being. You can believe that Prospero was a woman if you'd like, Adam," he said. "It makes no difference to Shakespeare, I am sure."

Jao, always practical, dedicated to action and problem solving, was suddenly a mystic when he talked about Candomblé. This philosophical side of him was softer, yet it made him seem even more distant. But as he talked to his traveling companions about the gods, Ada wanted him to keep talking. She wanted him to tell them everything he knew about this strange religion.

He told the stories of several other deities. Finally, his stories finished for the night, they fell asleep early and slept hard. But Jao woke them up near midnight. "We must pack the horses and donkeys now," he said. "We'll have to travel for part of the night to make up for our lost day."

"We're headed for the deep jungle," William told them. Ada was reminded of Edward and his habit of offering her information as if it were a great sacrifice to himself, or a largesse for which she should be forever grateful. It wouldn't have mattered if William had named the place. She didn't know where the deep jungle might be, or even where she was at the moment. Would they pass a city on the way? Would there be anyone there with whom she could communicate in English? In the end, would they finally reach the orchids they had come here to find?

"Good. So we'll stop in Juàzeiro?"

William nodded.

"Carnaval," Jao said.

"Yes. Carnaval," William answered.

They smiled as they said the word *Carnaval*, savoring the sound of it and whatever it signified to them. Ada knew of Carnaval only from gossip she had heard about Rio de Janeiro. Rio was renowned in Boston for its pagan decadence, its celebration of sexuality and wild music and dance. All the things that Victorian Boston was careful to dismiss or veil. "When will we be getting to the business of orchid hunting?" Ada asked. She felt, as she spoke, as if she were defending the puritan ways of her ancestors. There was an edge to her voice, which seemed, somehow, fitting. It was, after all, her money, meant to get them to the source of the orchids, not to carry them across oceans and continents so that they might immerse themselves in decadence.

"Carnaval is a good place to get information. A good place and time," Jao said. "People are happy, freed from their labors for a while. And they have been drinking and dancing and making love enough so that they feel generous. They'll tell us anything we want to know."

"And they won't be suspicious of us, either," William added. "Not now, at least. We need to go to Carnaval, Adam."

So they headed for Juàzeiro and Carnaval.

BY THE TIME they arrived in Juàzeiro, Ada hadn't bathed in days. Her duck suit was thick with dust, her hair stiff from her own oils and the earth she had slept on, her skin thickened by grime and burned by the relentless sun. Her whole body seemed to have lost its suppleness from sleeping on hard surfaces. Her scent couldn't be pleasant, though she had ceased being able to smell it herself.

"I need a bath, William. I need a room somewhere where there's a bath."

"That's fine. We all need one, I suspect."

It was nothing more than a hip bath in a small closet down the hall from her room, but the warm water eased her muscles, and watching the dirt roll off her skin and into the water offered her a kind of contentment. It was as if the process of rubbing the dirt from her skin was a concrete act of absolution, or simply accomplishment. She performed the act, there on her skin, and the results were visible, here in the water. Even Edward would approve of its simplicity.

Her breasts floated in the water, insisting on her acknowledgment of their existence. As she gazed on them, she was taken in by the wonder of the things. They were at the root of so much desire and satisfaction, and yet what were they really? A source of food for infants, infants who existed on some fantastical plane outside her own reality. So what did she need breasts for? She was no mother, and she was really not a woman at all anymore. Perhaps she would do well to slice them away, as the Amazons had reportedly done.

She dressed in her only remaining clean suit. As she pulled the undershirt over her breasts, and then buttoned the shirt on top of that, she remembered the ritual of lacing up her old corsets, and was glad to be free of it. She took a deep breath, allowing her waist to expand at will. The pocket of air in her belly tickled her, made her laugh. For an instant, she believed fully that she was living the life she was destined to live, that her choices were leading her to a kind of perfection that neither Alice Bunker Stockham nor Edward Pryce was wise enough to understand.

They passed two days and nights in which they did little more than eat, sleep, and wander the town aimlessly. The quest for orchids seemed to be an afterthought, a footnote to their travels through Brazil. "It's better to work this way," William told her. "Mr. Pryce and Mr. Locke and the others pushed us so hard, they were so insistent upon immediate results, we probably left many rare and valuable orchids behind in our rush to get back." Ada made no protest; she was learning to understand the idea of taking each day as it came.

ON THE THIRD DAY, in the early evening, William and Jao stopped at her door, inviting her to join them on a quest for food. They stepped from the small hotel into the streets, where Ada felt the music in her feet almost before she heard it. The vibration rose through her like a remembrance of the crisis of orgasm. Carnaval was beginning.

"It's the *batucada* of Carnaval," Jao told her. "The drumming."

People dressed in costumes and masks danced everywhere. The revelers undulated and writhed their bodies with an abandon that, had Ada tried it in her own bed with her own husband, would have earned her a special trip to Dr. Casey and his vibrating machine. Women swayed to the music, lifting their colorful cotton skirts above their knees, shaking their shoulders till their breasts nearly bounced out of their blouses. Men put their hands on the women's undulating hips, and the women laughed in response. This was what frightened people about Carnaval.

Many of the men and women wore costumes that mimicked colonial European fashions: low-cut dresses with huge hoop skirts, long, brightly colored jackets with gold buttons. "Why are they dressed like eighteenth-century plantation owners?" Ada asked.

Jao pushed his voice out over the sounds of the music. "Carnaval is a time when people play at being who they would rather be. The servant can become the master. The slave can become the slave owner. At the same time they are free to make fun of their masters. In a way, they make them look ridiculous when they turn their fashions into costumes." The clothing was almost comical in its imitation of the original. More elaborate, and at the same time less fine.

They passed women seated on the plaza with consecrated foods for sale, spread out on the ground before them. "Why don't we eat some?" Ada asked.

"I want something more substantial," said Jao.

"I want meat," William said.

They continued their pilgrimage across the crowded plaza. A young black woman moved onto their path, dancing right in front of Ada. She stopped, her back to Ada, but turned to look over her shoulder at Ada. She rocked her hips back and forth, allowing them to rub up against Ada. Jao laughed. "The girls like you," he said. "You need to show your appreciation." He held out his hands in a gesture that indicated Ada should put her hands on the woman's hips.

"No. I can't."

"Go ahead. She won't go away until you notice her."

Ada reached out her hands and placed them on the pair of hips in front of her. The woman put her hands over Ada's, moving her hips as if they were guided by Ada's hands. Ada closed her eyes, allowing the pulse of the drums to move through her fingers. She may not have realized that her own hips were beginning to pitch and sway. Perhaps this unfamiliar freedom to move unhinged her momentarily, and she forgot everything she had learned over a lifetime in Boston.

Jao and William were dancing now, through the streets on their way to a cafe. Ada released her grip on the woman and went after her companions. As her man's stride cut across the plaza, she was overcome by the rush of color from the women's costumes. Her suit felt too colorless, too absent of femininity. She wanted, more than anything, to wear a woman's costume, and dance through the streets in it.

They sat on the patio, watching the pageant of revelers, allowing the music to reverberate up from the ground and into their spines. The beautiful dresses swirling around her mesmerized Ada. She ate *churrasco*, a range of barbecued meats, that Jao ordered for all of them. Finally, without speaking to William or Jao, who talked now with the diners at the table next to theirs, she stood and went to the plaza, where she stopped the woman who had danced for her and asked her, in halting Portuguese, where she might find a costume. She had to shout to be heard above the music. Finally, the woman seemed to understand. She took Ada by the hand, leading her away from the plaza and down a narrow alleyway.

The music rose up and traveled across the buildings, settling itself down into the alley, shaking the walls and the cobblestones beneath their feet. The woman laughed, and danced her walk.

"O que é teu nome?" Ada asked her.

"Juliana," she said, her voice coming across the noise of Carnaval with the clarity of a small brass bell. *"E teu?"*

"Ada." She said it the North American way, with a long *A* first.

Juliana repeated it after her, as if it were an unfamiliar name. "A-da." She took Ada's hand again. *"Vem com mim."*

They arrived at a tall blue door that led them through a high wall flush with the alley. The wooden door creaked as Juliana pushed it open, revealing a tiny, lush courtyard. *"Vem,"* Juliana said again.

A few short steps, and Juliana opened up the French windows that led into the house. The room—the parlor, Ada supposed—was small. But the tile floors were cool, and the colorful furniture and tapestries, inviting. Ada imagined this room might make her feel safe if it were hers.

"Um vestido," Ada said, trying to make it clear to Juliana that she wanted to dress as a woman, not a man.

"Eu tenho assim muitos," Juliana said.

She pulled Ada through the front room and into the back, where a mattress sat on the floor. A blue curtain was strung across the back wall. Juliana pushed it aside, revealing a rod holding colorful dresses, set off by the whitewashed wall behind them. Ada hurried across the room, eager to touch the fabrics.

Juliana was speaking quickly now, and Ada failed to understand her. But she motioned to the dresses, an inviting gesture. Ada touched several before her fingers rested on a dress of a shimmering green with gold embroidery.

Juliana pulled it down and handed it to Ada, who took off her jacket and unbuttoned her shirt, not stopping to think about what she would soon reveal to Juliana.

As Ada pulled off her undershirt, Juliana's chatter ceased, and a long whistle eased out of her lips. *"Você é uma mulher,"* she said finally.

"*Sim.* I'm a woman." Juliana had thought Ada was a man who wanted to dress as a woman, and she had been totally accepting of her nonetheless. Now she knew Ada was a woman who had dressed as a man, and still she was fine. Woman, boy, wife, college graduate, lonely traveler, orchid hunter. Her identity cut so many ways now, all of it was beginning to seem just another piece of her. What she wanted for now was to put on the dress and go out into the streets to dance.

Juliana decorated the dress with shiny beads and a silver belt. The best piece of the costume, though, was the mask, a blue satin encrusted with rhinestones and elaborate feathers. It gave Ada a birdlike quality. She stepped in front of the looking glass that leaned against the wall to look at herself through the eyes of the mask. The dress hugged her body, revealing the swell of her breasts. Her hair was barely touching her shoulders, but still, there was no doubt she looked like a woman.

JULIANA TOOK ADA'S HAND and led her back to the streets. *"Você é bonita,"* she whispered into her ear. Ada felt beautiful, and tonight that was all that mattered. The rhythm of the music was as steady as the pulsing of the blood through her heart, and surely every bit as crucial. Without this pulsing, this loud beat, how would the world continue to spin? she wondered. She followed Juliana into the plaza, where she finally listened to the drums with every part of her body, and all those bits of her that had been sleeping for so long became thick with the blood of life.

People filled the plaza and the streets around it. Most of them were Africans. Many were Indian, or even Indian and African. Ada saw few other white people, but this absence caused her little discomfort.

Many of the dancers were drinking, but the music and the dance were all the intoxicant Ada would ever need. She danced near and around Juliana, she danced next to men she didn't know. Somewhere in the middle of her wanderings she saw Jao, then William. The dancing was like something she had always known how to do, had always been waiting to do, and yet as she danced, it was as if some other person had taken control of her body. Some part of her awareness knew it couldn't really be her, abandoning all sense of propriety in front of all these people, in a public place. No matter that everyone else was doing it, too. This simply couldn't be Ada.

But this other person, this Adam/Ada creature, was good at what she did. She enjoyed it, and it seemed to expand her. The more she danced, the more she knew how to dance, and the more she wanted to keep dancing. The drums were like some ancient language that she had spoken before she lost herself, and now as the vibrations inched through her, she remembered more than she had ever had time to forget. It was all so big, and it required that she increase in order to absorb it. She danced with an attention to the ground, and the way her feet moved upon it, that made her forget to notice the stars.

She danced her way across the plaza, and at various times she danced next to Jao, and William. Juliana was with her; she danced with Jao and Wiliam, too. William seemed unable to let her move away from him. He followed her as she zigzagged across the plaza. Ada felt oddly happy that William was drawn to Juliana.

A thin veil of sweat materialized all over Ada's body. For the first time she could remember, Ada felt beautiful because of the sweat. It made her desirable, she thought. It brought a sheen to her skin, and signaled her warmth, her heat. And it served as a conduit for the currents of the drums. It soaked them up, spreading them around the surface area of her skin, then under it, and into her inner organs. When she felt the drums there, vibrating in her veins, Ada believed that she had attained a moment of perfect grace. If only Alice Bunker Stockham had tried dancing to drums. *Karezza* would have been a very different book if she had.

Time expanded and shrunk back into itself, disappearing entirely. She danced, sometimes alone, sometimes with strangers. She moved in and out of knots of people, bumping up against Juliana, William, Jao at different points. She danced for a moment with Jao. And then Juliana was there, saying something to Jao in Portuguese. Jao laughed so hard his shoulders shook.

Ada went to him and yelled into his ear, her voice barely audible above the drums. "What did she say?"

"That your male spirit guide must have possessed you." Jao's voice was clear, vivid, in spite of the level of noise around them.

"What do you mean?"

"Your men's clothing. She explains it as spiritual possession."

Ada stopped dancing and looked around at all the dancing and singing people, listened to the wild drumming.

"It's not a bad thing to be spirit-possessed," he said. "Here, it's simply a fact of life."

She moved away from Jao then, and stopped thinking. She allowed her reactions to the evening to be purely visceral. She felt the blood move through her veins, she felt herself grow larger.

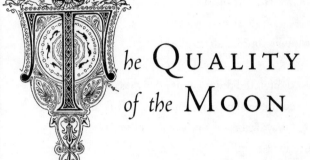

The Quality of the Moon

Her body began to betray her later in the evening. She sensed it growing tired; her feet were hurting, her dancing slowed. That was when she first saw the white man, on the far end of the plaza. He stood out because his dancing was awkward, yet somehow sensual at the same time. Ada's curiosity propelled her toward him. His mask was simple, covering only his eyes, so when she came close she realized almost instantly that this white man was Jeffrey. The man she had desired so fervently, and then had completely forgotten.

She stood directly in front of him and danced for him. He watched her. She saw the instant when he realized it was her, and in that moment her body seemed to move in synchronicity with all the drummers, as if her body were an aspect of the vibrations of the drums. Jeffrey moved closer to her, marking her movements by reflecting them back to her. It was another language, made up of signs that made more sense than mere speech. The crowd pulsed around them, taking them up in its forward momentum. Her tiredness had vanished.

Later, she wouldn't be able to remember how long she had danced. Time was stretched out and truncated in tempo with the drums, until it became meaningless. But sometime during that night, while the townspeople continued to dance, Ada took Jeffrey by the hand. She led him to Juliana's house, where she made him wait in the courtyard. He grabbed her around the waist as she turned to knock on Juliana's door.

"You won't slip away, will you?"

"Of course not."

He gripped her waist tighter and dropped his head onto her shoulder. "I don't know what will become of me if you don't come back."

She pulled his hands away, wriggled out of his grasp. "Don't worry. I will be back in five minutes. I promise."

Juliana's door was open. Ada walked in and closed the door behind her. "Juliana," she whispered. "It's me, Ada." The room was dark, save for a small slip of moonlight easing in through the window. Ada walked to the light it cast on the tile floor and stood in its circle. "Juliana." She said it louder this time. Now she heard a movement from the bedroom.

"Vem dentro," Juliana said.

Ada went into the room. The moon flooded the room, turning everything in it into a composition in silver and blue. Juliana was on her mattress, naked, a man draped across her.

"Perdoe-me," Ada said.

Juliana laughed and spoke quickly in Portuguese as she pushed the man's limbs aside. He didn't stir. Juliana stood in front of Ada, her skin glistening in the silver light. *"O que fazem você ned?"*

Ada patted her stomach. *"Bebê,"* she said. *"Não."* She patted her stomach and shook her finger at the same time, repeating the word *não* again and again. Juliana took her by the hand, talking quietly, soothingly, as she pulled Ada into her small kitchen. There, she lit a candle and set it on the table. Its glow cast a circle of yellow light onto the brown skin of Juliana's ample breasts and smooth stomach. Ada noticed the drums. They had been playing all along, but she had tuned them out. Now, as Juliana worked, naked, in the candlelight, she seemed to be performing a choreographed dance that was a part of the drumming, that was intrinsic to the celebration out on the plaza.

Ada had a sense that Edward stood behind her, observing this strange ritual. She could almost hear his strangled cough, his objection to all of it—Juliana's nakedness, the drums, the herbs, Jeffrey, Ada's fluid approach to her gender. "This will not do," he whispered in her ear. At first she felt the suggestion of fear begin to creep into her veins and along every nerve ending. But then she laughed out loud. Juliana turned and smiled at her laughter, joined in, not knowing what it was about but seemingly happy just to hear laughter.

Juliana gave her herbs, and a syringe for performing a douche. With her hands, she made a shoving motion and wiggled her hips. Her pantomime made it perfectly clear to Ada what she should do with the things. *"Obrigada,"* Ada said, hugging Juliana's naked body up against her own, Juliana's skin brushing the dress she had given to Ada to wear.

Back out on the streets, the drums were everywhere. They seemed to come from the plaza, the surrounding streets, inside houses, the distant hills. Jeffrey held her tight as they walked. "Don't leave me like that again," he said. "You frightened me." There was a sense of finality to his words, as if he were telling her they now were meant to be together, always, and she agreed.

When they reached the plaza, the pulse of the drums and the crush of the people pulled them into the collective dance. They wound their way across the space, their hips and shoulders propelling them forward as much as their feet.

Their lovemaking was a continuation of the dance. They moved with the drums that shook the walls of the inn and rattled Ada's small bed. There was no need to talk. The confluence of sound, rhythm, friction, and Ada's desire for Jeffrey brought her to climax quickly. This crisis was like a spiritual purging of unsatisfied desires. Her voice, she was certain, was louder even than the drums. Her hips pushed frantically against Jeffrey's. If she pumped them hard enough, she thought, perhaps she could make these brief jolts extend themselves out into a river of satisfied longings.

When they finished, though it was too fast, she felt cleansed, and ready for a deep sleep on a mattress.

But first, she took the pitcher of water from her bedside table and carried it with her syringe and herbs to the bathroom down the hall. There, standing in the empty hip bath, she performed her douche.

When she returned to her bed, Jeffrey was sleeping lightly. She climbed in next to him. Without opening his eyes, he wound himself around her, and they fell into sleep, tangled together in the narrow bed.

They woke with the first sun. Their sleep couldn't have been long. The music and dancing had gone on for hours into the night and the morning. But Ada felt rested. She turned to look at Jeffrey, to reassure herself that her memory of him here, in her bed, was real. He opened his eyes.

"Adam," he said. "Good morning."

The sound of the name stirred an undertow of satisfaction in her. She curled her leg around his hip, smiling into his eyes. I am Adam, she thought. Adam, the first man. Adam. The name, she remembered from somewhere, something she had studied in college, in the Bible perhaps, also meant earth.

She had no idea what *Ada* meant. It was good to know the meaning of one's own name. The brief vibration of the lips caused by that *m* sound added to her name made all the difference. The parsing of a name is, sometimes, all that we have left, or all that we have to go on.

"I believe I need food," Jeffrey announced.

THEY WENT INTO the street together, Ada in the cotton dress she had bought from the village woman. Jeffrey's smell rose up from the crevices of her body, slipping through the gaps between her dress and her skin. She was glad she hadn't bathed yet. The scent meant he had left remnants of himself for her to consume. She imagined it as a mystical source of energy. If she could maintain the smell about her person, she would have the strength to conquer the mountains of Brazil, to find the motherlode of orchids, to be a helpful partner to William and Jao.

The streets were damp with the morning dew. Their footsteps clicked on the cobblestones, their laughter lifted lazily across the plaza. Few people were about. They were all still sleeping off the revelries of the night before, no doubt. But Ada and Jeffrey managed to find a small cafe, still open from the night before. The sleepy-eyed waiter brought them a basket of breads and a plate of tropical fruits: oranges, mangoes, pineapple, guava. Ada ate little; the food distracted her from her hunger for Jeffrey. She felt satiated with looking at him, touching his warm skin, listening to the timbre of his voice as it beat against the silence of the early hour. As he spoke his eyes darted about quickly, rarely stopping to rest on her own. The restlessness of his focus made her nervous, made her feel the need to stay in physical contact with him in order to remind him she was there with him.

"I've only one more night here," he was saying. These were the words that drew her in to the meaning of his talk. "Then I'm going."

"But where are you going?" She remembered the two small, dark women he had tried to seduce on board ship, and his assurance, after he failed with them, that he would find a woman in Brazil. Was she that woman? Someone who would agree to sleep with him, and nothing more? And was he now moving on to the next?

"I have business here. You know that, Adam."

"What is your business? Will it take long? Will you go far?" She couldn't stop the questions; she wanted to know everything about him.

Jeffrey took a cigar from his jacket pocket and twirled it between his fingers for a moment before lighting it. Its musk drifted toward Ada and lingered there, clouding her other senses, while he spoke. "Did you seduce me just so you could get this information out of me?"

"I'm sorry? What did you say?" Had she simply imagined him hanging on to her last night, begging her not to leave him? Or had the alcohol and the drums together formed some sort of potion that rendered him helpless, needing her only for that moment?

"Come now, Ada." He put emphasis on her name, as if it were some grand secret shared between the two of them. "You heard me."

"I didn't realize I had seduced you," she said. "I thought you wanted me."

"Of course I did. But you led me there. Why do you want to know so much about my business? Tell me. Did William and Jao put you up to it?"

She slouched down into the spaces created by the absence of her corset. "I want to know because I want to know more about you. I'm interested in you. I care about you. I didn't bring you into my bed on a whim, you must realize."

"Tell me what your business is, and where you're going, and I'll consider doing the same."

Ada didn't fail to notice that he made no response to her admission that she cared about him. This refusal to appreciate her desire was so familiar to her, she suddenly felt tired. The comfort of familiarity could put her to sleep right now, sitting up in her chair. She closed her eyes.

"Let's just say I'm in the rubber business," he said. "And perhaps we could leave it at that."

When she opened her eyes, a shaft of the morning sun had moved its way into the small leaded window behind Jeffrey and was pouring itself right into her eyes. Jeffrey appeared only in silhouette. "Will you come back here?" she managed to ask.

"Of course I'll be back. It's hard to say when, though."

Ada had no idea when she herself would be back. There seemed to be no way to stay in touch with Jeffrey, or even to arrange a rendezvous. It was all too sordid. She was no different to Jeffrey than those two women on the ship. She would have done well to continue her charade with him, to let him believe she was just a boy. Perhaps then he would have revealed more of himself to her.

Before they parted company, Ada made the decision to invite him to her room again that night. Whether it was in the mistaken belief that he would become more attached to her if he had more of her, or if she just simply couldn't deny herself whatever she could get from him, she didn't care to contemplate. She simply asked him.

"Will you come to me tonight?"

His eyes fell squarely into hers for the first time that morning. "Yes. Of course," he said.

Later in the day, after she had tried, but failed, to sleep, Jao and William came to collect her. They sat together at a small outdoor cafe. Ada mostly watched while the two men ate. She still wasn't hungry, even though she had eaten almost nothing since the day before.

She watched as Jao devoured a plate of meats and eggs. "How can you eat so much?" she asked him, wanting to stop him so that she wouldn't have to witness it. The meat took on the aspect of something hostile to her, something that Jao had purposely chosen in order to threaten her. Her stomach felt unsteady, her head pounded.

"I suppose because I didn't drink so much last night," Jao said to her as he winked at William. William was at work on a large bowl of rice and seafood. He didn't react to Jao's goading. Ada held her tongue.

"How is old Jeffrey?" Jao asked. His voice was ridged with animosity.

Ada should have known they had seen her with Jeffrey, but somehow she hadn't allowed herself to imagine what they would think of it. And now she felt a sense of panic over the possibility of their disapproval.

"He's quite well." She sipped at her tea, poked at a piece of bread, pretended to be curious about a donkey that had refused to continue pulling its cart across the plaza, and the efforts of its master to get it to move. She avoided looking at her companions.

"Maybe he'll have dinner with us," William said. The very idea calmed Ada. So they weren't going to reprimand her, they even wanted to see him. This was good. Perhaps it was an omen. Perhaps Jeffrey wasn't a mistake, or a tragedy in the making.

She saw him later in the afternoon, when she had followed Jao to a home where he purchased burlap bags for orchid transport. Jao did the communicating and bargaining, while Ada approved the sum. She wasn't really needed. He knew how much money they had, and that there would be no more than that until they began to sell the orchids. He was better with figures than she was, but he brought her along as a sign of respect, she thought, and she appreciated the gesture.

As they were loading their donkey with the purchase of sacks, Jeffrey happened down the street. Ada stopped him and asked him to join the three of them for dinner. He seemed happy to agree, but he also seemed in a hurry to continue on his way. Jao watched him as he walked past them and on into the side streets of the town. "I wonder where he's going," he said.

"Why are you men all so curious about one another's work?" Ada watched Jeffrey, too. He turned around and glanced at the two of them as they watched him. He tipped his hat and hurried on.

"If we were to follow him now, he'd lead us astray," Jao said.

"Why would we follow him? Why on earth would we do that?"

"We'll get something out of him at dinner," Jao said as he finished loading the donkey.

"Is that why you wanted him to come to dinner?" Ada felt angry now, even used.

"We need to get on with this," Jao said, and pulled at the donkey, guiding him back toward the plaza. Ada followed, a step or two behind Jao. "We still have to buy food," he said.

THEY LEARNED NOTHING about Jeffrey's work at dinner. Not really. But Ada got a closer view of the strange game of subterfuge these three men were playing. When they were well into their meal, and talk of Carnaval had subsided, Jeffrey said to Jao, "I noticed today that you bought burlap sacks."

Ada watched the looks go all around the table. Jao to William, William to Jao, Jao to Ada, William to Jeffrey.

"We use them to pack breakables," William said.

"Ah, breakables," Jeffrey said, obviously not believing him. "When do you leave?"

Ada started to speak, but William interrupted her. "Day after tomorrow," he said. They planned to leave the next day. "And you?" he asked Jeffrey.

"Oh, I'm leaving tomorrow. I want to get things rolling, you know what I mean?"

"So what are you after?" Jao asked Jeffrey. "Gold?"

Jeffrey laughed till the table shook. "Hardly. That's not my business. I'm a rubber man."

"Ah, rubber." William and Jao both said it. The idea of rubber held much more meaning than the word itself could ever imply. Jeffrey nodded, as if he understood the layers of meaning there, and agreed. It was as if the three were in some sort of secret society, and when they uttered the secret words, a world of understanding passed between them. Ada remained outside the sense of their words. It might have been different if Jeffrey still believed she was a man.

It went on like that until the music started up again in the plaza and the table began to vibrate with the drumbeat. Ada no longer felt the desire to dance. She simply wanted Jeffrey in her bed with her.

Soon enough, but after what seemed hours, they were there, together on the thin mattress, the blanket kicked onto the floor, their legs winding around each other's bodies, their breath joined in the ethers around them. She was conscious of the number three. Jeffrey was her third lover. Three was a number substantial enough to notice. Before, it had been nothing more than her first lover and her husband. It seemed so paltry, the first and then the last, nothing more. But now she could roll that word off her tongue: three. Three lovers. Three men. A number that deserved to be considered.

Ada might have wanted the night to last forever, but she had had so little sleep the night before, she fell asleep soon after they reached their crisis and she had again performed the douching ritual.

They rose with the light, and Jeffrey, her short-lived but lovely number three, left soon after. He kissed her goodbye. "We will see each other soon." He seemed to want to reassure her, but Ada wasn't sure if he really wanted to see her again. She waited till he was gone to allow herself the luxury of tears. But her allowance was limited, the tears were brief. She felt the orchids, again, as they had in Boston, vying for her attention. She had work to do, too, just like Jeffrey.

That morning, she put away her cotton dress and took her linen suit out of the armoire. The two nights spent with Jeffrey had been an interlude, a sudden remembrance of her self as female. But it couldn't last. There was no one there telling her she had to continue masquerading as a man. Still, she sensed that it had to be that way. If she continued to move through Brazil as a woman, she would face all the diminished expectations that her gender commanded. She didn't want to live that way. She wanted to walk through the streets of cities and villages knowing that she could demand what any man was entitled to demand, anywhere he went.

William wanted to travel after the worst heat of the day was past, so they planned to leave in the afternoon. She would have time to take Juliana's dress back to her, and to tell her goodbye.

Carrying the dress and its glittering adornments, she turned right off the plaza onto a narrow dirt road. But the street Juliana lived on was cobblestoned. Ada remembered the feel of them under her feet. She turned back to the plaza and looked for a narrow cobbled alley. There were three to choose from. None of them had identifying features that Ada might have recalled. There were people all around; she could ask someone, but she struggled to find words in Portuguese. How did one say "Do you *know* . . ."? *Conhecer.* That was the word for *acquainted with.* She stopped a young girl carrying a basket of fruit.

"Conhece Juliana?" she asked.

The girl shook her head and spoke quickly, words Ada couldn't understand. She seemed to be telling Ada a story. Her Boston upbringing crept out from its shallow hiding place, and Ada stood, smiling, nodding her head at the girl. When the girl finally stopped to take a breath, Ada pointed down the road and waved goodbye to the girl. She didn't turn back to look at the girl, she could feel her disappointment without having to see it etched across her face.

Ada picked the closest street and walked across its stones in search of a tall blue door leading to a courtyard. Was her memory confused? Was it a blue door, was the street really paved with stones?

She saw red doors, yellow doors, orange and white doors. She even saw some blue doors, but the blue doors were so different from Juliana's door, there was no question that none of them could be the entryway to Juliana's house. Their color was not as deep, they weren't as tall, or they didn't open onto a courtyard. Some of them were open, and Ada could see inside. None of these places was like Juliana's magical little house.

Walking down another cobbled alley, Ada found the same thing. No tall, deep blue door opening onto a courtyard. Nor did the final alley off the plaza lead her to Juliana's door. She wanted to return the dress. She wanted to tell Juliana thank you. She wanted to tell her goodbye. How was it possible that Juliana's house, and the woman herself, had simply disappeared from Juàzeiro, from the face of the earth, even?

Ada carried the dress and its Carnaval decorations back to her room and packed it away with her cotton dress, ready to take it and put it onto the back of the donkey. Once the donkeys were tied together, they rode out of Juàzeiro, a small company of three humans, three horses, and three donkeys.

As they rode up into the mountains, Ada ventured a look back at the town where she had experienced two things: the love of a man, the friendship of a woman. But both the love and the friendship were off-kilter somehow. Frightfully different from the way she had learned to conduct her relations in Boston. Even Frederick had had more consideration for her than Jeffrey. And she had never danced to drums with a friend, or hugged the naked body of another woman. But she had never wanted to be near the people in Boston in the same way she wanted physical proximity to these two people.

The whitewashed buildings with their colorful doors, the open plaza surrounded by palm trees, after only three days settled in with her like a mystical yearning. She wanted to know this place better. She wanted to linger here and learn the secrets of the place. As she looked back at it, a horse and cart sped across the road just beneath them. She recognized the assured driver. Juliana. Ada turned her horse and stood up in her stirrups. "Juliana," she called. Juliana looked up and waved.

Ada pulled the dress from her pack. *"Vestido,"* she yelled, waving the dress above her head.

Juliana waved back, a gesture of dismissal. She called something out in Portuguese, but the words fractured on the breeze, and Ada caught syllables without meaning, containing only rhythms and melodies.

"Muito muito obrigada," Ada called out to her new friend.

Juliana blew her a kiss in response, but her cart continued along its route, heading away from them now. Ada turned her horse and kicked him, urging him to catch up to William and Jao.

• • •

WHAT LAY AHEAD for them was days of riding and camping out, cooking over fires, bathing in rivers, sleeping under nets in an effort to keep the mosquitoes and other creatures out. As they rode through the forest and into the jungle, the undergrowth grew thicker. The bamboo was so concentrated, they were forced to get down from their horses and hack a trail with machetes on several occasions. Ada's back and buttocks hurt, and she felt hungry and tired all the time, but she refused to complain. She had tried to bear all of the discomforts like a man, so that neither William nor Jao would be sorry they had agreed to bring her. But Jao remained distant most of the time, and Ada remained unsure of his assessment of her. What if she failed as an orchid hunter and Jao demanded that she be sent back? The alternative to this life was something she couldn't even contemplate, because it was an utter mystery. If the money she invested in the orchid venture didn't reap profits, she would have nowhere to turn, other than to beg Edward for his forgiveness. That, she knew, would never happen. Edward hadn't been able to forgive her for wanting to express her physical desires, and to satisfy them, with him. How could he forgive her for the transgression she had committed when she walked out his door?

Ada spent her days swatting the flies that buzzed around her face, swallowing the gnats that swarmed her mouth as she opened it to eat or to speak even, marking the time between rest stops in the shade. She was hot, her head throbbed. But still she refused to complain. At night, the temperature dropped, and she had to crawl into her sleeping sack for warmth. Once there, she would read by the light of the oil lamp from the books she had carried with her from Boston. By the time they arrived in Juàzeiro, she had begun *The Awakening*, by Kate Chopin.

One night, they set up camp next to a river. William didn't tell them its name. Was he keeping his place names secret from them? Was he afraid they would come back sometime, on their own, and steal orchids from him? Ada didn't ask him.

The river was wider than any they had seen, its water the blue of the ink she had used to write in her household journal at home. The far side of the river looked like a distant country. Beyond it was a valley, and farther still, another mountain. In the depths of the valley, a blanket of white mist hovered, giving the place a mythical quality. As she listened to the water gather and then move on, she read *The Awakening.* "The years that are gone seem like dreams—if one might go on sleeping and dreaming—but to wake up and find—oh! well! perhaps it is better to wake up after all, even to suffer, rather than to remain a dupe to illusions all one's life." The water's steady rhythms lulled Ada to sleep in the sack she had set up under the mosquito net. She slept deeply, still holding the book, without waking once during the night.

At first light, Ada was awakened by the sounds of Jao and William bathing in the river. They were splashing each other and laughing, like two boys at play. Still feeling tired, Ada tried to go back to sleep, but their laughter carried from the water and up to where she lay as if the distance amplified it. She got out of her sack and gathered her things to go down to another piece of the river, behind some thick shrubbery, to bathe herself, to wash away the blood and sweat.

The ground was slick with dew, and cold beneath her bare feet. At the bank, she took off her trousers to keep them from trailing in the mud. Her toes sank into the silky blackness. A low sucking sound rose as she lifted her feet—one, then the other. William's and Jao's deep voices floated up to her, their words indeterminate. Their voices comforted her; she wasn't alone, hadn't been alone at all since she left Boston. She had spent so many days alone when she lived with Edward. This was something different. It was almost enough for her, she realized.

Leaving her clothes on a rock, she stepped into the water and pushed off from the rocky edge. Suddenly, there was nothing beneath her feet, and a current was carrying her downriver, away from her companions. Ada began to thrash. She didn't know how to swim. She had stepped into the river assuming it would be as shallow as all the other rivers they had bathed in, shallow enough for her to keep her feet on the ground. But now she floated free.

She slapped her hands against the water and flailed her feet. It didn't seem possible these feeble movements would keep her afloat. Her chin went underwater, and her mouth filled. Forcing her face back above water, she coughed and spit it out. "Help," she called to her companions. She went under again. This time her eyes went beneath the surface. The sudden darkness, and the pressure of the water all around her, made her feel as if she were being constricted, pressed into a small, inanimate package, the life squeezing out of her under the weight. Sheer panic gave her the strength to lift herself to the surface. Her lungs beat against her ribs, struggling to expand.

Now the current held her, carrying her on its back. But how long would it hold her up? She called out again. This time she heard Jao respond. "Ada," he yelled. She saw him then, running along the banks, through the overgrowth, his body naked and moving swiftly, quietly. Her arms ached, her legs seemed not to be there at all. "Jao." His name came out in a whisper. Finally, he came abreast of her and dove into the water.

She was choking and sinking, her body exhausted, her movements wild, when he reached her. She fought the water, fought him. He wrapped his forearm around the front of her neck and forced her onto her back. "Stop fighting me," he said. "Relax. I'll pull you to shore."

The touch of his arm telegraphed some primal signal to her body. She relaxed. She didn't notice then that her body was naked, that her breasts floated up above the water, that his naked body swam under hers. When they got close enough to shore that he could walk, he let her go. "Go ahead. You can stand now."

She had just enough energy to stand; her body was still beneath the water. But she was too embarrassed to stand up and walk to shore with him there. Without moving forward, she wrapped her arms around her submerged breasts. Jao immediately saw her predicament. "Let me get out. I'll wait for you, in case you need help. But I'll keep my back turned."

"Thank you, Jao," she said.

It was silly, really, wasn't it? She knew Jao and William more intimately than she knew Jeffrey, and yet she had allowed him entry to her most secret places, and Jao she would not allow even a glimpse of her surfaces. But this remnant of modesty was important to her. Perhaps his viewing of her naked body would have been too problematic in light of her pretenses at manhood. If Jao saw her now, without her male trappings, whatever maleness she had succeeded in emanating would be forever supplanted in his mind by the image of her unclothed body.

When he stood on the bank, his back to her, some distance beyond her clothing, she walked carefully, still shaking and weak, out of the water and to the rock where her clothes waited. Grabbing her shirt and holding it against her body, she told him he could go.

"Are you certain you're all right?" he asked.

"Yes. Of course. Now go."

He walked away without turning back.

"And thank you, Jao. Thank you again," she said to his retreating back.

THEY TRAVELED FOR several days, following the river, sleeping near its banks. A sense of dread, even fear, of the river lingered about Ada as she moved along it. She could have so easily drowned there. It had a power over her that made her angry. It was such a simple thing, water. How could it be so treacherous? William and Jao bathed in the river again, but Ada declined, choosing instead to listen to their comforting voices from the safety of shore. She continued to read *The Awakening*. She felt as if Chopin was someone to whom she could talk about her own life when she read: "But the beginning of things, of a world especially, is necessarily vague, tangled, chaotic, and exceedingly disturbing. How few of us ever emerge from such beginning! How many souls perish in its tumult!" This world, in the jungle, with men, dressing as a man, looking for a rare orchid, all these things were chaotic beginnings for her. Chopin's words comforted her, and gave a sense of order to the chaos. But when she got to the sections in which Robert Lebrun taught Edna Pontellier to swim, Ada felt panic, and she put the book away without finishing it.

Before too long Ada began to stink. The film of sweat and grime that coated her skin was uncomfortable; it made her skin itch, it made her feel tired. She knew a dip in the water would invigorate her. But she was holding out, as if she were trying to prove something to the river, as if she could beat it in a battle of wills.

They cooked fish over the fire that evening, and supplemented it with a couple of cups of rice from the twenty-five-pound bag William had brought on his donkey. Jao sat next to Ada on a flat rock. When she reached her arm across him to accept her bowl from William, Jao pulled back.

"What?" she asked him.

"What do you mean, what?"

"Why did you jump back like that? Do I smell?"

William sat with them, relaxing onto the rock as if it were a soft, comforting thing. "Well, now, Adam. If I were you, I'd be a man and just admit it. When you go too long without bathing, you tend to get stale," William said.

Ada fought an urge to throw her tin bowl at him. Her hunger stopped her. She finished her food without speaking, then stood up and threw her bowl at the rocks circling the fire. It glanced off a rock, landing at Jao's feet. She walked out of the firelight and into the dark, where the stars above her were thicker, with a pattern more complex than Belgian lace. Footsteps crunched the decomposing leaves on the ground behind her, but she didn't turn, she simply moved farther afield.

"Ada, don't be angry." It was Jao. "William meant no harm. That's the sort of thing men like us joke about."

"Like us?"

"Men who live out in the open air. We aren't embarrassed by smells."

"But you leaned away from me." She turned to look at him for the first time. His dark skin vanished into the depths of the jungle around them. She could see only his eyes, and the silhouette of his clothes.

"I was surprised. It didn't smell like you."

"What do I smell like, then?"

"You smell like a woman. Usually."

Was it good to smell like a woman, or did men prefer the scent of other men? she wondered. "But now?"

"You are taking on the strong scent of a man." She could see him turn his head away from her, so that she couldn't look into his eyes as he spoke.

"Well, I guess that's not so bad, really. I am trying to convince people I'm a man." She stepped around him so that she could look into his eyes.

He laughed. "I've never seen you as a man."

This made Ada angry. For some time, she had believed that her companions saw her as a sort of honorary man, that her assumption of Adam's persona, that of a newly blossoming young man, had been convincing.

"Maybe you should let me teach you to swim," he suggested.

"Swim? What does that have to do with it?"

"You'll be able to give yourself a bath."

"I don't want to learn how to swim." The idea of lifting her feet off the riverbed and allowing her body to float free in the water was frightening to her. She knew the water couldn't be trusted.

"It's a valuable thing to learn, especially out in the wild," Jao said.

When Robert Lebrun taught Edna how to swim, it created a sexual bond between the two. What impact would such a sensual act have on Ada and Jao? She couldn't allow this man to have that sort of intimacy with her. Besides, didn't Edna end up drowning, purposefully, in the water in which she had learned to swim? It was all too much for Ada.

But by the next morning, her own stench horrified her more than the idea of learning to swim. William was building a fire when she stuck her head out from under her sack. "Where's Jao?" she asked him.

"Where else? In the water," he said. He blew on the embers until they licked into flame. "If Walter were with us, he would be down there with him. He was a swimmer, too."

Ada sat up and looked toward the river, leaving William a space of silence in which to reminisce about his friend before she spoke again. "I think I need to learn to swim today," she said.

"Ah, well. Walter would have been your best teacher. But Jao is second best. He's better at it than I am." She got out of her sack and stoked the fire while William prepared coffee. She felt a comfort in his presence that was solidifying. It was the kind of comfort that could lull her into believing he was someone who would always be there. Someone who would never grow old and frail, never die. He was the Dog Star. Bright. Constant.

"Coffee?" He held a metal cup out to her.

William made good coffee. "Thanks." The acidity hit her empty stomach in a warm rush that made her feel alive. "I'm sorry Walter isn't here with us. I would have liked to know him," she said.

William stopped fussing with the coffee and looked away from her, toward the river. "I think he was right about you."

His words were as good as an admission from William that he cared about her. Ada had never been much of a crier, and now that she had taken on the persona of a man, tears were even more infrequent. But she felt them coming on now, so she grabbed a bar of soap from her pack, then walked toward the river without responding to William. She could feel his eyes on her back, and her steps were heavy with self-consciousness.

When she came up on the riverbank, she saw Jao's head peeking out of the water. He waved at her. "Come on in," he said, then laughed at his joke.

"I am coming in," she said.

He stopped paddling for an instant and whistled. "Come on, then," he said. "Take those clothes off, first, though. They'll pull you down."

She took off her cotton shirt, and her long cotton drawers, and threw them on the bank along with the soap. They landed in the red mud, but she stepped over them without looking. She walked slowly into the water, her body fully naked, fully exposed to Jao. He watched her without blinking, without looking away, without moving toward her. When she had walked as far into the river as she could go and still keep her head above water, she stopped and waited for him. Only then did he swim to her.

He stood close enough so that he could take hold of her if the need arose. "Lift your feet off the ground," he told her.

Her feet were sunk deep into the muddy river bottom. It felt good to wiggle her toes in the soft earth. She had to steel herself as she prepared to pull her feet up. The anticipation made her heart race. This physical manifestation of her fear caused her to hesitate. She couldn't lift her feet.

"Come on," Jao said. "Let your feet come up here, where I can see them."

The Revealed Orixa

The Victorian woman's foot and ankle were always well concealed. No one ever saw those parts of her body, other than her husband and perhaps her maids. Yet here Ada was, completely naked, in a river with a man who was not her husband; she wasn't even in love with him. Now he was demanding that he be allowed to see her feet. Was her hesitation simply a left-over impulse from a quarter century lived in Victorian society? She knew Brazil was different. She had seen it already. They flaunted their bodies here. Some women wore skirts up to the knee and walked around in sandals that revealed their feet. So Jao was used to it; he probably thought nothing of her nudity. But this simple act, of lifting her feet so that he could see them, seemed to be such a crossing of boundaries, Ada could hardly contemplate it.

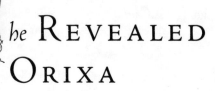

What would Edward think if he saw her now? Would he put her in an attic, as Mr. Rochester did his wife in *Jane Eyre*? The idea of it, of living out her life confined to a single room or cell, moved her. It filled her with purpose, and she was suddenly able to lift her feet. The sensation of weightlessness, the water enveloping her and separating her from the laws of gravity, made her laugh. But as she opened her mouth, her face dipped below the surface of the water, and she swallowed a mouthful. She choked and sputtered, and at the same time flailed her arms in an effort to keep from sinking. Finally, she put her feet back into the mud.

"Get your sea legs, and we'll try it again," Jao said. He waited patiently for her to finish coughing. "All right. Now this time, lift your feet and just grab onto my arm until you get the feel of floating."

The water sucked at her, resisting the movement of her legs through the water as she raised them toward the surface. She took hold of Jao's outstretched arm as she straightened her body and floated on her back. The blue of the sky slashed through the green canopy of trees overhanging the riverbanks. The world was upside down from this vantage point. She felt like a small thing in the vastness of the natural world. A parrot flew just above the tree line, its pure reds and yellows loud amidst all that green. The sun hid itself below the tree line, slipping out only when the tallest trees shook in a brief breeze.

Ada waved her free hand through the water while gripping Jao for stability. Her feet kicked, her body floated about with the easy current, her breasts rising and falling at the waterline. The cool water lowered her body temperature. Jao swatted the insects away, allowing her to rest there in front of him.

"Okay. Now you need to work," he said. "I'm going to let go. Stand up and watch me now." She let go of his arm and set her feet down. He moved his arms and legs at the same time, kicking his legs and pushing his arms forward, then out and away from each other. "Just try this," he said. "It's a simple movement, and it will keep you from sinking."

She tried, but she sputtered and flailed, and her face dropped into the water. She coughed, then tried again, with the same result. Jao demonstrated for her again. She imitated him again, unsuccessfully. Jao remained patient, showed her over and over what she should do, but she failed every time she tried.

Finally, after her arms had grown tired, and she began to believe her body was not designed for swimming, William called to them from their little camp. "I have food. Why don't you two come eat?"

"I'm hungry," Jao said. "You?"

Ada nodded. Jao started to swim toward the bank. He stopped when he realized she was not following him. "Come on. I don't want to have to jump in and save you."

"I'm going to try again." She turned away from him and began to paddle frantically. Jao swam toward her. "No. Go on. I'll stay where it's shallow. I'll be fine," she said. He got out, but watched her from the campfire.

She struggled throughout the men's mealtime, ignoring Jao's intent stare. She came to a point where she knew she was being ridiculous, and that it was sheer stubbornness that kept her in the water, and still she didn't stop. Her arms felt heavy, her legs were cramping, and the water had become a thing she was battling. But she continued to try.

Finally, all in an instant, the differing rhythms of her body came together, and the synchrony allowed her to stay afloat. Now, her body cutting through the water, she became aware of its sensuality as it moved across her bare skin. She let out a whoop. "I've done it," she called out. William and Jao cheered for her, shouting *Bravo,* and clapping. She felt like a child who, after much effort, has won the approval of her parents. It made her glow. After swimming about till she was too tired to go on, she walked to the shore and grabbed her soap, then went behind a bush to wash herself off.

Later, after they broke camp and headed onto the trail again, Jao pulled his horse up beside her. "Oxum should be your goddess," he said. "She is the goddess of sweet water. She watches over all the rivers of Brazil."

"Oh, I like that," Ada said. "Tell me more about her." Ferns brushed across her calves, tickling her as she moved over to make room for Jao in the narrow spaces between the undergrowth.

"She loves riches, and her color is golden," Jao said. "She's also the goddess of love."

Ada laughed. "That doesn't sound like me."

"I believe she's your revealed Orixa. Your hidden Orixa is someone else, someone who remains unrevealed." They rode together without speaking for a while. Then he leaned toward her and sniffed. "You smell good," he said, then kicked his horse in the sides, riding away from her before she could answer him.

. . .

AT LAST, they rode out of the jungle, toward a low mountain, and there, on its face, were waves of color. When she first laid eyes on them, Ada felt certain, for the first time, that she had done the right thing in running away from Boston and coming here to be an orchid hunter. For a moment, none among the party spoke. The only sounds were the sounds of the wild—the wind through the trees, birds calling, the horses' breath. Never, in all the hours she spent in Edward's Orchid House, could Ada have imagined they would look like this when she finally found them in their native habitat. She wanted to stretch herself on the ground amid them, to be enchanted by their magic. Red, yellow, and orange *Cattleya*, pink and white *Oncidium*, large and small, single flowers and long stems cascading with hundreds of blossoms. This was some kind of heaven William had brought them to. By the time they saw their first orchids, Ada had lost track of the number of days they had been traveling, but it made little difference. It was not important to be able to say when, precisely, they saw those flowers for the first time. What was important was simply that they had found them.

William broke the silent spell reluctantly and whispered to his companions. "We need to be very careful. I'm certain no one knows where we are. But from now on, we have to cover our tracks, and be wary of everyone we meet." It was discomfiting to Ada that the first words uttered about these creatures were words of warning. Was William being overly cautious, even fanciful in his fears?

"It's a crime that Walter isn't here with us," he said then.

Jao didn't speak, but his eyes shut tightly for a moment when William said Walter's name.

They stayed for three nights near the orchids. William never did tell them the name of the mountain. Each morning, when Ada awoke and saw the orchids all around her, she was newly stunned by their abundance, their vividness. The three travelers worked all day to lift them carefully from the rocks and branches on which they grew, and place them into one of the half dozen large burlap sacks they had brought. They took the plants whose flowers had not yet blossomed, in hopes that these plants would survive the boat trip back to New York, blooming just when they reached the northern shores.

"We must establish harmony with the spirit world as we take the plants from their home," Jao warned. William nodded in agreement.

Jao set up a small shrine, a pile of flat stones, on top of which he sprinkled leaves from a nearby tree. *"Akoko,"* he called them. "For luck, and to attract money."

During the three nights and two days they spent at the foot of the small mountain, they never saw another human. But William refused to relax his guard. "Ask Jao," he said when Ada questioned him. "John Jefferson and I came out of nowhere, didn't we?"

Jao dropped his eyes to the ground. William let out a long breath. "I'm not the only one who has tracked other hunters through the jungle."

"Stop, William. You had no idea what Jefferson was up to. I didn't even know."

William pulled his hand across his face and went about the work of collecting and sorting the orchids. There was no more talk of the incident with Walter, but it was clear to Ada that William was heavily burdened by the memory, that he stumbled into it constantly.

Many of the orchids grew on branches of trees that were too high to reach. William rigged a thick climbing rope that he threw up over the branch and tied in a loop. Jao taught Ada to shimmy up the rope. Her body had grown strong from the days riding horses, swimming, and setting up and packing camp. It wasn't difficult for her to learn. She let her feet do most of the work, sparing her arms. Nonetheless, at the end of the three days, her hands were blistered and her shoulders sore.

At night, Ada dreamed she had fallen into the world of a painting, or some ancient myth in which flowers were gods. The wild patterns and shapes of the orchids spiraled through the natural landscape of her dreams, creating a vortex that waited to envelop her, to suck her into its center. She wanted to go there, to become a piece of this world of color and texture and pattern. Being a human wasn't so important, she thought. Maybe it was really of no importance whatever in the scheme of things.

In the mornings, she woke up stiff but eager to get back to the plants, to touch them and see them all around her. Was this what Walter had felt? Did William and Jao feel it? She would have asked them, but she didn't know how to conjure the words.

When they had filled all the sacks, and the donkeys were weighted down by as much as they could possibly carry, there were still hundreds upon hundreds of orchids. All of the hunters felt contented that they hadn't cleaned the area of the flowers. They were leaving more than enough of them behind to propagate and repopulate the hillside.

Before they left, William made complicated marks on his map. "May I look at it?" Ada asked him when he had finished with it.

He handed it to her. "You won't understand it."

It was the size of an open newspaper. William had used topographic imagery, drawing a series of loops inside loops, and labeling them with numbers and letters that meant nothing to Ada. They could have signified any place in the world.

"Why don't you want your partners to be able to read it? What if something were to happen to you?"

"My sister has the code key."

"Why your sister?" The memory of William's sister, Harriet, and her welcoming home on Beacon Hill tugged at Ada, giving her an odd sense of disequilibrium. What if she had stayed in Boston and had gone to work for William's sister? She could imagine being the only white woman in Boston working for an African employer.

"Because I trust her," he said.

Ada folded up the map, being careful to crease it along the same lines where it had been previously folded, and handed it back to William. "Why don't you trust me and Jao?"

"It isn't that I don't trust you. I don't want our enemies to have three of us to go after if they get hold of the map. If only I know what it means, then they can only hope to learn its significance from me. And they can do nothing to you."

"It's true," Jao said.

Ada couldn't believe anyone knew where they were. Their meanderings across the country had been complicated. William's fears seemed improbable to her. But they were her superiors in this venture, so she held her tongue.

She and Jao followed William out of their jungle encampment, never knowing for certain where they were going or where they had been. The way back seemed longer than the way out. The donkeys moved slowly with their heavy sacks. And the food supply was scant. William began to ration their food. "We don't want to starve out here."

"That won't happen," Jao said. "There's plenty in the jungle to feed us."

"We don't want to have to put your knowledge of foraging to the test, though, do we?"

ONE NIGHT, after having eaten only a mango and some thin broth Jao had made for dinner, Ada woke, sick to her stomach, with a headache that made her dizzy. How could that simple meal have made her sick? she wondered. She tried to go back to sleep, but every time she began to doze, a new wave of nausea woke her.

By sunrise, Ada was so sick she couldn't see. Shivers ran through her, from her head to her feet, one after another, so that it was impossible for her to lie still. Jao was at her side, touching her head, but she barely noticed him. In between shivers, she vomited into the dirt next to her sack.

"Do you have lemons, William?" Ada heard Jao ask William. It seemed such a strange question, but she was too far gone to speak. Her back hurt; it felt like a burning poker was gouging her lower spine, digging into it, ever harder. Someone pressed a cup against her mouth. She drank the bitter lemon juice without bothering to open her eyes, and threw it up minutes later. The shivers jerked her about, hurting her back even more.

It went on like this for the entire day, into the night, and through the next day. Ada wasn't sure whether she slept or not, she only remembered many hours of torturous, wakeful pain. William and Jao both hovered around her, trying to force things down her throat, but through her fever they were an aggravation to her. Nothing they did could help her. The ground was hard against her burning back, her head felt on the verge of explosion, every muscle in her body ached with such exquisite definition, she thought it might be easier to die than to continue this way. It was far too painful to speak, but moaning seemed to dull the edge of the pain. She serenaded Jao and William on into the third night.

When she heard them talking, sitting nearby at the fire, her head seemed to expand with each syllable. "Stop, you must stop!" She screamed the words at them. They hushed instantly, but the silence was really no better.

The fourth morning, she was surprised to realize that she had, indeed, been asleep. She had no memory of the pain subsiding enough for her to sleep. Now, as she moved her limbs, she noticed that her aches were gone, almost completely. The men were still sleeping. Tendrils of sun, close to the horizon, showed through narrow openings in the trees. Ada lifted herself from the ground and went to start the fire and make coffee. The scent of the coffee woke her companions.

Jao saw her first. He didn't speak to her, didn't seem to know what to say. Instead, he reached under William's sleeping net and shook him by the shoulder. "Look. Look at her."

"I see," William said. "I see." The two men were grinning when they came to sit with her, to drink coffee and watch the sun white out the shadows of the distant mountains.

WILLIAM INSISTED THAT they not push themselves as they continued their travels.

"But the orchids," Ada said. "I'm fine."

"The orchids will survive. You're still weak," William said. Jao was silent.

"I feel good. Really, I do."

She did feel good. She had energy to ride even farther than they did each day. But William shook his head.

"But, William," Jao said, "we should try to make up the time we lost. Someone is going to figure out where we are if we add days to our travel time. I have a bad feeling about this."

William glared at him. "You and your bad feelings."

"I told you the same thing happened when Walter was killed."

William's face puffed up with anger. "You should have told him before he got killed."

Jao's back went straight and his mouth clamped shut. William rolled his neck and threw his shoulders up, then down. "Are you worried that someone has followed us?"

Jao looked first at Ada, then to William. "I'm worried about Jeffrey. I'm worried. I don't trust him. I think he was using Ada."

Ada felt sickened by the idea. She wanted to get off her horse and lie down on the earth, rest her head in the dirt and just sleep for as long as possible. "He's right," she said to William. "We need to hurry."

"Stop, you two," William demanded. "We'll go as quickly as I say."

"Since when do you decide?" Jao asked.

"Since I am the one with the map."

"I can find the way," Jao said. "I'll go ahead with the orchids. You stay back with Ada." So it was Ada now. Jao no longer counted her a man. It was as if her illness had made him angry, as if her sickness proved that women weren't up to this life.

Ada opened her mouth to speak, to say she would try to keep up, but William spoke first. "No. We will go slowly and carefully until we're sure she's all right. All three of us."

Jao gave in, but for the rest of the day, he didn't speak to either of them if he could possibly avoid it.

They stopped to make camp before it grew too dark for them to pick their way through the dense foliage. They ate a light meal, then Ada put her net around her sack and fell asleep almost instantaneously, in spite of her nearly empty stomach. She was still weak, and as she drifted off, she felt grateful to William for insisting they go slowly.

She woke in the morning when the first slash of sun topped the trees and lit her face. The forest was strangely silent. No birds called, no insects hummed, the trees didn't rustle. There were no human voices. The absence of sound made Ada wary. Her ears tuned in to the silence, her eyes looked about, peering sharply into the recesses of the brush and trees. Time seemed to bend itself out in front of her, reaching away from her, curving around behind trees, trying to confuse her.

She pulled herself out of her bed, stealthily, so she wouldn't make a noise, and walked away from the campsite. Her feet took her; she put no thought into the direction she took. Seconds or minutes or aeons later, she saw it. The problem. The thing that had gone so horribly wrong. Beyond their sleeping sacks and nets, by the closest group of trees, were their three horses, and a single donkey. Two of the donkeys were nowhere to be seen. Jao and William were already there, speaking in voices so low she couldn't hear them.

"What happened?"

Jao's face was pinched with anger. "Someone came. Someone followed us. They took the orchids. They took them." His shoulders shook as he hissed the words out. He spat them at her, pointing them like a finger at her.

"But there's still one. Why is there still one?" Perhaps if they could make sense of that, they would realize precisely where the other two donkeys must be, and they would find them, unharmed, still laden with orchids.

"Something frightened them off before they got this one. Maybe one of us stirred in our sleep," William said. "They wanted what they had badly enough to refuse to gamble it."

"I told you. Didn't I say this? I felt it. I felt they were coming after us," Jao said. "I knew they were coming. If you hadn't insisted upon pampering her, our orchids would not be gone," he said to William, his words slicing through his gritted teeth. Then he turned to Ada. "What did you tell Jeffrey?"

Rage had been welling up in Ada as Jao berated William. Now, at the suggestion that she had said something to Jeffrey, it spilled out. "I said nothing to him about what we were doing or where we were going. How dare you suggest I might have?" Her words were shouts echoing in her skull.

"It was a terrible idea for you to be with him. The man can't be trusted."

"How do you know?" Ada asked. "How do you know?" She balled up her fists and took a step toward Jao.

She would have hit him if William hadn't stepped between them. "You two stop. This will get us nowhere."

"You should have listened to me back in New York," Jao said to William. "How can you expect anything but bad to come of our taking a runaway along with us? A runaway who is also the wife of a murderer." He glared at Ada then, his mouth clamped shut, his eyes angry slashes. Ada heard the whir of a group of hummingbirds before she saw the brilliant red birds cross in front of Jao's face, half a dozen of them, happily oblivious to this human drama. He waved at them, as if they were an irritation. That small gesture triggered something in Ada. She lunged forward and lashed out with her left fist, catching him across the jaw.

William tackled her before Jao had a chance to strike her back. She was on the ground, her face in the dirt. William held her wrists while she kicked and grunted. "Don't move," he ordered her. She continued to kick, and he shouted at her again. Finally, her energy drained, she lay still, but he continued to keep her pinned down.

"Let me up," she said.

"Not until you calm down."

"I am calm. Let me up. I can't breathe." William loosened his grip, but didn't let her up. "Please, William."

"Let her up," Jao said. "If she tries anything, I'll cuff her but good."

When she was at last able to sit up, she saw Jao rubbing his jaw. The sight made her chest swell out. She had to gulp for air. "Did I hurt you?" she asked Jao.

"Yes, damn it. It hurts."

Ada laughed. She had hurt a strong man. She laughed so hard, it knocked her onto her back. She laughed so hard, William couldn't resist joining her. Jao watched the two of them for a moment, then turned away from them in disgust, or perhaps shame.

"Don't feel bad," said William. "It was Adam who hit you, not Ada."

They ate then. Mangoes from the forest, and some dry bits of bread. Jao remained silent throughout their simple meal. When they were finished, they set out again. "At least we've got some of the orchids. At least we will make something out of this," William said.

"Not enough," Jao insisted. "We'll have to come back. We can't fill our orders with what we have."

"Of course we'll come back," William said. "I never doubted that."

THE EVENING OF the second day after losing the orchids, as dusk blanketed the hills and the trees began to recede into the darkness, Ada felt suddenly ill again. A dizziness overtook her, and she nearly fell off her horse. Jao rode up beside her. "Are you all right?"

"I don't know," she said.

William came up on her other side. The donkey stopped where it was, its sacks balancing across its back. He put his hand on her forehead. "You're hot."

"No. No. I think I'm okay." As she said the words, blood seeped into the corners of her mouth.

"Shit," William said. "Jao."

Jao leaned alongside Ada's horse. "Look at me," he said to her. She turned to look at him. His eyes and forehead lifted high in an attitude of panic.

"Do you know herbs for this?" William asked Jao.

"Manaca. We need manaca. Do you know it?"

Ada felt a metallic taste in her mouth. She reached to wipe it; her fingers came down covered in blood. Jao grabbed her face, looked into her eyes and mouth.

"I know manaca." William turned his horse and headed off into the jungle.

Jao got down from his horse and pulled Ada from hers. "What is it?" she insisted.

"Your eyes are bleeding. Yellow fever," he said as he rifled through her pack. He put Ada into her sack, setting up the mosquito net around her. She became disoriented. Her skin was changing, turning a pale yellow. Jao poured water from his water bottle onto her forehead. He built a fire.

"Am I going to die?" she asked him. He didn't answer her. "Oh, well. Oh, well," she said.

William finally came back, carrying a branch covered with white flowers. Jao grabbed it from him, putting the bark and leaves into a pot of water on the fire. They fed her the tea, but she vomited blood almost immediately.

They talked about her. She heard them, but the words held no meaning for her.

"We have to get help. People who get to this second stage often die." Did one of them just say she was going to die? She didn't think she cared. The pain in her stomach reached itself out toward all the extremities of her body. She was one continuous rope of pain.

Somehow the men put her into Jao's saddle, and Jao rode with her seated in front of him, bound to his torso with twine meant for wrapping the orchids. As they rode, she passed out, vomited, and moaned by turns. She didn't remember arriving at the little compound in the forest.

When she came to, she was on a thin mat on the dirt floor, and an old Indian woman was leaning over her, her face almost touching Ada's. Ada was naked, her body covered in wet linen. The woman's face opened into a wide grin when Ada's eyes opened. The grin cut a long line into the length of each of her papery brown cheeks. The lines were valleys containing the history of the woman's life, a record of her smiles and tears.

"Como está você?" the woman asked.

Ada moved her head, looking around the room. A slant of light heavy with shimmering dust cut from the window and across the room to her feet. She had to think for a moment to be clear on what light was, what dust was, what a window was. When she had settled on it, remembering the significance of these things, she looked at the woman. "I'm all right," she said. *"Estou muito bem."* She thought she was all right. But who knew? She wasn't sure what she was doing in this small room, with this stranger leaning over her.

Jao came into the hut then, as if he had been summoned. *"Está acorda?"* he asked the woman.

"Sim, sim." The old woman looked proud, Ada thought. Her smile lifted and spread to every inch of her face.

Jao moved his face into the small space around Ada. "She cured you," he said. "She's a powerful healer." He sat on his haunches next to her. "Her name is Izabel."

Ada nodded at the woman. *"Obrigada, Izabel,"* she said to her. "What was wrong with me?" she asked Jao.

"You had yellow fever. Jungle fever. It comes in two stages. The first time you were sick was just the beginning of it. When you got sick again, I knew you had a bad case. We worried."

"I slowed you up again, then. What has become of the orchids? How are the orchids?"

"William should be in Juàzeiro soon. We'll meet him there. He'll ship the orchids out and the money will be wired to the bank there. Once we get the money, everything will be fine. We'll take a little holiday, and then we'll come back to find more orchids, to fulfill our orders."

"So the plants were all right? They didn't die?"

"Everything is fine."

Ada tried to rise up on her elbow, but the effort was immense. She leaned closer to Jao. "Do you think he was safe, going alone?"

"Izabel's sons went with him." Jao lowered himself all the way to the floor, allowing his white pants to fall into the red earth.

"You trust them?"

"Of course. They're good people. As you can see." His head nodded to her, suggesting that she was there due to the goodness of this family.

Ada reached out to Izabel, who was running linen rags through a dark liquid in a basin next to the mat. *"Muito, muito obrigada,"* she said to the woman, allowing her hand to rest on Izabel's arm as she spoke. The truth was, she didn't really know what she was thanking her for. She didn't feel so alive, nor did it seem real to her that she had almost died. She was more grateful to the woman's sons for helping William with the orchids.

Izabel began to take the linen from Ada's body, replacing it with the newly moistened rags. Jao didn't look away as bits of Ada's body were exposed, then slowly, carefully covered. For a moment, it occurred to her that Jao was lacking the basic social skills that would cause him to turn his head. But in the next instant, she realized these social skills were irrelevant to the situation. Let him look.

As Izabel's gentle fingers peeled away the linen from Ada's right breast, her nipple extended itself, and Ada wondered if Jao enjoyed looking at her body, if he found her attractive. His eyes rested on the exposed nipple.

"You can't take your eyes off me," she said to him.

His eyes widened, startled. "Your skin is so white. It's fascinating to me."

"Do you like it?"

"I don't know. It's so different from the skin of my countrymen."

Ada wasn't offended by his response. The body was so weak, she felt as if she were no longer part of it. It was stretched out before her on the mat, right in front of her eyes, but it wasn't her. It was some other thing that couldn't be trusted or controlled. This much she knew, after all her body had been through in its life. "But you lived in America a long time," she said. "Aren't you used to our skin by now?"

"I never touched a North American woman. Or saw one without clothes."

"Oh," was all Ada said to him.

Izabel covered Ada's right breast with fresh cloth and pulled the linen from her left. Ada watched Jao's eyes slip across her body to gaze on the left breast now. He hadn't looked at her like this when he taught her to swim. What was different now? She looked down at his arms. A thin line of musculature ran across his forearm. Without a forethought, Ada reached out and touched his dark skin. His muscles contracted at the instant of contact. "I like your skin," she said. Then, "I'm sorry about the orchids. I'm so sorry."

Jao's eyes closed, his chin lifted. For the first time since she had known him, and after all the days and nights in such close contact with the man, Ada felt a tightening in her groin and an electrical charge running up into her abdomen. The sensations made her angry. How could she be so sick and yet feel this desire, especially for this man? She took her hand off Jao's arm, turning her attention to Izabel. She watched the woman's careful ministrations. She felt Jao rise from his place on the floor, but she refused to look at him, or speak to him. When he had gone, she thought the empty space next to her, the place where he had been sitting, retained a trace of his warmth.

Hours later, when Ada was strong enough to get up, Izabel had her stand naked on a small bed of smooth pebbles, while the old woman brushed her down with a leafy branch. They communicated with hand gestures, Ada's few words of Portuguese, and Izabel's long monologues in Portuguese. But they understood each other. Ada knew that she was getting a leaf bath, and that the leaves the woman used had curative properties that were both physical and spiritual. There was a summoning of a protective deity, whom Ada understood to be named Omulu. She knew nothing about this deity, but later, on the way to Juàzeiro, Jao would tell her that Omulu was the god of smallpox and other illnesses. "The deities choose you," Jao would tell her then. "Omulu sought you out for some reason."

What mattered here, in this little room, was that when Izabel invoked the deity, Ada was overcome by a jolt that pushed her torso forward, causing her to snap her neck and throw her arms up over her head. She yelled out, as if some other person were speaking through her, and she walked about the room for a moment as if she owned the place, as if she were lord of the realm. It lasted only an instant, but in that instant, Ada thought she had experienced the spiritual awakening that Edward had pushed her toward for so long. Why was it so impossible for her to find with Edward, and here, without meaning to, she had simply given herself over to it?

When the strange force left her, she turned to look at the old woman. Izabel's teeth sparkled through her generous smile; she began to speak rapidly. The words were lost to Ada, but there was no doubt they contained a kind of joy.

Ada reached out her arms to Izabel, hugging her tightly. *"Obrigada,"* she said, again and again.

Afterward, Ada felt inspired to wear a dress. She chose the turquoise cotton. She left her feet bare.

Izabel served food to Jao and Ada that night. Jao directed most of his conversation to the old woman. He spoke very little English to Ada. She wondered if she had offended him when she asked him if he liked her skin. She wanted to draw him back, force him to talk to her again. But hadn't he always been reticent in his dealings with her? Weren't his words always brief, even carefully considered? Was this any different?

Izabel seemed to sense Ada's discomfort. She tried to talk to Ada, including her with hand gestures and glances even when Ada couldn't understand a word of the conversation. It was only when the Brazilians laughed together that Ada felt hurt by her inability to understand the language. As their laughter rose up and spread out across the room, reverberating for long minutes, Ada felt profoundly lonely. She tugged at her skirt, ran her fingers through her now shoulder-length hair, stared at her naked feet, trying to block the jarring sound of laughter from her consciousness.

THEY WERE ON their horses with the first sun. Jao wanted to wait another day, give her time to regain her strength, but Ada felt anxious. She wanted to be in Juàzeiro, to be reassured that the orchids were on their way, that they had earned money, that she was free to decide what to do next.

They were able to travel faster without the donkey. It would take them only six or seven hours to reach Juàzeiro. Ada rode beside Jao, but they didn't speak unless they had to. It was difficult for her to take her mind off the silence. It tugged at her awareness. But even though there was this tension between them, Ada felt safe with Jao, comforted by his presence.

Riding in a dress with bare legs was a new experience for Ada. The space where the saddle ended and her leg touched the horse grew tender. The contact of skin against leather and horse hair reminded her again of how lucky she was to be free of corsets and petticoats and stockings.

In the late morning, they stopped beside a small river to eat. Jao had simply turned to her and said, "Are you hungry?" She nodded, and so they ate.

The mangoes and bananas and even the strange fruits she had never eaten before soothed Ada's still tender stomach, their juices cooled her in the heat. The tumbling of the river water across stones and around low-lying bushes replaced the sounds of conversation. A monkey called out, its high-pitched voice echoing across the treetops. Birds flashed overhead, calling attention to themselves and then disappearing almost before they could be located. Ada swatted a swarm of mosquitoes away.

"They say once you've had yellow fever, you can never get it again," Jao said. "You're lucky in that way."

"Well, if the mosquitoes get you, I'll take you back to Izabel," she told him. "I'll make sure she heals you."

"She's a high priestess," he said. "A *mãe de santo.* She can cure anyone."

Ada wanted to tell Jao that she loved this about Brazil. Female deities, women priests. Katie would love it, too. She wished she could share this country with Katie. She wanted to tell Jao how much she missed Katie, and how she thought her maid would love Brazil, but she didn't know where to begin. So instead, she ate in silence. Jao fell into the quiet with her. The sounds of the jungle accompanied their dinner.

When Ada had finished eating, she grew restive; she needed to stretch her legs, move them about before returning to that stationary position on her horse. Without saying anything to Jao, she wandered away from him, walking along the banks of the river. Where the river narrowed, a grouping of large smooth stones spanned its width, making a neat natural bridge. Holding her sandals in her hands, Ada crossed over, disappearing into the brush on the other side. It felt as if she were testing the bond that attached her to Jao. She knew it was foolish to go too far alone in these wild places, but she needed to be away from his silence. She wanted the space of silence to be her own, not his.

CRIMSON-LIPPED LABELLUM

Smatterings of lavender on the slope of a nearby hill drew her eye. Wanting to get close enough to see the source of color, Ada left the bank of the river and walked toward the hill. As she drew closer, she could see that these were orchids. Her heart beat a little faster. She had stumbled upon another source, one William apparently knew nothing about.

It wasn't until she stood in the center of the orchids that she realized what they might be. Here, far from anywhere, all by herself, could she have stumbled upon Edward's beloved *Cattleya*? There were twenty or thirty of them across a small patch of ground, scattering their color haphazardly about. They let off a sweet scent that thickened the warm air. The flowers were as big as her open hand, with lavender sepals and petals, and a crimson-lipped, wavy labellum. Edward had told her the labellum was a landing platform for the pollinating insect. This ruby stain that extended from the inside of the lip across its bottom half would lure many insects, Ada thought. As she gazed into the flower's deep labellum, past the crimson and up to the point where it faded to yellow, Ada tried to compare it with her memory of drawings of the *Cattleya labiata vera*.

This had to be it. She was certain of it. The plant that had been shipped to Edward in the wooden box had turned out not to be the *vera*. All those men who had been chasing after this flower for the past seventy years, and here it was, in front of Ada Pryce, née Caswell, formerly of Boston, now of parts unknown.

These were cheerful flowers. Ada didn't then imagine them as commodities to be shipped back home. She saw them as they were, here in the middle of a jungle rarely visited by humans, appreciated only by the sun and rain, the birds and insects. Why should they ever have to leave this place? No one knew they were here, and perhaps that was as it should be. Ada spread herself out on the ground, so that her head was below the tops of the plants and she could look up at the bottoms of the flowers. Her turquoise dress in the midst of all their purple, red, and yellow was like an offering of color to soothe the gods. The flowers seemed to reach into infinity, allowing her a sense of the idea of a world or a universe without end.

She didn't know how long she lay there, but Jao must be wondering what became of her. She got up to take her leave of the flowers. As she stepped between the plants on her way back to the river, it hit her that Edward would kill for this particular flower. Maybe he had already killed for lesser flowers than this. What would he say if he knew she was here, in a field of his most coveted objects? It was with a sense of power that she leaned over and plucked two of the plants from their habitat and wrapped them carefully in her skirt. She had what he would never have, she told herself. And this made her feel like she was something more than she had been just an hour ago. Maybe her Orixa had called her, after all. Maybe Omulu had made her sick so that she would stumble upon this place, and find the mysterious *vera*.

Without speaking, she held her skirt out to Jao, showing him the plants that nestled there. He looked, and looked, and looked again. Finally, he whistled slowly. "Could it be?"

"I'm certain it is," she said. He reached his fingers out to touch them;

she held her skirt higher. A subtle breeze lifted up into the open space, cooling her thighs and making her smile.

Jao didn't say it, but she knew what he was thinking. This discovery could end up being worth much more than the orchids they had lost, if they could come back and gather enough of them. Or, if they could keep the location secret, just a handful of the plants could be valuable as well. "It's a shame William isn't here with his map," Jao said as he examined the flowers. "These could make us rich, you realize this?"

"Let's make our own map," Ada said. They both knew, without discussing it, that they couldn't carry more than a few of the plants back. There would be a danger in trying to take too many. They had only the packs on their two horses. William had taken the other packs and burlap bags with him. Whoever took their orchids might be nearby, watching them still. If they saw them gathering the few orchids they could carry, they would simply take the rest as soon as Ada and Jao were gone. If they just rode away now without the plants, chances were no one would know they were there. And even if they weren't being watched, if they took a number of the orchids with them now, and word got out that they had found *Cattleya labiata vera*, others would be out looking for them in no time. And they might discover that someone else had found the plants before they themselves made it back. They needed to leave the plants, and they needed a good map to get them in and out quickly. Both of them understood this.

"I'm not a cartographer. I don't have the skill William has," Jao said.

"You got us here, didn't you? I mean, you do know where we are, don't you?" The look he gave her was remarkably sheepish, his laugh one of embarrassment. "Are you trying to tell me you don't know where we're going? But you told William you knew the way." The words came out slowly, stuttered by her disbelief.

"I wouldn't say that I don't know. I do know. I just don't know as well as William would know."

The flowers seemed to weigh her skirt down more than was possible for their size and number. As she looked at them, she felt her heartbeat speed its tempo. If Edward saw her here, he would be angry that she was alone with Jao, angry that she was dressed in such an immodest fashion. But he would be angriest that she, not he, stood there, holding the *Cattleya labiata vera*, and that the plant he had tended at home was not the real thing. These were.

"Let me try. I'll draw something to get us back here." She gave the orchids to Jao. He looked as if she had suddenly handed him a newborn baby. He seemed stunned by the fragility of the creatures. But he handled orchids for a living. Why would these particular plants confound him?

She ripped a blank page out of the back of *The Awakening*. She looked about her, studying the countryside, then drew on the paper. The rough approximations of the hills and the trees surrounding them would be a jog for the memory, at least. "You can get us to Juàzeiro, can't you?" she asked him.

"Of course. Of course. That won't be a problem."

When she was satisfied that her map was as good as she could make it, she helped Jao to wrap the orchids in a small piece of burlap and then tie them to her saddle. As they wrapped them up, they kept their florescences hidden from possible watchers, and at the same time tried to act as if they had nothing special, as if they were simply going through a routine collection. Both Ada and Jao were alert to every sound. Every small animal made them turn to examine the forest, searching for signs of a human following them. But no man ever revealed himself to them.

Jao got them safely to Juàzeiro, in spite of the fact that he stopped several times to debate with himself whether or not they were on the right route. As they rode, the burlap containing the orchids bumped gently up against Ada's calf. Each contact reminded her that she had in her possession flowers of immense value, of a variety that was desired by many rich and powerful men. What if she were to show up at Edward's door with the things? Would he forgive her and take her back into his home happily? Or would he demand the orchids and throw her out, cursing her to live out her days in her mother's home?

The questions were always there, just waiting to pose themselves. The problem was, Ada so rarely had answers. One question seemed to lead to another, and then finally away from anything that resembled assuredness.

But it had always been this way. She never fully embraced the work of her fellow suffragists, she was never overjoyed in her role as wife. Motherhood she had rejected outright. And now that she was an adventurer, she couldn't be sure even of her gender. So what did the *Cattleya* mean to her, really? She didn't hunger for it the way Edward had. Its beauty was admirable, but there were so many other beautiful orchids. Perhaps the problem was that she wanted something beyond what they could offer. Perhaps all she really wanted was to be an adventurer, like William and Jao.

THE SUN WAS beginning its decline into the hills as they rode into Juàzeiro. The journey without William's help had been longer than it would have been with him, but at least they made it. The hills looked purple against the play of shadow and light in progress above them. A sense of comfortable familiarity settled into Ada's ribs as her horse set its nose for the town. She was glad to be back here.

The clouds were rippled, as if the wind had cut across them in a perfectly timed up-and-down pattern. Near the horizon, the clouds broke just below the dipping sun, sending out a tricolor strip of light—yellow to orange to green—refracting off its rays.

The gentle breezes coming up the hill carried the vibrations of drumbeats.

"They're still celebrating?" Ada asked.

Jao smiled with an air of pride. "Carnaval lasts a long time in Juàzeiro."

Their horses hurried now, as if the drums called to them, urging them to come home.

They found William waiting for them in the same pension they had stayed in on the way out. They went together to his room, where Ada showed him the *Cattleya labiata vera.* He considered them in silence, but he seemed agitated. Ada realized she was beginning to be able to read both men's silences. Finally, he said simply, "Walter was killed for this sort of thing. These plants are dangerous." The drums rolled over his words.

"I'll keep them in my room. Who would know?" She raised her voice to be heard over the drumbeat.

Jao squirmed but remained silent. William rubbed his face.

"We can make money with them, can't we?" Ada was still determined to secure a future for herself, to know that she could support herself, a woman on her own. Money was essential.

"You keep them," William said. "You make the money."

"But I don't know who to send them to. Who would buy them? I don't know where to go."

Jao laughed. "So you do need us."

"Of course I need you. Did I ever say I didn't?" Ada felt confused now. She had been so proud when she found the *Cattleya.* Now these two men were acting the way she might have expected Edward to act. As if she had stolen their thunder. She wrapped the plants up again and stood to go.

"They are beautiful," William said. "I'll help you find a buyer. But we need to hide them for now. Don't keep them in your room. It isn't safe. I worry about you. You're too often in some sort of danger."

"Oh, I see," Ada said. William was right, perhaps. "But where can we hide them?"

"Perhaps your friend Juliana?" William suggested.

It was only then that William asked after her health. Maybe he hadn't thought to inquire because she seemed so healthy. And it was true; she was confident when she told William she had been cured. William assured Jao and Ada that their orchids had been shipped without difficulty. The drums pounded over their conversation, and soon all of them were distracted by the downbeat that shook the pension and tickled the soles of their feet.

Ada took the *Cattleya* to her room, where she stepped into the dress Juliana had loaned her.

When she met up with her companions again, Jao was washed and wearing a clean suit. She realized she hadn't seen him so clean since they left Juàzeiro. He smelled of a scented water. The three companions went out into the square together, allowing themselves a final assignation with Carnaval. They danced and drank, and moved away from one another. Ada was flushed and sweaty when she saw Juliana, like an apparition, at a small table on the edge of the plaza, tapping her feet and shaking her shoulders as she talked to a man. When Juliana saw her, she jumped from her seat and threw her arms around Ada.

Juliana put her hands on Ada's skirt. Ada signaled to Juliana, pointing at the skirt, then in the direction of Juliana's house. She wanted to return the dress to Juliana. But she needed something to wear home. *"Espera mim,"* she said to her. Wait for me. Juliana nodded and turned to go back to her man. But she stopped before she reached the table. "William?" she asked Ada.

"*Sim.* He's here. Wait. I'll be back."

When she returned, she was carrying her lightest linen suit and the wrapped plants. Ada's gender meanderings were becoming second nature to her. She could be one sex as well as the other. It almost made no difference now. The suit was the first thing in her trunk, so she took it.

She found Juliana leaning against a wall, William in front of her, showing off for her. He spoke Portuguese to her. His voice was easy in the language. He didn't seem to struggle to find the words. Juliana laughed. They both laughed. But the sound of their laughter disappeared in the roll and rumble of the drums. Ada waited for them to notice her there.

"Ah, Ada," Juliana cooed at her. "Come," she said. "You wait," she said to William.

Ada was glad he wasn't going to come with them. He would be a distraction for Juliana.

Juliana's blue door shone in the moonlight, the entryway to a hidden world. A place where magic was possible, like in the fairy tales Ada's governess had read to her when she was small.

Ada put the plants down in the kitchen, removed them from their wrappings. *"Podem estar aqui?"* she asked. *"Puoco tempo?"* A little while.

Juliana nodded. *"Sim, sim. Quão bonito,"* she said. How beautiful.

"Yes. They are," said Ada. Beautiful and dangerous, she thought, but she didn't say it aloud. She didn't look back at them as they walked away.

Inside Juliana's room, Ada stripped off the dress, then handed it to her friend. The moon lit the room as if this were its home, the place it rose and fell for. Juliana went to the curtain, disappeared behind it. As Ada put her suit on, Juliana reappeared, carrying several dresses over her arm. *"Não, não,"* she said as she grabbed Ada's hand. She shoved the dresses at her. *"Faça exame destes,"* she said. *"Por favor."*

Ada understood now that Juliana meant to give her more dresses. She thought Ada had asked for more. "*Não.* No more dresses." She continued to put on her suit.

"Mas você é bonita neles," Juliana said, holding the dresses out to Ada again. What should she do? This woman had given her so much already. Ada wanted to do something for her. But she had no idea what.

"Take," Juliana said. She held one dress out and shook it at Ada.

"You're learning English?" Ada asked her. She still didn't reach out to take the dress.

Juliana smiled. "For William."

Perhaps this is what she could give to Juliana, then. The gift of William. "William? Ah, yes. Good man," she said. "He's a good man."

"I try English before, but not good. I try more now."

"I will help you," Ada said.

Juliana threw her arms around Ada. "Oh, yes. *Obrigada, obrigada.*" Again, she pushed the dress at Ada. "Now. Take."

Ada took the pale blue dress from Juliana.

"Two," Juliana said, and handed her a dress of saffron and crimson.

"Later," Ada said. "After Carnaval." She put the blue dress down and picked up the crimson. This would suit her for a night of dancing.

They went back to the plaza together and found the two men waiting for them, alone together at a table on the edge of the plaza. Jao stood when he saw Ada walking toward him, her ankles showing beneath her dress, her shoulders bare, glistening in the moonshine and the lamplight. She shook her shoulders to the drumbeat. Jao went to her and took her by the hand. "Dance with me," he said.

She moved into the crowd of dancers with him, letting him lead her with his hand. Dancing with Jao seemed somehow deviant. His touch, on the small surface where his skin met hers, unbalanced her. In order to regain her balance, she closed her eyes and allowed the rhythm to guide her, to sway her hips for her, to slide her feet across the stones, to roll her belly.

When she felt solid again, she opened her eyes to find Jao's face too close to hers. Too close for her to see him clearly. She backed away, he followed, staying close in. Taking a step forward, she dared him to stand his ground. He gave just enough to keep the distance between them steady. Finally, she crossed her foot over his and rolled her hip up against his thigh. He put his hand on the small of her back, holding her body against his.

All those times he had seen her sick, naked, unconscious, dressed as a man, dirty, stinking, she had never felt he saw her as a woman. Now he seemed to be struggling to keep her attention, to force her into his orbit. Flashes of light bounced off his black eyes. She leaned her face in closer to his. He put his hand on the back of her head, pressed his lips into hers. The kiss was so easy to slip into, she didn't even stop dancing. Was this a mistake? Did one do these things with one's business partner? It didn't matter. It couldn't. She wound her arms around his neck. He let his slide down her back, onto her buttocks. She touched her lips to his neck and sucked at it, letting it nurse her.

"Ah, Ada," he breathed onto her neck. "Ada." Her name was a sigh, a moan, it embodied all the sounds she had longed for Edward to make. Here they were, in a single note, dissonant, jarring, but lacking in the undertone of humiliation that had been so familiar to her in her marriage bed.

"Say my name again," she said.

It came out in a slow expulsion of breath, from deep inside him, a death moan. This was so easy. The way it should be. The way it should always have been. Her name. Ada.

"Jao," she said.

He stepped back to look at her, still holding her around the waist. "What are we doing?"

"What we want to do, what else?"

"But you are married to a powerful man. And we are business partners. You're a dangerous woman, aren't you?" His forehead creased, his eyes narrowed. He seemed worried about the danger, rather than tempted by it.

"Let's not try to stop it. I have had enough of locking up my desires to last me into eternity." She took his hands from her waist, and stepping out, she pulled at his hands. "Come with me." It never occurred to her that he would resist her invitation. He acquiesced to the tug of her arms, and walked with her toward the pension. He put his hand on her back. The contact heated her skin through the crimson dress.

As they moved through the crowds, Ada saw a man, separated from her by just three or four others. He was a white man, wearing the same mask Jeffrey had worn when she saw him here for the first time. Ada looked into his eyes, but the man turned away and continued to dance to the drums. She didn't mention anything to Jao. Why make him jealous when he was already so tentative about her?

They walked down a narrow alley on the side of the pension. Before they reached the corner, Jao stopped and turned her toward him. His brown face was lit by a sliver of moon on one side, the other was in the dark, his features erased. "Let's think about this," he said. "I don't want to do anything that will compromise our partnership, or the respect we have for one another."

Ada's stomach deflated, as if the air had been sucked out. This had the aura of déjà vu. Hadn't she been in this precise scenario with Edward too many times before? And in the end, hadn't Frederick and Jeffrey both resisted her, walked away from her, just this easily? Perhaps she should consign herself to being Adam. It was so much easier to be a man.

"So do you respect me now? After all those times you claimed I would be nothing but trouble to you?"

"You know I don't feel that way anymore. You must know that."

She turned, to step away from him, probably to run, just to move away from this humiliation as quickly as possible. He was still holding on to her arm. The drums confused her. Their music demanded passion. Instead, she was poised to run from her desire. The percussive music moved up through her torso and into her sternum, causing it to vibrate with the downbeat. She tried to wrest her arm free. Her eyes clouded over, making it difficult to see where she was going. Before she took a step, though, something hit her on the back of the head. The force sent her to her knees. She felt her arm free from Jao's grip. The drums grew louder.

Jao yelled something. She didn't know what. The palms of her hands slapped down against the cobblestones; her face landed on top of her hands.

The back of her head seemed to be pressing toward her face. The burning sensation on her palms came only as she was being lifted from the ground by strong arms.

"Ada!" Jao was shouting, but from farther away. This wasn't Jao who held her, then. She twisted to look back, but whoever had grabbed her head was holding it straight, preventing her from turning it. She heard fighting, bodies struggling, hard breathing, groaning from behind her. Another man came at her from out of the shadows, carrying rope. The man who carried her set her down, and together, the two, both black Brazilians wearing plain masks, spoke to each other quickly in Portuguese as they tied her arms behind her back.

"What are you doing? How dare you?" The anger in her voice was mitigated by the pulsing drums and the pain in her head. As they tied her, she turned and saw Jao, struggling, trying to fight off two other strong black men. They each took turns dealing blows to his stomach, until he was doubled over and could no longer speak. "Stop it!" she screamed.

One of the men put a hand over her mouth, pushing her lips against her teeth till they bled. "Shut up," he hissed. "Do not speak."

The first man threw her over his shoulder, like a heavy sack. She kicked. The man stopped walking and allowed the second man to do the talking. "You must shut up if you want your friend to survive."

Ada thought of the *Cattleya* in Juliana's house. Was that what they were after? Was Juliana safe? An image of Walter's face settled into her consciousness. He was dead. Had he struggled? Was that why they killed him? If he had given them what they wanted, perhaps he would be alive, here with them now.

"What is it you want?"

"Shut up so you will live to find out," the second man said. They were moving quickly to the other end of the alley. The sounds of the beating the other men were giving Jao were growing fainter, the drums dominated Jao's groans now. Ada, her head hanging over the man's shoulder, lifted herself to look back at him. The last thing she saw was one of his attackers dealing a final blow to Jao's solar plexus, while the other pushed him from behind. Jao fell onto the cobblestones, face-first, and did not move. Ada felt the will to fight slip out of her as if she had been dealt the same blows Jao had received, and their force had simply been too much for her body to bear.

The two men carried her to the edge of the town, where their horses waited. They put her onto the second man's horse, and she rode behind him. They rode through the night. Ada's back hurt, her head pounded, her hands burned, she was tired and wanted to sleep, but the idea of sleeping in the vicinity of her abductors was abhorrent to her.

They finally did stop when the horses were too worn to continue.

As she got off the second man's horse, the first man, the bigger one, pulled a pistol from his trousers. "Do what we say at all times, and you will be treated well," he said.

She leaned her stiffened back against a tree, as directed, and watched as they built a fire and took food from the horses' packs. The chill of predawn settled into her bones as she sat, immobile. She took the food they offered, hot cornmeal and cheese. She was thirsty, so she drank greedily, but she had to pee just minutes later.

"Right here, where we can see," the second man said.

She spread her legs, and reached her hand under her skirt to spread the pee-hole in her cotton pantaloons. She had been traveling and sleeping in the woods long enough so that urinating standing up wasn't difficult for her to do. But the eyes of her abductors infuriated her. She wanted to scratch them out with her fingernails. She hadn't relieved her bladder in many hours. It took forever to empty it. The sound of her urine puddling in the dirt was louder than all the noises of the jungle. It echoed in her ears even after she was finished. When she was done, she simply dropped her skirt and walked back to her place under the tree. The stray drops of urine ran down her thighs. The feeling would have disgusted and shamed her when she was a lady in Boston. Now she hardly noticed.

The men took turns sleeping so that one could watch her at all times. She spread herself out on the dirt and undergrowth, and finally slipped into sleep as the sun gained the tops of the trees.

They spent many days like this, riding in silence, then stopping to eat and sleep. The men gave her orders in English; the rest of the time they spoke to one another in rapid Portuguese that Ada never understood. Ada withdrew into herself, protecting herself from them by refusing to let them see any part of her. She spoke only when she had to eat or urinate, or when they demanded an answer to a question. The rest of the time, she listened to the sounds of the jungle, and the earth beneath her, and waited. What she was waiting for, she didn't know. Was it death? She didn't care. Her abductors didn't harm her in any way. Ada knew they could have raped her, and she would have been defenseless. Apparently they were concerned with delivering her intact to whoever had commissioned the kidnapping.

They never asked her about the orchids; evidently they weren't interested in or didn't know about the *Cattleya.* Certainly Edward had sent them after her. But how had they known where to find her? She survived the days by imagining that Jao and William were not far behind, riding day and night to catch up with her. The fantasy contented her. It was preferable to wondering what the end result of her abduction might be, or what had become of Jao.

Finally, they arrived in Salvador de Bahia one late afternoon. Ada wasn't sure how many days it had taken to get there. It was better to simply let the days flow through her. She was exhausted from the nonstop travel. She had barely had time to recover from jungle fever before these men kidnapped her. If she collapsed and died on the spot, it wouldn't surprise her one bit. She had nothing with her but the crimson cotton dress and a thin blanket the men had given her. She didn't even know what month it was.

The big man had showed her his pistol as they rode through town. "Remember. Do as we say. Speak to no one. Then you will be fine." They rode on to the edge of the bay, where they dismounted and waited in silence. Ada sat in the sand and watched the men throw their fishing nets, and the small boats that traveled between the ships anchored beyond the bay. The warm sand soothed her tired muscles, the salt air eased her breathing. This was the beach where she had revealed herself to Jeffrey. Perhaps if she had not committed that simple act, she wouldn't be here now. She imagined the two men gone from her. If she could just sit here, alone, perhaps she could reel time back and blot out the moment when she let Jeffrey know who she was.

Soon, a boy rowed up in a small boat, pulling it to shore right in front of them.

"Get in," the bigger man said. She climbed in. The boy rowed, the two men rode lookout.

"Who are you?" Ada could stand it no longer. "Where are you taking me?"

"Your husband has been looking for you. He will be happy to have you back." She knew. She knew it all along. But hearing him say it out loud sent an icy sensation up her spine and into the center of her skull.

A good breeze chopped at the water. They weren't making quick progress in their little boat. Ada looked to the shoreline. It wasn't far. She could make the swim if she jumped out before they went much farther. There were other boats on the water, and there were the fishermen. She could call out to them if the big man tried to shoot her.

Before she really thought it through, before her brain actually sent the signal to her muscles, she was on her feet and diving into the bay. She swam hard. She summoned every bit of strength, and pictured Jao's face, urging her on. Her dress dragged at her shoulders, but she swam hard anyway; she swam until her arms grew weak, and then she kept swimming. The shoreline was creeping closer. Kicking her legs harder, she tried to rest her arms. She swallowed too much water and began to choke. As she spat and gulped air, she felt a hand at the back of her neck.

They had caught up with her. Arms were all over her, and she was hauled back into the boat. Her brain registered no pain as her body bumped up against the side of the boat repeatedly. She didn't cry out. No one in the entire bay seemed to notice her attempted escape.

Once she was back on her seat, the big man took a knife from beneath his shirt and pointed its tip at her. "Don't do that again. You have nowhere to go."

"Nowhere," the second man said.

When they reached the ship, out at the edge of the bay, they waited in the boat until a man lowered himself down the side and joined them in their small craft.

The man was Mr. Wirt, Edward's business acquaintance who had appeared on the *Sea Witch*. She had worried about him then, and had subsequently forgotten all about him. How had he found her? He addressed the men without acknowledging Ada, who stood quietly by, her wet dress clinging to her slouched body. "You did everything according to my orders?"

"Yes, of course, sir," said the big man.

Wirt turned to Ada. "Did they abuse or molest you in any way?"

Ada shook her head. Wirt gave the men money, and then ordered Ada to climb the ladder up to the deck of the ship.

Once on deck, he took her by the elbow and proceeded to talk as he walked her toward the first-class deck. "You are registered as my wife. We are sharing a suite. You will take the inner bedroom. As you are ill, you will spend the entire voyage in the cabin. There is a steamer trunk in the bedroom, with proper clothing sent to you by your husband. You will dress as a proper lady on an ocean voyage would dress, even though you will not be dining with the other guests. There should be no confusion about these instructions. I have aides strategically located throughout the ship. There is nowhere for you to go." He squeezed her elbow tighter and tighter as they walked. Wirt hurried her along, but the people they passed noticed her wet dress and bare feet, and stared at her as if she might be an escaped lunatic. Maybe that's what her fabricated "illness" was supposed to be. Lunacy. She was relieved when they finally reached the suite and he locked her in her room.

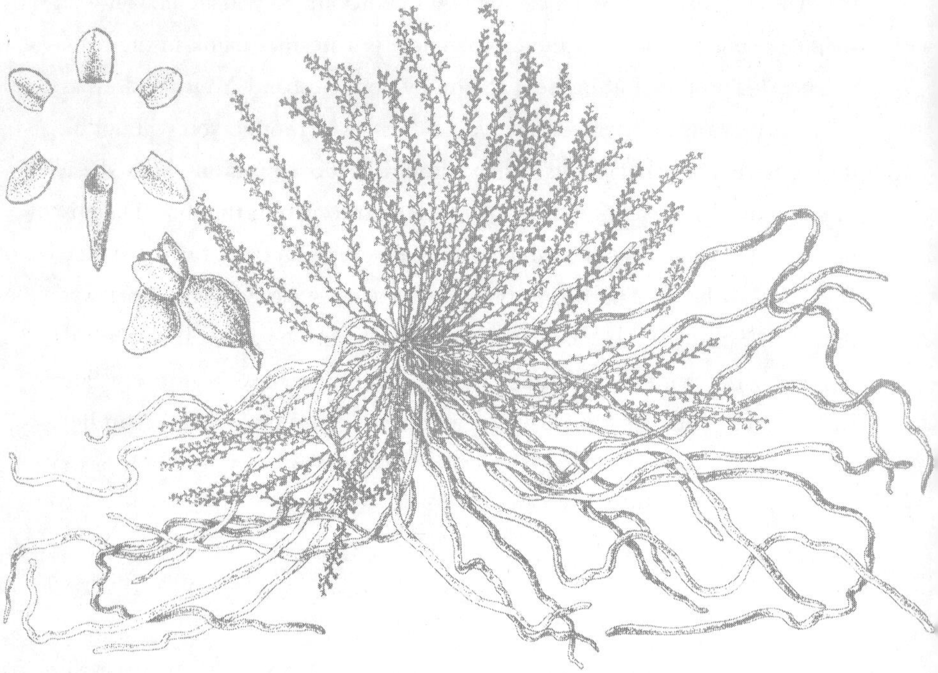

VICTORIAN SPLENDOR

The cabin walls were mahogany inlaid with cherry. Thick Oriental rugs covered the floors in reds, blues, and golds. An embroidered silk bedspread and a dozen pillows dressed the bed. Ada peeled off her wet dress and fell into the bed, naked. It was thick and soft, the linens were smooth against her tired body and her salt-sticky skin. The late afternoon sun coming in through the portal sent a tube of light across the room, turning everything in its path a silvery shade. She hadn't been in the company of such luxury for months now. The bed cradled her body, and in an instant she was sleeping.

Her sleep was deep, but troubled by dreams that oozed out into the room. The different parts of her life butted up against one another, as if her college years, her marriage, and her brief escape all joined together there in her cabin. The sound of Edward's authoritative voice, ordering William and Jao about, startled her from her sleep.

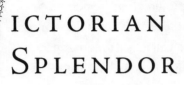

When she woke, the room was dark and the ship was under way. Her body was stiff. She walked, naked still, to the bathroom, where she found, luxury of luxuries, a full-sized bath. As she soaked her aches and the dried salt and dirt away in the warm water, it was easy to forget that she was a prisoner, that this was her jail cell. The soap smelled of lavender and the shampoo of rosemary. The towels she used to dry herself were plush and soft. She could feel her desire for adventure slipping away as she basked in the comforts of her cabin.

Wearing only a towel, she went back into the bedroom. The sun was rising, the bright early light shone in the porthole. Someone had left a tray of food while she was in the bath. It sat on the stool at the foot of her bed. Ada ate the eggs and ham with boiled tomatoes and toast. Even though her long journey had made her ravenous and she ate every morsel, the food somehow tasted wrong to her. She had already grown accustomed to the diet of an adventurer.

She went to the trunk to find clothes. Edward, or Katie no doubt, had packed a dozen dresses, her silk bathrobe, corsets and petticoats, stockings, toiletries, brushes, a mirror. How considerate of them, she thought. But she would have preferred a simple linen suit. Instead, she pulled on her silk robe, eschewing corsets and stockings and muttonchop sleeves.

Someone had put books in the bottom drawer of the trunk. Ada pulled them out eagerly. Shakespeare sonnets, *Jane Eyre*, and finally, the book at the bottom of the stack, *Karezza*. She settled herself onto the floor, leaning her head against the trunk. This book, this single book had wreaked so much havoc in her life. She was so hungry for the crisis, she had slept with another man without giving it a thought. She was returning to her husband, and if he ever touched her again, he would be touching her where Jeffrey had touched her. Would he know somehow, and condemn her as a slut? She threw *Karezza* back into the trunk and carried the other books to the bed.

Her days on board went like this: sleep, eat, bathe, read, eat, and sleep again. Wirt came to check on her two or three times a day, but never said more than a few words to her. Her door was always locked from the outside, but three times a day, a ship's steward brought her food, and once a day a maid came to clean her room and ask her if she needed anything. Ada's only view of the world was what she could see of the decks and the ocean from her single porthole. When people came near enough to her porthole for her to hear their conversation, she listened intently to their boring talk, just so that she would feel connected to some sort of living beings. By the time three days had passed in this way, she was bored to the point of rage, and she would have done anything to go out on deck.

Finally, on the fourth day, when Wirt stuck his head in the door and uttered his routinely cold "Cheerio," Ada ran to the door. "Mr. Wirt, please, I simply must get some fresh air. I shall be sick if I don't. Can someone walk the decks with me? Please. I just need air and sunshine."

He tugged at his muttonchops, considering her in silence. Finally, he answered: "All right. Once a day you may stroll, with two companions. And if you need to use the toilet, you will come back here. You may not speak to other passengers other than to say hello. You must give them no information about yourself, and do not give them a chance to invite you to dine with them. If they do ask, you must politely decline, telling them your health won't allow it. Understood?"

Ada nodded, appalled and relieved at the same time. She would now get to go outside. That was all she had wanted. But his catalog of restrictions reminded her that this entire ship was her prison.

One man walked on each side of her as they circled the deck. They were a Mr. Fielding and a Mr. Jensen. That was all she knew about them. They were big men, who no doubt served as some sort of security agents for Mr. Wirt. They must have made an odd-looking trio, Ada in her Boston finery, and those two in their ready-made suits and cheap shoes. Ada grew tired of walking with them and avoiding eye contact with other passengers. She moved to the rail and looked down, past the lower decks and out across the endless reaches of blue sky and sea. As she leaned over, her corset cut into her skin.

Jao and William, and her trunk of men's clothing, seemed a world away from her now. She didn't try to fool herself into believing it would be easy to get back to them. Perhaps her partnership with the orchid hunters had been nothing more than a brief interlude, as her college career had been. Another thing to remember and pine for, but never to know again. The waters reached back to Brazil; she longed to dive in and let them carry her there. Soon, Mr. Fielding tapped her shoulder, and the men escorted her back to her room, where she would pass the twenty-four hours that stood between this stroll and the next.

On the tenth or eleventh day of the voyage, during her on-deck stroll, the seas grew rough. On the way back to her room, Ada was thrown against the passageway wall. When she finally made it back to her room, she crawled into her bed. Her sea legs seemed to have left her. She was so sick she thought she might die. A Brazilian healer with a tree branch might save her now, she thought. Even Juliana would probably have an herb to give her. At the height of the storm, when Ada's stomach was the weakest, her dizziness the most acute, she allowed herself, finally, to cry. It didn't occur to her then that she would look back on her time alone in her cabin with longing.

THE SHIP TOOK THEM directly to New York, where Mr. Wirt and his aides, Mr. Fielding and Mr. Jensen, hurried her onto the train to Boston, leaving some other underling to deal with the luggage. Ada didn't care about her trunk. It held remnants of her life in Boston. What she wanted were her suits and Brazilian dresses. In the first-class compartment she shared with the men, Ada kept her head against the window, staring out into the landscape of the Eastern seaboard, but seeing Brazil. She saw herself there, wearing her trousers, riding horses, swimming in the river, kissing Jao. She laughed out loud when she imagined Edward finding her, trouser to trouser with Jao as they embraced. He wouldn't know what to make of it. His sense of reality would be so upended, he wouldn't even recognize his own wife. She didn't allow herself to wonder if Jao was all right, if he had survived the beating given him by the men Wirt hired.

Instead, she shifted her thoughts to her mother. What if her mother saw her dressed as a man? The thought of arriving at one of her mother's dinner parties dressed in a man's suit distracted her from images of Brazil, and saved her from feeling sorry for herself for a moment, at least.

Mr. Wirt called Edward at his office from a telephone in the train station, arranging to meet him at the house. Wirt's own driver picked them up in a carriage and drove them to the front door of the Pryce house. In the carriage, as a sense of doom closed in on her, Ada finally asked the question she had been afraid to ask until now. "How did you know it was me? How did you know where to find me?"

"I came across your friend Jeffrey Stipes. He told me he had had the unbelievable luck of learning you were only posing as a man. That you were really a woman. He was thrilled to have the opportunity to bed such a creature, he said. I knew then that it had to be you. What other explanation could there be?" Wirt smirked at her as he relayed the information, as if it pleased him somehow.

"And Jeffrey told you I was back in Juàzeiro?" she asked.

"I had men there. I told him to let them know if he saw you again. It all turned out quite well."

So it was Jeffrey she had seen briefly that night. When he saw her, he must have immediately contacted Wirt's men. And he must have known no good would come of it for Ada. This was the man who had shared her bed for two nights.

They pulled up in front of Edward's house then. When she stepped out of the carriage and stood in front of the imposing Gothic structure, it was as if she were seeing it for the first time. What went on inside those walls? Certainly it had nothing to do with her. Wirt's hand on her elbow guided her to the front door. As she crossed the threshold and entered the foyer, her legs were moving of their own accord, free of her will. She felt strangely disembodied and uninvolved in the simple physical actions involved in walking.

Suddenly, Katie was in the entryway, followed by George, and then, hovering behind him, partially blocked by George's bulk, Edward. Ada thought she felt herself take a sudden deep breath. The floor was somehow coming closer to her face, and then she made contact with it, without feeling anything, without realizing she had been falling.

She heard Katie call out, "Oh, Mrs. Pryce. Oh dear." Then she felt hands on her, and someone was picking her up. It was George. Yes, those were George's arms around her. All the while Edward hung back.

Finally, he spoke. "Take her to her room, both of you. I'll see to Mr. Wirt."

George carried her upstairs and set her down in her rocking chair. "You should get her out of those things," he said to Katie before he left the two women alone.

Ada allowed Katie to handle her as if she were a baby incapable of the simplest purposeful movement. The heavy dress, the petticoats, the corset fell away under her maid's deft touch. Once the silk nightgown was on, Ada fell into her bed, allowing Katie to tuck her into the covers as if she were swaddling her mistress. The things that kept the world ordered, like language and time, purpose and memory, were all out of Ada's reach. The only thing she could respond to was the simplicity of Katie's touch. Katie said words to her, but Ada couldn't place the meaning of the words, so she didn't answer.

Katie's face seemed to fall out of its usual alignment as she spoke to Ada, but Ada couldn't assign significance to its shifting shape. Was this anger, fear, sadness? She didn't want to know. She wanted to sleep. And dream of Brazil.

WHEN KATIE FINALLY LEFT, she did sleep. But she woke herself up in the middle of the night. Something had frightened her in her sleep. It was a black moon; no light leaked through the curtains, and the dark caused her fear to linger. Something had been chasing her through her dreams. Or someone. Was it Wirt? It was hot in the room. Gulping for air, afraid that she would pass out, she went to her window. She pushed the bottom window up, but it stopped after rising only a few inches. It was impossible for her to put her head out the window. This panicked her. She lit her lamp and brought it to the window. When she shone the light on the frame, she saw that someone had driven nails into both sides so that she couldn't open the window all the way.

The door behind her was suddenly the only thing in the room. She had to get to it, open it. She ran with her lamp, nearly tripping on her gown. Grabbing at the doorknob, she twisted and shook it, but the door refused to open. It was locked from outside.

So this was what Edward had brought her home for. Simply to imprison her. When would he have the courage to come speak to her face-to-face? she wondered.

• • •

IT WOULD BE seven days before he appeared. By that time, she was so used to being locked away in a bedroom, Ada felt she was adopting the instincts of an animal. She spent her days listening to the sounds of the household, responding to them on a purely primal level. Should she be afraid of any given sound, or did it offer no threat to her? When she heard the voices of the household staff in the garden below or in the hall outside her door, she didn't even try to understand their speech. She dismissed their conversation as background noise. Even when she could hear Edward in his room, the only thing she cared to know was whether or not he would leave his room and come to her door. When his footsteps moved away from his room and toward the stairs, she was unfailingly relieved. She was afraid that when she saw him, she would spit in his face, even kick him in the testes. She would jump on him and tear the hair from his skull. She would beat his head against the wall. It was better that he simply leave her alone.

Katie brought meals to her three times a day. But George always escorted her, locking her in the room with Ada for a few minutes, then opening the door and ushering her out. Ada could hardly speak to Katie. She was still comforted by her presence, but she didn't know what to say. She only wanted to be able to tell her maid how much she ached to return to Brazil. But if she opened her mouth to utter such thoughts, she would surely begin to cry and never, never stop. Being in this room, in Edward's house, made her feel as if she had crossed out of physical existence and entered some strange metaphysical dimension where nothing held meaning. What was there for her to say about such a state?

But finally, on the third morning, Ada spoke to Katie. When the maid came in with a tray of breakfast food, she looked so tired. Suddenly, Ada wondered how she had been these months, and what her life had been like.

"I'm happy that Edward kept you on. Has he treated you fairly?" The words felt strange in her mouth, as if they filled it up and she needed to chew and then spit each one out.

"Oh, ma'am." Katie's voice caught and she had to stop for a moment. "It's good to hear your voice."

"But how are you, Katie?" Ada reached out to take her hand. Katie sat next to her on the bed.

"I'm perfectly fine. But it's you we're worried about."

Ada stroked Katie's hand, remembering all the times she had wanted to speak to Katie while she was gone. "Are you married yet?"

"Yes. We married. I received word from a messenger who said you were fine and that you had asked after me, and that he meant to contact you. I gave him our wedding announcement to give to you. We've been fine, but Liam wants to leave and start his own business. Blacksmithing."

"Katie, that's wonderful." Ada felt profound envy in that moment. It would be far better to be a blacksmith's wife than to be a caged woman in a mansion.

"But never mind me. What became of you?" She petted her mistress's hand.

"Oh, I don't think I can talk about it," Ada said. She almost said that it was too painful. But there was a rap at the door before she opened her mouth again.

Katie jumped up from the bed. "I'll be back with your dinner," she said. George threw the door open just as Katie reached it. He glared at Ada, then locked the door after Katie.

The complexities, the unreliability, of time crushed Ada's spirit more than any of it. Some afternoons wound out before her like a never-ending line snaking its way toward the possibility of something. But that something could never, ever be reached, and she waited on that line, knowing there was no end to it. Some nights, she fell asleep, and when she woke in the full sun of the next day, it seemed as if she hadn't slept at all. But time's worst conspiracy against her was in its refusal to allow her knowledge of the date. In Brazil it hadn't mattered; life was lived out in the sun and the moon, and the subtly changing seasons were in the air, and she felt part of the natural movement of time, so the date, when she did know it, was an interesting abstract.

Here, she couldn't even put her head out the window. Knowledge of the month and day seemed a way to stay attached to the rhythms of the earth. But Ada had been cut away from its movement. She rested above it, up here on the second floor, and it no longer had any contact with her. She still wasn't sure what month it was. It was enough to drive anyone mad.

This desire to be back in tempo with the earth caused her to take out a notepad and scratch off the days, one by one. That was the only way she knew without doubt it was on the seventh day that Edward opened the door and walked into her room. When she saw him, standing in the thin light of her lamp, all the blood rushed out of her head and down to her feet. She sat up in her bed, but her dizziness caused her to fall back into her pillows. Edward walked slowly to her bed. His boots clicked across the wood, then silenced when they stepped onto her carpet. She held her breath, closed her eyes, fearing the moment when he reached her side. The bed moved, dipped down under her. She opened her eyes to see him, sitting on the mattress, almost touching her left hip. The desire to scream flushed through every vein and electrical circuit in her body. But she held it in.

"Ada," he said. "My vanished wife." His voice was even. She detected no intense anger. Perhaps it was simply puzzlement. In any case, it was too calm. Too calm to bear.

Ada found herself suddenly up on her knees, kneeling over Edward and pummeling his back with her fists. She hit him hard. She had grown strong during her time as a man. "You have locked me up in my room like a common criminal. Why? Why? What are you trying to do to me? Do you want to kill me?" She didn't stop hitting him until he grabbed her wrists and threw her onto her back. He held her there, by the wrists, his knee holding her thighs down, as he spoke through his teeth.

"You are a common criminal." He lifted himself off the bed and left without another word.

The next evening, he came and sat in her rocker. He pushed the floor with his feet so that the chair began to glide back and forth. He looked at her as he rocked. They didn't speak to each other. He watched her through eyes that were narrowed down to angry slashes. She turned her head from him and read her book.

He did the same thing for two more evenings. The next evening, the eleventh since her return to Boston, when he sat in the rocker, he spoke to her.

"Why? Simply tell me why."

Ada rolled over in her bed, readjusting herself to avoid bedsores. Her body ached from inactivity. She tried to exercise in her room, but it couldn't replace getting out for a walk, going for a swim, or riding a horse through the countryside. She looked at the wall and never said a word to her husband.

"Perhaps you need more time," he said to her. "I've decided that I'll sit here for a while every day. When you decide to explain what you have done, I will be here." He got up and walked out then, leaving the chair rocking for some time after he had closed the door behind him and turned the key in the lock.

At first his silent visits infuriated Ada. Her body remained tense, her jaw clamped, for so long after he left each time, she was certain his appearances were going to destroy her health. She refused to speak to him. He had called her a common criminal, he had imprisoned her in her room, before he had bothered to ask her why. As far as Ada was concerned, he had already judged her, and nothing she could say was going to lead him to an understanding. But the worst thing about all of this was, he had stolen Brazil from her. If she were to talk to him, the only thing she would want to tell him was that she had begun to be somebody, she had been forming a distinct identity during the time she was in Brazil, and she needed to get back in order to complete the process. He had arrested the most important development of her life.

ONE EVENING, as he sat rocking in her chair, Edward informed her that they would return to the sexual practices that had been interrupted by Ada's sudden departure. "We are husband and wife, after all. Perhaps the responsibilities and joys of motherhood will bring you to your senses."

Ada spoke to him for the first time since she had attacked him, since the day he called her a criminal. "You mean to impregnate me? You will allow a common criminal to bear you a child?"

The chair stopped rocking. Ada had to concentrate to absorb the words he said to her now, even though he pronounced each one carefully, slowly. "You had some sort of breakdown. I admit I don't understand what happened. But I have sought advice from the best people. They say I should do my best to act as if our marriage is as it should be, and in time you will return to being the woman I married. We should start right away with sexual relations. Today, in fact."

He rose from the chair and began to take off his clothes. As he removed each article, it was as if he were performing a part that was scripted for him. Some stage director, Ada imagined, had told him exactly where to stand, and which piece of clothing to take off first, which last. He seemed conscious of what he was doing, and of being observed as he undid the buttons of his shirt, peeled away his trousers, untied his underclothes, and pulled them down his legs. A chill shook her shoulders and set her teeth to chattering as she watched him. He placed all his clothes, neatly folded, onto the overstuffed chair. When he was at last naked, he walked slowly toward her. With each step, his penis grew, so that by the time he reached her he was fully erect.

The strength of Ada's shivers increased. He climbed into the bed, pushing her away from the edge. He pried her legs apart with his knees, while pulling her gown away with his hands.

"No," she said. "Please stop."

"You are my wife," he said. "I have this right, by law."

He put his fingers inside her and moved them quickly. They scraped against her dry, tender skin. It hurt, but her vagina moistened in spite of the discomfort his fingers caused.

"You will practice your Karezza techniques. You will not allow yourself to reach crisis. But I shall ejaculate," he told her as he removed his fingers and mounted her. "We are here to create a child."

She lay, motionless, on her back. As he pounded himself in and out, Ada choked down the urge to scream. She counted his parries. He began to ejaculate on the tenth thrust, and was finished by fifteen. The instant he pulled himself off her, Ada rolled away from him and refused to look at him. She sensed, without seeing him, when he picked up his clothes and walked out of her room, still naked, apparently unconcerned if any of the staff should see him. Or perhaps he wanted them to see him, like some wild animal proclaiming his prowess.

THE SIGHT OF KATIE bearing the silver tray laden with dinner brought Ada back from a cascade of dark thoughts. She brightened enough to greet her maid with a barely audible hello.

"Oh, Mrs. Pryce. How are you?" Her smile must have been meant to encourage Ada, to pull her into Katie's cheery orbit. But to Ada it was a reminder of all that Katie had, and all that Ada lacked.

"I might as well be dead, Katie."

Katie sank down onto the bed next to Ada. "Please don't think that way. What can I do to help you? I'll do anything."

"I need to get out of here."

"I'm certain Mr. Pryce means to let you out soon. He's still nervous, is all." Katie couldn't lift her eyes to Ada's face as she spoke. She kept them trained on the bedcovers.

"Even if he intends to let me out of the room, I need to get out of this house. Away from Edward." Ada grabbed Katie by the hands. "I need to get out of here."

Katie patted Ada's hands and finally looked her in the eyes. "George will be knocking on the door in a minute. Your mother was here several times when you were gone. She was worried. You should see her. Let her come talk to you."

Ada dropped Katie's hands. "Certainly. Tell her to come. What difference will it make?"

Katie hurried toward the door. "I must go. I'll speak to you in the morning." She left, and George immediately locked the door, leaving Ada with nothing but the echo of the brass key against its escutcheon.

The next morning, Katie suggested that Ada bathe. Ada acquiesced, not imagining there was anything behind the request other than the desire to keep Ada functioning according to the laws of polite society. Or perhaps

Edward had requested it so that Ada would be fresh when he came to her room that evening. But once they were both inside the bathroom, with the water pouring into the tub, its heat filling the chilly room with warm steam, Katie revealed her true intentions. "I thought this would give us an opportunity to speak for more than five minutes," Katie said. "But we must speak quietly, in case George is listening at the door."

Ada removed her gown and stepped into the tub. "What shall we talk about?" Her question was listless.

"I want you to speak to your mother. I'm certain George will leave you alone to talk with her. You tell her what you want." Ada lowered herself into the bath and relaxed into the water. Katie spoke in a low voice, leaning over the tub far enough for her mouth to settle close to Ada's ear. Ada laughed and swooshed at the water with her palm. As she disturbed the surface, creating a small wake, she imagined the Brazilian rivers, and her first time swimming. What would Katie think if she swam the six feet to the other end of the tub? Would she be surprised? "Will you, Mrs. Pryce? Please?" Katie asked.

"Will I what?" Ada pulled her gaze away from the rippling water.

"Speak to your mother."

"But what would she do? She has never been concerned about my life. She has always been far too busy with her social activities to mind what becomes of me." Ada's voice was growing louder. Katie held her finger to her lips.

"Shh," she warned, looking toward the crack under the door. She whispered into Ada's ear. "She was angry with Mr. Pryce. She told him it was his fault entirely that you left."

Ada pulled away, then dropped her face under the surface, listening to the sounds of the water pressure all around her. She opened her eyes and looked up at Katie's rippling face above the water's skin. Finally, she ran out of breath and emerged.

"I'm stunned she summoned up the energy to care," Ada said.

"With your permission, I'll tell her to come tomorrow."

"All right. To make you happy, Katie, I'll talk to her."

. . .

That afternoon, as Ada stood at her window, gazing into the garden, she saw Katie and Liam meet there for a moment. Liam quickly kissed Katie's neck. Katie put her hand around his head, then pushed him away and hurried about her tasks.

Edward came to her room again that night, and she again submitted to a brief and unpleasant sexual congress. The entire duration of the act, she was acutely aware of the possibility that he was impregnating her. She hoped that by sheer will she could prevent such a thing.

When Katie brought her breakfast the next morning, Ada begged her to bring her contraceptive herbs.

"I don't know how I can do that. What if I'm caught?"

Ada flung herself across her bed and beat her arms against it. "You must. I will die if I bear his child. Please."

"I'll try. I promise." She stroked Ada's hair. "Your mother will be here for lunch," Katie said. "Be kind to her."

At the lunch hour, George threw her door open. Beatrice Caswell swept into the room, her skirts rustling, her perfume sweetening the air, her necklaces clanking. Beatrice was followed by Katie and Edith, who carried trays of food. Even this simple visit to Ada's cell was bound to be a grand production since her mother was involved. Ada fluffed up her pillows and sat up straight.

"Oh, do get out of the bed," her mother said. Beatrice seated herself in the overstuffed chair and waited for Ada to settle into the rocker. She waved Katie and Edith away. "We'll serve ourselves," she said.

They ate while Beatrice talked. Ada had no idea what to say to this woman.

"My Orphans' Fund is winning a Governor's award. I can't tell you how fulfilling this is to me. I had hoped you would grow into the same sorts of involvements. It has been profoundly disappointing to me to watch you turn into someone so difficult to understand."

Ada shrugged and took a bite of meat pie. Her appetite was small, but her mother's conversation drove her to eat more than she wanted.

"These months that you were missing, I came to a new understanding, I believe. I have come to accept that you are a rebel. You always have been. There is simply nothing to be done about it."

Ada felt a tickling in her solar plexus. The sensation bordered on pleasurable. "I'm glad you recognize that about me."

"I don't approve of Edward's keeping you locked up here. He is making a laughingstock of your marriage." Beatrice straightened her back, all the better to glare at her daughter. "I think he should end this charade."

"But he won't."

"I realize that. We argued while you were gone. I see how stubborn he is."

Ada leaned back in the rocker and settled into its rhythms. "But there is nothing to be done."

"I simply want you to know if there is anything I can do, tell Katie, and she'll get a message to me. I can't reason with the man, and I have no legal recourse, since he is your husband. But perhaps there is some other way we can get to him."

"Get me back to Brazil. Give me the money to go to Brazil, Mother." Ada got up from her chair and went to her mother's side. She put her head in her mother's lap, as she had on a couple of occasions in her childhood. Beatrice gave Ada's hair a single pat, then pulled her daughter to an upright position.

"I can't do that. You know that's unacceptable to me. I don't believe you belong in Brazil." Beatrice got up and walked away. But then she stopped and turned back to her daughter. "But I will do what I can to get you out of this room and back into the world."

Ada knew that any return to the world would require her performing her role as Edward's wife to perfection. The farcical nature of the role sickened her almost as much as the prospect of a life of imprisonment.

Before her mother left, she took a package out of her handbag and held it out to Ada. "Katie informed me that you don't want children." Ada shook her head at her mother. "I can't say that I blame you." Perhaps at another time, that hard statement would have hurt Ada. But now it seemed to be nothing more than a simple truth. Beatrice handed the brown paper package to her daughter. "Douche with this after every time," she said. "You won't get with child."

• • •

THE HERBS HER MOTHER brought her improved her mood for a while. Sexual relations with her husband seemed less horrific knowing that she would not get pregnant. But every time Edward came to her room, climbed onto her bed, and straddled her in the same, repetitive fashion, Ada felt a little more desperate to get away from him forever. She closed her eyes throughout the ordeal so that she could imagine something other than the debasement she was suffering. But Edward's smell, an admixture of sweat, hair pomade, French cologne, sour breath, cigar smoke, and semen, signified Ada's own loss of self, her sinking into this narrow space where her own desires had no meaning.

George watched her vigilantly. There was never an opportunity for her to leave the house. Her doors and windows were locked against her. And even if she could leave, she had no money. Where would she go? How would she get there?

The image of Mr. Rochester's mad wife in *Jane Eyre* had always seemed chilling to Ada. But she had always seen Mrs. Rochester as some evil burden that had made her husband miserable. Never until now did it occur to her that perhaps Mr. Rochester had locked up his wife unjustly, and the imprisonment was the thing that had driven her mad. She felt a kinship with Mrs. Rochester. She herself was now that madwoman, hidden from the world by her controlling husband. If only there were a Jane Eyre to free her from Edward's grip.

Maybe her only recourse was a good fire. She looked at her lamp, imagined tipping it over under her curtains, allowing the spilled oil to ignite the fabric. But death by fire was too frightening. And she wouldn't want to harm anyone but herself. She longed for a small pistol, a quick shot to the brain. That would be so much more pleasant.

She counted off four more days after the visit from her mother. Every night, Edward came to her room. She endured his stinginess, the way he stole bits of her when he entered her without concern for her desires. And every night, as soon as he left, she took the concoction she had infused with the hot water from her dinnertime tea, and douched with it as she squatted over her chamber pot.

She spoke briefly to Katie three times every day. She walked between her bed, her chair, and her window one hundred times a day. The garden was garnished with a delicate, late snow now. But the Orchid House was difficult for her to look at. There it was, so close to her, yet she wasn't allowed to enter it, to revive herself with the sight of all those orchids, with the scent of the loam and the flowers. When she stood at her window, she looked only at the garden and out toward the carriage house. The Orchid House was the one thing she feared might make her lose her will to survive this imprisonment, so she worked to make it invisible.

And she read as many books as Katie brought to her, hidden inside her apron. When she wasn't reading, she hid the books in her trunk. The routine settled into her unconscious, propelling her through her days. But there was still a certain slipping of her grip on reality, and a certain disorienting of the mind. She thought often of Mrs. Rochester, and the thoughts were unsettling. Sometimes she dreamed of flying out her window, other times she dreamed of fire licking at her feet. She refused to think about Jao and William. When they appeared in her dreams, she was awakened by a constriction in her throat, as if she had been sobbing or crying out in her sleep.

On the fifth day after her mother's visit, after Katie set the breakfast tray down in front of Ada, the maid reached into her pocket and pulled out a small package. "Someone from the African Meeting House came to the back door this morning. Esau was his name."

Ada's heart raced so quickly she was sure it would simply cease to work. She grabbed at the package. "No one saw him but you?" She tore the paper from the small bundle.

"I don't think so," Katie said.

Inside the package was a piece of paper, wrapped around another small bundle. Ada opened the paper, and a stack of bills tumbled out. She ran her hands across the money, counting it quickly. Three hundred dollars, in fifties, twenties, and tens. More than enough to get back to Brazil. She picked up the paper that had held the money, and read the words there:

We are in New York. Same place.

She knew now that Jao was all right. Wirt's men hadn't killed him. The relief she felt surprised her. And the two of them must have gone back for more orchids, and succeeded in shipping them out and receiving payment for them, or they wouldn't have this much money to spare. Ada felt distraught that she hadn't been there with them to make up for the part she played in the loss of the first batch. She felt bereft at having lost time that could have been spent roaming the forests of Brazil, sleeping on the ground, defying disease and hardship in the pursuit of a parasitic plant that so many people desired. She recognized the outlaw nature of her reaction, and in that moment, she understood that she really was what William, Jao, and Walter, and for that matter, even Jeffrey, were. She didn't simply imagine herself an adventurer, she was one. Ada was no longer in her room in this home in Boston. The home that belonged only to Edward, and was controlled by Edward. She was already in a ship, headed south, breathing the salt air, watching dolphins jumping. With William and Jao at her side.

Katie cleared her throat. "What are you going to do, ma'am?"

Ada jogged herself back to the present. "What's the date, Katie?"

Katie's eyes widened, but she answered the question politely, as if it didn't worry her a bit. "It's April ninth, ma'am."

"I've been here for quite a long time, haven't I?" Katie nodded, waited. "This is what I would like to do," Ada said. "I would like to give you and Liam one hundred dollars to start your business." She had had more money when she ran away the first time. Why had she not thought to give Katie money then? Her thoughtlessness embarrassed her now. Katie's mouth moved, but she seemed unable to speak the words that were roiling there.

Katie was crying now. Ada took Katie's hands and kissed them. "Congratulations on your marriage, Katie. The message must have come after they took me. I'm sorry I wasn't here. But now at least I have a proper present to give you."

"Are you sure? That's such a lot of money, Ada."

"I am going to be making my own money now, Katie. I'm certain. Don't worry. And the orchid, my Ghost Flower? Is it thriving?" Ada asked her.

"I've taken good care of it. It made me think of you."

Ada hugged Katie. "I have missed you, Katie," she said.

The two women clung to each other until Ada pushed herself back. Katie's eyes were still wet, but Ada couldn't succumb. She had too much to do. "Take the orchid to Van Oot's greenhouse," she told Katie. "He'll give you something for it. My guess is you can get at least seventy-five dollars from him. So hold out. But before you do that, you are going to get me out of here."

IT TOOK THREE of them, Katie, Liam, and Beatrice, to work out a foolproof plan. First, Katie altered two of Liam's suits to fit Ada. Katie was a skilled seamstress; somehow she was able to find time in her busy workday, and she finished the suits within two days. Next, she invited Beatrice to come visit Ada.

But two days before Beatrice arrived for her second visit to Ada's cell, Edward came to her room, ready to attempt to impregnate his wife again. When George first opened the door, and Edward appeared there, Ada imagined that her planned escape would make the mechanical coupling her husband came for easier to bear.

But she was wrong. Edward was hard before his trousers were off. When he mounted her, he grunted loudly. He pressed his legs hard against hers, hurting her. His peregrinations across her body were clumsy and turbulent. How had she ever enjoyed sexual relations with this man? As he lunged toward and away from her arrhythmically, the desire to be free of him swelled up into her throat. She thought she would suffocate if she didn't get him off her. Twisting her body away from him, she pushed on his chest with her arms.

"Stop," she said. "You've got to stop."

"Not now."

"You must. I'll be sick." She pushed at him harder.

Mercifully, she thought, he stopped and looked at her. "Sick? Are you with child?"

It might save her. "I think so. Please, Edward. I feel terribly ill."

He pulled himself out of her. The suction caused by his quick withdrawal skinned her insides. He sat on the edge of the bed, hovering, as though he might want to speak to her.

"Please. Could you send Katie up with something for my stomach?"

He dressed and left without trying to engage her in conversation. She turned to face the wall until he was finally gone.

Katie brought her peppermint tea, and they talked for five minutes. Ada luxuriated in the double bliss of having rid herself of Edward before he ejaculated inside her, and of having an extra moment with Katie.

The next afternoon, Edward came to her room early. He should have been at work, or at his club, at such an hour. She imagined he had come to check on her fecundity. But his face was dingy with anger. What had she done now?

He sat in the rocker and kept his eyes trailing the floor as he pitched the chair forward and back. "I went to the Club for lunch today. I learned something very odd. Something very disturbing."

Ada felt her legs and arms tense, her breath flutter above the surface of her lungs. She waited for him to continue.

"Franz was just back from New York today." He leaped out of the chair, which continued to rock, and as it did so, suddenly started to squeak for the first time. He spoke loudly, over the screech of the chair, and riding a wave of rage that seemed to be swelling as it approached the surface. "I received a strange message some months ago claiming that William and Jao had discovered the *vera*. Someone in New York, a competitor of mine, has purchased two *Cattleya labiata vera*, and is claiming discovery." He slammed his fist into her armoire. Ada flinched, and pulled herself back against the headboard, trying to disappear into its chiseled surfaces. "Do you have any idea how much this meant to me? I have people in Brazil, right now, still looking for them. Who knew that they had been found?"

Ada stared at him, shaking her head, not speaking. But her heart lurched inside her rib cage. They must have sold the plants. Perhaps they shared the profits with Juliana. The thought made Ada feel contented.

"Did Jao and William find them? Or were they simply taunting me?" he asked her. She felt her eyes pop open, startled out of her imaginings.

"No," she managed. "They only found standard species. No *vera*."

"Don't lie to me." He hissed the words, and spittle fell on his chin. He moved suddenly toward her, as if he were about to strike her. But he stopped suddenly. "I received a strange message while you were missing. I didn't understand it then, but now it seems clear."

She leaned toward him, her chin out, a challenge. A man's response. "I'm not lying." She looked straight into his eyes as she spoke. The move provoked him. He treated her now, she thought, as he might treat a man whom he intended to best.

"I have believed, ever since I first began collecting orchids, that I was destined to become the man to rediscover the *labiata vera.* I have invested thousands of dollars in the quest. I have sent men all over South America searching for it." He leaned over her then, constrained menace stiffening his torso. "A true wife would understand this desire. And she would grieve for the husband who was thwarted in its pursuit."

"Maybe your desire wasn't strong enough."

She had said precisely the wrong thing to him. She knew it the instant the words were out of her mouth. His face went the red of a vibrant sunset. "But William and Jao, was their desire strong enough? Did they find my orchid?"

"I said no to you before, and I say it again."

"And I still do not believe you. I have gone to great lengths to locate the *vera.* If you have destroyed my chances, Ada . . ." He stopped then, as if the words couldn't be uttered.

"What would you do to me if I had?"

"I stopped Walter. I can certainly stop William and Jao."

In her mind's eye, Ada saw that smiling picture of Walter again. "What did you do to Walter?"

"Let me just say that his death was no accident. And there is nothing anyone can do about that. No one will touch me. I have the power to see to that. Your friends should be wary of toying with me."

Fear compelled Ada to change her tack, to be acquiescent now. "No one wants to toy with you, Edward. I swear it. You deserve to find the *vera.* I would never stand in your way." She praised him then, and his orchid collection, and she talked about looking forward to having a baby. By the time he took his leave, Edward was calm again. But he left Ada with a heightened sense of fear, and a renewed desire to get out of his house at the earliest opportunity.

AT LAST, her mother came. While Beatrice was in the room with her daughter, for an apparently routine visit, Liam called George away to see to some crucial business in the carriage house. The two women could hear Liam through the door. "There is a problem with the saddle that Mr. Pryce ordered. They won't listen to me, they insist I take it as it is. Mr. Pryce will be furious. You must talk to them." George opened the door and stepped in.

"Mrs. Caswell," he said to Ada's mother, "I need to step away. I must lock you in."

Beatrice jumped up from her chair. "Whatever are you saying, man? Lock me in?"

"Why, yes. I've been instructed by Mr. Pryce. Mrs. Pryce mustn't leave the room." Beatrice glared at him, so he stumbled on. "For her health, you understand."

"Of course. I know all that." Beatrice took a step toward him. Her gait was solid, her boot heel struck the floor loudly. She squared herself to face him. "I'm her mother. I want her to get well every bit as much as Edward does. But you can't lock me in here. I have engagements. I don't have time for this. Give me the key. I'll lock the door after myself and give it to Katie before I leave."

George hesitated just a beat too long. Beatrice pushed at his arm. "Stop dillydallying and give me the key. I'm in a hurry." He gave her the key then, throwing his head back and jutting out his chin in an empty gesture of defiance as he handed it to her.

The instant he was gone, Beatrice set to helping Ada get out of her housedress and into Liam's suit. When she was dressed, Ada pulled a carpetbag from behind her curtain. Beatrice opened the door a crack, then pulled it wide. Katie stood outside the door. "Are you ready?" she asked. Ada nodded. "I'll go down and guard the back door. You come through."

"Quickly," Beatrice said. Ada stopped and turned to hug her mother. "It's all right. Just have a good life." Beatrice pushed her away.

"I'll write to you, Mother. And perhaps one day you'll visit me in Brazil. It would be an adventure."

Beatrice's eyes clouded a bit. "I might do that." She patted her daughter's cheek. "Now go."

Once Ada was gone, what happened in the Pryce household was this: Beatrice closed the door and went back to the overstuffed chair, where she began a monologue designed to make anyone who might pass the door believe that she was still visiting with her daughter. She would keep it up for the next thirty minutes, then pass through the kitchen to hand Katie the key on her way out. Katie would return the key to George, who was still quite entangled in a mix-up involving a missing order for new saddles. Later, Katie would carry a dinner tray to Ada's room and bring the empty tray out again. It wouldn't be until late, when Edward entered the room to sexually molest his wife, that Ada's disappearance would be discovered.

Edward would berate his staff for days, and he would accuse Katie and Liam of complicity. But Katie and Liam would take their savings, the one hundred dollars from Ada, seventy-five dollars from Ada's Ghost Flower, and the fifty dollars they had managed to save over the last year, and leave before Edward could decide on a punishment for their failings. Edward would also confront Beatrice, but his social standing was no match for her venerable position, and so, in the end, he had no choice but to leave her be with her own grief over her daughter's second vanishing.

The Return to Away

It was almost dark when Ada stepped off the train in New York. After so many weeks locked up, first on board ship and then in Edward's house, the sound of the trains, of people yelling and carriages careening, the scents from people hawking food, of steam, of horses' droppings, and of this great press of people, all made Ada feel small. Her knees knocked together when she stepped onto the street. But within all this activity was also a sense of security. Nothing could hurt her here in the city, inside her man's suit. She was free to go anywhere, and Edward would never find her here.

She took an omnibus up Fifth Avenue, jumping out just before Twenty-third Street. The sun had dipped behind the buildings. Ada tried to remember where the rooming house was, but the churning activity confused her. By the dimming light, children played hoops in the streets. Women hawked rolls and sausages, fruit and live chickens. Tired men and women returned from work on the omnibuses and on foot. Old people wandered aimlessly. Horses, carriages, omnibuses clopped and skidded across the bricks. Smoke spewed from factories and chimneys. Boys called out the headlines from the evening newspapers. Ruffians leaned against walls, lingered on street corners. A prostitute in limp blue taffeta, her brown hair greasy, her lips a flaking red, rounded the corner just ahead, and aimed straight for Ada.

"Eh, Johnny." She grabbed Ada by the lapels. "I'll fuck you, right now, in the alley, just there. Two dollars." She tugged at Ada. Ada grabbed the woman's fingers, pried them from her lapels.

"No. Not me," Ada said.

"What, I ain't lady enough for you?" The prostitute tried to put her tongue into Ada's ear. "Just give it a go," she said. "You'll see. I'm the best."

Ada swatted at the woman's hot tongue. "You have the wrong man," she said, trying for her gruffest, most resonant tones. After she spoke, her own voice echoed in her head. She stepped out of the whore's path and hurried on, hoping to find the rooming house before it was fully dark.

The prostitute hurried after her. "Okay, just for you. One dollar."

Ada shook her head and hurried on.

"You're a Nancy boy, ain't ya?" the whore called after her. Others joined the woman in her derisive laughter, but momentarily, so much activity filled the gap between Ada and the whore, the woman's scorn was subsumed by the other sounds of the streets.

She looked down every narrow alley, but none seemed to be the right one. The first time she was here, she hadn't been terrified of the streets. But Jao and William had been with her then. And they were here now, somewhere very close. If only she could find them.

It was still cold. Spring hadn't really begun. Ada stuffed her hands into the pockets of her trousers. Her nose was cold. Her feet hurt. Her carpetbag felt heavy, and too obvious. Would someone try to steal it from her? The sense of security she had felt just moments before vanished. At least there were still plenty of people about. There was comfort in that.

She bought a roll from a woman in a dark dress with a thin shawl around her shoulders, who carried her basket of rolls as she walked. The woman shivered as she tried to count out Ada's change. Ada waved her hand at her. "Keep it," she said. "Go home and get warm."

"God bless you, sir." The woman smiled, then hurried away.

Ada was certain she would never find the rooming house. Soon, only prostitutes and cutpurses would be about. She decided to get a room. She stayed on Fifth Avenue, hoping to find a decent place there. The first sign she saw advertising rooms was in the window of a three-story wood-frame house. The parlor was dark and cold, but Ada was too tired to keep looking. The landlord was a short, round man who had better things to do than chat with his guests. He took Ada's dollar and gave her a skeleton key, pointing at the ceiling to indicate which side of the house the room was on.

The room was big enough, with a window onto the street. But it smelled of mildew, and cold air leaked in through the single, small window. Ada spent the night shivering, and never quite fell over the edge of sleep.

She left the rooming house just after sunrise, bleary-eyed, exhausted. The streets were already busy with people and vehicles. There seemed to be no landmarks from her earlier stay here with which to orient herself. How different the world looked when one was all alone, she thought. Perhaps she had paid scant attention to her surroundings because there was no primal need when she was with her partners. She didn't need to note the territory because there was no fear of getting lost when she was with William and Jao. Now a fear of wandering like this forever, or until her money ran out, gripped her. Her fear overrode her exhaustion and propelled her down the streets and alleys along Fifth Avenue.

Before long, her stomach demanded that she find food. She stopped at the first street hawker she saw and bought a roasted sweet potato, which she ate standing next to the old woman's table. As she blew on the potato, nibbling at it carefully to avoid burning her mouth, she remembered Oxum, the goddess of fresh water and of love. Her revealed goddess, Jao had said. Oxum's color was gold. The sweet potato glinted in the early morning sun, gold, consecrated food, an offering to Oxum. Just as she bit into it again, her eyes lifting, she saw the building. The same blackened brick, halfway down the alley across from her. It had to be the one. She ran across the street, skipping over manure, gripping her potato. She held on to the potato as she hurried into the building, knocked on the proprietor's door, and then found her way up to William and Jao's room.

William opened the door. Her heart pushed itself toward her sternum at the sight of his smooth, wide face. Jao got up from his bed and, still in his long underwear, moved toward the door. The two men laughed and clapped Ada on the back, pulling her into the room.

"Adam," they were saying to her as the floor seemed to bolt and buckle underneath her. "Adam, old man. We knew you'd make it. We never doubted it for a second."

Acknowledgments

I want to express my sincerest gratitude to my editor, Molly Barton, for her many insights, her delicate touch, and for believing in the book from the beginning; and to my agent, Lisa Grubka—who also championed the book from the start—for her support and unbridled enthusiasm. Thanks to Ivan Held and Catharine Lynch for their support, Lisa Amoroso and Andrea Ho for the gorgeous jacket design, Claire Vaccaro and Nicole LaRoche for the luscious interior, and also my thanks to Meredith Phebus, Marie Finamore, and Alaina Mauro. I am indebted to writers and poets Linda Alcorace, Judith Blazer, Margarita Cardenas, Gayle Elliott, Kitty Forbes, Ed Frankel, Joyce Griffin, Rebecca Martin, Janet Mendelsohn, Virginia Reiser, Janie Spataro, Shawne Steiger, and Janice Striddick, for generating creative heat that I am always honored to bask in. Also, thank you to my advisers and workshop leaders at Vermont College of Fine Arts—Xu Xi, Ellen Lesser, Phyllis Barber, Robin Hemley, David Jauss, and Sue Silverman—for thoughtful critiques, and for much-appreciated inspiration. And to the Vermont College of Fine Arts Writing Program, I am grateful for an unforgettable writing experience. Many thanks as well to Greg Sarris for his early reading and comments. Finally, my love and gratitude to Courtland, Kelsea, Mr. Jones, and Neil, for everything.

I would like to acknowledge some of the books and other sources I consulted during my research for *The Disorder of Longing.* For insight into orchids and their collectors, I found these books to be entertaining, educational, and inspirational: *The Orchid Thief: A True Story of Beauty and Obsession,* by Susan Orlean; *Orchid Fever: A Horticultural Tale of Love, Lust, and Lunacy,* by Eric Hansen; and *A History of the Orchid,* by Merle A. Reinikka. For Victorian sexual practices, these books were invaluable: *Karezza, Ethics of Marriage,* by Alice Bunker Stockham; and *The Technology of Orgasm: "Hysteria," the Vibrator, and Women's Sexual Satisfaction,* by Rachel P. Maines. For a look inside the workings of Candomblé, I watched *Ile Aiye (The House of Life),* a film by David Byrne, and read *Sacred Leaves of Candomblé: African Magic, Medicine, and Religion in Brazil,* by Robert A. Voeks. Finally, I would like to thank the following museums and events for the contributions they made to my research: Heritage Square Museum, a collection of Victorian houses in Pasadena, California; the International Orchid Show in Santa Barbara, California; Dennis Severs's house in Spitalfields, London; The African Meeting House in Boston; and the furniture and housewares collections in the Metropolitan Museum of Art in New York City.

Note: I have taken some license with the historical, botanical, and geographical facts I represent in the novel. For instance, the search for the lost *Cattleya labiata vera* was a real one, but I have changed the date of its rediscovery, its location, and, of course, the identities of the people who again found that elusive plant. The year that Katie is reading *The Woman's Bible* does not quite coincide with the year in which it was published, nor does the year in which Ada reads *The Awakening* coincide with its publication date.

A NOTE ON TYPE

The text of this book was set in Bembo,
based on a roman cut by
Francesco Griffo
in Venice in 1495.

This book was designed by
Nicole LaRoche.

This book was printed and bound
by R. R. Donnelley
in Bloomsburg, Pennsylvania.